General fiction

DATE DUE		

People
of the Raven

People
of the Raven

Kathleen O'Neal Gear
and
W. Michael Gear

A Tom Doherty Associates Book
New York

PEOPLE OF THE RAVEN

Copyright © 2004 by Kathleen O'Neal Gear and W. Michael Gear

This book is printed on acid-free paper.

Maps and illustrations by Ellisa Mitchell

A Forge Book
Published by Tom Doherty Associates, LLC
175 Fifth Avenue
New York, NY 10010

www.tor.com

Forge® is a registered trademark of Tom Doherty Associates, LLC.

Library of Congress Cataloging-in-Publication Data

Gear, Kathleen O'Neal.
    People of the raven / Kathleen O'Neal Gear and W. Michael Gear.—1st ed.
       p. cm.—(The first North Americans series)
    "A Tom Doherty Associates book."
    ISBN 0-765-30855-X (acid-free paper)
    EAN 978-0-765-30855-9
    1. Prehistoric peoples—Fiction. 2. Race relations—Fiction. 3. Caucasian race—Fiction.
    4. North America—Fiction. I. Gear, W. Michael. II. Title.

    PS3557.E18P486 2004
    813'.54—dc22

                                                                2004047178

First Edition: September 2004

Printed in the United States of America

0 9 8 7 6 5 4 3 2 1

To
Howard and Belenda Willson
With
Fond Memories of Elands and Africa,
Fine Meals Shared,
And
Hale and Hearty Drink.
All the Best, Dear Friends

Acknowledgments

We could not have written *People of the Raven* were it not for the work of Jim Chatters, Doug Owsley, Robson Bonnichsen, Alan Schneider, James Dixon, Richard L. Jantz, Silvia Gonzalez, Jose Concepcion Jimenez Lopez, W. A. Neves, and others who have worked to recover meaningful information on early Caucasoids in the Western Hemisphere.

The Hot Springs County Library ran down obscure articles that were critical for this work. Our thanks go to Tracy and B.J. You are an asset to our community.

The efficient staff at the Holiday Inn of the Waters in Thermopolis reserved our special table when we escaped for Guinness, succulent buffalo patty melts, and jalapeños. Thanks to Mary, Jake, Dawn, Jimmy, Kenny, Karla, Howard, and the crew.

Finally, we wish to thank our editor, Bob Gleason, for his enthusiasm for the book, Eric Raab, for tending the manuscript, and Deanna Hoak, for her superb copyedit.

13,000 B.C. 10,000 B.C. 7300 B.C. 6000 B.C. 5000 B.C.

Paleo Indian

Early Archaic

People of the Wolf
Alaska & Canadian Northwest

People of the Raven
Pacific Northwest & British Columbia

People of the Fire
Central Rockies & Great Plains

People of the Sea
Pacific Coast & Great Basin

People of the Lightning
Florida

Paleo Indian

Archaic

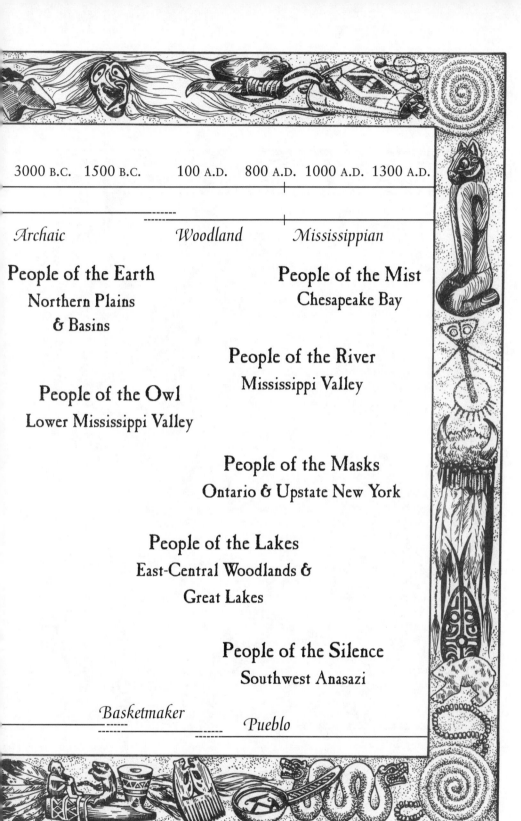

| 3000 B.C. | 1500 B.C. | 100 A.D. | 800 A.D. | 1000 A.D. | 1300 A.D. |

Archaic   *Woodland*   *Mississippian*

People of the Earth
Northern Plains
& Basins

People of the Mist
Chesapeake Bay

People of the River
Mississippi Valley

People of the Owl
Lower Mississippi Valley

People of the Masks
Ontario & Upstate New York

People of the Lakes
East-Central Woodlands &
Great Lakes

People of the Silence
Southwest Anasazi

Basketmaker   *Pueblo*

1994 E. MITCHELL

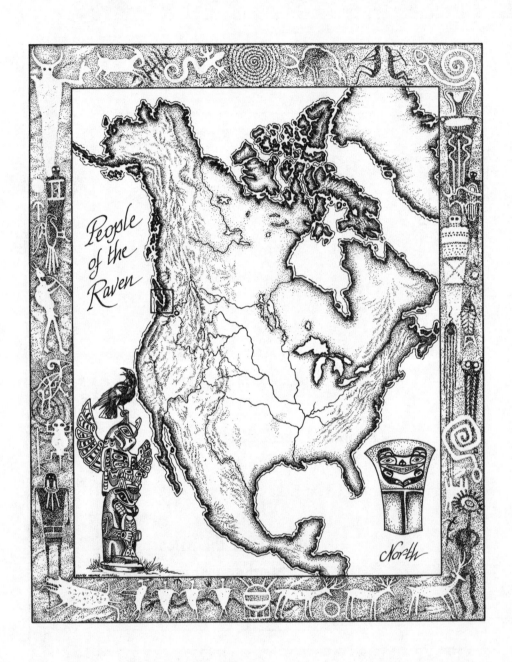

People
of the
Raven

North

Deer Meadow
Village

Wake's
Nose

Shell Maiden
Village

Raven
Bay

Cupped Finch
Village

Sandy Point Village

Orphan
Village

War Gods Village

Antler
Spoon's
Village

Eelgrass Village

Sea Lion
Village

Wasp
Village

Fire Mountain

Salmon
Village

Fire Village

Guuu
INLET

Tortoise Shell
Village

Trailing
Raspberry
Village

NORTH

Foreword

In the fall of 1996, Dr. Jim Chatters, adjunct professor at Central Washington University and deputy coroner for Benton County, Washington, sent an urgent e-mail to several American anthropologists saying, "Subject: Need Help ASAP."

He had in his hands an archaeological discovery that would rock the nation, and he knew it. The specimen would come to be called "Kennewick Man," and prove to be one of the most controversial archaeological finds in the history of the world.

When Kennewick Man was discovered eroding out of the banks of the Columbia River, it appeared to be a simple case. Obviously he was a Caucasoid male, forty-five to fifty-five years of age, probably a White pioneer.

Then a CAT scan revealed a "Cascade" point—a distinctive leaf-shaped prehistoric spear point—embedded in his hip. Shortly thereafter, the radiocarbon laboratory at the University of California at Riverside returned their analysis of the date: Kennewick Man was between 9,200 and 9,500 years old.

A Caucasoid man in America more than 9,000 years ago? Weren't we all taught that only "Indian" people, that is, Mongoloid people, were here that long ago?

This was a stunning find that had the potential to completely rewrite our understanding of the peopling of the Americas.

Five days after the radiocarbon dates were released to the public, the Army Corps of Engineers—upon whose land Kennewick Man was found—ordered Jim Chatters to immediately halt all scientific studies and relinquish the bones. In the end, the Corps would defy orders from both Houses of Congress to leave the site alone and would cover the Kennewick Man archaeological site with six hundred tons of earth and debris. They even planted thousands of trees on top of the fill to stabilize it, very effectively concealing any undiscovered evidence that would spark additional questions about who Kennewick Man was and what he was doing in America more than 9,000 years ago.

You may think this smacks of lunacy, or at least a loathing of scientific inquiry that borders on madness. But we're dealing with a complicated story here. Let's talk about the facts.

After the radiocarbon dates became public, an alliance of five northwestern tribes—the Umatilla, Yakima, Nez Perce, Wanapum, and Colville—claimed the remains under the 1990 Native American Graves Protection and Repatriation Act, demanding that the bones be turned over to them for reburial without further study.

Why would the tribal alliance claim a White man?

Armand Minthorn, Umatilla leader, said, "Our oral history goes back 10,000 years. We know how time began and how Indian people were created. They can say whatever they want, the scientists. They are being disrespectful."

Eight scientists, in *Bonnichsen et al. v. United States of America,* sued to be able to study the remains.

The meetings of the Society for American Archaeology and the American Association of Physical Anthropologists were spiked with bitter acrimony. Since no scientists were allowed to see the remains—because they might be able to study Kennewick Man with their eyes—the vast majority of conference attendees were high on hearsay.

Next, enter the Asatru Folk Assembly.

The Asatru, based in northern California, trace their ancestry to pre-Christian Scandinavian and Germanic peoples. In their publication, *The Runestone,* they wrote, "Native American groups have strongly contested this idea, perceiving that they have much to lose if their status as the 'First Americans' is overturned. We will not let our heritage be hidden by those who seek to obscure it." They filed suit to have Kennewick Man—whom they believed to be *their* ancestor—turned over to them.

Archaeologists around the world shouted their approbation.

Not so much because they agreed, but because the Asatru lawsuit begged a very important question: Do some religions in America have precedence over others? Do certain racial or ethnic groups have the right to certain archaeological sites? Should Canada return the Viking archaeological sites dating to around A.D. 1000 to Canadians of Scandinavian heritage? Should the United States return all Hispanic archaeological sites to people of Hispanic heritage? Should the African-American sites administered by the federal government be turned over to African-Americans? If so, which people or persons? Is one-eighth blood enough? Does it have to be based on ethnicity? What about the beautiful historic Catholic missions in the California State Parks system? Should the state of California be forced to turn them back to the Catholic Church? And what happens to those sites once they're turned over? Is it all right if these groups destroy them?

The debate isn't finished by any means.

The battle over Kennewick Man has been long and arduous. As we write, a federal judge has just overturned the Department of Interior's decision to give the ancient remains to the coalition of Indian tribes for reburial. The Department of Interior has appealed.

Will we ever know the fate of the Caucasoid peoples who first inhabited the Americas? Who they were? How they got here? What happened to them?

We may still have a chance. British scientists working in Mexico have discovered two skulls, both older than 12,000 years, which appear to be Caucasoid. Dr. Silvia Gonzalez, of John Moores University in Liverpool, says, "It looks like some of the most ancient Paleo-Americans were not of Mongoloid affinity and therefore perhaps not directly related to modern Native Americans." Working in conjunction with Jose Concepcion Jimenez Lopez, curator of Mexico City's National Museum of Anthropology, she is in the process of analyzing the remains, including doing DNA research. No matter what they find, their work will greatly enrich our understanding of the ancient peoples of the Americas.

Will we ever have the freedom to do that kind of study in the United States?

It is clear to us now that the only people who can answer that question sit on the bench of the Supreme Court of the United States of America.

We hope that the Court will see that the rich "melting pot" history of America is too precious to allow it to be annihilated by religious fundamentalism—of *any* variety.

—KATHLEEN O'NEAL GEAR and W. MICHAEL GEAR
January 2004

Prologue

The call comes at 10:32 P.M. I know because I look at the digital clock on the white wall of my basement laboratory. *Ten thirty-two and twenty-four seconds.*

While I dry my sweating hands on my blue jeans, my three colleagues around the room straighten. Dr. Kim Lacey, recently retired as chair of the Anthropology Department at McGill University in Quebec, wets her lips. Kim seems to be working very hard to ignore the ringing phone. She bends over the skeleton and continues measuring the femur, the thighbone. Peering over her glasses, she jots in her notebook as fast as she can. Beads of perspiration glisten on her wrinkled forehead and mat her short graying brown hair to her temples.

Dr. Sam Collier, twenty-eight years old, with blond hair and bright green eyes, squints at the ringing phone, then resolutely returns to measuring the orbits, the eye sockets, of the skull.

My basement laboratory in Lynden, Washington—just a few miles from the Canadian border—stretches twenty by thirty feet. One window, high on the wall, looks out at the street—but tonight it's draped with a heavy dark blue curtain. The lab is dim, and every wall is covered with shelves filled with books, archaeological specimens, artifacts. Only the fluorescent bar hanging from the ceiling glares to illuminate the ancient skeleton laid out on the stainless steel table in the middle of the room.

I glance at the old man sitting on the stool in the dark corner. Moss Pale Horse is a stoop-shouldered little man with a round face and hooked nose. He frowns at the concrete floor. His gray braid drapes his shoulder like a fuzzy snake. He is gently rubbing the "medicine bag" that hangs from a leather cord around his throat; it's filled with sacred things, things his Spirit Helper told him to collect when he went on his first vision quest at the age of twelve.

I pick up the receiver on the tenth ring. "Dr. Catherine Garren."

"Cathy, they're coming," my friend, the archaeologist at the local BLM office, says. *"Somebody told them you took the remains to your home. You've got twenty minutes maximum."*

I close my eyes. "Thanks, John. I know it'll end your career if anyone finds out you called me. I mean it. *Thank you.*"

He hangs up, and the loud click of the phone seems to echo around the quiet lab.

I put the receiver back in the cradle.

Sam takes a tentative step forward. "How long?"

He finished his Ph.D. last summer. He's barely started his career in forensic anthropology. I hurt for him.

"Twenty minutes. Maybe." I lift a hand and point to the video camera on the paper-strewn shelf behind Kim. "We're not going to have time to finish this. Let's videotape as much as we can."

Sam picks up the camera. As he lifts it to his eye, he asks, "Where do you want to begin?"

I tuck a loose lock of damp black hair behind my ear and try to think. I was born in Ontario forty-three years ago. I have shoulder-length straight black hair and the broad face and brown skin of most Iroquoian peoples.

"Here," I say, and carefully lift the skull. My hand shakes.

This is one of the most important archaeological finds in the world—the only mostly complete skeleton dating to this time period ever found in North America. But he's about to be destroyed, re-buried in some secret place, out of context with his past. Within a year, the acidic soils of the Pacific Northwest will have done their job. I'm losing him to religious zealots with lawyers.

I turn the skull to face the camera. A century from now, if anyone is alive to care, if the laws have been changed so that this isn't a crime, someone will look into his empty eye sockets and say, *Dear God, what was a White man doing in North America nine thousand years ago?*

I have to brace my elbows on the table to keep the skull still for the camera. "As you can see from the long, narrow shape and marked constriction of the forehead," I narrate, "this is a Caucasoid male.

The sutures on the braincase are closed, almost obliterated, suggesting a man of advanced age, forty to fifty." I tip the skull to show the backs of the teeth. "Note the dental morphology. He is not a Sinadont. I mean the backs of his incisors are not 'shovel-shaped,' which is typical of Indian peoples. They are flat, a characteristic common to many European skulls."

I tip my chin to Moss. "Get a close-up of Moss's face, will you, Sam?"

Sam walks across the lab, and Moss looks up. His dark eyes are sad. He has a deeply seamed brown face—one of those elderly faces in which all the world's despair seems to be concentrated.

For the camera, I say, "Gull Man proves there were at least two racial groups in North America at the end of the last Ice Age. Moss's people were Mongoloids, traditionally called American Indians. They generally have broad faces, round heads, straight black hair, and shovel-shaped incisors." I tip the skull again. "Pan back to me, Sam."

Sam walks the camera back and stands looking down, filming my hands as I turn the skull. "Gull Man's people were related to modern Caucasoids."

I'm having trouble focusing my eyes. I squeeze them closed for a second, then open them and continue. "We're discovering that the peopling of the Americas is a lot more complicated than we thought. The first arrivals, both in North America and South America, must have been ancient mariners of extraordinary skill. They also must have used the stars to guide them on their long journeys, indicating detailed astronomical knowledge. They were scientists and explorers par excellence."

I gently place the fragile skull on the table and move to the spine. As I run my finger down the table beside the shattered vertebrae, I feel nauseous. When did I last eat? I can't remember. "A short time before Gull Man's death, he was speared in the hip. His chest was also apparently crushed by a powerful impact."

Kirk adds, "Proving that interpersonal violence between humans is nothing new."

I pause to check the clock. Have seven minutes really passed?

I blink. I've started seeing a ball of light flashing at the edge of my vision. I fight to shake off the exhaustion.

A car screeches to a stop on the street outside, and everyone gasps and stares at the curtained window. A man shouts, *"Goddamn deer, get out of the road!"*

Breath escapes my lungs in a gush of relief. I constantly have deer in my yard, especially in the winter.

"What's wrong, Cathy?" Kim asks and frowns at me over her glasses. "You look like you're about to pass out."

"No, I—I keep seeing a ball of light. It bounces around the room, just at the corner of my eye."

"You're exhausted. You haven't slept in two days. Just stay on your feet and recording for another ten minutes, kiddo. Let's get as much information as we can."

I nod and see Moss shift on his stool.

"Is it one ball of light or many?" he asks in his gentle old voice.

"Just one, Moss," I say as though in another couple of hours I expect to see thousands of them. I run a hand through my hair.

Moss slides off his stool and quietly pads across the floor to stand beside the table, near Gull Man's feet. He glances at the window before turning back to me and softly saying, "My father was Lakota, but my mother's people, the Onondaga, believe that deer have a special purpose. They guide the spirits of the dead to the afterlife."

I love Moss. He's my great-uncle and he's been a friend for forty years, but in the most inappropriate times, like now, he often goes into long tribal stories that seem to have no relevance whatsoever to the job at hand.

I say, "Sam, film the long bones. Get a really good shot of that stone point embedded in the innominate, the hip bone, and the cranial lesion where he was struck in the head."

"I'm on it," Sam says, and moves down the length of the body to the andesite spear point they had dated to around 9,300 years ago.

Moss pushes closer to me. He has his wrinkled face tipped up, staring at me with kind eyes. He continues. "Sometimes a person's spirit becomes lost when it's trying to find the star road to the Village of Souls. You may see such spirits wandering through the forest or down busy streets. Sometimes a soul must wait for a long time because of the things the person did when he was alive."

"Moss," I say, barely able to keep tears of frustration at bay. "We have a lot of work to do, and our time has almost run out."

I edge by him and point to the spear point for the camera. "When we were first called in to analyze Gull Man, the coroner thought he was a White pioneer. But in the process of analysis, we discovered this point. The Stemmed Point tradition is contemporaneous with the Pebble Tool Tradition in the Pacific Northwest. Both date to between nine and eleven thousand years ago. This Stemmed Point is a classic examp—"

Moss softly interrupts. "When a soul leaves the body, it takes the shape of a ball of light. Most humans can't see it, but the deer can.

When the deer see a soul wandering around, lost and confused, they chase after it. The deer catch the light in their antlers and throw it into the sky, so the soul can see the star road better, and start its journey."

My eyes are inevitably drawn to the open newspaper spread on the counter behind Kim. The big bold headline reads: COURT RULES SCIENTIFIC RESEARCH VIOLATES TRIBAL RELIGION. In slightly smaller letters the subtitle proclaims: *Bureau of Land Management officials say, after the recent court decision, there will be no more study of the remains of Gull Man! Science is sacrilegious!*

"Forgive me, Moss." I look back at him and try to apologize. "You know I love that story. I've loved it my entire life. It's just that religion got us into this mess."

He smiles sadly. "I know."

As he slowly ambles to the head of the table to peer into Gull Man's empty eye sockets, I say, "Okay, Sam, let's get some pictures of the—"

Down the street sirens wail.

No one makes a sound, but we all look at the clock. Eighteen minutes have passed.

I say, "Kim, hand me the phalanx fragment."

Kim lifts the plastic bag containing a tiny piece of finger bone and tosses it to me. I tuck it inside my jeans. If I'm very lucky, I'll be able to sneak it out to a DNA lab somewhere. Then maybe we'll know if Gull Man's people interbred with the Mongoloid population, the American Indians. I suspect they did. After all, people drop their "genes" at the drop of a hat. If they did interbreed, Gull Man may be an ancestor to most people currently living in America and Canada.

"Thank you," I say in a trembling voice. "Now, grab your notes and get out of here before they come. I pray none of you gets caught."

Kim tucks her notebook under her arm and swings her coat around her shoulders. On her way out, she grabs my hand and stares into my eyes. "Never be ashamed of standing up for what's right, Cathy. Fact is fact. I don't care what religious 'truths' the fanatics try to push on the public."

Hastily, she climbs the basement stairs, and I hear her sprint for the back door.

"Hurry, Sam. Moss?"

Sam stuffs everything, including the video camera, into his backpack and kisses my cheek on the way out. "Thank you, for all you've taught me about what it means to be human," he says with genuine affection. Fear lives in his eyes.

"Thanks for caring, Sam."

The sirens are growing louder.

Sam runs. He must have flung open the back door, for it slams twice.

"Moss?" I look down into his elderly face. "You have to go."

He takes my hand in a tender grip and seems to be examining the freckles that dot my skin—the legacy of my Irish father. "It's a form of murder, you know?"

"What is?"

"These crazy fundamentalists, they're killing the history of a continent. It's . . . geographic genocide," he says thoughtfully.

Geographic genocide. He may have just coined a new phrase.

I think of the great lengths to which governments have gone to erase the multiracial heritage of their nations: the Chinese with their Caucasian warriors, Americans with the Indians, Europe and the Jews . . .

Loud knocking starts on the front door.

"Oh, my God, Moss." Tears tighten my voice. "It's too late now. Why didn't you go?"

His smile wilts. "You shouldn't have to stand up for our peoples alone, Niece," he says, and his gaze darts around the room as though he's watching something. "And I wanted to see his soul go free."

"Whose soul?"

He looks at Gull Man. I finally understand. The ball of light. The deer in the street outside.

"Do you think you released it, when you prayed over him at dusk?" I ask.

"Yes, he was calling to me. He needed to hear the old Songs, before he could—"

A man shouts, *"Dr. Catherine Garren! FBI! Open this door!"*

Moss drops my hand and turns to face the basement stairs. "Government soldiers," he says in a distasteful voice. "Just like in the old days."

"In the old days, Moss, they hunted our people down because they thought we were bad guys."

His eyes fill with despair again. "We're still bad guys. At least the fundamentalists say we are."

I take a moment to make sure the plastic bag is tucked securely in my underwear. I am going to be arrested for doing scientific research—does that mean I'll be a political prisoner? Like Andrei

Sakharov? I suppose they'll search me. I just pray the bone fragment is small enough that they won't notice and reach into my panties to get it.

Moss's wrinkled lips curl into a smile. "I think you should let me have it. My old friend, Lydia, works at the University of California in Riverside. She can get it to the DNA lab there."

He may be right. I'm the real "bad" guy here. When I was ordered to stop studying Gull Man and turn him over, I didn't.

As I pull the bag out and hand it to Moss, my front door explodes and what sounds like dozens of feet stamp the wood floor of my living room.

"Dr. Garren!"

I look at the bag. "Where are you going to hide it, Moss?"

He slips it inside his medicine bag. "Medicine bags are sacred to my people," he says as he tucks the leather bag back into his shirt. "I'll make a fuss if they say they want to 'study' it!" He grins toothlessly at me.

I'm not sure it will work, but the phalanx is probably safer there than in my underwear.

Heavy feet pummel the stairs, and two burly agents rush into the room. Their blue FBI jackets look faintly purple in the dim light. A local police officer follows them. The tall red-haired man marches toward me. "Dr. Catherine Garren?"

"Yes." My knees are shaking.

"You are under arrest for the theft of federal property and violations of the Native American Graves Protection and Repatriation Act."

He pulls cuffs from his belt. I hold out my hands as he rattles off the Miranda warning.

Moss does the same, but they seem reluctant to cuff him. They look at him as though wondering what an old Medicine Man is doing here—as though he shouldn't care about the history of his people or his nation. Moss fought in World War II. He cares very much. He walks forward, smiling, and stretches his hands out until they almost touch the officer.

The man obligingly cuffs him.

"Let's go." The officer pushes me toward the door.

Before I climb the stairs, I take one last look at Gull Man and softly pray that somewhere, sometime in the future, we will find another one of his people and Americans will care enough about who he was and what happened to him that we will be allowed to tell his story.

As the officers lead us out onto my dark front lawn, I see the deer.

They are frolicking, leaping and tossing their antlers toward the heavens.

Moss smiles and stares up at the star road.

The Milky Way is brilliant tonight, like a fluttering white veil stretched across the sky.

After more than nine thousand years, we have sent a soul home.

Early Morning

*S*eagulls squawk high above me. I cannot see them—my eyes are too heavy to open—but their cries comfort me. Their voices and the wet muddy scent of the river are all I have now.

"You haven't forgotten me, have you?" the old man sitting beside me asks.

"You were teaching me about compassion," I say, and try to breathe. It isn't easy. I feel as though a huge block of granite sits atop my broken ribs.

"Yes, good. Stay with me now," he says in a gravelly voice. "Here you are, dying more every moment, and you still believe compassion is some sort of sentimental self-indulgent whining. That surprises me."

I try to listen, to focus on the Soul Keeper's words, but it's growing harder to distinguish his voice from the rattling leaves and the rushing blood in my veins. All are unbearably loud.

"I don't think that's exactly what I said." A tired smile touches my lips. "But, I'm listening. Tell me what it is."

"Let me ask you another question first. You feel pride when you believe you are acting compassionately, don't you?"

"I am proud to be a compassionate man, yes."

In a darkly ironic voice, the Soul Keeper says, "I know few people who would consider you compassionate, Chief."

"You're a hermit. How many people can you know? Five? Maybe ten?"

I can almost hear the thunderous lowering of his thick gray brows. "True compassion does not make a man feel pride. Its core is humility and *sacrifice. If you feel pride after an act of compassion, you've clearly only sacrificed enough to make yourself feel good."*

I struggle to lift my eyelids to look at him, but they are too heavy. "I like feeling good after I help someone."

"Feeling good is not the goal. The heart of compassion is sacrifice." He halts long enough to inhale a deep breath, then adds, "When a human being sacrifices so much for another's sake that he feels empty and bereft, he has, for one shining moment, been truly compassionate. All other acts of 'compassion' are simple selfishness."

The seagulls dive closer, squealing and fluttering. On the fabric of my souls, I can imagine their white wings flashing in the sunlight. In my memory, my wife's face flickers, and I wonder what compassion has ever gotten me.

I tell him, "If what you say is true, it's a miracle anyone is ever compassionate twice."

The Soul Keeper scoffs, "It's not supposed to be easy."

Wind Woman swirls around me, and I breathe in the sweet scent of the cottonwoods that cover the grassy floodplain. It's summer, isn't it? I think it's summer. I try to imagine buffalo grazing in belly-high grass and wildflowers.

"Well," I say through a long, congested exhalation, "you are here to teach me what I must know to travel to the House of Air. So. Teach."

He reaches out and uses a blunt obsidian scraper to cut off a lock of my hair. Soon he will light a fire and smoke the lock in sweet grass and cedar, then wrap it in a buffalohide bundle and place it in a beautifully painted box. He will Keep my soul. Finally, after four days, he will carry it to the sacred center of my people's Council Lodge, where I will forever advise and bless them.

At least I pray that is what he will do.

One never knows with this old man. He's unpredictable at best.

If he does not Keep my soul, it will stay locked in my bones, alone, crying out for salvation and never finding it.

Because that's what happens to the souls of bad people.

Or I should say the souls of people who ignored every opportunity for that "one shining moment. . . ."

One

The pale blue halo of dawn arced over the eastern horizon and shimmered on the high snowcapped peaks. Mother Ocean still lay in shadow, her voice soft this morning, a bare purl of sound. White breakers pounded jagged rocks, then washed onto gravelly beaches. Offshore, fir-covered knobs of rock jutted from the wave-streaked water.

Just to the north, along the precipitous shore, Waket's Nose—a spear of basalt—thrust up. Streamers of morning mist shredded on the mossy rock and drifted through the few stands of firs that had taken root in the steep sides.

The grizzled warrior known as Red Dog scratched his bent nose and curiously studied the ancient Soul Keeper, Rides-the-Wind. The old man had seen more than five tens of summers. They must have been hard ones, for deep lines engraved his oblong face and criss-crossed his broad flat nose. His elkhide cape swayed in the fading starlight as he adjusted a set of sticks on the ground, moving them from one place to another.

"Elder," Red Dog bravely tried to interrupt for the third time, "Starwatcher Ecan sent me. I have urgent news."

"Ecan considers his bodily functions to be urgent news," the old man snapped.

"Yes, Elder, but this is different. He—"

"Don't tell me this is different. I know him. I remember once, three summers ago, when his guards rushed in and pulled me from my robes. They dragged me kicking and scratching to his lodge. I was certain he'd ordered my death. It turned out he'd discovered a star-shaped object in his morning phlegm. He wanted me to kill the evil Spirit before it had a chance to leap back inside him." Rides-the-Wind arched a white eyebrow. "He's an imbecile. Imbecility runs in his family."

"Well, perhaps, but—"

"Not yet." The old man aimed a crooked finger at Red Dog. "I'll tell you when I'm ready to listen."

Red Dog gruffly folded his muscular arms and let his gaze drift to the small fire behind Rides-the-Wind. The hair-stuffed bodies of three toads perched on the hearthstones, where tendrils of smoke bathed them. What on earth did the old man use them for? Their bulging eyes seemed to be glaring right at him.

Mist had just begun to form a tufted rime along the shore. Every now and then, he caught glimpses of orange fire bobbing out on the ocean—whale oil lamps, perched in the bows of fishing canoes. A few seagulls hunted along the surf, their calls shrill in the darkness.

Rides-the-Wind moved another stick less than a fingernail's width from where it had been. In the bare breeze, his long gray hair and beard fluttered, rising around his wrinkled face as though alive.

Red Dog shook his head. Only pure-blooded North Wind People had hair around their mouths. He'd never liked it. So far as he was concerned, beards had one use: soaking up soups and stews. Though his father had been one of the North Wind People, Red Dog thankfully looked more like the Raven People, who did not have beards.

"What are you doing, Elder?" Red Dog asked.

"You're blind, are you?"

"Well . . . it didn't seem as though you moved your stick very far, so I was confused."

"What does it look like I'm doing?"

Red Dog frowned and followed the old man's gaze. The stony point was bare of the ever-present stands of fir and spruce. Rock cairns made black humps on the eastern horizon. The Star People rose along the line between the humps and the sticks he'd planted in the ground.

"Seeing where the Star People are rising?" Red Dog ventured a guess. "Which sounds a little silly to me. I mean, they rise in about the same place every day, don't they?"

Rides-the-Wind tipped his antique face up. His brown eyes resembled stones under water, round and shiny. "You know, I think that when Song Maker was pulling threads of sound from the heavens to Sing the world into existence, a few flat notes stuck in your soul."

"Well, Elder"—What did a man say to that?—"I'm a warrior. My heart has different concerns. While your eyes are trained on the sky, mine are generally scanning the forest for people who might wish to kill me."

"Given your ability to irritate people, your constant need for vigilance isn't surprising."

As the Soul Keeper struggled to stand, Red Dog gripped his elbow and helped him up. Rides-the-Wind, though so much older, towered over him.

The Soul Keeper waved a hand to indicate the mist-lashed cliffs. "This is a sacred place. The Star People often come down to earth on this very spot. On certain days, they dance on Waket's Nose. And if you are careful and observant, you can calculate when they will arrive because they move a little closer to us every day. Hence the sticks. Each morning I measure their approach."

Red Dog scowled at the eastern horizon. Only a few Star People remained visible against the gleam of dawn. At death, the souls of North Wind people traveled to the Above Worlds, where they became stars. Soul Keepers, like Rides-the-Wind, spent their entire lives trying to seek the wisdom of those ancestors. Such elders never fought, or used a knife, no matter for what purpose, but dedicated their lives to seeing beyond this world.

Red Dog asked, "Which one of our ancestors is planning on dropping out of the sky?"

Rides-the-Wind lifted a gnarled finger and pointed. "That one. See how his hair is blowing out behind him? He's flying toward us very fast."

It did look like long hair streamed out behind the Star Person. He glanced back at Rides-the-Wind. "When will he arrive?"

"When he wishes to. The Star People travel in far greater time circles than we do. I think it will take him a few moons. But when he arrives . . ." Rides-the-Wind turned toward Waket's Nose; the rocky point jutted out over the water like a giant's beak. "He will soar down right there—at least, that's what my calculations indicate."

Red Dog's eyes widened. Waket's Nose was noted for strange happenings. As a boy, Red Dog's own grandfather had seen one of the giants appear there. Grandfather had been canoeing with friends when the giant had stepped out onto Waket's Nose and leaped into the sea. They hadn't been able to see the giant's face, but as he plummeted into the water, his hands shook like a Dancer's. A tremendous splash rose when he hit Mother Ocean, nearly swamping his grandfather's canoe and hurling spray for hundreds of body lengths. Summers later, two women from Red Dog's clan had seen a huge mountain goat walking on the water at the exact spot where the giant dove into the ocean. When they stood up and gasped at the sight, a storm rose that overturned their canoe and drowned them. He'd heard the story from the very person onshore who'd seen it happen.

Worried, Red Dog said, "I pray I am far away when the Star Person arrives."

Rides-the-Wind gazed up at the deep blue sky. "Oh? You irritate him, too?"

"No, Elder, of course not, I—"

"Myself, I pray to be right here. I would give my very life to speak face-to-face with one of the Star People. The miracles they must see from up there. I can't even imagine."

For a while, they just stared at the twinkling lights of the ancestors; then Rides-the-Wind heaved a breath and said, "Very well. What news do you bring from Fire Village?"

The North Wind People—who had been here since Song Maker created the world—centered their affairs at Fire Village. There, the Four Old Women, the ruling Council, met, decided the law, and governed not only the North Wind People, but also the Raven People, upon whom they relied for tribute.

Red Dog said, "Chief Cimmis sent me to tell you that the woman, Evening Star, is gone. Escaped from Ecan's lodge."

Rides-the-Wind's dark eyes blazed. "Fools, you should have never meddled with her. She is more than you know." A pause. "Wasn't Ecan's young brother one of the guards assigned to her?"

"Kenada is dead, Starwatcher. She slit his throat with such vehemence she almost severed his head."

For a time, Rides-the-Wind just stroked his long gray beard, as though deep in thought. He smiled warily. "Next you will tell me that Ecan has sent a pack of his mangy guards out after her."

"Yes, Elder. Runners were sent immediately. I'm sure they've caught her by now, but Ecan orders you to curse her. He wants it done where the Raven People can see you do it. Just in case."

The old man's withered mouth pinched. "Curse her? In a way that makes the Raven People fear to help her?"

"Yes, Elder. Exactly."

"And just why should I do that?"

Red Dog made an airy gesture. "Well, if you don't, Starwatcher Ecan will kill you."

Rides-the-Wind closed his eyes and chuckled under his breath. "Humans. Such strange creatures. They forever remain a child in one part only: their fear of death. That's why they dwell on it. Death is the only thing in our lives that never fails to fill us with childlike wonder."

Red Dog tucked a windblown lock of graying black hair behind his ear. Rides-the-Wind rarely made sense to him. "Which means . . . what?"

Rides-the-Wind gave him an annoyed look. "You wouldn't understand. When did the woman escape?"

"Two days ago. It has taken me that long to find Ecan, and then you. Oh, and Chief Cimmis orders you to return home immediately. He says that while Ecan is away leading the war party, he needs your services in Fire Village."

"Ecan is leading a war party? He's the Starwatcher, a priest. Or has his appetite for the holy been subsumed by his appetite for blood and terror?"

"I don't know, Elder. All I can tell you is that the Four Old Women sent a war party to punish some North Wind People who incited disobedience among the Raven People villages."

"You mean the *starving* people who defied Chief Cimmis's orders to turn over the tribute owed to Fire Village."

"Yes."

"The fools," Rides-the-Wind said softly. "They dance on the tip of Waket's Nose, not knowing how treacherous the footing is."

Did he mean the Raven People? Or the Four Old Women who ran the Council? Red Dog cocked his head, but the Soul Keeper asked, "How long has Ecan been gone?"

"Perhaps ten days."

Wind Mother rushed up the slope and beat her way through the twisted spruce and fir growing at the edge of the cliffs. Their sweet evergreen fragrance bathed Red Dog's face and carried the damp scent of the sea.

"It is the beginning of the end." Rides-the-Wind shivered, tugged his elkhide hood up, and held it closed beneath his chin.

"The end of what?" Red Dog asked.

Rides-the-Wind didn't seem to hear, but added, "Tell Cimmis that I'm not coming. I wish to be left alone."

Red Dog examined him in detail. "Are you ill, Elder?"

Rides-the-Wind gave him a look that would have withered polished stone. "Why? Did you become a Healer while I was away?"

"Uh . . . no."

Red Dog chewed his lower lip. Over the past sun cycle, Ecan had become the most powerful holy man in the North Wind Nation—mostly because he enthusiastically supported the Council's decisions to make war upon the Raven People. Rides-the-Wind, on the other hand, had opposed the Council, and had abruptly left Fire Village just after fall equinox. Was it because he'd seen his influence dwindle, and he couldn't stand the humiliation?

"What should I tell Chief Cimmis about the woman? Will you curse her for Ecan?"

"On the contrary." Rides-the-Wind reached down for his walking stick where it rested on the ground near the Star sticks. He propped both hands on the use-polished knob. "I will be praying night and day for her safety."

Red Dog shifted uncomfortably. "Well, prayers aside, I don't see how she can be. Once people discover she's Ecan's escaped slave, no one will dare to help her."

In the furred frame of his hood, Rides-the-Wind's seamed old face resembled a dried berry. He turned to his fire, picked up his smoked toads, and gently placed them into his pack. Finally, he reached down and plucked a small stone from the ground, holding it up for Red Dog to see.

"Tell Chief Cimmis that I have a message for him. He stands on the precipice . . . and if he doesn't watch his step, he and Ecan are going to fall. The drop will cost him everything he holds dear."

With that, the old man pitched the stone out, over the cliff. In the purple light, it arced down, shattering into slivers as it struck the rock below.

Two

The droplet formed on the damp rock. It hung in front of her eyes, clear and crystalline in the soft light. She tried to shrink back into the stony recess in which she hid. Angular shale gouged her back.

She froze, refusing even to breathe, when a warrior stepped out of the ferns and bracken opposite her. He wore a woven sea-grass cloak and had a conical rain hat on his head. His spears and atlatl were clutched in one callous hand. He knelt, keen eyes on the damp soil next to the small forest pool. He found her tracks immediately, stepping over to crouch and run the fingers of his free hand over delicate imprints. Like a wary panther, his eyes began to take in the damp ferns and thick grass surrounding the pool.

She dared not stare straight at him, willing her gaze to fix on the bent grass to his right. Each beat of her heart thundered like a pot drum. Gods, he could hear it, couldn't he?

He rose on stealthy legs and inspected the bruised grass. Yes, that was it. Follow the sign. She had carefully lain a false trail, walking across the grass to a slope of bare stone beyond.

Soundlessly he slipped through the ferns and brushed back the fir branches to the rocky slope. She could just see his partially hidden form as he started along the slope, searching for signs of her passage.

She dared to take a shallow breath, her chest rising as cool air entered her burning body. How could she feel so hot when chilly water was seeping into her deerhide dress?

If she closed her eyes, horror played behind her eyelids, conjuring images of the last two moons. The wail of her dying daughter still echoed in her ears. She could see her husband's face, streaked with blood and disbelief. The stench of burning lodges clung in her nostrils.

So much lost. How did a soul bear it? Or the humiliation of her captivity? Even now, so much later, she could feel the pain as, one after the other, Ecan, and then Kenada, pried her legs apart to drive themselves inside her. Her skin crawled with the memory.

Perhaps it is better to die. Her fingers tightened in the gritty moss carpeting the hollow. Hot tears began to leak past her eyes, a painful knot forming under her tongue.

Her daughter's high-pitched wail rose again in her ears.

But if you die, Cimmis and the Council will have won. They will continue to kill, enslave, and murder, until nothing fine and beautiful is left.

She swallowed hard. It would be so much easier to die.

Movement.

The warrior eased back through the trees, stepping softly, crouched, eyes alert. A hunter on silent feet, he slipped back to the place where her tracks could be seen. Then, patiently, carefully, he began to search the pool and the fern-covered shale wall behind it.

Evening Star's heart began to race again.

The droplet of water rounded, elongated, and fell. A silver streak before her eyes, it spattered on the stone, a finger's width from her cheek.

The warrior cocked his head, a foot lifted, as he listened to the forest. Then, with the faintest of grunts, he turned and eased back into the tangled vines before trotting off between the swaying fir trees.

Wind Woman whistled down the mountain and batted at Cimmis's long gray braid as he walked the starlit path through Fire Village. This place, Fire Village, was the home of his ancestors. It nestled high on the southwestern slope of Fire Mountain, the great volcano that dominated the land. From the cliff that lay just behind the village, a sweeping panorama of the surrounding country could be seen. On those heights, the Soul Keepers and Starwatchers could greet the morning sun and chart the track of the stars across the sky. The expanse of ocean to the west—dotted by thousands of islands—

could be seen in the shimmering afternoon. Here his people lived among the clouds, forever blessed by moist ocean breezes ameliorated with the damp scents of the surrounding forests. The village itself was surrounded by a twenty-hand-tall palisade of cedar that wound around boulders and trees, creating a serpentine oval that protected not only the Council, but the four tens of bark lodges where the most powerful of the North Wind People lived.

Cimmis glanced over his shoulder at the three old women ducking out of the Council Lodge. They wore buffalohide robes over their shoulders. The fine brown hairs twinkled in the light of the Star People. Old Woman North hesitated and shot him a look of irritation. Of them all, she was the most recalcitrant and insidious. By force of will, she dominated the others and insisted that her senseless notions be adopted as policy.

Even as he walked away, the memory of her shrill voice grated on his ears: *They shall pay! Of course there's food! There's always food! They owe it to us.*

No matter what insane orders the Council gave, he would enforce them. If Old Woman North was mad, so perhaps was he to follow her? He glanced down in the darkness to his strong right fist. Throughout the known world, people trembled and quailed at that fist. Gods, how had that come about?

Looking at it, he saw only muscle, bone, and sinew wrapped in age-leathered skin.

"You will regret this decision you have made tonight," he grumbled to himself.

He cradled his weak left arm against his chest. He'd seen fifteen summers since the buffalo had charged him during the hunt. He'd tried to leap out of the way, but the big bull had slammed into his arm, flinging him four tens of hands before dashing away in a cloud of dust. The arm still worked; it was just weak and much smaller than his right.

The beaten path curved around the plaza fire and continued up the slope. Bark lodges created a perfect circle around him. Each was made from a large pole frame covered with bark; life-size paintings of the gods decorated the exteriors. The enormous white eyes of Buffalo Above flashed as he passed Old Woman North's lodge.

"A pleasant evening to you, my Chief," a young slave woman called.

"And to you," Cimmis replied sourly.

Even at this time of night slaves scurried about, dressed in brown sea-grass capes, carrying food or firewood. Most just bowed as he passed. Others felt obliged to speak. As he walked in front of the plaza fire, its light threw his monstrous shadow over the lava cliff behind the village; it danced like a leaping ghost.

He ignored it, his mind on the Council. If they kept making the sort of decisions they had made this night, that's what they would all become: dark, lonely shadows. He could feel the truth knotting his belly.

His North Wind People had been here since the beginning of the world. Didn't anyone remember the old stories? About the Creation? About Singing the World into existence? About the coming of Wolf and Coyote, Eagle, and Killer Whale? About Raven, the Trickster, and his dark-haired children?

He tugged his lynxhide cape closed and glowered.

"I remember the stories," he whispered. "I remember them well."

Around the winter fires, his grandmother had told many stories of the Beginning Time when their people first arrived here. Glaciers had covered most of the world. The people, guided by the North Wind, had paddled their canoes down the icy coastline, looking for a sanctuary, and found it on the islands off the coast. Everything they could have wanted was there—a paradise of fish, sea mammals, berries, tubers, algae, and kelp. In the springtime, the islands had been rich with tender shoots and greens. In summer and fall, the raspberries, blueberries, cranberries, and others had filled the baskets.

Generations passed in peace and plenty, and the people split, becoming Cougar People, Buffalo People, and Elderberry People who moved off in different directions. Finally the Raven People had appeared in the north, wearing their black hair in buns, reddish brown of skin, with round heads and high-cheeked faces. Few in numbers, they drifted down the coast. They'd been timid, awed by the North Wind People.

At first, the North Wind People gladly shared their fishing and gathering grounds. There was plenty for everyone. But the elders hadn't realized that the Raven People bred like meadow vales. Within a few cycles, they had begun moving east, south, and north. The Buffalo People retreated farther eastward to the grassy plains; the Elderberry People headed south along the shore. The Cougar People had retreated into the rugged mountains, crossing the passes and heading inland. Others had made their homes on distant islands to the north.

With the burgeoning population, it didn't take long for the resources to run short. The Raven People no longer wished to share. Fights broke out. Many died.

The North Wind elders decided to move their villages inland to Fire Mountain. A strange choice for a maritime people, since the terrain was steep and uneven and there weren't many resources, but they'd been trying to get away from the greedy Raven People. Every summer for tens of tens of tens of cycles, the North Wind People had moved higher and higher up the slopes. Ever closer to their ancestors, the Star People.

The Raven People sought them out. It was little wonder. The North Wind People had been in this world longer; they knew the best places to gather berries, tubers, nuts. They knew the best fishing coves and where to find elk and buffalo, even in the worst winters. And most importantly, they knew the Healing plants.

Seven tens of cycles ago, when Cimmis's mother had led the Council, she'd started to demand payment for such valuable knowledge. They'd exhausted their own mountain resources and needed supplies. She'd told the Raven People they could come to the North Wind villages twice a cycle, on the solstices, and ask anything they wished, but they had to bring "tribute" or they would not be allowed to return.

His mother had never dreamed what a wealth of food, exotic shells, furs, and other precious things would pour in—including slaves. When the Raven People could not afford to send food or other valuables, they sent some of their children. Many Raven People served here as cooks, wood carriers, basketmakers, weavers, and warriors. Lately, others had been captured in raids and brought back as additional slaves.

"May the gods curse you, Mother. You made a terrible mistake. We are at war because of tribute."

After seven tens of cycles, tribute had freed the North Wind People from the drudgery of finding food every day and had allowed them to pursue grander things. Nearly every elder here was an accomplished Dreamer, Healer, painter, carver, or weaver. They could cure many diseases, and when they couldn't, their Dreamers could fly to the House of Air where the ancestors lived and seek the advice of ancient holy people who'd been dead for cycles.

As Cimmis walked around a massive lava boulder, he glimpsed old Red Dog talking to the guards at the western entry—a gap in the circle of lodges—and Cimmis continued up the trail. The runner could find him sitting before his fire just as easily as standing out here in the cold night wind.

When he neared his lodge flap, he heard his only surviving daughter, Kstawl, say, "Oh, Mother, please try to eat."

Cimmis took a deep and despairing breath before he lifted the lodge flap and stepped into the soft yellow glow.

The lodge measured four paces across. The interior wood had been smoked to a deep brown, and the dark walls provided a stunning background for the white buffalohide shields that hung from the lodgepoles. Each had served him in battle over the years, but they still looked new. He constantly repainted the images of the gods who had blessed his weapons: Wolf, Cougar, and Bear had given him strength for the land battles he'd fought; but out on the ocean, he'd relied upon Killer Whale, Dolphin, and Sea Lion. Their painted eyes seemed to follow him as he removed his lynxhide cape and hung it on a peg beside the door.

His wife, Astcat, the great matron of the North Wind People, leaned against a pile of hides to his right. Kstawl had dressed her in a bright yellow wrap. Ascat's jaw gaped, and her beautiful green-brown eyes jerked from place to place. Gray hair framed her long, narrow face. He thought he saw the slightest flicker of a smile on her lips when she looked at him.

"How is she?" he asked.

"Not well, Father." Kstawl had seen three and ten summers. Her whiplike body was still a girl's, with only the first hint of womanhood beginning to bud on her chest. She wore her long red hair in a bun coiled over her right ear and fastened with a beautifully carved buffalo-bone pin. "The Matron hasn't eaten since this morning when you left for the Council meeting."

She'd been trying to feed the matron spoonfuls of fish stew. Stew had dribbled down the front of Astcat's dress.

Cimmis walked across the lodge and untied his belt pouch. It hurt to see his wife like this. Only a few moons ago, she had been bright and happy, her smile like sunshine in his soul.

"When did her soul fly?" he asked as he placed his pouch beside their bedding hides.

"Father, it was as though when you left this morning you took her soul with you."

Cimmis nodded.

Before leaving, he and Astcat had discussed what to say to the Council. They had agreed it would be better to limit attacking recalcitrant villages that refused to send tribute; it was better to wait until they could call in favors from the other North Wind villages. Perhaps gather additional warriors before pushing the Raven villages.

She'd reached up and tenderly touched his face. *My husband, the fact is, they cannot pay. These are difficult times for all of us. If we continue to harm them, they will strike back.*

Kstawl rose and returned the bowl to the stew bag that hung on the tripod by the fire. As she poured the bowl's contents back into the bag, he watched her. Her innocent oval face wore a perpetual frown.

Apparently nervous beneath his gaze, she wiped her hands on her brown dress and lifted the water bag beside the fire, preparing to wash the bowl.

"No, Daughter, don't wash it," he said, and walked over for the bowl. "Perhaps I can get her to eat."

"I hope so."

Cimmis stirred the stew and ladled the bowl full again. Kstawl stood quietly, awaiting further instructions.

"It's late. Go and sleep. Thank you for trying to feed her."

"I'll return first thing tomorrow, Father." She ducked through the flap.

Cimmis took the warm bowl to Astcat. Her eyes had stopped jerking uncontrollably. Now she stared vacantly at a fixed point in space. A small improvement.

"Here, my wife," he said softly, and sat down beside her. "You must eat something or you'll be as skinny as a weasel. I'd have to set your belongings outside my lodge."

They always joked about divorce—about setting the other's belongings outside the lodge—because it was simply unthinkable. Since their Joining day, he had taken captive women to his bed, even married them to establish beneficial political alliances, but he'd never loved them. His love for Astcat was like his heartbeat, constant and necessary.

Cimmis put his weak left arm around Astcat and hugged her shoulders. "Please try to eat. You know how it upsets me when you stop eating."

He carefully raised the polished horn spoon full of fish stew to her lips.

She dutifully opened her mouth, chewed twice; then her mouth gaped and chunks of fish fell down the front of her dress.

Much practiced, Cimmis used the spoon to scoop up one of the chunks, and fed it to her again. This time, she chewed and swallowed.

Cimmis smiled. These were the small victories that made him happy. Not exacting the tribute owed them. Not leading war parties, or winning Council arguments.

Cimmis ate a bite of fish stew and gazed around the lodge. Blue-gray smoke spiraled up from the fire, hovered near the smoke hole, then escaped into the cold night beyond.

Most of their belongings were gone. A moon ago, when it became clear they could not survive the winter without additional tribute, the Four Old Women had made the decision to move to Wasp Village. He had ordered everything except what they needed every day to be packed and sent on ahead.

He hadn't realized that on those rare occasions when Astcat's soul returned to her body, she would need those things. Not so much because of what they contained, but because the baskets reminded her of where she was in the lodge. He'd come home right after dispatching the warriors with the first litter loaded with their things and found her wandering the lodge like a lost child.

He finished the stew and hugged her shoulders again.

"Well, I had another difficult meeting with the Elders. They needed you there to guide them, my wife." He hoped she could hear. "They dismissed our argument and voted to continue the attacks." He exhaled hard, feeling hollow. "I have been ordered to send the Wolf Tails after any North Wind person who has sided with the Raven People."

Astcat made a tiny sound of dismay, but she still stared blankly across the room. Her fingers, however, had tightened on her yellow leather skirt. Cimmis gently tucked locks of her gray hair behind her ears—she'd hate looking so untidy.

"I explained your fear that more attacks might force the Raven clans into an alliance against us, but they refused to listen." He clenched his good fist and made a face that resembled Old Woman North's scowl. In a voice that sounded very much like hers, he croaked, "They owe it to us! It's ours and we need it!"

He lifted her hand, kissed her fingers, then clutched them to his heart.

Moccasins shuffled on the trail outside, and a man called, "Chief Cimmis, I bring a message."

Cimmis gently removed his arm from Astcat's shoulder, made certain the hides supported her, then went to his door. As he shoved the hide aside, a rush of cold air swept in, rattling the shields.

"Yes?"

Gray-streaked black hair draped Red Dog's burly shoulders and framed his round face. In the firelight, his bent nose seemed to jut unnaturally to the left. He wore a tattered deerhide cape and carried a stone-headed war club. He'd clearly been running since Cimmis had first dispatched him; his face was streaked with dirt and soot, and his legs trembled.

"Forgive me for arriving so late, my Chief," Red Dog said, and bowed. "As ordered, I passed Starwatcher Ecan's party. He wished you to know that they were victorious at Shell Maiden Village. They took the tribute owed us and are heading to Sandy Point Village."

"Sandy Point Village? Why? They've sent their tribute."

Red Dog brushed a stringy mass of graying black hair from his brow. "Ecan said he wished to pass through Sandy Point Village on his way to the Moon Ceremonial at War Gods Village."

Cimmis smoothed his hand over his gray beard. Ecan always attended the Moon Ceremonial as a sign of support for Weedis the North Wind Healer, whom the Four Old Women had sent to live in the village. This journey, however, was different. Weedis had defied the Four Old Women, refused to demand that her villagers turn over the tribute they owed. For that reason—no matter the wisdom of the act—Ecan had other orders.

"Did Starwatcher Ecan tell you why he was going through Sandy Point Village?"

"No, my Chief."

Cimmis could see the reserve in his warrior's eyes. "But you don't think it's a good idea?" He smiled. "Go on, speak."

"Chief Rain Bear . . . well, I knew him well when he served here. He has struggled to keep the peace. Starved his village to pay tribute. His wife is recently dead. It would not be smart to act in a way that would alienate him."

"You and I agree on that. What of Rides-the-Wind?" Cimmis asked. "I expected him to return with you."

Red Dog winced. "He's not coming."

"Why not?"

"My Chief, I am only a messenger."

"Yes, yes."

"He says he may never return."

Cimmis felt a cold wind blow past his soul. "Did he give you any reason?"

Red Dog, nobody's coward, swallowed hard, a pained look on his face. "He said you and Ecan were dancing on the edge of the abyss, my Chief. And that if you weren't careful, you would both fall."

Cimmis narrowed an eye. "I will flay the skin from his body." To Red Dog: "And the young matron?"

"Rides-the-Wind was being very cantankerous. He said he would not curse Evening Star for Ecan. In fact, he'll be praying for her safety."

Cimmis rubbed his wrinkled brow. He had a headache building. "I shall show him a thing or two about falling into the abyss when I use cooking stones to roast his intestines in his living body." He paused. "I need you to find Wind Scorpion."

Red Dog shifted uncomfortably. "My Chief, I've been running for days."

"I must see him *now*. Then get a good night's rest. Tomorrow morning I want you to run a message back to Ecan. New orders from the Council."

"Yes, my Chief."

Red Dog bowed and shuffled toward the slave lodges that huddled together lower on the mountain.

Cimmis let the flap fall closed. He felt old beyond his four tens and seven summers.

Every muscle felt pulled from its socket as Red Dog made his way across Fire Village to the low lodge where Wind Scorpion lived. By the gods of the sky, that had been a close one! He had seen the anger boiling behind Cimmis's eyes when he'd been told that Rides-the-Wind wasn't returning. The threat Cimmis had made about cooking the old man's guts hadn't been an idle one.

Stones were heated in a crackling fire to white-hot, and a slit was made in a man's belly from the chest to the groin. With smoking sticks, the stones were plucked from the coals and dropped through the slit into the living intestines. The screams twined with the sizzling. All in all, it was a most gruesome way to die, smelling your guts as they cooked inside you.

Red Dog pondered that as he walked. The world was slipping sideways like a boulder on a mountain. How long before it slid and tumbled into the abyss Rides-the-Wind had mentioned?

He approached Wind Scorpion's lodge, low and menacing, like something crouched in the darkness.

Red Dog hadn't liked the man from the moment they'd met four summers ago. Wind Scorpion came from the east, from out in the sagebrush country beyond the mountains. It was said he'd lived with the Striped Dart People, but he had obviously once lived here, among the North Wind, and even in Fire Village itself.

Whenever Wind Scorpion looked at Red Dog, it made the hairs on his neck stand up. Something about the man, including his very smell, gave Red Dog the ghost-shivers.

Flickers of light could be seen around the door hanging as Red Dog called, "Wind Scorpion? Chief Cimmis calls you."

Nothing. Only the sound of scurrying from inside the lodge, and a worried gasp, as though someone had been caught unawares.

Under normal circumstances, Red Dog would have waited, curious to see what happened, but tired as he was, he bent and ripped the hanging aside to see a naked slave girl jerk a red wig from her head. Her skin was painted white, dabbed with clay. She had a lithesome body, perfectly formed. She stared at him in horror, the firelight playing on her strained face.

"What are you doing?" Red Dog demanded. "Why are you here?"

She swallowed hard, crossing her arms over her breasts, shrinking down to hide her nudity. "I—I am Wind Scorpion's slave, warrior. He—he was called away. I thought . . . thought you were—"

"Where is he?"

She was trembling now. "A runner came. A man. I didn't hear what was said. Wind Scorpion just smiled, as if in triumph, and packed his things." She was almost babbling. "He left just like that, and said nothing to me about when he'd be back. It's been almost two days now."

Red Dog scowled, stuck his head into the lodge, and peered around. To his amazement, images of white-skinned women with flowing red hair had been drawn on the walls. Each had oversized breasts and exaggerated hips around swollen vulvas.

Red Dog made a face and asked, "And you have no idea where he went?"

"No, warrior." She was wringing the red wig with one hand as she stared at him.

"Well, if he comes back, tell him the great chief wants to see him *now!*"

Red Dog ducked back into the sanity of the darkness and sighed as he turned and started wearily back for Cimmis's lodge. Now he had more bad news to deliver.

He had seen a man's guts boiled, could still smell the stench of it. As he approached Cimmis's lodge, his belly began to crawl inside him.

Gods, what could he do to save himself from this madness? Or was salvation already beyond his ability?

Three

The stars were nowhere in Starwatcher Ecan's thoughts as he lay slumped on the weeping woman. She was really just a girl. If she was lucky, she'd seen ten and three winters. For all he knew, he might have been the first man to ever take her.

What was it about a weeping woman that made coupling so much more satisfying? Her sobbing body trembled beneath him. Was it that in that moment he had no doubts about himself? And, as Song Maker knew, he had overcome so many doubts. He and Kenada. Dead Kenada. Murdered Kenada.

In the flickers of firelight her eyes glinted, vacant, as if her soul had fled at the hot rushing of his seed inside her. Waves of her long black hair lay tumbled about the woven-bark matting upon which they lay.

How could a woman sob without leaking tears?

The same way I do, when I think of Kenada. He hadn't shed a tear at the news. A cold emptiness had yawned inside him, like a falling of water into a black lava tube. He hadn't known that such a small thing as a man's body could hold such a bottomless pit.

He reached out and wound his fingers around the girl's silky black hair and remembered the smile on Kenada's lips. He'd been two summers younger, never the leader, but always a willing accomplice. To know that he had been brutally ripped from Ecan's life was like suddenly living with only half of his soul.

Ecan shifted, rising to stare down at the girl. Her round face shone with a copper tint in the firelight, the vacant eyes like glistening obsidian. No movement stirred her lips. But for the sucking sobs that shook her, she might have been as dead as Kenada.

The last time he'd looked down on a woman like this, it had been Evening Star, daughter of Matron Naida, heiress to the Ash Fall Clan. Unlike this shining black hair, he'd looked down on red curls, stared into blue eyes, and run his fingers down her pale cheeks.

A woman, North Wind or Raven, was still a woman. Just as warm, just as lifeless. Except that Evening Star hadn't wept when he drove his hardened manhood inside her. Jaw locked, she'd fixed her sight on something to the side, and lain there, lifeless but for the occasional blink of her eyes.

Who would have thought that she could kill Kenada?

He had been so careful to break her soul into submission. He had carefully planned the attack, using every element of surprise. When it was over he had brought the surviving captives into the plaza, where burning lodges illuminated the scene. He had watched Evening Star's expression when he walked behind her mother, Matron Naida, and used a razor-sharp obsidian blade to slit her throat. Then, drenched in the matron's blood, he had walked to Evening Star's struggling husband, stripped him, and gutted him like a living fish so that his intestines tumbled into the fire.

Evening Star had withstood it, face set against the horror. It was her daughter's screams that had finally broken her. Ecan would have sworn he saw Evening Star's soul leave her body. She had been like clay afterward, compliant to orders. So much so that he had taken her as a slave, an example of his Power, a warning to anyone who would challenge his rising authority.

And this girl? He wondered as he searched her face for any expression. Had he truly driven her soul from her body, or might it return sometime? If he could just get it right, think of the incredible Power he would wield. No one would challenge them. No . . . him. There was no more they. Kenada was dead.

"Are you like her? Can you come back to yourself?"

The girl didn't answer. The tremors running through her body massaged his manhood, and he felt himself stiffening again. Was that where Kenada had made his mistake? Had he rolled off Evening Star's body, satiated? Ecan could imagine his brother, flaccid after his release, perhaps with his arm over his head, eyes closed, as Evening Star, like a wraith, rose from the robes. He could see her long red hair falling around her pale body as she hovered over Kenada. At the thought of her striking, Ecan thrust his hardened manhood into the girl beneath him. She made no noise; only the opening of her mouth betrayed any awareness at all.

At a slight moan, War Chief White Stone turned, staring uneasily at the shelter where Starwatcher Ecan lay with the captive girl. Ecan made him nervous. Something about the man had changed over the last year, as if his soul were decomposing from a faint fuzz of mold to downright rot and corruption. Ecan had grown from dislikable to dangerous. And now, Kenada, who had balanced his moods, was dead.

He checked his guards, each positioned to cover the approaches. The canoes had been pulled up on the beach beyond high tide. The rest of his warriors lay rolled in hides and matting, blissfully asleep.

He wished that he, too, could lose himself to Dreams. White Stone rubbed the back of his neck and stared out at the fluorescing surf. Above, clouds covered the Star People. And what, he wondered, did the North Wind ancestors think of this current lunacy?

As war chief, he knew full well that Matron Astcat had lost her soul, and Old Woman North—an aged halfwit—had the force of personality to whip the other old women into obedience.

We're losing ourselves. White Stone stared helplessly at the night sky. The Council didn't understand. They remained, locked away on their mountain, unaware of the reality building against them.

White Stone turned his attention back to the surf. It would be so easy. Just push one of the canoes out past the surf, and then paddle north. There were still islands out there rich in berries, roots, fish, and shellfish, where a man could make it by himself.

"Father?" the faint voice called.

White Stone sighed and turned his steps toward the other side of camp, where Ecan's beautiful painted hide lodge stood. He stopped short of the colorful image of Killer Whale and said, "Your father is discussing matters with some of the warriors, Tsauz. He'll be here soon."

That was another thing. What kind of nonsense was it to bring a *blind* boy on a war party like this? The child was a constant nuisance and was never allowed near the fighting, but Ecan still demanded at least four warriors be left to guard the boy.

"I had a bad Dream," Tsauz called from inside.

"We all have bad Dreams. Go back to sleep, boy. Your father will be here soon."

"I saw a man, half human, half coyote. He was winding souls out of people. Pulling the souls out with a string."

What did a blind boy see? The thought sent a chill through White Stone. "And what did he do with them?"

"He put them into stones, War Chief."

Evening Star shoved a dripping spruce bough out of the way and continued, half running, half stumbling, down the foggy mountain trail. The tortured terrain here consisted of long ridges thick with timber, steep slopes, and rushing white streams that carved deep ravines. In places, sandstone, shale, and limestone lay canted; in others, lava flows and volcanic mud had flattened the land. Covering it all, the riotous tangle of ferns, vines, brambles, lodgepole pine, fir, and spruce made travel perilous as she picked her way westward toward the sea.

She hadn't slept in three days. Tired, cold, and wet, she plodded on. The small pack holding her matron's dress and few remaining belongings swayed on her back. Her bruised and cut feet felt as heavy as the stones that abused them. Tangles filled her long red hair, and her finely sculpted face was blotched with mud and scratches. When she stared into pools, haggard blue eyes reflected the nightmares that filled every waking moment. The real horror didn't start until she fell into fitful sleep.

She stopped, bracing a hand against the smooth bark of an alder. Overhead, squirrels chattered. The winter forest seemed to wait, anticipating her next move.

As did she.

She laughed bitterly, and massaged her aching breasts. Her moon was coming. Thankfully Ecan and Kenada hadn't planted a child inside her.

She stared around at the somber forest. A larch, red-brown in winter drab, mocked her.

The Raven People would almost certainly refuse her sanctuary. Worse, Ecan's warriors were on her trail. But there was one hope, one woman who might make the difference.

A stick cracked.

She spun around to look.

There's no one there. Just keep running.

The heady confidence she'd felt after her escape had drained away like water through a cracked shell cup.

Run. Run.

As though to spur her onward, Ecan's eyes watched from her memory. No lines marked his lean, pointed face. He might have been North Wind, but his hair was straight and obsidian black, like that of the Raven People.

His low laugh echoed in her heart—so vivid he might actually have been standing in the spinning mist, behind her. A chill ate into her like a badger into a carcass.

She forced herself to run harder.

As she entered a forested section of the trail, the odor of smoke came to her. Giant spruces rose around her like black spears. The barest of breezes stirred the massive branches. She stopped and braced her trembling legs.

They will probably kill me the moment I step into their village, but what other choice do I have? If I can't find sanctuary, Ecan will kill me.

Wind Woman gusted up the slope, and with her came the sound of voices. The Raven People's language had a breathy, lilting quality.

Evening Star clenched her fists to bolster her courage. The idea of going to Dzoo, the strange Raven People Healer, had come to her two moons ago, just after Ecan took her captive. He'd claimed her as his slave while the fires of her burning village raged around them. He had stripped her, forced her to the ground, and taken her there, amidst the wreckage of her dreams. Then she was prodded, kicked, and dragged back to Fire village, shoved into a small lodge, and left to relive the memories.

One guard had watched her during the day, another at night. They followed her everywhere. She couldn't even walk into the forest to relieve herself without a leering audience. When she wasn't "entertaining" Kenada, she spent her days hauling firewood, weaving seagrass capes, and carrying Ecan's, Cimmis's and Kenada's waste out to the midden in the forest.

For a while, she had believed Ecan when he claimed he was part god. Then one day she had been carrying out his waste. She'd looked down into the wooden bowl before splashing it onto the other trash below the palisade; his feces had looked no different from those of a slave. He was a man. Nothing more.

It had taken another moon to lull her guards into believing she'd accepted her fate. One night, after he'd finished with her, Kenada had dozed off. In that moment of vulnerability, she'd eased the obsidian knife from his belt and begun hacking at his throat. Naked, covered with his blood, she had dressed. Casting around for her few belongings, she had rolled her beautiful dress and stuffed a few supplies into her small pack before slipping out into the night.

Now, trembling, she eased around a bend in the trail and stared at the village she could see through gaps in the trees. Breakfast fires winked and sent blue smoke toward the morning sky. Dark shapes passed in front of them: moving humans who might, within a hand of time, be smiling over her dead body.

Bark huts wavered in the veils of fog, and patches of silver-crested waves crashed onto the shore to the west. First she would wash, then put on her fine dress and don her jewelry. She might be seeking asylum, but she would do it as Naida's daughter, not some ragged forest sprite with fir needles clinging to her hair.

She didn't see any guards.

But very soon . . . they would see her.

Four

Rain Bear, great chief of Sandy Point Village, rarely found time to enjoy the morning. Generally the demands of his people left him in the midst of a maelstrom. Either someone was sleeping with someone else's wife, or a miscreant had stolen a fishing net or just perhaps borrowed it without asking. Sometimes it was a fistfight that had broken out between friends, or the division of household goods during a divorce that had to be solved while the bickering clans waited in the wings and fingered their war clubs.

This morning he had risen early, awakened by Dreams of his wife, Tlikit. She had been staring down at him, warning in her light brown eyes, urging him to do . . . what? He couldn't remember that part. Only that something was about to happen.

Not that it took a ghost to remind him of that. His world was changing before his eyes.

So he had dressed, walked down to his heavy canoe, and perched on the bow to watch dawn purple the sky over the forested ridges behind Sandy Point Village. In that moment of peace, he could reach back with his memories and smile once again as he and Tlikit relived some of the tumultuous events of their life together. She had been in line to follow Astcat as matron for the North Wind people. A stunningly beautiful woman, with hair the color of burnished wood, light brown eyes, and a mischievous smile, she had surrendered her heritage and run off with him over ten and six summers ago.

During the following years, she had borne four children, of whom one, his daughter Roe, still lived in Sandy Point Village. One, a boy, had drowned at the age of six, and his second daughter had been taken by an infection of the bowels at the age of ten.

He was pondering that notion when War Chief Dogrib emerged from the trees and picked his way down the beach, stepping between exposed rocks and brown bits of kelp that dried in the cool air. Dogrib had been specially touched by Song Maker. Long white hair framed his round face, and his skin was unnaturally pale, like sun-bleached wood. Long muscles ran down his arms and legs, and rippled on his broad shoulders.

"Many people have made it onto the water before us." Dogrib walked up, propped his hands on his hips, and studied the canoes bobbing out on the waves. The dark hulks of forested islands appeared and disappeared as the mist shifted.

Old Woman Above had not stepped out of her lodge and begun to carry the ball of the sun across the sky, but a faint yellow gleam now haloed the east.

"Well, forgive me for saying so, War Chief," Rain Bear said with a smile, "but I had to wait for you *again* this morning."

Dogrib smiled apologetically. "Algae and I spent the past several nights together. Finding time to be together is difficult. We are still desperate to hold each other. It's like a fever."

"I wish you two would marry; then you wouldn't have to sneak into the forest to enjoy each other. You could move her into your lodge."

"Her grandfather doesn't like me. He thinks she should marry Blackbird." Dogrib shrugged as though it didn't matter. He'd seen two tens and four summers and had already lost a wife and two children to North Wind raiders. Unlike Rain Bear, he seemed to have come to terms with his grief.

"Well," Rain Bear said in sympathy, "she has only seen four and ten summers. Her grandfather is just trying to protect her."

Rain Bear rose from the bow of his elaborately painted canoe, thoughts returning to Tlikit. Her death had been so senseless. A fall in the forest. He had seen where her foot had slipped in the moss, tumbling her down a steep slope. She was dead when he finally found her, the terrible lacerations in her head long dried and crusted. Though his clan kept insisting he remarry, he'd just never found anyone that interested him.

"I know. It's just . . . difficult," Dogrib said.

"What isn't, my friend?"

Tall and muscular, with long black hair and deeply set brown eyes, Rain Bear had seen three tens of summers. The fringed hem of his otterhide cape swirled the mist as he stowed his harpoon and fishing pole, then bent to touch the red, beautifully stylized face of Grizzly Bear painted on the prow. Softly he prayed, "Grandfather, I ask that you help us today. Call the fish and the sea lions. Bellies are empty, and our children are crying. If the creatures will surrender themselves to us, we will honor their souls and pray for their kind."

Even at this time of morning, he could see the brown swath of runoff water that extended several tens of paces from the shore out into the ocean. Indeed, the world was changing. Everyone could see it. The Ice Giants had been melting at ever-faster rates, swelling the rivers over their banks, spilling silt into the ocean. The fish had moved farther out, past the islands and into the blue water. The coves and deepwater niches where they used to harvest mussels, crabs, clams, and fish were mostly empty. The salmon runs had dropped dramatically, leaving the weirs and traps to clog with mud, sticks, and detritus.

Dogrib had gripped the gunwale to push the canoe into the water, when a voice called, "Rain Bear! My Chief! Wait!"

A skinny man pelted across the rim trail that led from the sea cliffs to the canoe landing. He was waving his arms as he disappeared into the trees. They caught glimpses of him as he hopped from root to rock on the steep trail before dashing out onto the beach.

"Is that your son-in-law?" Dogrib asked, and straightened.

"That's Pitch, all right. I wonder what's so important that he would interrupt our attempts to catch breakfast."

Pitch careened down the trail as fast as he could, his arms out for balance as he negotiated the slippery rocks. He had a wild look, his eyes huge, mouth open. The woven sea-grass cape flapped behind him.

Dogrib said, "Something's wrong."

Rain Bear started up the slope, calling, "Pitch? What's happened?"

Pitch cupped hands to his mouth. "You are needed at the village!"

Rain Bear sighed and retrieved his fishing gear and his harpoon with its toggling point. He carefully wound the cord into a loop and followed after Dogrib.

Pitch was gasping. "The northern villages were attacked three days ago. Refugees are beginning to trickle in. Roe thought you should be warned. They've been traveling all night to get here. According to the reports, the wounded are following as quickly as they can."

"Refugees?" Dogrib asked. "I pray they brought their own food. We have none to spare."

A sense of unease ran through Rain Bear's veins. "How many, Pitch?"

"At least five tens—but maybe more. The first reports are hazy."

Rain Bear strode forward and took Pitch's arm in a hard grip. His skinny son-in-law had a beaked face with soft brown eyes. "How many dead?"

"We don't know yet, my Chief." Pitch gave him a penetrating look. "And that's not all. Moments after the first refugees came straggling in, the guards on the ridge trail intercepted a woman."

"What woman?"

"She says she will give her name to no one but Dzoo, but she's North Wind . . . and high-born from her jewelry and dress."

Rain Bear narrowed an eye. "Explain."

"She has at least two tens of polished shell bracelets on each arm. She wears carved abalone shell necklaces and copper earrings that would buy enough food to feed a Raven village for a season. Her dress belongs to a matron—the finest leather, buffalo calf, if I'm not mistaken, and beaded with dentalium. Even the fringe is adorned with red obsidian fetishes."

Rain Bear's gaze rose to the towering trees that thrust up like spears above the beach. During the night, mist had dusted the branches, turning them into glittering silver giants as the morning sunlight poured over them. "Did you tell her Dzoo is away on a Healer's journey?"

"We have told her nothing, my Chief."

"Where is she being held?"

"In the Council Lodge."

Rain Bear shoved past him and took the slick trail up through the trees to the loamy bench where Sandy Point Village nestled amidst the towering firs, spruce, and alders. Smoke from the morning fires hung low, giving the impression that the round bark lodges with their grass-thatch roofs were hulking, shaggy beasts. A handful of refugees crowded around the central fire, filthy and haggard looking, some with bandaged injuries.

Rain Bear avoided them, needing time to think. By Raven Above, who was his woman? Why was she here? Was she another messenger from chief Cimmis? Blood and tears help them if she was, because any messenger from Cimmis meant trouble.

He frowned when he neared the Council Lodge. At least two tens of warriors stood around. Each held a weapon of some sort; all looked nervous as they paced, talking in small groups.

"Why are so many warriors here?" he asked Pitch in a low voice.

"As soon as the sentries brought her in, men leaped from their robes and hurried to look at her. That's when I ran for you."

"I want five guards at the Council Lodge"—Rain Bear swung around to face Dogrib—"and the rest dispatched to the high points around the village." In a harsh whisper, he added, "Cimmis's warriors could be following on the woman's heels—and the refugees could be the excuse he needs for an attack. Do you understand?"

"Rotted dogs," Dogrib growled as he sprinted ahead. "I should have thought of that myself."

Rain Bear took a deep breath and used the moment to look around, searching for anything out of place. He nodded to people who bowed to him and continued toward the Council Lodge.

Twice as large as an ordinary lodge, the circular Council Lodge measured six body lengths across. It sat at the eastern edge of the village in a copse of leafless alders. The winter-brown leaves were spongy beneath his feet as he approached the entry.

"I took a quick look inside," Dogrib said, and drew the leather door hanging aside for Rain Bear to enter. "No one is here but the woman."

"I thank you, my friend."

A freshly built fire burned in the central hearth and cast a pale amber gleam over the soot-coated walls. Power Boards leaned side by side around the circumference. These were elaborately carved planks painted with the image of a clan totem or family's Spirit Helper. Every family in Sandy Point Village had a board here. Rain Bear preferred the huge carving of the Light Giver, Raven. In this depiction, Raven had obsidian-bead eyes that glinted in the light and a painted beak as long as Rain Bear's arm.

She stood at an angle to him, her face half obscured by a thick wealth of wavy red hair that fell to the middle of her back. He instantly understood Pitch's comment about her jewelry. Her many bracelets clicked with her slightest move, and her abalone shell pendant was huge, a full hand across. Immaculately carved, the pendant might have been the finest Creation Maze he'd ever seen. Creation Mazes told the circuitous story of how Song Maker had pulled different threads of music from the fabric of his own garments and woven them together to make the world.

"You are Chief Rain Bear?"

"I am. And you?"

She turned to face him, and her polished copper earrings flashed bloodred in the light. Had he ever seen such a beautiful woman? She had bright blue eyes and a perfectly sculpted heart-shaped face. "Where is Dzoo? I am here to see her."

"Dzoo's away . . . on a Healer's journey. I don't think she'll be back for several days. If you'll tell me who you are, and what you want, perhaps I can help."

The news struck her like a physical blow. The haughty air slipped; her face paled. "Dzoo is gone? Where? Please, I—I have come a long way to find her." Her struggle to hide the desperation in her voice touched him. Was she ill? Is that why she'd Come? "The last we heard, she was among the Cougar People—at Chief Antler Spoon's village. A strange fever broke out there. Some time ago, they sent a runner to beg her to come Heal them."

Rain Bear crossed the floor toward the fire, knelt, and checked the teapot hanging on the tripod. Empty. There was no Council meeting scheduled, and no one had thought to make tea for her.

The young woman took three quick steps toward him. "Chief Rain Bear, forgive me, but once I explain, I hope you will understand my fears. I am Evening Star, daughter of Matron Naida, of the Ash Fall Clan of the North Wind People. My mother—"

"Is dead. Her village was destroyed over two moons ago, on her brother, Cimmis's, orders. If you are her daughter, you were taken slave by Ecan. A lesson to the other matrons who might be inclined toward disobeying Cimmis's orders." He rose to his feet and studied her. "But I am curious. Your name—it's not one of the North Wind People's."

Evening Star nervously wet her lips. "My mother spent most of her life among Raven People. When I was born, it was a different time. Attitudes were different. Evening Star was a friend to my mother, a woman who helped her in a time of need. I was named in her honor. Matron Naida taught me your language and something of your beliefs and manners as a way of preparing me since I would be responsible for the Raven People in my territory. She had great respect for your people. I think that's why she's dead. Neither the Council nor my uncle could allow her such traitorous extravagances."

A log popped in the fire, and the sudden wavering burst of light painted her stunning face and sent fiery threads through her hair. It was the color he imagined a dye master could achieve if she blended red coral with polished copper.

"Why would your uncle spare you? With your mother gone, you are the next matron of the Ash Fall Clan, are you not?"

She nodded, and glistening red waves fell over her shoulders. "I would be, if I had a clan."

"How many survived the attack?"

"I think a few of my kinsmen escaped. I don't know how many. No word has come to me of where they might have gone." She glanced at him, a wary curiosity in her eyes.

Rain Bear inhaled a breath and let it out slowly. The survivors would come looking for her. If they found her here . . . "I have heard, Matron Evening Star, that those of your kin who survived fled eastward, across the mountains. Beyond that, I know nothing more."

"Matron?" Her expression strained. "Please, Chief Rain Bear, do not call me that. The last man who did . . ."

Grief briefly tightened her features; then she lifted her pointed chin, and hatred shook her voice. "Starwatcher Ecan took me as his slave while I was standing in a pool of my mother's blood. I'm sure Cimmis thought it was the ultimate insult to my mother's memory."

"How did you escape from Fire Village?"

She studied him through steely blue eyes, as if trying to gauge how much she could safely say. "That need not concern you, only that I did, and I am here now."

He, too, considered. The story he'd heard was that Kenada himself was keeping her captive. He had a reputation for cutting babies from the living wombs of captive women. Yet she had slipped past his watchful eye?

His expression must have pinched.

"You think I'm lying?" Her blue eyes sharpened.

"Well, it just seems unlikely, that's all. Kenada is legendary."

Defiantly, she said, "A legend is all that he is now. And the sooner forgotten, the better."

"You mean he's dead?"

She walked around the fire and stopped less than a pace from him. Her cape swayed around her lithe body. When she looked up into his eyes, he swore his heart began to flutter. Rot take it, he hadn't had such a reaction in years. What was it about her?

She said, "I slit his throat and ran."

"You *killed* Kenada?"

"Just tell me how I can find Dzoo, and I will be gone from your village immediately. I do not wish to place you or your people at risk."

"It's a two-day run if you travel by trail across the passes. You might make it in three days if you go by canoe to the mouth of the Wolverine River, then take the north trail along the bank." He made a gesture at her blank look. "No matter. You'll never make it. Refugees are arriving as we speak. Ecan burned their villages, and his war party is between you and Dzoo."

He could see her wilt inside, like a popped fish bladder.

"Matron . . . excuse me, Evening Star, traveling anywhere will expose you to capture."

She seemed to will herself erect again, and then stepped close. She searched his eyes, asking, "You were husband to Tlikit?"

He nodded. "For ten and five years."

"She gave up everything for you."

"We gave up everything for each other," he corrected.

Her searching gaze continued to probe. For long moments, they stood in silence, each trying to see into the other's soul.

Finally she said, "I came here to ask for Dzoo's protection. Since she is not here, I must ask for yours. Will you give it, or should I go elsewhere? I haven't much time. Please tell me quickly."

By midday every village for a day's walk would know who she was and that Rain Bear had denied her sanctuary. By nightfall, villages within a day's run would hear. By the time she made it that far, someone would have captured her to gain favor with Ecan and Cimmis.

But if he offered his protection, could he see it through? Guards would have to protect her day and night. What if Ecan showed up at the head of a war party demanding her back? Could he face down Ecan, Cimmis, and the might of the North Wind People? So many things could go wrong it was stunning.

"Why would you ask this of me?"

"Were she alive, Tlikit would be my cousin. What would she have told you to do?" She arched a delicate eyebrow. "I can help you, Chief. I know some of the things that are being planned by the Council. Orders that Cimmis will be giving."

"Such as?"

"You are right about Ecan's war party. They'll be here soon."

"Why would he come here? We delivered the tribute we owed Cimmis. I had to strip my village to . . ." And it hit him. "He'll be coming for you."

She smiled grimly. "I'm only incidental. He is headed for War Gods Village, and passing through your village will give him a chance to analyze your strength and disposition before they attack this place. You only think you're safe, Great Chief."

"Why attack us?"

"Because they must. You're too dangerous to ignore. You're a leader, a man trusted by the people. You alone could rally the Raven

People to resist. Even some of the North Wind People would back you."

"I have no desire to rally my people against yours."

"Not yet, perhaps, but you will, Rain Bear. One day, sooner or later, you will lead the Raven People against them, and the Council knows it."

Five

Evening Star studied Rain Bear as he removed his cape and stalked a few paces away to throw it atop the pile of grass mats stacked near the entry. Long black hair fell around his broad shoulders. He looked angry and incredulous.

He was lean at the waist, broad-shouldered, and quick on his feet. He stood a little taller than she. The red leather knee-length shirt conformed to ripples of muscle as he moved. Several pouches, a stone-headed ax, and deer-bone stiletto were belted at his waist.

She said, "You have three, maybe four days before Ecan arrives."

"Three or four days," he said. "Are you sure?"

"Yes."

The lines around his eyes and mouth deepened into a fiercely predatory expression. "How do you know he plans to attack us?"

Evening Star told him boldly, "I heard Kenada speaking with a runner. The man was very excited about the attacks on your northern villages. Kenada said, 'Good. Within a quarter moon, my brother will take the struggle into Rain Bear's own lodge.'"

Rain Bear's unblinking gaze bored into her. "Why should I believe you? You are no friend to my people."

"Friendship has nothing to do with it. I am bargaining with you. Information for protection."

Rain Bear thought for a moment. "How many warriors does he have?"

"It was reported to Kenada that he had assembled ten tens."

Rain Bear closed his eyes for a moment. "Sandy Point Village has barely three tens of warriors, and that's if I pull every old man and boy from his house and force him to fight. Blessed Spirits, how can we—"

"You will defeat him."

"Really? How?"

"Because now you have me."

He didn't speak for several moments. "Is your information that valuable to me?"

"*I* am that valuable to you."

She couldn't tell if it was amusement or suspicion that danced in his dark eyes. Rain Bear crouched, pulled a branch from the woodpile, and roughly tossed it into the flames.

Her heart hammered hollowly as she waited.

He appeared to be concentrating on the sparks that danced up from the fresh tinder. Then, suddenly, he rose to his feet and swung around to glare at her. His long black hair, bluish in the firelight, fell over the front of his red shirt.

"Matron, what makes you think I won't turn you over to save my village?"

Fear shot ice through her heart. She hoped that no sign of the terror in her breast betrayed itself on her face. She took her most desperate gamble. "Because I am more valuable to you alive than dead at Ecan's hand. I think you're smart enough to know what my support will be worth to you. When you are pushed into war, you are going to need a woman from the Ash Fall Clan, someone who gives your cause validity with the North Wind People."

He weighed her words before asking, "What kind of life do you imagine you will have here, Matron? If I give my people reasons to protect you, I think they will, but you will be forever Outcast. No North Wind man will ever dare speak to you, let alone consider marriage. You will grow into a lonely old woman."

Evening Star turned away.

"Your life here will be miserable," he continued. "If you help us, your people will label you a traitor. You will never be able to leave Sandy Point Village. Never see relatives again, Cimmis's warriors will always be waiting somewhere nearby, hoping you will expose yourself." He hesitated. "And then there are the Wolf Tails."

Tears pressed hotly at the corners of her eyes, but her voice came out strong. "Kenada talked in front of me as though I was not there.

He repeated many of the things said in Council by our Four Old Women."

Rain Bear's expression didn't change, but the gleam in his eyes betrayed a new level of interest. Unlike the Raven People, the North Wind People traced descent through the female. The Four Old Women were the most powerful individuals in the North Wind world. They made all of the important decisions in Fire Village. Chief Cimmis just carried them out.

Rain Bear said, "For example?"

Evening Star struggled to control her emotions. How long would he torture her before telling her yes or no?

"They are considering replacing Cimmis as chief."

"But . . . how can they? Matron Astcat is the leader of the Council."

"That may not last long. My aunt is not well, Rain Bear. People have begun whispering that her soul is loose." Which to the North Wind People meant either she was insane or unconscious.

Rain Bear rubbed his forehead. He looked sick in the soul, like a man who had just discovered his wife had been unfaithful to him and who couldn't figure out how to shove his guts back inside.

Now was the time to make the last cast of the gaming pieces. "As to how I would live among your people, another North Wind woman did quite well here. Her name was Tlikit. I hear she had a most satisfying life."

He strode briskly to the door, a decision made.

Evening Star watched him, her heart aching. Gods, why wouldn't he face her?

When he reached the exit, he pulled the leather curtain aside without looking back, and said, "I grant you sanctuary in Sandy Point Village, Matron. Do not make me regret it."

She found enough breath to whisper, "Thank you, Great Chief."

As he stepped out into the misty morning, she heard him order, "Dogrib, pick five men. I want them to build a suitable lodge in the space next to mine. And I want it done right, not a slapped-up mess. Pitch, you must find Dzoo and bring her here. Accept no excuses. Tell her we are about to be attacked. Get your things and go immediately." A pause. "Oh, and you'll have to avoid Ecan's war party in the process."

Evening Star tilted her head back, spilling her hair down her back. She took a deep breath, the memory of Ecan's cackling laughter deep in her soul.

Six

Rides-the-Wind, propped by his walking stick, carefully made his way down the slick trail that wound along the rim. Below him, the cliffs dropped away, ragged rock supporting green patches of moss and winter-bare currants. Fog tufted the shoreline one hundred hands below him, and far out on the water, dugout canoes rose and fell, riding the waves with the grace of dolphins. If his sense of direction was right, Capped Finch Village lay just ahead. Because of the terrain, he could not see it yet, but he smelled the sweet fragrance of their alder fires.

The trail dipped, and Rides-the-Wind had to pay special attention to the damp moss-covered stones. He took them one at a time, propping his walking stick, lowering his foot, and propping his stick again. At his age, the slightest fall could mean a broken bone, and despite his Healing powers, that could mean death.

Since his meeting with Red Dog, the Spirits had been disturbing his sleep, plaguing him with peculiar Dreams. He had seen lightning flash around him, and heard a voice whispering in the darkness. A man's voice, rich, raspy, and full of menace.

"Power is loose," he muttered under his breath, and glanced up. A cow and calf elk vanished into the dense brush that skirted the black timber.

Something wasn't right. Rides-the-Wind could feel it on the wind. An old evil, malignant and insidious, drifted on the breeze.

The source of it baffled him. He could almost suspect a witch was loose upon the land, but where? As a Soul Keeper, he knew most of the Dreamers, Healers, Soul Keepers, and Soul Fliers. He knew who had trained whom, and what their skills and talents were. But beyond that, there were the stories, the rumors that seemed to trot up and down the trails of their own volition.

"If you need to make a girl love you, see so and so." "If you want to contrive a man's death, contact you-know-who." "Unlucky in gambling? This man will provide a charm." And so it went. People liked to talk about witches. Better yet, witches liked to be talked about. How else did they ply their craft?

Rides-the-Wind had heard many such rumors in the time he had been away from Fire Village. Each time he ran one to ground it turned out to be a midwife skilled in the use of herbs, or some old man with more imagination than skill.

No, he was looking for a man—and yes, he was sure it was a man—driven by obsession. Ecan, of course, had come to mind early, and despite his brave words to Red Dog, Rides-the-Wind had no illusions about the danger the Starwatcher presented. Ecan, however, was concerned with political prestige and authority, not the ways in which Power could be turned to evil.

When Rides-the-Wind looked up from the treacherous footing he glimpsed a young man trotting through the wind-sculpted grove of spruce trees where the trail rounded the brow of the hill. Beneath his elkhide cape, the young man wore the long red leather shirt of a Sandy Point warrior.

He continued edging down the trail until he reached the last rocky step, then sat down, propped his walking stick across his lap, and waited. The pack on his back felt like a sack of stones. He shifted it to a more comfortable position and studied the ferns that sprouted from every crack in the rocks. Delicate and lacy, their fronds glistened with dew.

Below the cliffs, where the water poured into the sea, the beaches had been cut back, the rocks scoured clean. The water appeared murky. Every drainage that ran to the ocean was flooded and had been for three sun cycles. No wonder the salmon no longer swam up the rivers to spawn. No wonder the numbers of mussels and clams had dwindled to the point that a woman was lucky to be able to collect enough in a moon to feed her family a single supper. Even the terns and gulls had declined. He could count on one hand the number of terns wading in the surf below.

"Hello!" Rides-the-Wind lifted a bony hand in greeting as the youth trotted closer.

The youth lifted a hand in return, but the smile died on his lips when he recognized Rides-the-Wind. The Soul Keeper wasn't like other people. He was a revered elder of the North Wind People—a man of great mystery and Power. It was tiresome.

The youth glanced around as though looking for another trail, but seeing none, plodded forward. Long black hair whipped around his shoulders.

"Pleasant morning to you," Rides-the-Wind began. "Have you traveled far?"

The skinny youth halted five paces away and gave Rides-the-Wind a wary scrutiny. He had a narrow beaked face with soft brown eyes, kind eyes. "I've been running for a day, Soul Keeper. I'm on my way to Antler Spoon's village."

"Well, then, you should be there by nightfall. You're from Sandy Point Village, aren't you?" He gestured to the youth's shirt.

"I am called Pitch, of the Sea Whistle Clan."

"You are married to Roe, are you not?" When Pitch nodded uneasily, Rides-the-Wind added, "I know of you. A young holy man. You are of Chief Rain Bear's family. He has a reputation as a peacemaker."

Rain Bear often angered his people by giving far more in negotiations than he received. They didn't seem to understand that in these perilous times, that was the reason they were alive and their village intact, not a burned heap of rubble. Rides-the-Wind had never met Rain Bear, but he'd admired him for many winters.

"A peacemaker? Yes, in the past." Pitch shifted uneasily. "We have received word, however, that Ecan comes to make war."

"War?" Rides-the-Wind arched his bushy gray eyebrows. "I have been away for a time, tracking the stars. Please tell me what's happened." At Pitch's obvious hesitation, he added, "I understand your reluctance, but I bear your people no malice. On my soul, I seek only to know what I might be walking into."

The youth sighed and plopped his butt on a boulder. Sweat beaded his hooked nose. "All I can tell you is that we received news that Starwatcher Ecan is about to attack Sandy Point Village."

Rides-the-Wind stroked his long gray beard. "I don't understand. Why would Ecan do that? Rain Bear always faithfully delivers the tribute he owes Fire Village. Ecan has no reason to attack."

Pitch seemed to have relaxed a bit. "I agree, but that's what the North Wind woman, Evening Star, told Rain Bear. He can't ignore it."

Rides-the-Wind clutched his walking stick hard. "I heard that young Evening Star had escaped. Did Rain Bear grant her sanctuary?"

"Yes. She came looking for Dzoo, but when she discovered Dzoo was gone, she asked for Rain Bear's protection—which he gave in exchange for information."

Rides-the-Wind let out a relieved breath. "At least she's safe."

Pitch looked skeptical. "For the moment, but no one likes it. Why did she come to us? Harboring her is dangerous. If Ecan didn't have a reason to attack before, her presence might just goad him to now."

"You're suspicious of her, are you?"

"Of course," he said, half angry. "Why would a North Wind matron, even an escaped captive, come to us with these tales? Things she supposedly overheard her guards saying."

"You think she's trying to trick you?"

"Elder, in these days of treachery and deceit by the North—" He suddenly realized what he'd been about to say to the Soul Keeper. His thin face flushed.

Rides-the-Wind smiled. "No, young Pitch. She's an honorable young woman who just saw her husband and two-summers-old daughter slaughtered before her eyes. I can't guarantee the accuracy of her information, but I'm sure she is faithfully reporting what she heard."

Pitch made a soft skeptical sound and rose to his feet. "I had better be on my way. A pleasant day to—"

"You said she was looking for Dzoo?"

"I have been sent to bring the Healer back to Sandy Point Village, Elder."

"Then you should be about your business. Travel in safety, young Pitch." Rides-the-Wind propped his walking stick and struggled to stand up. "We shall talk some more when you return to Sandy Point Village."

Already started up the trail, Patch whirled, his brown eyes huge. "We—we will?"

"Yes. If Rain Bear will permit, I would like to spend a few days in your village. Perhaps we'll be neighbors."

"Neighbors?" Fear and dismay edged his voice.

"Yes. Why? Does that concern you?"

Pitch didn't even try to act casual. "Why, Soul Keeper? Among us, I mean."

Rides-the-Wind gingerly took a step down the trail. Over his shoulder he said, "Something is coming, Pitch. I need to have counsel with Chief Rain Bear."

"Counsel?" A hostile tone lay in Pitch's voice.

Rides-the-Wind didn't look back as he called, "About how to keep the wind from whistling through his chest."

Seven

The forest had not yet given up the night's numbing cold. Frost glittered in the towering fir trees and covered the beach. Even Mother Ocean seemed to have frozen in place. Her waves washed the shore in soft, quiet strokes.

Rain Bear pulled his otterhide cape closed at the throat and followed the trail through the crowded refugee camps. Behind him, Dogrib carried a net bag full of crabs they had collected from a trap. One of the camp dogs had died, and Rain Bear had used the carcass to bait his crab trap in a tidal pool. He would use the remains to catch crabs until it was exhausted. Today's catch wasn't much, but they were going to need every scrap of food given the unending trickle of people limping in from the northern villages.

Dogrib shook his long white hair back and muttered, "Our lookouts say Ecan's war party is two days to the north. What are we going to do?"

Rain Bear glanced at his war chief. Dogrib's unusual pale skin had reddened with the chill, and a somber weight lay behind his blue eyes. "We must speak with the other war chiefs. See what they say. Then, we'll decide."

Rain Bear took the southern trail through the Orphan Village camp where people, filthy from days of fighting on the run, hunched over their breakfast fires. Some were boiling strips of bark and fir needle tea—their only source of sustenance. A constant staccato of coughs peppered the air. They cast longing glances at the bag of crabs visible through the netting.

"I don't understand any of this, Rain Bear. Why would Ecan attack us? We paid our tribute. Did Evening Star give you any reason?"

"No."

"Then why do you believe it?"

"I'm not sure I do. But I can't very well afford to ignore her warning, can I?"

As they passed another group of villagers, conversations halted; then awed whispers broke out and heads turned, following them.

"Is it true?" A young warrior staggered to his feet and called to Rain Bear. A bloody bandage wrapped the right side of his head. "Is Starwatcher Ecan coming?"

The weary people around him whispered and glanced fearfully at the surrounding forest.

Rain Bear lifted his hands reassuringly. "His war party is two days away. Our scouts are keeping a close eye. As we receive more news, we'll send runners to notify every chief."

The man nodded as he sank back to the log where he'd been sitting.

Rain Bear started to walk away, but an old man's frail voice stopped him: "Where is Dzoo, Chief? Why isn't she here to protect us?"

At the sound of Dzoo's name, quiet descended. People stared wide-eyed at Rain Bear.

He turned and saw the old man standing in front of his makeshift lodge—little more than deerhides sewn together and draped over a cord strung between two trees. He resembled a knotted twig. White hair straggled around his gaunt face.

Rain Bear replied, "Dzoo is away on a Healer's journey, Elder. I have sent Singer Pitch to fetch her home."

The old man heaved a tired sigh. "How long do you think it will take?"

Dzoo was legendary. A creature of darkness and moonlight, she moved silently through the shadows like a hunting wolf, Healing, praying with people who had lost everything. It was said that she could read the future in the patterns of sea foam. Some considered her a living Spirit, others, a god.

Rain Bear added, "She promised to help Matron Weedis with the preparations for the Moon Ceremonial at War Gods Village. I'm sure she planned to be home by then anyway, but perhaps my son-in-law can persuade her to return sooner."

Her name passed through the camp like the hiss of rain: *Dzoo* . . .

The old man squared his bony shoulders. "I brought my people here because I believe in her Power, Great Chief. I will feel better when she walks through my camp."

Rain Bear nodded sincerely. "As will I, Elder." He looked around at the ragged people. "War Chief Dogrib will leave this catch of crabs with you. Please, Elder, see to it that they are distributed as far as they will go among the most needy."

Dogrib unslung the net bag and offered it to the old man. "We should go, my chief. We dare not be late."

They continued along the path, stepping over roots and rocks to the makeshift lodge set up at the edge of the clearing. One guard and three attendants already stood outside. They watched Rain Bear's approach with narrowed eyes.

It was an old warrior's ritual. No chief wished to arrive first and be made to endure the dishonor of waiting for his opponents, so he sent in his guards ahead to search the makeshift lodge and surroundings. When all was ready, the guards signaled so that all chiefs arrived at the same time.

A scar-faced warrior ducked out of the lodge and lifted a hand.

War Chief Talon appeared through the trees, his chin up, his old eyes like daggers. Red images of mountains and soaring eagles decorated his hide cape. He had seen four tens of summers, and wore his white hair twisted into a bun at the base of his skull. Abalone shell hair combs kept it in place. Two slaves followed him, both Elderberry People caught while raiding the southern coastal villages. He turned to his guard. "Make certain that no one comes close. We do not wish to be overheard."

"Yes, War Chief."

Talon warily scanned the camp, gave Rain Bear a hostile glance, then ducked under the lodge flap, leaving his guard and slaves standing outside.

Dogrib entered next. When he reappeared, he nodded to Rain Bear and took up his place two tens of hands from the lodge.

Rain Bear ducked through the doorway, stripped off his cape, then untied his weapons belt—which held his deer-bone stiletto and stone-headed ax—and dropped it beside the door. After the clear cold air of the forest, the heat from the central fire felt stifling.

Winter hides from bull elk covered the floor. Poles had been raised to create a framework to which fir boughs were lashed. Rain Bear took a position opposite Talon and nodded to the other occupant.

Sleeper, war chief of Deer Meadow Village, sat cross-legged, a martenhide cape over his shoulders. He placed a hand to his heart in greeting. Sleeper might only have seen two tens and five winters, but gray already touched his temples. Rain Bear returned the greeting, then looked at Talon.

"I thank you both for coming. I wasn't sure you would."

Talon settled himself on the hides, unlaced his cape, and let it fall from his broad shoulders. "Well, I couldn't stay away. I'm tired of all the whispers."

"As am I," Sleeper said. "Have you asked the North Wind woman to come here?"

Word of both her presence and her warning had spread very quickly.

Rain Bear placed his palms in his lap. "No. I felt these were matters best discussed between Raven People. If we deem it necessary, I will ask her opinion on our decisions."

"Do you believe her?" Talon narrowed his crafty eyes. "Is that why you granted her sanctuary?"

Rain Bear considered. "Let me put it this way: I don't disbelieve her. Given what has happened to the northern villages, I can't take the chance that she is mistaken."

"But, why?" Sleeper demanded. "You've paid the tribute to Astcat and the Council. Much to our mutual disgust, and at no little risk to yourself and your reputation, I might add. Why would they alienate you, of all people?"

"I don't know." Rain Bear glanced from face to face. "I've heard, though, that Matron Astcat has lost her soul. Perhaps they have all gone a little mad."

He reached for one of the wooden bowls near the roasting stick. The stick had been arranged perfectly, propped up with stones so that the large chunks of meat cooked slowly right at the edge of the flames. Rain Bear slipped several chunks of elk off the stick into his bowl. "Please." He gestured to the others. "We have had many long and sleepless nights. Eat."

Bowls clacked as each man stripped the steaming meat from the skewer.

Talon turned, and his white hair gleamed orange in the fire's glow. "All right, Rain Bear, we're here. What do you wish to tell us?"

Rain Bear set his bowl in his lap to let the meat cool. "There are three matters I wish to discuss. The first, of course, is what to do about White Stone and Ecan if they appear tomorrow."

Talon's sharp old eyes glinted. "After what they've done to us, I say we kill them on sight."

"Starwatcher Ecan is a holy man," Sleeper said; reverence tinged his voice. "He has the right to pass if he intends us no harm."

Talon bit a hunk out of the steaming elk tenderloin. "I owe him no such courtesy, Sleeper. He lost all worldly rights when he burned my village."

Sleeper's mouth tightened into a white line, and Rain Bear could feel the tension building. They had been adversaries for so long, clan against clan, village against village; it was difficult even to speak without rancor, let alone about killing the great Starwatcher Ecan.

Calmly, Rain Bear asked, "If we allow him to pass, Sleeper, what should we do to assure our own safety? My scouts report he is traveling with over ten tens of warriors."

Sleeper's expression darkened. "If Ecan comes in peace, I say that we take the opportunity to speak with him. Perhaps we can arrange a meeting between our chiefs and Cimmis."

Talon grunted and bolted another mouthful of the tender meat. "You may do as you wish, but I'm taking my warriors and setting up an ambush. If the ancestors smile, perhaps we can kill him and his entire war party."

Sleeper grimaced. "An ambush would be foolish. And unnecessary. This is now the largest village on the coast. Including refugees, we have almost two times ten tens of people here. Out of sheer desperation, they would tear Ecan's warriors to pieces. He knows that."

"Does he?" Talon asked with a vague smile.

"He's not dimwitted," Sleeper insisted.

"Really? I've heard he's an imbecile."

Rain Bear leaned forward to warm his hands over the flames. "I think we should be more concerned about his assassins than his war party."

Talon nodded. "Now there we agree. It is far more likely that he will send his Wolf Tails to pick off our elders one by one. Curse them. They seem to be able to slip through our defenses like field mice." Talon ripped another mouthful of meat and stretched out on the thick hides.

Rain Bear grimly lifted a piece of elk and tore off a bite. Grease coated his lips. The taste was rich and satisfying. For many moons, he'd denied the existence of the Wolf Tails, believing Cimmis too smart to take such foolish chances. Now, however, after hearing some of the stories circulating, he had to accept their existence.

Talon twisted to look at Rain Bear, and his abalone hair combs glistened. "Grinder, war chief of Salmon Village, told me that he had two tens of guards around Matron Gispaw's lodge, and when he went to check on her the next morning, he found her lying in her bed with her head missing."

Sleeper added, "I heard a similar story from the war chief of Sea Lion Village. He said he found his headless matron, Kirzo, leaning against the wall of her lodge with a teacup still clutched in her hand. That's why we must try to speak with Ecan. This has to stop."

"I will speak with Ecan," Rain Bear said, "if we agree that is the way. But I think we should consider another alternative."

"What?" Talon asked.

The meat had started to warm his empty stomach. He glanced at each of them and said, "An alliance."

Talon's brows lowered suspiciously. "An alliance? With Ecan? Are you mad?"

"Not with Ecan. An alliance between our villages."

Talon grunted suspiciously and gave Rain Bear a defiant look. "My people do not trust yours, Rain Bear. We've raided each other's territories for cycles. They won't agree."

"None of our villages can fight Ecan alone. That should be obvious by now. At most we each have a few tens of warriors. If we join forces and put our warriors under the command of one person—"

"Who? You?" Talon asked defensively, and sat up. The wrinkles across his forehead deepened. "You've always argued against war."

Rain Bear said, "Actually, I was thinking of you, Talon. You command twice as many warriors as I do, and have been a war chief much longer than Dogrib or Sleeper. You are best suited for the position."

The crow's-feet around Talon's eyes tightened. He seemed somewhat mollified and stretched out on the hides again. "I'll consider it."

Sleeper stared at the meat in his bowl, his expression thoughtful. "Rain Bear is right. No matter what is behind us, we must join forces and start defending ourselves. So far, we have turned our heads, left each individual village to defend itself. That must stop. But . . . you would make a better leader, Rain Bear. You were married to a North Wind woman. Plus, you have Matron Evening Star close. With her counsel, you should be able to anticipate the North Wind People's moves better than anyone else."

Talon gave Sleeper a hot glare.

Rain Bear lowered his gaze and peered at the steaming meat in his bowl. "Truly, I do not wish to lead the fight against the North Wind People. My wife, Tlikit, was one of them. According to their ways, my daughter and grandson are North Wind People."

Raven People traced descent through the male, but North Wind

People considered Rain Bear's daughter and grandson to belong to his wife's Dragonfly Clan.

Sleeper said, "But your daughter and grandson live among our people. They consider themselves to be part of your clan. So does everyone else."

"For now." Rain Bear looked up. "But if we join forces and attack the North Wind People, the fighting will get worse before it gets better. People will be killed, inflaming hatred. That's what war does. It creates an 'us' and a 'them.' I do not wish my family to become 'them' to my people, Sleeper."

Talon asked thoughtfully, "Does that mean you do not wish to fight with us?"

"I will fight," Rain Bear said. "But if we choose this path, we must all understand that killing Ecan is just the beginning."

Sleeper sat up straighter. "Go on."

"If we destroy Ecan's war party, the North Wind People will be forced to retaliate. We can't let that happen. So we must attack Fire Village as quickly as possible and with as much force as we can muster. To succeed, I believe we must ally our forces under one war chief." He paused to let this sink in. "But there is one more thing we must have."

"Which is what?"

"A spy in Fire Village."

Talon and Sleeper chuckled softly.

"Well, yes, that would be very nice," Talon agreed with exaggerated interest, "but I have no spies I wish to sacrifice. Ecan already has enough of my people's heads on his wall."

"Without someone inside we won't know when they're the most vulnerable, Talon," Rain Bear answered.

Sleeper asked, "Whom do you have in mind for this dangerous task? Perhaps we could send a slave as tribute, or are you thinking of a slave who is already there?"

Rain Bear tore off another chunk of elk and chewed before he said, "I was thinking of Dzoo."

Talon jerked so suddenly a piece of hot meat rolled from his bowl into his lap. He leaped to his feet to brush it away. "Blessed gods! Have you lost your senses? Half of our people think she's a witch, and the other half that she's one of the virginal Comet Women!"

"Our *enemies* think she's a witch." Sleeper leapt to Dzoo's defense. "Most of the people in the Raven villages would die for her."

"Yes, but . . ." Talon's gaze darted as if searching for another reason. "Isn't she in mourning?"

Rain Bear nodded. "Her husband, Pearl Oyster, died three moons ago."

As Sleeper leaned forward to refill his bowl, the long leather fringes on his sleeves hissed across the hearthstones. "What difference does it make if Dzoo is in mourning? Can you point to a single person in our camps who hasn't lost someone?"

"But"—Talon hesitated—"why her? Surely there must be someone more . . . appealing?"

"Who?" Sleeper asked.

At Talon's blank look, Rain Bear said, "She was born in Fire Village. She knows the place."

"She was taken from there as a child, you'll recall," Talon muttered. "And that's a strange story if I ever heard one. Foreigners taking a little girl like that."

"They knew she had Power," Sleeper countered.

"And that's another reason she's perfect," Rain Bear continued. "She's sympathetic to us. With her reputation as a Healer, she can go anywhere, talk with anyone. A spy's first duty is to listen, and no one listens like Dzoo."

Talon studied the piece of meat that had fallen from his plate, then popped it into his mouth. After he'd swallowed it, he added, "I don't see why Cimmis would allow her past the walls in the first place."

"I do," Sleeper countered. "He'll see it as an opportunity to demonstrate his Power over a legendary witch. His reputation would soar."

Talon's sun-bronzed face appeared pale against the background of the soot-colored lodge. "I hadn't thought of that."

Sleeper steepled his fingers. "Will Dzoo do it?"

Rain Bear lifted a shoulder. "I'll talk to her when she and Pitch—"

Shouts erupted outside.

Talon rose into a crouch. "Hallowed gods, what now?"

Rain Bear reached for his weapons belt and slipped it around his waist.

Dogrib jerked the flap aside. "A runner just came in. Ecan's war party has split. Eight tens of his warriors are headed in the direction of Antler Spoon's village."

Sleeper frowned. "Isn't that where Dzoo went to Heal?"

"It is." Rain Bear swung his cape around his shoulders and ducked out into the cold morning air. Warriors had already begun to gather, all shouting questions at Dogrib. Their frightened eyes fixed on Rain Bear as he asked, "How long will it take us to get there?"

Dogrib shrugged. "Given their head start, my chief, too long. Besides, we would need to send at least five tens of men to have a chance against his forces. We can't afford to pull that many away from Sandy Point Village. If this is one of Ecan's ruses, these people will be slaughtered like dogs while we're away."

"Yes, you're right, War Chief." Rain Bear's gaze went over the hungry children sitting around the smoky fires and the old people huddled beneath mounds of tattered hides.

In a weary exhalation, he added, "Blessed Song Maker, I should have known he'd do this. Dzoo is our strength, and Cimmis knows it. Of course he'd take the opportunity to snatch her when she's outside Sandy Point Village's protection."

Dogrib gave him a searching look. "I just pray she has foreseen their coming."

Late Morning

*O*h, *I have seen many things in my time. But most of them, I admit, I did not wish to see," I whisper.*

The old Soul Keeper rises to his feet, and I hear him walk a few paces away. His voice is dimmer, muted by the rushing wind through the cottonwoods and the riot of birdsong that fills the day. "Seeing is good, Chief. Most humans sleep from the womb to death. They never fully open their eyes. Oh, a few are startled now and then and forced to really look at the world, but they quickly choose to return to sleep. Not seeing is so much easier."

"I, too, have spent a good deal of time sleeping, Soul Keeper. I blame them not."

He pauses as though not sure what to say to my admission. He thinks everyone should wake up. That there is no place for sleeping in a world such as ours.

"Did not seeing comfort you, Chief? Weren't you afraid that there were others stirring around you who were awake and watching you?"

I laugh softly. "People who are truly awake are engaged in great suffering. They didn't have time for me."

He turns, and his long robe flaps in a gust of wind. "Are you awake now?" he softly asks.

"More awake than I have ever been."

He walks back and sits beside me. The scents of wood smoke and wet leather cling to him. For a long time I just lie still, trying to memorize the fragrances. I have smelled these things every day of my life, yet they smell new, fresh, and pleasant. I want to keep them.

"Do you mean you are suffering physically, or in your soul?"

"Both."

"Great suffering," he says with a sigh, "is not usually physical. Abandonment, isolation, loss of hope—those are the real torments. So many people these days have outlived their beloved spouses and companions. Their children are absorbed in their own lives. They cannot bear to stare into the eyes of someone who is truly awake." He reaches out and takes my hand. His fingers have a knobby, skeletal feel, like knotted ropes. "Are you lonely?"

"I wish my wife were here. I yearn to look into her eyes."

"She would not look back. You have become the entire universe. The naked unbearable universe. All that there is."

Is that what Death is? Looking into the naked unbearable eyes of the universe?

It takes a great effort, but I manage to slit my eyes, and I find him gazing down at me with infinite kindness through a blaze of white-hot light.

How strange.

If occurs to me for the first time that he is wrong. Looking upon great suffering is not the most frightening thing in life. It is not what is naked and unbearable.

Great kindness is.

Perhaps because it is harder to accept.

I close my eyes and work very hard to keep them closed.

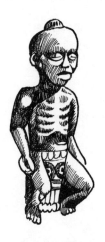

Eight

The man known as Coyote prowled the starlit forest trail that wound around Antler Spoon's village. He carefully stepped over snow-covered ferns that might rustle beneath his fur-trimmed moccasins. He could not afford to misstep or be heard. Not tonight when old dreams were about to become real.

He lifted his nose to sniff the chill air, and his long hair blew around the magnificent coyote mask he wore. Human scents rode Wind Woman's breath: cooked food, moldering hides, the fever-sweaty bodies of the ill, and the tangy odors of boiling Spirit plants.

Beyond the dark spruce to his left, smoke clung like a blue veil to the towering gray cliff. There the villagers had taken refuge in the lava caves that riddled the rock like wormholes. They'd come here six moons ago. Three tens of refugees from famine-struck villages in the north. The children had been filthy and starving. Many of the elderly had barely been able to walk. For a time, this narrow mountain valley must have seemed like one of the Above Worlds to them, beautiful and free, impervious to the raids that savaged the villages along the shore and on the islands out in the sound.

When his duties allowed, he had come here to watch them. They were people with no local kin, no one to call upon for aid. Isolated and vulnerable. From that the plan had been born. One night he had crept among them and sowed the deadly fever. He had trickled scrapings of a red-brown fungus into their stews, sifted it into sacks

of dried food. Within days, people started to lose weight and com-
plain of chest pains. Some died before Chief Antler Spoon asked for
help.

As he had hoped, *she* had come.

Now, as the frost of his breath silvered the muzzle of his Coyote
mask, he watched from beneath a spruce tree's dark skirt. A shadow
moved across the firelit roof of the largest cave. Coyote let his tall
body melt into the dark trunk.

Is it her?

The shadow wavered, as if blown by the wind, then continued
across the roof until it slipped into the black edges of night.

Is that you, Dzoo?

Fear and excitement tickled his belly.

It was said that she could point at a star, and it would fall to earth
in a streak of fire. She had reddish brown hair and the perfect body
of a Sea Spirit.

His gaze caressed the cave for a time; then he forced himself to
step out and follow the snowy trail toward the rendezvous. If the
terms of his bargain had been met, Dzoo would be his tonight.

If I can just see her . . .

He *needed* to see her. Sometimes the need was overwhelming. It
became an ache so desperate he thought it would cause his very
bones to splinter. As a youth he had been a trader. Though he had
heard of her childhood capture, he had been unprepared for her
Power and beauty. Then, one day, he'd met her in Pearl Oyster's
camp, stared into her eyes, and lost his soul to her. He had watched
her from afar after that, kindling even more need. In desperation he
had gone to an ancient Soul Flier—a man of great renown among
the Striped Dart People—and honed the skills of Power and obsession. Then, when he had come down from the mountains, it was to
find her vanished. The people said that she had returned to the
coast, to her home. So he had come, searching, until he found her.
Through careful planning, he had placed himself where he could finally have her for his own.

Once, he'd been close enough to breathe in her fragrance and
touch her hair. But the path to greatness—as his mentor had taught
so diligently—was not to be wasted by an idle move or lack of discipline. He was Coyote. Cunning, Powerful, and patient.

He balled his fists and shoved them beneath his woven sea-grass
cape.

Until recently, Dzoo's husband, Pearl Oyster, had guarded her
like an old wolf. He'd never left her alone. No matter where she

went, he was standing there with his weapons, eternally vigilant. The man's cool eyes took the measure of anyone who came near her.

Of all Coyote's challenges, killing Pearl Oyster had been the most difficult. From the protection of the Mossy Cave, he had thrown attack after attack at the stern warrior's soul. Then news of Pearl Oyster's death had spread like wildfire across the land, and Coyote had known.

It was his turn.

The snowy trail through the trees ended in a small meadow ten tens of body lengths from the village. The gleam of the Star People and the near-full moon silvered the snow and played in the fir needles.

He wiped his clammy palms on his cape and drew an intricately engraved deer-bone stiletto from his belt. As he knelt behind a boulder, he heard the faintest of scuffing sounds and willed himself to become one with the stone. It might just be an animal. An owl or—

A foot crunched the wet snow.

Only Coyote's eyes moved.

In the firs, much closer than he'd have thought possible, a man rose and whispered in an accented voice, "Coyote? Is that you? I've brought her."

His gaze surveyed the dark shapes of the forest, searching for any hidden threats. "Show me."

"She's over here. Come and see." The man braced his feet and clenched his fists at his sides, as though expecting a fight. "I dragged her here just moments ago."

The newcomer had seen perhaps three tens and five summers, but he had a wrinkled face and silver-streaked black hair. His moon-washed expression tightened in fear as Coyote walked toward him.

"You dragged her out here by yourself?"

"No one must know what I do." The accent of the Cougar People made him almost unintelligible.

The idea of gazing into Dzoo's eyes again sent a tingle through Coyote. It was like looking into an endless black abyss—only to have the abyss look back. She stirred something deep in his soul, something that had brought him here, to this place—the end of a long and arduous journey.

She lay on her side on a black-and-red painted hide. A tangle of long hair obscured most of her face.

But it *did* look like her.

He tried to keep his voice from trembling. Cold shakes were running through his hands and fingers. "This is Dzoo?"

"Would I cheat you after what you promised to do to my family if I failed?"

Coyote willed control into his muscles. His need was a soul hunger that nibbled and sucked at his bones and nerves. "What did you give her to make her soul fly?"

"A small sip of nightshade, Coyote—just enough to make her sleep."

"Nightshade! You gave *Dzoo* poison?"

The man reached out pleadingly. "How else could I bring her to you? I had no choice! Her Powers are very great!"

Coyote thrust his hand into his belt pouch, pulled out the bag, and threw it at the old man. As the old man caught the small bladder sack, the delicate tinkle of glassy stone could be heard. "With those precious objects, Broken Sun, you could buy an entire village." *For all the good they will do you in the end, old man.*

Broken Sun turned the small bag to the moonlight and stared at the tiny red coyote paw prints painted on the leather. He offered it back. "Take it. I don't wish it."

"That was our bargain. And you do wish it, my friend." Coyote paused, and carefully pronounced the following words: "Betrayal is a costly business. Costly in every way. Remember that your own people might thank you for saving them, but the Raven People will kill you for what you have just done. You may need those fetishes to buy your life."

Coyote knelt, and the large spear point pendant he wore on a necklace swung forward. As long as a man's hand, and almost as wide, it had been carefully chipped from translucent brown chert with two deep channel flakes driven out of each side like flutes.

He tucked it back before reaching out to stroke her hair with a shaking hand, then quickly wrapped her in the blanket, slipped his arms beneath her body, and lifted. She felt as light as a sparrow's feather.

Dear gods, I'm holding her.

His arms started to tremble, and he could feel the first ecstatic prickling at the root of his hardening penis.

Broken Sun's eyes narrowed. "I've kept my part of the bargain. Do not forget what you promised. My village is safe, yes? The sickness will leave us, and no warriors will come here."

Coyote clutched the slender body against his chest, and a fiery wave flooded through his pelvis and along his veins. In a soft voice, he answered, "It will be just as I promised."

Broken Sun scurried away like a rabbit freed from a snare, tripping, falling, running again.

Coyote waited—listening to the darkness, feeling the need throbbing through each fiber of his soul—until he knew he was alone with her.

Then he tenderly kissed her silken cheek and carried her away into the forest.

Nine

Pitch?" A voice pierced the Dream like a sharpened stick. In it, Pitch had been conversing with Rides-the-Wind on a windblown shore. Strong white waves had battered the rocks below them while dark Power slipped and dove, flitting about them like a falcon on the stiff wind. In the Dream, the old man had been tossing a soul, like a glowing orb, from hand to hand.

Pitch blinked, shoved the tanned elkhides down around his waist, and raised himself on one elbow. His red war shirt was rumpled, and his skin itched where the thick fabric had eaten into his flesh. How long had he slept? The heaviness in his limbs told him it couldn't have been too long. "Who is it?"

"It be me, Whisker."

He blinked in the faint glow of the fire and saw the young woman standing in the cave's rounded entry. She must have run to get here. Sweat glistened on her catlike nose, and black strands had torn loose from her bun and straggled around her oval face.

"Please, come, Pitch. Elder Ragged Wing say for you to come. *Now.*"

The Cougar People, distant relatives of the North Wind People, had a strange accent that had always been difficult for him to understand. They were hunters who lived for the most part east of the mountains at the edge of the plains, rarely fished, and insisted that fish did not feed the blood.

Pitch clambered unsteadily to his feet. "What's happened?"

She wrung her hands. "Dzoo gone."

"What do you mean? Where did she go?"

"Don't know. Men hunt for her."

Pitch pulled his cape from the floor and swung it around his shoulders. When he'd arrived at dusk, Dzoo had ordered him to get some sleep before they began their journey back to Sandy Point Village.

"She must be somewhere close by, Whisker. She wouldn't have left the people in the sick cave for long."

"Hope so."

Whisker's right hand rose, to clutch the little fetish tied around her throat, and revulsion ran through Pitch like a cold wave.

Witches' fetishes had become so valuable that even ordinary people had begun to prowl the burned villages, collecting ears, toes, sexual organs, or a lump of human liver from the dead to make fetishes to sell. Those who bought them believed that the gods could not protect them from the North Wind People, so they had to protect themselves. Only that morning, a passing Trader had shown Pitch a hideous doll made from dried seaweed mixed with human fat and baked hard. He'd said the maker was a Powerful witch called Coyote. The Trader promised that if Pitch carried the doll, no spear would be able to penetrate his body.

"Dzoo probably just needed a moment alone to gather her thoughts, Whisker."

"Yes. Please, hurry." She grabbed his wrist and dragged him out into the cold wind, then rushed ahead.

Pitch tied the laces of his cape as he walked.

The night smelled pungent—a mixture of wood smoke and boiling willow bark tea they had Traded for from the far south. Big bags bubbled near the fires in the sick cave ten and five paces ahead.

Whisker sobbed suddenly and looked at Pitch over her shoulder. Her wide eyes were startlingly black in the firelight. "My mother gone, too."

"Your mother?"

"Yes, I go to cave to talk. She gone."

A chill settled on Pitch's heart. In a gentle voice, he asked, "Did your mother's soul fly, Whisker?"

"Don't know."

Whisker broke into a run, heading away from the caves and out into the forest.

Pitch stopped. "Whisker? Where are we going?" He could see that other feet had beaten a path into the snow.

"This way. You come this way." She waved him forward. "Elder Ragged Wing needs show you something."

"Show me what?"

The shake of her head looked more like desperation than a refusal to answer.

As they entered the forest, Pitch heard voices and caught the glimmer of a shredded-bark torch. A group of six or seven people stood near a large boulder. They had their backs to him and, for the most part, resembled dark, amorphous figures floating in the halo of torchlight.

"What are they looking at, Whisker?"

"Skinned . . . wings," she said, and hesitated as if she wasn't certain that was the right word. "Bloody feathers. You must see. Come. The elders wait for you."

"The elders want me to see skinned wings?"

"Not all. Broken Sun not here."

"Maybe he and Dzoo are together."

Maybe your mother died and the carried her body out into the forest to be ritually prepared for the journey to the Underwater House.

People cleared a path for them. Two of the elders stood speaking softly. Behind them, a shape lay on the forest floor. A body, human from the looks of it. His heartbeat quickened.

"Who is it?" He stepped forward. "What happened?"

Chief Antler Spoon glanced at him, then walked a few paces to one side. Thin white hair matted his head, as though he'd just risen from his bedding. A pale caribouhide cloak hung down almost to the high wolverine leggings that covered his moccasins.

Elder Ragged Wing stood in front of the body. He had a sunken, withered face that reflected horror and disbelief. The elder put a gnarled hand on Pitch's arm as he came forward, and said, "Whisker thinks this her mother, but I am not so sure. You know Dzoo better than any of us. . . ."

Pitch bent over the corpse where it lay in the track-pocked snow.

At first he could make no sense of what he saw. She lay on her side with a bloody white cape covering her torso, but nothing was in the right place. She looked deformed or . . . contorted.

"Skinned wings," he murmured.

The murderer had wrenched the victim's arms and legs from their sockets and twisted them behind her back at unnatural angles; then he'd peeled the skin from her arms and smoothed it out flat on the snow. Pitch swallowed hard. They did resemble wings.

In the past twelve moons of raiding, the North Wind warriors had committed a great many atrocities, but nothing like this. Hate-filled warriors often mutilated their victims, but they did it in haste, hacking and slashing. This had been performed with grisly patience. "Bring me a torch."

Elder Ragged Wing took a torch from someone and held it over the body.

The killer had cut out her eyes, leaving bloody gaping caverns, and her cheeks bulged hideously from the fatty flesh stuffed inside her mouth.

Pitch's hand hesitated over the cape before he nerved himself to pull it back. She was naked. Her breasts had been cut off—not with the quick hacking of a warrior, but with the surgical slicing of a practiced Healer with a freshly struck obsidian blade. He glanced at the flesh in the woman's mouth and realized what it must be: breast tissue.

Pitch wiped his mouth with the back of his hand. Weakly, he asked, "Did you find any clothing or jewelry? Anything that might identify her?"

"No, just this beautiful cape."

The longer Pitch stared at her bloody face, the more his fear grew. He turned to the milling crowd. "Did anyone see Dzoo leave the village?"

Heads shook, and murmuring broke out. People huddled against each other as if in protection from some misty vapor that hung on the night.

"Someone must have seen Dzoo leave. Or seen Whisker's mother leave. They cannot both have just vanished without someone noticing!"

"He did it for us," Antler Spoon whispered fiercely. *"For all of us!"*

Pitch twisted around to look at the elder. Wind Woman blew wisps of Antler Spoon's white hair. He was fingering a caribou-bone fetish carved in the shape of a great northern owl.

"What are you talking about?"

"He Traded her."

"Traded who?"

Antler Spoon's jaws clamped, as though he was afraid to say more.

"Who?" Pitch shouted. "Who did you Trade?"

Antler Spoon pointed to the dead woman. "We had to give him someone!"

"Antler Spoon, answer me. Is this Dzoo?"

"No. Sweet Grass! We were too afraid to give him Dzoo! Broken

Sun, he say, Dzoo's Spirit Helpers swoop down upon us and tear us to pieces!"

A small tendril of relief wound through Pitch, to be followed by guilt. He could hear Whisker crying softly somewhere behind him.

"Who did you Trade Sweet Grass to?"

Antler Spoon's sticklike arms flailed uncertainly. "We call him 'Coyote.' Don't know his real name. Or even what he looks like. He wear a coyote mask! He been coming here for moons, watching us. We knew he out there. Many of our people seen him. But he never tried to harm us or speak to us, so we don't worry about him. Then, two nights ago, he came down from the forest and found Broken Sun."

Coyote? Pitch frowned. The same Coyote of whom the Trader had spoken?

Antler Spoon stepped forward, and his grip tightened on Pitch's arm. "He ordered us to bring him Dzoo! There was nothing we could do! He say if we didn't give her up, witch sickness and his warriors would kill my people. Broken Sun told me the whole thing." He took a deep, shuddering breath and let it out slowly. "We protect our village! Protect Dzoo! Sweet Grass dying!"

"Look! Out in the trees!"

A soft rasping sounded as stilettos and knives were drawn clear of leather sheaths.

Pitch's blood began to pound. He followed the pointing fingers to a spot in the darkness. A slender black shape wavered among the shadows cast by the firs.

Ragged Wing shook his head. "Who is it?"

Pitch muttered, "I don't know, but he's coming straight for us."

"Is Broken Sun?" Antler Spoon asked and lifted a hand to shield his eyes against the glare of the torch.

Pitch blinked, trying to make the darkness congeal into a recognizable shape. After several moments, he let out the breath he'd unconsciously been holding. "It's . . . it's Dzoo."

"You certain?" Antler Spoon's voice quavered.

"Yes." Pitch took a steadying breath. "No one else moves with that inhuman grace."

Dzoo seemed to float around the boulders, her black buffalohide cape swaying around her tall body. The hair had been turned in for warmth, and magnificent designs decorated the exterior suede: black lightning, spirals, strange birdmen, and huge rainbow serpents. A dreadful stillness possessed her. The Cougar People began to shift uneasily.

Pitch called, "Dzoo? Are you all right?"

She entered the halo of torchlight. "Gather your things, Pitch. We have no more business here." Then her gaze faxed on Antler Spoon.

A curtain of long reddish brown hair swayed around Dzoo as she silently marched toward the old man. Not even the snow crunched under her feet. Antler Spoon went still, like Crab suddenly coming face to face with Seagull.

Dzoo stopped three hands short of the chief and stared at him through eyes as black as polished obsidian and strangely luminous.

A dripping sound caught Pitch's attention. He looked down and saw drops of blood speckle the calf-deep snow at Dzoo's feet.

"Dzoo, are you hurt?" Pitch reached out to her.

Dzoo's delicate brows arched as she bent closer to Antler Spoon, extended her arm, and let something fall from her hand. It sank into the snow like a hot rock.

She whispered, "Betrayal is a costly business, Antler Spoon. Costly in every way."

Antler Spoon stammered, "Wh-what are you talking about? I don't understand."

Dzoo turned, met every eye in the crowd. "Run. While you still can."

Silently, she walked away toward the village.

No one moved; then they surged forward, asking questions, shoving each other to get a better look at what she had dropped.

Elder Ragged Wing dug it out of the snow: A globular thing, heavy, and covered with thick black—

A cry lodged in his throat as he scrambled backward. "Oh, Blessed gods. It's someone's head. It's . . . it's Broken Sun!"

Pitch couldn't turn his gaze from it.

Astonishment filled the wide, dead eyes, as though at the very last instant, Broken Sun could not believe what he was seeing.

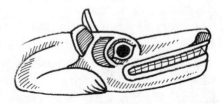

Ten

Evening Star chafed in the confines of the small lodge Rain Bear had ordered built for her. Round, with a bark roof and walls, it measured but three paces across.

Yesterday afternoon, dour-faced women had brought her supplies: blankets, food, cooking pots, even hair combs and drab but serviceable dresses. She'd stacked everything along the east wall. In the pale amber gleam of the flames, the place looked shabby, rude, and unfamiliar—the sort of thing a hunter would throw up as a temporary shelter.

Her anxious fingers caressed the fine buffalo calf leather of her formal dress. Sense would have dictated that she wear one of the others, but this one reassured her, reminded her of who she was, or at least had been. Dropping another stick of wood on the fire, she stared at the flames. "What am I doing here?"

Her Dreams had been tortured. All night long, she'd run through her burning village trying to find her husband, Toget, and their little daughter, Bright Cloud. Now that she was warm and safe, she couldn't stop thinking about them. Couldn't banish the memories of that terrible night. She kept seeing Toget's head as Ecan lifted it in the light of burning lodges.

The knot of grief in her chest seemed to be strangling her heart.

Her marriage to Toget had been arranged by her clan. They had never really loved each other, but had gotten along given the roles life had dealt them. He had been a good husband, as dedicated to Bright Cloud as he had been to his sister's children. She would miss him not as a dead lover, but as the kind man he had been.

She shied away from thoughts of Bright Cloud—tried to block the scream that lingered in her ears. That memory was too painful.

She stared around the dismal little lodge, wondering what had induced her to ask Rain Bear's protection.

"You should have kept running. You have relatives in the north." Could she still go? Was that prudent, given the number of Cimmis's warriors who would be on the trails looking for her?

She dropped her face into her hands. Long red hair fell around her. If she had only known how to find Dzoo. She might have avoided this dangerous and dingy place.

The wind moaned in the trees beyond the lodge. She lifted her head, wondering. Did she dare wait until night to creep away? She could travel north, avoid the war parties and scouts. Perhaps steal a canoe and paddle to some distant island.

"Stop it. You don't have the strength, and you know it."

She massaged her tight neck muscles. So much had changed. Two moons ago, she'd been looking forward to the day when her mother stepped down as clan matron and came to live in her lodge. Mother would have cared for Bright Cloud while Evening Star took over her fated clan responsibilities.

Now . . . none of that would happen.

Evening Star propped her chin on her drawn-up knees and gazed at the painted box of food that rested near the hearth. The box bore the intertwined images of a red killer whale and a blue cougar. Like her, they were animals out of their elements.

Why hadn't she known that Cimmis was going to attack them? Why hadn't Mother known? Naida's web of spies rivaled anything Cimmis could arrange. Surely Mother had heard rumors.

She wouldn't have believed it, no matter who told her. Cimmis was her brother. She loved him.

Cold hatred spread along her veins.

Cimmis, my uncle . . . my greatest enemy.

She picked up the wooden comb the women had brought her and began pulling the snarls from her wavy red hair. She'd bathed and washed her hair, but it was still damp and felt cool beneath her fingers.

When she'd finished, she opened the food box to find two neat stacks of dried berry cakes and a wooden cup covered with a bark lid. She bit into one of the cakes. The mixture of blueberry, coastal red elder, and highbush cranberry tasted delicious. She finished three cakes before she picked up the wooden cup and removed the lid. The rich smell of salmon oil caressed her nose. Taking another bite of the dried, berry cake, she washed it down with a sip of salmon oil. The blend of flavors sent delight through her. The North Wind People made something similar: a dried cake of black huckleberries and bunchberries: they served the dish with warm bear grease. For the moment, this tasted better than anything she'd ever eaten.

Voices rose from outside, and a man called, "Evening Star? It's Rain Bear. May I speak with you?"

She stood and smoothed her hands over her fancy calfhide dress. Olivella shells gleamed on the bodice, and expensive dentalium ringed the collar. In the fire's wavering light, the shells glittered. "Come."

Rain Bear ducked beneath the door hanging and looked around. "Is your lodge satisfactory?"

"More than I deserve, given the animosity between our peoples." She smiled dryly. "And no matter what, Chief, it beats sleeping under a rotting log while cold rain drips on you."

Rain Bear gave her a knowing smile. The otterskin cape he wore seemed to have been sculpted over his broad shoulders. Worry carved lines around his deeply set brown eyes. He propped his hands on his hips, revealing the long red shirt beneath. "I spent time last night consulting with the refugee war chiefs and the various elders of their clans."

"And?"

A derisive smile came to his lips. "Most of them don't believe you."

"They think I'm lying to further my own ends?"

"No, they think you're lying for Cimmis."

Anger speared her veins. "That's—that's ridiculous! Cimmis burned my village and slaughtered my family! Why would I—"

He held up a placating hand. "Please, Matron. I've done a good deal of thinking since I first spoke with you. I can find no logical reason why you'd spy for Cimmis."

But he *had* considered it. She crossed her arms defiantly. "So, you're making plans to defend yourselves against Ecan's attack?"

"We are." But he tilted his head as though uncertain about something. The firelight shone on his high-arching cheekbones and drew a line of gold along his strong jaw. "Before we proceed, however, I have a few more questions."

She said wearily, "I'll tell you whatever I know."

Rain Bear frowned down at the open food box beside the fire. His eyes fixed on the half-empty cup of salmon oil. "Forgive me for disturbing your breakfast. If I could, I would come back later, but I must attend a Council meeting shortly."

"You are not disturbing me, Chief." She gestured helplessly at the small lodge. "My universe is no longer the pressing place it used to be."

He paused. "Did you sleep well?"

"Does knowing how I slept help you defend against Ecan?"

He walked around to stand on the opposite side of the fire, looking suddenly self-conscious. "I just thought you might want to spend a few moments talking about something that didn't matter."

She squeezed her eyes closed. "Then my nightmares are *not* a good subject. What's the weather like this morning?"

"Foggy and cold. Not a fit day for humans or animals. Wear your mittens when you go out."

"I can go outside?" She enjoyed a sudden leap of hope.

"Go anywhere you like. But I want your guards to be close at hand."

Evening Star arched a challenging eyebrow. "Ah, indeed? Worried about my safety, are we?"

The earnest look he gave her left her oddly unsettled. "Yes, Matron, I am. And not just because some of my people might wish to cause you harm. I suspect that if Ecan can't take you back by force, the Wolf Tails will be sent sniffing."

A sudden chill went through her. To change the subject, she said, "Ask your questions, Rain Bear."

He folded his arms. "You said Ecan had perhaps ten tens of warriors."

"Yes."

"He's split his forces. Eight tens of them are headed toward Antler Spoon's village. I've also heard that Ecan's son was with the war party."

"Splitting his forces is a diversion."

"Perhaps."

"He must know that I'm here, warning you. It's a game, Great Chief. Strategy to keep you off your guard."

"And the boy? Why is he along?"

She seemed puzzled by his concern. "Kenada spoke of that. It's the boy's first War Walk. What difference does it make if his son is there?"

He slowly walked around the fire toward her. She tried to read his expression, a combination of unease and hope. "Under the right circumstances, it might make a great deal of difference. How old is the boy?"

Comprehension edged through her. "Ten summers. But Tsauz will be well guarded. I suspect that capturing him will be more difficult than defending your village."

"Tsauz? That's his name?"

"Yes." She gave him a curious look. "He'll have ten or more guards around him. Do you know why?"

"Because he's Ecan's only son, isn't he?"

"The little boy is blind, Rain Bear."

"Blind?" His surprise was complete. "Scan took a *blind* boy on a War Walk?"

"Apparently."

"Why haven't we heard, this? Surely one of the traders would have mentioned that Ecan's son was blind?"

"His blindness is recent. He lost his sight in a tragic fire. His mother—and most of her family—was burned to death. That Tsauz was rescued otherwise unharmed by a passing warrior was a miracle."

Through a long exhalation, he said, "Well, that does complicate matters. What about Ecan? Is there a chance we might be able to capture him? Does he have any curious behaviors, like bathing alone, or walking out by himself for morning prayers?"

"He insists on placing his lodge in the very middle of the camp so that he's surrounded by warriors, but he only goes alone up the cliffs to deliver the morning prayers because he has to. People hate him, and he knows it."

Rain Bear seemed to be staring at her hair. At the way the light glittered through it when she moved. Absently, he said, "Every man is vulnerable, Evening Star. Is there anyone else he cares about? Perhaps a relative in one of the nearby North Wind villages?"

She lifted a shoulder, perplexed by the softness in his eyes. "I don't think so. He seems to hate everyone except his son. And I'm not even sure about that. I've heard that he beats the boy."

As he had beaten her. Evening Star glanced away as a flashback of Ecan stabbed through her memory. She remembered the ripping sound as he tore the fabric dress off her body, and she could feel his hot flesh against hers as he pried her legs apart. Flickers of firelight in her lodge mixed with those of a burning village. An unbidden shiver ran up her spine.

"Matron, I must go, but I thank you for speaking honestly with me."

She jerked a nod. "If I can be of help again . . ."

He inclined his head, said, "I will," and walked for the door.

Thankfully he was gone before her knees went weak and she sagged to the floor. Behind her clamped eyes, memories ran free and terrible.

Rain Bear stepped out into the fog and looked around. Bark lodges wavered in the mist. On either side of him, Evening Star's guards cast curious glances his way. They undoubtedly questioned his sanity for granting asylum to such a potentially dangerous woman.

Although he'd almost convinced himself she wasn't a spy, he couldn't be absolutely certain. Was he supposed to be attracted to her? Was that the trap? Well, may Fishing Eagle strike him dead, he was. He just couldn't get the image of her odd blue eyes out of his head, and he had been dazzled by the firelight shooting burnished copper glints through her luxurious hair. He'd fought with the desire to reach out and touch it. Touch her.

When she moved, he had to make a conscious effort to keep from staring at the way her dress conformed to her round breasts and slim waist. Her soft and slim body had begun to insert itself into his waking Dreams. Those he could control. How long before her image invaded his sleep to tease his manhood?

Had his enemies bet that her very presence would be enough to make him drop his guard?

Eleven

Though it was well past midnight, neither Pitch nor Dzoo could sleep. Snow gusted out of the darkness in glittering white veils to soak Pitch's cape and the tangles of hair that crept out beyond his conical hat. They had left Antler Spoon's village immediately, trudged through the snow for four hands of time, and finally made camp in this grove of alders near Black Rock Creek. Water trickled beneath a thin crust of ice two body lengths away, sweet and melodic.

Pitch smoothed his fingers over his wet teacup and studied Dzoo. She sat across the smoking fire from him, eyes focused on their back trail as though she expected to see a war party at any instant.

An exotically beautiful woman, she drew a man's eye. Pitch couldn't say why exactly, but he caught himself staring at the curved hollow of her cheek, at the full red swell of her lips. A man might flounder in those large dark eyes. Her brow, high and smooth, balanced her upturned nose, pointed chin, and delicate jaw. But her long hair was her crown. In bright sun, it was a deep red with golden highlights, but in the firelight tonight, it glinted like polished red cedar. Though Dzoo had seen two tens and nine summers, she had never borne children; her body was still perfect, her breasts, small waist, and long legs the stuff of male fantasy.

Pitch smiled at that, aware that he liked to fantasize about her. Dzoo was a perpetual enigma, more a creature of other worlds than this one. He could see it in the way she walked, almost floating above the soil, each step placed with a feline grace. An unsettling energy flowed through her, around her, and into her. Something she could project through a look or a touch. In her presence, no one was complacent. Being close to her reminded Pitch of sitting on a peak during a lightning storm. He could feel his skin prickling and his hair starting to stand on end.

"I am not lightning," she whispered as she remained motionless.

Pitch swallowed hard, wondering where that had come from. "Did you hear my thoughts?"

She just gave him the vaguest of smiles. The silence of the night began to press down around them.

"Who do you think this 'Coyote' is?" Pitch smoothed his hand over his wooden cup. As the snowflakes struck the warm surface, they melted and ran down to pool around his fingers.

Dzoo's eyes fixed on some point out in the snow and held, motionless. She might not have heard.

Pitch took a long drink of his tea, then tugged his cape more tightly about his shoulders. "Do you think he's one of the Raven People?"

Dzoo shook her head. It was a bare movement, as if, over the decades, she had grown weary of extravagant gestures. "He's of the North Wind People."

"Why do you say that?"

"He has their long, narrow head and pale skin."

Pitch's cup froze midway to his mouth. Like him, the Raven People had broad, flat faces on round skulls, but the North Wind People were characteristically long-headed, with sloping foreheads and thin faces. "Are you telling me that you . . . you *saw* him?"

Dzoo turned her gaze on Pitch, and a tingle went through him. Looking into her large black eyes was like gazing into the eyes of a Spirit Raven. He could almost feel his soul begin to drift.

"I'm almost certain he lives in Fire Village," she said. "Or at least he was born there. He is broad of shoulder and has a curious scent, like the moss that grows at the base of the lava cliff above Fire Village."

Her hand lifted to the pendant she wore, and she gently smoothed her fingers over the red spear point. "He wears one of these."

Pitch stared at the pendant. The fluted points were magnificent, as long as his palm, and so finely flaked they had a vitreous glitter. They were called fluted points because the very last thing the maker did was to "flute" the base: that is drive a wide, thin flake of stone down the long axis of the point. Only North Wind People were allowed to possess them. The points were part of their Power as a people. They claimed their ancestors had made them from the blood of long-dead monsters. It was considered a grave offense to even be found trying to copy them.

"Then," Pitch said, "Cimmis probably sent him after you."

"There is more to Coyote than even Cimmis understands." Her smile was cold and crystalline. "Oh no, Pitch, he is more dangerous than a desperate chief, or his soul-sick Council. He has touched blackness. It lingers on his soul, taints the very air with his every breath."

That sent a shiver down Pitch's back. Chief Cimmis and the Council of Four Old Women was scary enough. The Four Old Women had felt no pity, suffered no mercy in their decisions to punish those who defied them. Reprisals had been immediate. All along the coast Raven villages lay in charred ruins, and refugees filled the trails, fleeing their wrath.

And Coyote was more dangerous than that?

Her lips parted slightly as she studied him. "He and I will meet in the end. One of us will possess the other. I wonder who will be the stronger? He . . . or I?"

"Dzoo, you don't have to deal with him alone. There are a great many of us—"

She raised her hand, fingers a golden brown in the firelight. "Listen to me. Power is shifting, Pitch. People are being swept up in the passion and madness of the gods. Our souls hang in the balance."

"How? I don't understand."

"The future," she whispered as she fixed on the night beyond their camp. "We will decide that in the coming weeks. The Raven and North Wind Peoples will begin their Dance together, shuffling . . . step by step. . . ."

An owl hooted out in the forest. Pitch tipped his head, letting the water drip off to the side as he studied Dzoo. "How will the Dance end?"

For a long time she seemed oblivious; when she finally spoke, she said, "In the end, we all make love with Death. We wrap ourselves in the most intimate of embraces. As we thrust ourselves inside Death, so does Death thrust into us." She paused, eyes alight, lips parted as if on the verge of ecstasy. "And then the release comes, tingling through us like a burning delight."

"I've never heard Death described that way before."

She glanced at him as if she hadn't quite understood him. "Pardon?"

"Death," he added, "as a lover."

Her only reply was a sad smile.

Pitch tossed another branch onto the flames and watched the sparks twirl upward through the dark filigree of alder branches. Snow frosted the tops of the limbs, but the bottoms remained as black as night, creating a stunning interplay of light and dark set against a background of scudding starlit clouds.

"Broken Sun must have been waiting for me to leave the cave," Dzoo said.

"That's when he took Sweet Grass?"

"Yes. He Traded her for these." She reached inside her cape, took a small leather bag from her belt pouch, and tossed it across the fire to him.

He hefted the bag, finding it heavy and decorated with beautifully painted red paw prints.

"Open it."

Pitch set his teacup aside, and poured the contents out.

Two tens or more obsidian fetishes glittered on his palm, and his skin began to crawl. Magnificent things: coiled serpents, bears, howling wolves, eagles with spread wings, and several images he couldn't discern in the dim light. The longer he looked at them, the more he felt it. Strange Power filled the fetishes, as though the master flint knapper had breathed part of his Spirit into the objects.

But there was something else—a voice, frail, childlike, but there. Pitch held them for as long as he could, studying them; then he shoved the fetishes back in the bag and set it on one of the hearth stones.

"Hallowed Spirits." He shivered. "Who made these, Dzoo?"

A cold smile touched her lips. "He's Powerful, isn't he?"

Pitch wiped his hands on his cape, but he could still feel the man's presence, a fetid prickle, like hungry maggots crawling around his bones. "Who is he?"

"Coyote, I assume, but I'm not certain."

Pitch washed his hands in the freshly fallen snow. "Where did you find them?"

"Broken Sun offered them to me."

In a heartbeat he saw the entire thing on the fabric of his soul. Broken Sun must have known the instant Dzoo found him that she had seen everything.

"Where did he get them?"

"That was the bargain. Coyote gave them to Broken Sun in exchange for me."

Pitch flinched. "Dzoo? What did you do with . . . I mean, Antler Spoon searched . . ." He made a face. "The warriors backtracked you through the snow. They found blood, but no body. No other tracks but yours."

The wind shifted, and snow plummeted out of the sky, creating a thick white veil between them. The fire sizzled and popped.

Dzoo answered, "He would not have been welcome at the Underwater House. I just spared his ancestors the trouble of telling him so."

He squeezed his eyes closed. If a person's body was not properly cared for, the soul became a homeless ghost, wandering the earth forever, trying in vain to speak with people, watching loved ones die. Most homeless ghosts went mad and took out their vengeance on the very people they loved most.

"What he did was wrong, Dzoo, very wrong, but he thought he was saving his village. I wish you had—"

"A man who will sell a sick woman's life for a handful of trinkets is capable of anything. I couldn't let him go."

It sounded like something Pearl Oyster would have said: *Who will he sell next? Hmm? You? Me? His own daughter?*

Pitch asked, "What does Coyote want with you?"

"Possession."

"Possession? Of what?"

"My body. One of us will devour the other. We will embrace each other, and one of us will suck the other dry." Dzoo stood, and her black buffalo cape billowed in the gale. "Why don't you try to sleep? I'll take the first watch."

Pitch finished his fir needle tea and placed the cup beside the tripod. "I think you should sleep first. In two days, you are supposed to lead the Moon Ceremonial at War Gods Village. You will need . . ."

Dzoo turned suddenly, eyes searching the storm.

He followed her gaze to the trees five tens of paces away. "What is it?"

The reflection of the firelit snow wavered over Dzoo's beautiful face. She said nothing, staring in knowing silence.

An elusive wink of light flashed in the alders.

Pitch grabbed the fetish bag, stuffed it into his pack, and gathered his things.

"Back away. Slowly," Dzoo said. "When you're two tens of paces up the trail, turn and run. I'll be right behind you."

"But it might just be a messenger from Antler Spoon, or Rain Bear. Perhaps we should—"

She turned. *"Go. Now!"*

Twelve

Evening Star picked her way carefully down the path, placing each foot so that she didn't slip and fall among the exposed roots and rocks that clogged the trail leading to the beach. She glanced back to see her two young guards following carefully, half of their glances for her, half for the surrounding forest, and a couple stolen for themselves, as if to express their unease at escorting a matron of the North Wind People.

Evening Star stepped out from the lowest trees that masked the beach and strode forward. She wore a bulky bark hat, a rain-slick grass cape, and a snug badgerhide dress that one of the women had supplied her. It was really quite cleverly made, strips of badgerhide having been twisted and then woven together to create a warm but light garment.

Through the gray drizzle, she could see Rain Bear bent over the gunwale of his canoe, placing long slender poles into the craft. As she walked closer she made out the painted red grizzly bear that decorated the canoe's side; the head had been carved into the bow, where the eyes could look out at the water. The clawed paws rose up, following the tall prow as if about to pounce on whatever lay beneath the waves.

Rain Bear caught movement from the corner of his eye and looked up. She saw surprise quickly replaced by curiosity, and then a sort of dread.

"Matron? Can I help you?"

She came to a stop beside him, looking out over the gray water. A pair of gulls wheeled and dove over the surf. "Are you going out?"

"I am." He was eyeing her two guards, who had stopped several paces short of the canoe.

"May I accompany you?" She met his penetrating gaze as he tried to divine her motive. "Chief, I have been locked in that tiny lodge for too long. You said I could go where I wished." She nodded at the boat. "I can think of no safer place than in a canoe with you. I certainly can't spy out secrets, let alone communicate them to my bastard uncle."

He shifted, his moccasin-shod feet sliding on the gravelly sand. "It's a cold, gray day. This drizzle isn't going to let up. It's not likely to be pleasant."

She knotted her fists, tilting her head to see him better from under the bark rain hat. "I want some time to be myself. I can't do that while these guards follow at my heels. Nor can I find a moment's relaxation when I am the center of everyone's attention. Wherever I go, people stare, and I see fear in their eyes as they whisper behind their hands about me." She pointed at the water. "No one will stare out there."

He considered, his craggy expression betraying a deep-seated indecision.

"What?" she demanded. "Surely you're not afraid of me." She batted her sides with fists of frustration. "Search me if you like. I carry no hidden stilettos, no war clubs or spears. I give you my word, as matron of my clan, I won't try to brain you with one of your paddles before fleeing to the far ends of the ocean."

He gave the guards a wave of dismissal. "It's all right. I'll take the matron out. If she wants to suffer in cold misery, I do not object."

The two youths nodded, gave her one last suspicious glance, and helped them push the heavy canoe into the waves.

Evening Star leaped in as the craft surged seaward with the receding surf only to buck as it met the approaching wave. She clambered to the bow and took up one of the pointed paddles, throwing herself into the task of driving through the breakers.

She grinned, let out a whoop. Her muscles corded and pulled as she took bite after bite with the paddle. It had been years since she—as the pampered daughter of Matron Naida—had been able to exert herself thus. As they cleared the last breaker, she found herself slightly winded, a warm tickle playing through her muscles.

Rain Bear's canoe was made of split cedar planks. Caulked with pine pitch, it cut the waves straight and true, without listing to either side. She tilted her head, drawing the salty smell of the ocean into her lungs.

"Feeling better?" he called from behind.

"I am."

"That was some war whoop you let loose."

She turned, grinning, then glanced at the long poles on the canoe floor. "Where are we headed? Fishing? Are those spears?"

He chuckled. "I suppose you could say it's fishing of a sort."

"Do you always go out alone?" She cast a glance over her shoulder in time to catch the irony in his expression.

"Actually, I've been spending every waking moment building this alliance between the clans. It looked like a lull, so I thought I would get away before the next runner comes in to report Ecan's whereabouts." A pause. "I needed time to think without interruptions."

"And then I came along." She considered that, knowing full well what time alone could be worth to a leader. "Perhaps, Chief, I could help you think. And if not that, I would be willing to listen."

"Listen?"

She watched the gulls as they glided past, craning necks to see if the long canoe offered any chance of food. "Sometimes Mother just needed me to listen. She would talk, rehash the problems she faced, while I just sat there weaving or twisting cordage. Sometimes I would ask a question and send her thoughts in a different direction. She used to tell me it helped."

"It probably did."

"I miss my mother. I miss the life that was taken from me. All of the lives."

They paddled in silence then. She perched herself in the bow, easing into the rhythm of stroking with the paddle. She found solace in the constant motion of the sea, in the rise and fall of the murky brown swells and the soft whispers of water splashing off the bow.

"I fear that we are never going to live like we did," he finally said. "Something has gone sour in our world. The council has given up wisdom for terror. The Four Old Women are afraid, and in their fear, they lash out. Now, in order to save ourselves, we must plunge our world into chaos."

"Fear?" she asked.

"That's what Dzoo told me. And after dwelling on it for half a moon, I suspect that she's right."

"What do they have to fear? They live behind the palisaded protection of Fire Village, surrounded by the finest warriors that have ever lived."

"It's the future, Matron. It's 'what if' that frightens them the most. They see the world they knew becoming something different. Of all our deep-seated fears, the fact that the future will be different frightens us the most."

They continued for another half hand of time, Rain Bear steering them toward a gap between two small forested islands that rose above the surf. He shipped his paddle, standing in the stern to study first one shoreline and then the other.

"You fish here often?"

"Yes." He squinted at the rocks. "This looks pretty close. We'll know when we put the poles in the water." He glanced at her. "Would you like to help?"

She shipped her paddle and carefully picked her way to the center. Rain Bear raised what looked like a flexible three-pronged harpoon from the floor. He handed it to her while he pulled out one of the long poles.

The odd harpoon was like nothing she had ever seen before. Its prongs were blunt, and it had an unreasonable amount of spring to it.

"You'll never get this to stick into any fish."

"Here, watch this." He shifted closer, took the harpoon, and fixed it onto the end of the long pole. "You are about to see something I don't think any North Wind person has ever seen."

His strong brown hands pulled a cord tight, binding the pronged head to the long pole. Next he picked up a round stone about the size of her two clenched fists and tied it a hand's length above the binding. This done, he slipped the harpoon over the side and let it sink until only a forearm's length of pole extended. "Very carefully, without tipping us over, pull out another of the poles."

She worked a second of the narrow poles free and maneuvered it around.

"Can you lift it upright?" he asked. "This is the tricky part."

Tricky indeed. She managed to raise the pole, holding it against the slight breeze. "You wouldn't want to do this when the wind was blowing."

"No, you wouldn't. In fact, you can't." He grinned in a boyish way. "The stone acts as a weight to carry the entire length to the bottom. Without it, the wood buckles and floats to the surface." He maneuvered the end of her pole into a hollow carved atop the first and fitted them together. This, too, he tightly bound, adding, "The lengths have to be tied together. If it comes apart, you still need to be able to retrieve all the pieces."

"I see." She reached for yet another of the endless lengths of pole. "How deep are we fishing?"

"You'll see."

"Are there crabs or clams that live so deep?"

"Oh, yes. We sink our traps very far down and catch crabs. As to clams, we haven't figured out how to dredge for them at these depths." He stared at the murky water. "If we could, it might alleviate some of the hunger in the camps."

One by one she helped him tie the lengths of pole together and watched them vanish over the side. Water slapped at the hull, and the gentle drizzle fell from the sky.

Finally, as he was lowering the long contraption, she saw it stop, the shaft quivering. He looked up at her, one eyebrow cocked inquisitively. "There we go. Bottom. And perfect for our purposes."

"How do you know?"

"By the feel through the wood. It's sandy, soft. If it were rock, we wouldn't find what we're looking for."

"And just what is that, Chief?"

"Well, let's see. You ready?"

She glanced around, taking in the five bald eagles that perched on a dead fir tree on the island across from them. "Sure. Ready for what?"

He smiled at the tone in her voice and began pulling the pole from the depths. One by one, he laboriously untied each pole as he drew it from the water, and Evening Star maneuvered the unwieldy length back into the canoe without capsizing them. Finally, Rain Bear lifted the pronged head with its stone from the murky depths.

"And there it is. Two of them in fact." He shot her a dazzling grin. "You're good luck, Matron."

She bent down, aware of his warmth as she knelt by his shoulder. Two white slivers were caught between the prongs. Rain Bear wiggled the first loose and handed it to her.

She took the thin white shell in her hand, immediately recognizing it. "Dentalium."

"Dentalium," he agreed, and stared at the murky water. "The only place they come from is down there. If you lay the poles out on the beach, it's about the same distance that a strong man can throw an egg-sized rock. They live that deep."

She sat back on her haunches as the canoe rocked and studied the delicate shell in her fingers. "That's how you've done it. That's how you've survived this long. You've used dentalium to buy food and tribute for Sandy Point Village."

He nodded as he withdrew the second denticulate white shell and placed it in a pouch at his belt. "In the past we'd get lucky and find a dentalium shell lodged in a deep water crab pot or fish trap. They wash ashore so very rarely, and even then they're usually broken."

She nodded. Of all the wealth, dentalium shells were the most sought after. The ten that ringed the collar on her good dress had been part of her bride price. Toget had offered them on the night of their marriage, fully aware of the fact he was marrying into the Ash Fall Clan, the most prestigious of the North Wind clans. His clan had scraped and sacrificed to be able to accumulate that wealth.

Her vision blurred as she thought back to that night, to the world that was no longer hers.

"So, now you know," Rain Bear said as he began fitting the poles back together.

She shook herself to clear her head, and lifted the next of the poles up and into place for him to bind. "Why me?"

"Excuse me?"

"Why do you show this to me?"

He sighed. "I'm not sure, really. Perhaps it is because you have placed your trust in me."

"That doesn't make sense."

"Of course it does. How do you know I won't turn you over to Ecan in return for something like dentalium?"

"Because you gave your word."

"One's word can be broken."

"Or maybe because you were married to Tlikit for all those years."

He gave her a wary sidelong glance. "That was in a different world."

"At the time she left Fire Village, she was in line to rule the Council. People still can't understand why she did that—gave up her heritage to marry a slave warrior. For a long time, it puzzled me, too."

His jaw muscles jumped as he pulled the knots tight.

She studied him with narrowed eyes as she pulled out another of the wet poles and lifted it high. "I don't think the man that Tlikit placed that much faith and love in is the type to break his word."

"Perhaps not." The muscles in his brown forearms corded as he pulled the knots tight. "We were so young then." He smiled at the memories that lay just behind his eyes. "I used to worry that over time her regrets would accumulate. If they did, she never let on. Until the end, she was . . . well, let's say that everyone deserves at least one remarkable love during their lifetimes."

The longing in his voice touched her. Had she ever had a remarkable love? With her mother and daughter, yes. But certainly not with Toget. She could have traded him for another husband without a thought had circumstances required.

She blurted, "I've never loved like that."

He studied her, a softness in his vulnerable brown eyes. "You have a long life ahead of you, Matron. Finish your mourning; find some peace for yourself. Only then can you begin to build your life again."

"Have you found peace for yourself, Chief, or are you still in mourning?"

He didn't answer her, turning instead to the long length of pole he lowered into the water. "It's a remarkably tedious chore, this fishing for dentalium. Don't expect that we'll bring up two shells with every try. I've done this for days and only recovered one or two."

She nodded. "You never know, Great Chief. Sometimes you get lucky more than once."

He said nothing in reply, and she felt a curious stirring in the darkness of grief and pain. What was it about this taciturn man who wore the cares of his people like a cape of stone?

Fear rode like a burden on Pitch's shoulders as he trotted up the trail, barely making a sound. Almost invisible shapes—silhouetted against the snow—slipped between the dark trunks behind them, there one instant, gone the next. In the falling snow and darkness, it was almost impossible to see them.

"Dzoo, where are they?"

"Stay in front of me," she whispered. "Don't look back."

The trail, a white slash in the darkness, narrowed and wound through a thick grove of firs, brush, and boulders taller than a man. The baleful eyes of crows glared out at them from the limbs. Their occasional caws broke the predawn quiet.

Pitch whispered, "Why is he just following us? Why doesn't he attack?"

She turned slightly. Her pointed nose, full lips, and a single dark eye shone against the dark rim of her hood. "He is like Brother Wolf.

Patient. He knows our final Dance will come. For the moment, it is you we must protect."

The stealthy crunch of footfalls behind them affected Pitch like fists in his belly. He hated being driven like a blacktailed deer into a surround. And truth be told, he chafed at having to rely on Dzoo for protection. It should be the other way around. She was the more valuable, a great Healer and Soul Flyer, while he was but a practicing young Singer.

He lifted his spear and nocked it in his atlatl—a throwing stick about as long as his forearm. Dawn was breaking. If they were going to try to kill him, it would be now.

"You're sure they won't harm you?"

"Coyote would cook their livers inside their gutted bodies if any harm came to me." A pause. "So don't let your masculine pride goad you into doing something foolish. You are an important piece in the game to come. We need you alive."

"What game? You speak in riddles, Dzoo."

"Riddles are everything and nothing. Circles within circles, round and round without end."

Far away, farther than could be real, he caught a glimmer of dawn light on a wind-stirred hide cloak, and a strange scent filled the air.

"Dzoo?" Pitch whispered urgently. "Is that the smell you spoke of?"

"We're a half hand's walk from Sandy Point Village. Keep the pace."

"Maybe that's what he's waiting for! He wants to kill us close to camp so people will find our bodies. The villagers would panic. You know how it would affect them. Let me fishhook back, I might be able to ambush—"

"They're watching every move you make. Obey me and *walk.*"

He marched around a wide curve in the trail with his heart pounding. By the time they emerged into a small snowy meadow, his hand ached from clutching his spear.

The forest was dim, quiet. Empty. His gaze darted over the snow-sheathed rocks and brush, searching for a glimpse of skin or hide clothing. Somewhere behind them, snow fell in a white shower from a high fir branch.

"Where did he go? Do you see him?"

For a time only the melodic sounds of the dawn answered him, the trill of a gray jay from the top of a fir, the strange cooing of Wind Woman playing in the trees.

"He's still there, Pitch."

"How can you be sure? We're only a stone's throw from the cutoff to Sandy Point Village. Maybe he grew frightened. As soon as it's light, our scouts will see him."

Dzoo lifted the hem of her cloak to step over a log that had fallen across the trail. As she continued up the path, she said, "That just means Coyote has to be more careful."

She said his name softly, as though along this snowy trail, covered with coyote tracks, the animals who bore his name might awaken and join him in the hunt.

"Do you think he's circling around us?"

"Probably. He wants me very badly."

Pitch frowned. "Who does?"

"He's there!"

Pitch jerked his spear up and saw the shadowy figure approaching through the trees to his left. "Dzoo, run!"

Dzoo's talonlike grip tightened on his arm. "No. Back up. Let him come to us."

Dzoo loosed the war club from her belt and backed into a grove of alders. Pitch took cover behind one of the wet trunks. As he waited, sweat trickled down his face.

A man moved no more than two tens of paces from Pitch's position, weaving silently between the trunks, taking his time.

Pitch slid his arm back, took aim, waiting for a clear shot—

Then he heard it and spun. "There's another one behind us!"

Instinctively his arm slid back, muscles rolling as he cast. He lost the flashing dart in the dim dawn light. The man staggered away, into the forest, and Pitch pulled his stiletto from his belt.

A second warrior ran out of the trees screaming and jabbing his spear at Pitch. Pitch dodged sideways, thrust his stiletto into the man's belly, and ripped upward.

He heard the long dart as it cut the air and sliced into his left arm. The force of the impact spun him around and knocked him off his feet. He sat down hard in the cold snow, staring at the bloody length of dart point that stuck out through his arm above the elbow. "Dzoo, for the sake of the gods, run!"

But she just stood there, tall and straight, her haunting gaze on the forest. After several heartbeats she said, "They're gone."

"What?" Pitch cradled his wounded arm, dazzled by the pain each time he moved and the long shaft pulled at his flesh. "Where did they go?"

Dzoo knelt and examined the spear that pinned his cape to his arm. Without a moment's hesitation, she reached into her healer's pack and rummaged for a long obsidian blade.

Pitch blinked, feeling light-headed, seeing the world start to spin around him. His stomach lurched, tickling the bottom of his throat with the need to vomit.

Dzoo gripped the blood-slick shaft and began sawing at the binding that held it to the stemmed point. Even those faint vibrations sent waves of sickness into his soul. He cried out when the point came free. Dzoo stepped behind him, grasped the shaft, and pulled it slowly from his flesh.

When Pitch screamed, he caught the hazy image of the Noisy Ones. The misshapen spirits looked like ugly children, whirling each other around, flying into the sky while snow drifted down behind them.

Pitch gasped, bent double, and threw up. His gut wrenched once, twice, a third time. Then he collapsed to the blood-spattered snow, panting. Hot blood soaked his shirt and cape. He had no idea how long he lay there, soaking cool relief from the snow. His arm moved as Dzoo bound it, feeling numb, oddly removed from his body.

"Come on. We have to get out of here." Dzoo pulled his good arm over her shoulders and dragged him to his feet. Pitch threw up again, vomit burning his throat.

"Go ahead," he whispered. "Get away while you can."

"It is already too late for that, Pitch. He knows I will be his in the end. It is only a matter of how."

She propped his good arm over her shoulder, and together they staggered down the trail toward Sandy Point Village.

Thirteen

The Dreams were terrible as they wrapped around Tsauz's soul in those last chaotic moments before wakefulness. . . .

He fell through images of fire and lightning. A dreadful emptiness filled him, knotting at the bottom of his throat. As he fell, the sick sensation of weightlessness grew in his gut. Flashes of light lit the sky around him.

He screamed, having never felt this terror before—not even that terrible night he had almost burned to death.

Fire flared yellow in the sky, but this time, it did not sear his flesh. He screamed again, venting his soul into the rushing air.

"It is your decision to fall, Tsauz. Reach out! Grab the wind! Clutch it to you, and save yourself!" *A voice boomed in time with the thunder.*

Tsauz reached out, seeing his hands, fingers grasping for a bruised and wounded sky. He could feel the air tearing through his fingers. As he closed them, the rushing air screamed in agony, a loud whistling wail that sent shivers through him. He could feel the pain.

Crying in terror, he let go, his body spiraling, falling, falling . . .

Tsauz bolted awake, blinking in the darkness. His body shivered; the pit of his stomach still tingled with the sensation of his weightless plummet through space. The roaring sound was gone with the Dream, replaced by the hollow clunking of wooden bowls and the murmurs of the warriors beyond the walls of his lodge.

Tsauz clutched his knotted blanket and pulled it up to his chest, sniffing the familiar scent of the fabric. Mother had given the blanket to him. He remembered what it looked like: the chocolate brown of woven buffalo hair with dyed porcupine quill decorations done in chevrons over one side.

With one hand he reached down to where Runner, his little puppy and only friend in the world, shifted and began scratching behind his ear. Tsauz could tell by the flapping sound the puppy's ear made.

"Bad Dreams, Runner," he whispered as the puppy licked his hand.

Mother, dead. Afterimages of her blistered and peeling face, her melted hair like wet leather against her scalp, lingered as his last memory of sight. He sniffed his blanket again, using its odor to blank the stench of fire.

In the Dream, he had fallen through fire. And the voice had called out to him: *Reach out! Grab the wind!* But whose voice had that been, booming even louder than the thunder?

He cocked his head, as if the echoes of it lingered somewhere above.

A worried voice from beyond caught his attention. Then came the familiar strains of a baritone voice. Yes! That was Father! He was back.

Tsauz pressed his ear close to the leather door hanging, trying to hear what Father was saying to the warriors assembled around the morning fire outside. Father spoke softly. He'd been gone for several days, and it surprised Tsauz to hear his voice.

"How many made it to Sandy Point Village?" Father asked.

War Chief White Stone answered, "More than we thought. Perhaps ten tens."

Red Dog's gruff voice added, "They ran like wood rats through the brush, Starwatcher. Some we ran down and dispatched; others, well, had they gone in a group, we could have killed more."

Father said something Tsauz couldn't make out, but the tone

frightened him. He was used to hearing Father shout in rage when angry; this quiet, seething fury made Tsauz's heart race. Sometimes when father spoke like this, it was because someone had been bad. When Tsauz was bad, Father had to hit him. It was for his own good. Father said so.

He fingered the tender bruises left from when Father had taken a piece of firewood to him several days ago. He'd been bad, slipping out of the tent one night when he was supposed to stay inside. It had been so hard to know what was right. There had been whimpering sounds, like someone in trouble would make. Tsauz had crept out into the night and felt his way to the sounds. He'd found blankets and had heard a woman's voice whimpering "No" over and over as the blankets moved and Father grunted, as if in pain. He'd asked Father if he was all right. He could hardly remember what had come next. Only the sound of the blows, and the crying woman, mixed with the guilt because he'd been bad.

Beyond the tent, Father's voice still had that sibilant quality. He wished he could see what was going on. He'd only been blind for two moons. It frustrated him not to be able to see facial expressions.

He leaned his head against the doorframe. Yellow flashes played behind his eyes as they had since that night. Yellow flashes, tongues of fire, forever burned into his last vision.

He'd been sitting at Mother's side in Grandfather's Salmon Village lodge. Her entire family—brothers, sisters, parents, and grandparents—had been there. He had gone with Mother that night. Once again he remembered the worry he had felt when Grandfather, a stern old man with snowy hair and an age-lined face, had said, "The time has come for us to leave this place."

Tsauz had felt a bolt of fear run through him. He had lived his entire life on Fire Mountain. Why would they go? He had looked around the lodge again, wondering why Father was not present, too.

"It must be done with great care," Grandfather had said. "No one must know. Tomorrow, when the sun rises, they must find our lodge empty. We must be ever careful to leave no trail."

Tsauz remembered the concern with which everyone had looked first at Mother, and then at him. Their pity hadn't made sense to him, any more than had Mother's excuse that she had fallen while hauling water, and that that was how she'd gotten so badly bruised and dislocated her arm.

Grandmother had looked at him and said, "He will be coming for the boy. We must all remember that."

Tsauz had been about to ask who would be coming when a strange fire had literally exploded in the lodge entrance. No one really knew what had happened, or what made it burn so hot, but a spark must have caught in the dry bark roof.

The blaze had been bright and hot. Tsauz ran his fingers over the scars on the backs of his hands. Had he ever felt such pain? After that, not even Father's beatings hurt.

A man's hand had grabbed him from behind and dragged him outside. He'd caught a glimpse of Red Dog before the man ran away into the darkness. The last thing he'd ever seen was Mother's face peeling and shriveling as her hair burned.

Tsauz let out a pained breath. He kept that image locked deep in a secret place in his soul. When he felt lonely or afraid, he pulled it out and looked into her eyes again—frightened eyes, filled with desperation to save him.

Tsauz shifted, and his head brushed the sloping roof. Though only ten summers had passed since his birth, Tsauz had grown tall. He had a long narrow face with a pointed chin and shoulder-length black hair that had grown out after being singed short in places.

Outside the lodge, an unknown man whispered, "What do you wish us to do, Starwatcher?"

Tsauz could hear fir needles crackling as Father paced back and forth. He knew that careful, measured tread. Before he'd gone blind, he'd seen Father pace often enough before their lodge at Fire Village.

"We carry out the plan," Father said.

A brief silence. Then the man said, "But, Starwatcher, we can't possibly win."

"*Yes,*" Father hissed, "*we can.*"

"But how?" That was White Stone.

"By misdirection, deceit, and surprise."

Tsauz wondered what misdirection and deceit were. He hadn't heard those words before.

Father continued, "Antler Spoon's village plays a role in this great hoax. The bulk of our forces are headed that way as we speak. Suspicion will be allayed while they circle, working their way on stealthy feet." A pause, and then Father's voice almost sounded joyous. "I can hear the gathering of raven wings, my friends. And they shall be blown away by a great northern wind!"

Grab the wind! the Dream voice echoed inside Tsauz.

Feet shifted, and several conversations broke out.

Father's voice suddenly burned with rage. "Do not ever let me hear you say we can't win again. Do you understand? Now take the remaining warriors and begin your circle. Make certain everything has been prepared for War Gods Village. And do not allow yourselves to be discovered." A pause. "I will be most displeased if that happens. Do you understand?"

"Yes, Starwatcher."

Steps padded away from the fire: One man at first, then many followed.

Runner snuggled against Tsauz's leg and whimpered. When Tsauz reached down to pet him, the puppy wagged his tail and pawed the ground. Runner had a black body with a white face and spotted ears.

Tsauz patted the little dog on the head. "Shhh, Runner, I'm trying to hear Father."

Runner may not have understood the words, but he knew a reprimand when he heard it. He circled on the blanket and curled against Tsauz's side, then propped his chin on top of Tsauz's thigh.

War Chief White Stone asked, "And the rest of us, Starwatcher?"

"The final stroke of genius, War Chief. We leave immediately for War Gods Village . . . and we are going straight through Sandy Point on the way."

"Gods! Sandy Point? Are you crazy?"

A sudden silence made Tsauz tremble. Across the distance he could hear White Stone swallow dryly.

When Father spoke it was with a deadly fury. "If you ever use that word with me again, I will cut your tongue from your body, no matter who you are, or what you are to Cimmis. Pack your men; we move out now."

"Yes, Starwatcher." Feet pounded as White Stone turned and raced off.

Tsauz crawled out of his blankets and pulled the lodge flap open a crack to listen. Down the valley, he heard tens of warriors moving and smelled the scents of their breakfasts cooking: roasted venison and lady ferns. From Father's position, he heard nothing, only a long and lingering silence, as if Father was lost in deep thought.

Runner licked Tsauz's moccasin, and Tsauz gently stroked the puppy's side. "Are you hungry?"

Runner perked up. He knew the word "hungry."

Tsauz felt his way across the lodge to the bag where he kept the extra fried clams the slaves had fixed him for dinner. Runner trotted at his heels, whimpering.

Tsauz pulled out some clams and petted Runner's side while the dog gulped them down.

"Now, be quiet. Father thinks we're asleep. He might be angry if he knew we'd sneaked out of our hides to listen to him."

When Father got angry, things died. That's what had happened to Tsauz's last puppy. Mother must have said something that angered Father, because he'd kicked the little puppy so many times he'd killed it. The squeals had been terrible. Then, the following night had been the fire, but Father had been gone. Chief Cimmis said he was high on Fire Mountain speaking with the stars that night, and could not be reached. Father hadn't returned for days.

Tsauz had been so alone. The strange new darkness had pressed on his eyes and ears like granite weights. The warriors who'd guarded him hadn't dared to speak with him. Neither had they made so much as a sound when he called out his dead mother's name, or that of his puppy.

Only Chief Cimmis, passing by, had stopped. Tsauz had heard him, felt his penetrating stare, and then the old man had walked away. A half hand of time later he had returned with Runner, saying in an ominous voice, "Here, boy. This one is a gift. No one will dare to harm him."

Tsauz tiptoed back to his bedding and quietly pulled the hides and buffalo blanket over him. Runner curled up on his chest.

"You would not have believed my Dream. It was so terrible, filled with Power. And this voice . . . it called out of the storm."

Runner wiggled and stomped, weaseling his way up until he could lick Tsauz's chin. The wagging of the little dog's tail brought joy to his heart.

"We will be together forever, Runner. You will be my best friend. We'll always take care of each other. And if you get lonely, I'll hold you. Just like this." He wrapped his arms around the squirming puppy.

Runner made soft sounds of joy, his tail lashing the air as he snuffled and tried to lick Tsauz's chin.

Who was that other man Father had been talking to? War Chief White Stone and Red Dog he had recognized, but that last voice? It had been so low that even if Tsauz had known him, he doubted he would have recognized his voice. He—

Father's steps pounded the ground, and he tugged the lodge flap aside. "Tsauz? Get up, my son. I need you to travel with me today."

"Yes, Father!"

Tsauz sat up so suddenly, Runner scrambled as he rolled across the hides.

Father ducked into the lodge. "I'm sorry my journey took so long." He seemed to be ignoring Runner. Tsauz could hear the puppy snuffling at Father's moccasins.

"Don't be sorry, Father. I'm just happy to be with you." Tsauz dutifully began rolling up their bedding hides. "When did you get back to camp?"

"Hmm?" Father said distractedly, then, "Just a short time ago. Were you asleep?"

"Yes. The sound of your voice woke me. I'm glad to see you." Tsauz smiled his love at Father.

"And I to see you. I know this trip has been difficult for you. I'm often away, and you are alone with our slaves in Fire Village."

"I have Runner, Father. I'm not alone."

Runner heard his name and galloped over to lick Tsauz's hand.

Father said, "Well, you're very brave, but I won't take you on my next trip. It's too dangerous for you to be away from Fire Village. More and more villagers have been flocking to Rain Bear. Any one of them would love to harm you, and . . . and I couldn't stand that."

Tsauz beamed, finished rolling the hides, and tied them with a sea-grass cord. "Why do people flock to him? Why don't they come to us for protection?"

Father paused, and Tsauz could feel his rage; it made the very air seethe.

In a clipped voice, Father said, "Rain Bear offers them things that we cannot. He has been pillaging villages for a long time. He has amassed great wealth, especially dentalium, and uses it to pay them to fight against us."

"But we have great wealth, too, don't we?"

"Yes, but we cannot afford to give it away to the filthy Raven People. We need everything we have to purchase food for ourselves. Our fishing and hunting last autumn produced barely half of what we needed to survive the winter."

Tsauz edged closer to Father, eager to repeat the words he'd overheard. "Father, is that why we're leaving Fire Village, because there's no food?"

Father went still. Angrily, he snapped, "Who told you we were leaving Fire Village?"

"I—I heard you say it. I'm sorry. I couldn't help it. When will we be moving to Wasp Village?"

Tsauz could hear Father's breathing turn shallow. "Very soon, my son. Wind Scorpion arrived last night with word that Old Woman North has had a vision. She said the North Wind People must abandon Fire Mountain. But no one is supposed to know. Do you know why?"

"No, Father."

"Because if the Raven People knew that the North Wind People were going to abandon the Fire Mountain villages, they might take the opportunity to attack us. It would be easy enough. We will be traveling, strung out on trails for several days to get down to the coast." Father turned and seemed to be staring across the lodge. "According to Wind Scorpion, Old Woman North said that if we travel at night the Meteor People will lead us. Wasp Village will be the rebirth of the North Wind People."

Tsauz stroked his puppy. Runner's fur felt soft and warm. "We will have all of our warriors on the journey, won't we?"

"Yes, but the Raven People still might be tempted to attack us. They hate us, my son. Hate with a passion that you will never fully understand. That's why the North Wind People have been packing in secret. We don't want to give the Raven People time to plan and prepare an attack."

"Are we safe here, Father?"

"I'm not sure we're safe anywhere. And today I need you to be very brave. A huge camp of Raven People is just a short distance away."

Tsauz's belly clenched. "B-but we'll be safe when we get to War Gods Village, won't we? And we'll get there today?"

Father patted Tsauz's cheek. He always seemed to use a little too much force; it hurt. Nothing like when Father really got mad. Then it hurt for days afterward.

"It will depend upon how much snow has fallen on the trails, my son. But we will be there tomorrow morning for certain."

"Then matron Weedis will give us shelter, won't she? She's one of the North Wind People. She won't let anyone hurt us while we're there."

"Of course not." But something hid behind his voice.

Tsauz turned blind eyes on his father. "I am looking forward to the Moon Ceremonial. Will there be many people?"

"I suspect the entire mountaintop will be infested with Raven People," Father said distastefully. "But we will make the best of it, won't we?"

Tsauz nodded. Father had hated Raven People for tens of summers, since the day Raven warriors destroyed his village and he saw his parents slaughtered before his eyes. He said Raven People weren't really human beings. More like vermin with a language. It had always puzzled Tsauz that his mother had been one of the Raven People. But she had been very beautiful. Father had often shouted that men always watched her with longing in their eyes, and that she was his alone. Perhaps that explained it.

"Will I be able to touch the stone bodies of the gods, Father? I have always wished to touch them. The Traders speak of them with such awe."

"That's why I wished you to come with me on this journey. I think you will be astounded. The twin War Gods are enormous and perch right on the very edge of the mountain overlooking Mother Ocean."

"Can I help you with the Moon Ceremonial? You said I could if matron Weedis didn't object."

"Are you certain you wish to fast and pray while everyone else is feasting and dancing?"

"Oh, yes, Father," Tsauz said reverently. "Someday, I plan to be a very great holy man, just like you."

"Well, if that's true, we'll have to start looking for a proper teacher for you. Old Rides-the-Wind has recently placed himself in a most precarious position. As a way of making amends, I'm sure he will be willing to instruct you."

Tsauz stared in blind disbelief. "Rides-the-Wind? Truly?"

"We will try, my son, but I can't promise anything. He is old . . . and he recently gave me a hint that his health might be in jeopardy."

Tsauz sat back on the hides and let the sense of wonder fill him. Very few boys received instruction from the old Soul Keeper. The idea made Tsauz's thoughts swim. In a hushed voice, he said, "I would like him to teach me, Father."

"I'm sure. I would have given my very life to have been taught by that crazy old man." Bowls clattered as though Father were stuffing them into a hide bag.

"Didn't he wish to teach you?"

"Well, he might have, but my grandmother said he was dangerous. She wouldn't allow it."

Tsauz wondered about that. Wouldn't allow it? Rides-the-Wind was one of the most holy men in the world. Why would any matron not jump at the chance of having one of her descendants taught by such an august man?

Father finished tucking their few possessions into the bag and said, "We must hurry. The slaves have prepared breakfast around the central fire. Let's eat so we may be on our way. I want you to be very brave today. In fact, I'm counting on it. Just keep this one thought in your head: We are going to War Gods Village for the ceremonial. Nothing more. Understand?"

"Yes, Father." But he had to ask himself what more there might be than the ceremonial.

Fourteen

Pitch blinked. Disbelief had just begun to set in. He'd been hit. The sticky blood cooling his skin, the stinging agony and insult to his flesh, couldn't be denied. Blinking again, his vision blurred as Dzoo rushed him toward the village.

Am I going to die? The question slipped sideways through his mind as he hurried down the familiar path. Sudden nausea gave him the slightest warning. His stomach lurched, and he pulled away from Dzoo to vomit. She didn't even allow him the simple relief of wiping his mouth. The bitter taste of bile and acid lingered on his tongue as she propelled him forward.

Woozy and wobbling, he stumbled along. Voices were shouting. He caught the image of one of the young warriors, a village guard, as he stepped out of the trees. Dzoo seemed to be speaking from a great distance, giving orders.

The world began to spin, and Pitch whimpered in fear.

Am I dying? Was that the hazy loose sensation that curled into the pain?

They passed more trees, vision jerking with each step. Then they were in the village. He should have been relieved at the sight of the familiar houses.

"Easy, Pitch," Dzoo told him firmly as she lowered him to the ground. Glad to rest, he hunched forward, holding his wounded arm. A crowd gathered, whispering, asking questions.

He looked into Dzoo's eyes as she bent over him, inspecting his wound. Her words seemed to vibrate in his bones. "You're safe now. I must go after him."

"No!" he had wits enough to protest. "Wait! Take warriors with you."

Dzoo ran cool fingers down his cheek, her smile like a sunrise. "It isn't that easy."

He pressed his eyes closed, forcing himself to concentrate. "Dzoo, you can't . . ." But when he opened them again, she was gone. Vanished.

He stared around at the gathering people, searching in vain for Dzoo. Then Roe pushed her way past the gawking crowd. He smiled up into her face. It was all right. He could die now. Looking terrified, she leaned over him, fingers probing his blood-soaked wrappings.

"I've sent for Father," Roe said. "He'll be here soon."

She was tall and slender, with a triangular face and slanting brown eyes; she looked older than her ten and six summers. The hood of her eagle feather cape waffled in the wind as she threw his clothing back to better examine the wound.

"How bad is it?" His voice stuck in his vomit-choked throat.

"You're bleeding."

Roe pulled the obsidian knife from his belt and sliced the wrapping Dzoo had put on him. Blood immediately began to well in the two punctures.

"Gods!" she cried, and cut a long strip from the bottom of her leather dress. When she began wrapping it around his wound, the pain almost blinded him.

Roe cut the ends of the leather bandage and tied it; then she wiped her blood-slick hands on her red leggings. "When the bleeding stops, we'll remove the bandage and clean . . ."

A din went up from the crowd, and Pitch saw his father-in-law shoulder through the press with War Chief Dogrib close behind. Dogrib's long braid hung over his shoulder like a glistening white snake. His pink skin had an eerie yellowish glow in the morning light. It took a moment for Pitch to place the North Wind woman who walked at Rain Bear's left: Matron Evening Star.

"Pitch!" Rain Bear dropped to one knee and said, "Roe, what happened?"

"Dzoo dragged him into camp, called me to tend his wound, and left. I don't know anything else."

"We were attacked," Pitch said through gritted teeth. "Just outside of the village. We thought we'd lost them yesterday, but apparently not."

Rain Bear said, "Where's Dzoo?"

"She went after them."

Rain Bear swung around to Dogrib. "Take a war party. Go."

Dogrib left at a run.

Rain Bear looked at Roe. "How is he?"

She shook her head. Long red-brown hair draped the front of her cape. Roe looked a great deal like Tlikit, right down to her light brown eyes. "Once the bleeding stops, I'll take a good look at the wound. The spear didn't break the bone, though it may have nicked it. The important part now is to stop the bleeding."

"Who attacked you?" an old gray-haired man demanded from the edge of the crowd. "Was it one of Cimmis's assassins? Or Ecan's warriors?"

The crowd went silent. Several people backed away, muttering with worry.

"I don't know," Pitch said with a gasp.

Rain Bear rose and faced the crowd. "We don't know anything yet. I want you to stay vigilant. Know where your children are. Make sure that your elders are safe. There may be one North Wind warrior out there, or five tens."

Some of the women pushed away through the crowd and sprinted for their lodges. The gaps they left were quickly filled as people jostled for new positions.

Rain Bear knelt again. "Pitch, you said you thought you'd lost them. So you knew you were being followed?"

"Yes."

"How many were there?"

"I saw two, but there had to have been more."

Rain Bear looked up when War Chief Talon pushed through the crowd, glared uneasily at the silent Evening Star, and turned his attention to Pitch.

Talon shoved his hair away from his dark eyes and squatted beside Rain Bear. "I sent my best trackers with Dogrib. We'll find them."

Rain Bear nodded in gratitude, his eyes boring into Pitch's. "Tell me what you saw. Every detail."

"Just glimpses of hide capes. I managed to cast my spear before I was wounded. I'm sure I got him. I stabbed another."

"Were they Wolf Tails?" Talon asked. "Assassins?"

"Maybe. I don't know."

Rain Bear's gaze went to the crowd, as though searching for the culprit, expecting to see him out there leering at them.

Pitch pulled his wounded arm forward, trying to ease the pain. Blood leaked around the edge of the bandage. Rain Bear scooped up snow and packed it onto the wound. Pitch shuddered, woozy, and wondered if he'd throw up again.

"I know it hurts. I'm sorry."

Pitch bit his lip.

"Tell me about Antler Spoon's village. Were you followed when you left? Is it possible that you were attacked by his villagers?"

"It's possible . . . but not likely. We had problems . . ." He flinched when Rain Bear pressed harder on his wound. "Someone tried to kill Dzoo."

Talon's brown eyes slitted with deadly intent. "Who tried to kill Dzoo?"

"It's . . . it's a long story. A man they called 'Coyote' tried to buy Dzoo's life from the elders."

Rain Bear asked, "Buy her life? Are you telling me the elders had the audacity to try to *sell Dzoo*?"

Pitch groaned softly as he dug into his belt pouch and removed the bag of fetishes. "They tricked Coyote. Traded another woman in Dzoo's place. For these."

Rain Bear took the bag and poured the fetishes into his palm. Talon sucked in a worried breath. People moved forward, trying to see.

Talon murmured, "Hallowed Ancestors, don't let anyone see those, or you'll be the target of every starving person within a moon's walk."

Rain Bear cupped a hand over them, shielding them from sight. He shivered, as though chilled by the gorgeous obsidian fetishes. "Coyote made these?"

"Dzoo thought so." Pitch paused to clench his jaw. "But whoever made them is very Powerful. I wouldn't touch them for long, if I were you. They drain a man's strength."

Rain Bear shoved the fetishes back into the bag. "Was it Coyote who speared you?"

"Maybe."

At a call, Rain Bear stood, looking beyond the crowd. "It's Dog-rib," he said, and tucked the bag into his belt pouch.

Pitch forced a swallow down his dry throat. He glanced up, seeing Evening Star. She kept shooting furtive glances at Rain Bear. Thinking what?

Dogrib elbowed his way through the crowd and shot a measuring glance at Pitch. "We found a dead man. Pitch's spear was sticking out of his guts. He was wearing this." He removed an object from his pocket and held it out to Rain Bear.

The chief took it and turned it over in his palm. The glorious fluted spear point shimmered. Evening Star's quick intake of breath wasn't lost on either Rain Bear, Dogrib, or Talon.

Rain Bear said, "I need to see the corpse."

Talon stood up and propped his hands on his hips. "I have heard that all the Wolf Tails wear those points." He gave Evening Star a distasteful glance. "They are supposedly gifts from the North Wind People."

Rain Bear nodded. "Yes, and highly unusual ones at that. Do you know what they would do to you or me if we so much as touched one?"

"Kill us quick, I suspect."

A man could Trade one of those pendants for a cycle's supply of food. If the pendant's Spirit was properly cared for, it was supposed to bring Dreams of the future.

Dogrib knelt beside Pitch and gave him an approving look. "Excellent cast. Your spear took him through the chest."

Pitch blinked, trying to focus. "What about the other? Did I kill him?"

"He's wounded." Dogrib shoved white hair behind his ears. "I don't know how badly. We found a spatter of gut blood."

"And the others? There had to be others. Someone hit me from behind."

"We found a third set of tracks. Evidently the man who wounded you. After he cast, he turned and ran."

"Where's Dzoo? Is she all right?"

"She's tracking the wounded man up the trail to War Gods Village." Dogrib's eyes glinted when he turned to Rain Bear. "We have to find her. She's going to need help."

"Bah!" Talon bellowed. "Pity the poor bastard she's tracking. You can bet that by this night, his soul is going to be wailing, lost among the forest shadows."

Rain Bear turned to stare, as though he could see War Gods Village through the layer of clouds that cloaked the mountaintop. "Yes, find her. Tell her that Matron Evening Star and I must speak with her immediately, before the Moon Ceremonial. I need to hear her side of what happened in Antler Spoon's village."

"I'll be back by nightfall." Dogrib trotted away, motioning to several of the warriors to follow him.

Pitch tried to muster enough strength to think. His senses seemed to be flowing out with his blood. Memories flitted behind his eyes, but nothing he hadn't already—

He stared hard at Rain Bear. "One of the last things Dzoo said to me was 'He knows I will be his in the end.' "

"What did she mean?"

"I'm not sure, but I thought she meant that they knew each other, or at least she knew him."

Rain Bear looked at Talon. "Let's see this dead man."

As he rose, Talon caught his arm in a rough grip and hissed. "This is just a distraction. You know that, don't you? This *is* Ecan's work, and he wants our attention focused here, around the camps. Why?"

"Probably because he . . ."

A low hiss of surprised voices began and built to a frightened roar. Villagers ran in all directions, scattering like a school of fish at a thrown rock.

"What's happening?" Talon asked as he drew his stiletto with a gnarled fist.

Pitch craned his neck, trying to see as Rain Bear growled, "Speaking of your demon, Talon, here he is."

Rain Bear stiffened when he saw Ecan. The Starwatcher walked straight down the main trail. He had placed himself in the middle of a group of armed warriors, his white leather cape shining. A head taller than any of his men, Ecan's dark gaze fixed on Rain Bear, then on Evening Star. An amused smile crossed his lips.

Instinctively, Rain Bear reached out, placing a reassuring hand on Evening Star's elbow. He could feel the tension rising within her. "You all right?"

She swallowed hard, eyes narrowing. "I'd forgotten how much I hate him."

"Hallowed gods," Talon whispered, "I can't believe he's this insolent! Does he think he can walk right in here and we will do nothing?"

Rain Bear noticed the little boy holding Ecan's hand, then surveyed Ecan's warriors. It was a small party: five and ten men. White Stone led the way, his jaw hardening when his gaze met Rain Bear's. A long time ago, when Rain Bear had been a lowly warrior in Fire Village, he'd often butted heads with White Stone. The man was a tough and shrewd opponent, but honorable. Or, at least, he had been.

The villagers who'd fled had begun to return in ones and twos, each bearing a weapon, even if it was but a piece of firewood. Their voices built to a hostile din, shouting challenges and accusations.

Ecan didn't reply. He held the boy's hand and kept his eyes locked with Rain Bear's. He stopped five paces away and in a clear voice said, "Greetings, Chief. I enter your village openly to speak with you." Then he glanced at Evening Star, the barest flicker of an eye betraying the cold fury burning within him.

People said Ecan had the soul of a weasel, and it was true. He had a handsome face with glistening, inhuman green eyes.

Rain Bear gave the man stare for stare. "Why are you here?"

"Matron Weedis has invited me to attend the Moon Ceremonial again this year. I have come as I have every year. But given the current unrest, I wanted to stop and ask your permission to pass in peace."

"That is all you want?"

"I see you've captured my escaped slave." Ecan turned fierce eyes on Evening Star. "What do I owe you for her return?"

"She has sanctuary here." Rain Bear could sense the growing desperation in Evening Star.

Ecan's smile didn't extend to his eyes. "I will give fifteen pieces of dentalium as a token of my appreciation for her return."

Evening Star's fists balled; back stiff, she glared her hatred. Rain Bear placed a hand on her shoulder. The muscles beneath were like rock.

Ecan's smirk grew as he added, "And I might be able to guarantee some extra rations—food for your people here, Great Chief. You know, something to tide your village over during these trying times."

In a commanding voice, Rain Bear stated, "She has sanctuary."

Ecan's green eyes seemed to swirl with implied threat. "Think carefully about what you do here today, Rain Bear."

"The subject is closed." He inclined his head toward the menacing crowd. "Unless you want to test your luck, Starwatcher."

Ecan, fully aware of the volatility, smiled knowingly. "I assure you, we will revisit this problem on another day."

"Do you have any other business here?"

"Why? Did you hear I'd come to attack you?" He waved a hand at the small party that accompanied him. "With my five and ten warriors?"

His men, despite their half-panicked eyes, forced a laugh. To Rain Bear, it sounded staged, hollow.

The villagers pressed closer, hissing questions, their eyes daggers of hate. Talon was shifting from foot to foot, as if in his mind he was driving a long bone stiletto into Ecan's whip-thin body.

Rain Bear glanced down at Pitch. His son-in-law, wounded and half dazed, had drawn his stiletto from his belt and held it out of sight against his belly. It would only take a gesture, a single wrong word, and this could degenerate into a massacre.

Rain Bear considered the little blind boy behind Ecan, wondering what kind of arrogant fool would lead a child into a mess like this. In a calm voice, he said, "I think you should leave, Starwatcher."

Talon's gruff old voice rose above the din. "Where are the rest of your warriors? Circling to hit us from behind? That's the sort of sneaking cur thing you'd do, isn't it?"

Ecan was either totally oblivious, or exercised incredible control as he answered, "They are on their way back to Fire Village with tribute. I am here on a peaceful journey. To attend to spiritual matters." He gave Evening Star an oily smile. "No matter what you might have heard."

Talon stepped forward, his stiletto up. "You murdering filth!"

Rain Bear reached out with a restraining hand, hissing, "Easy, old friend. This isn't the time." He met Talon's eyes. "Trust me."

Talon growled and stepped back, his upper lip twitching.

White Stone's warriors were fingering their weapons, many damp with fear-sweat as they took the measure of the hostile crowd. Ecan's expression did not change. "Circling to attack? Where did you hear that? From my *slave*? Ah, yes, the pitiful Evening Star. Are you telling them lies? In return for what? Hmm? Bedding Raven People to save your pretty neck?"

The look on Evening Star's face was one of disgust and loathing. Rain Bear realized she was trembling, sensed the fraying of her rawhide control.

Talon gave her a slitted look, and Rain Bear said, "What are you talking about?"

"Don't play the fool with me, Rain Bear. The instant the news reached me that she was here, I was certain she would be filling you with stories about my wicked intentions." He spread his arms. "That's *why* I came. I wanted to assure you that I had no plans to attack your village. You fulfilled your obligations to Fire Village. Neither I, nor any of my people, wish you harm."

"*Lying slug!*" Evening Star hissed.

Rain Bear raised a fist. "Refugees flooded in all day yesterday and for most of the night, fleeing your attacks. Do you—"

"I want to speak with my slave," Ecan rudely interrupted. "Alone."

Ecan's son gripped his father's war shirt and stared blindly at Talon as a deafening roar of disbelieving voices rose from the crowd.

Someone shouted, "There are tens of us! Let's kill them!"

Rain Bear swung around, but saw only a swimming sea of hateful faces. "Stay where you are!" he ordered. "Ecan and his party are under my protection until we've finished speaking! Back away!" He signaled several of his warriors.

Shouts and curses rose as they used their spears to move people back.

A small smile curled Ecan's lips. He petted his son's hair, but said nothing. Something wiggled and whined inside the pack on the little boy's back. A puppy?

Evening Star shook her head, stepping forward. She seemed to have found her control. "We will speak here, piece of filth. Where all can hear, and where no warrior will sneak up and slip a stiletto into my back."

Blessed Spirits, she was beautiful. Her long red hair hung in thick waves to her slender waist, and she had skin like white chalcedony.

Ecan tapped one of his warriors on the shoulder, and the man opened a space in the protective circle. Ecan and the boy walked through. The Starwatcher bowed respectfully. "Slave, I come at the invitation of Matron Weedis to attend the Moon Ceremonial. That is all. Since I must pass through Rain Bear's village, I came to ask his permission. Did you tell these people I was going to attack them?"

She nervously wet her lips. "Where are the rest of your warriors?"

"I thought it might be provocative to arrive with such a large party. I told no lie when I said they were on their way to Fire Village."

"More like Antler Spoon's village," Talon muttered under his breath. "Which is close enough that they could double back and strike us at any time."

Ecan's green gaze shifted smugly to Talon. "Then I'm sure your scouts will give you ample warning, War Chief. All the more proof that my story is true." He sniffed in derision. "My slave, here, wouldn't know truth if it caressed her in the daylight."

The hissing of the crowd grew louder, and people began to glare at Evening Star, as though angry that she'd lied to them about Ecan's intentions.

Evening Star shot Rain Bear a pleading look. "Don't let him pass. He's not on a holy mission. You must believe me."

Before Rain Bear could respond, Ecan said, "As you see, she knows nothing about me or my plans. We stand here at your mercy, Rain Bear. Would I bring my son into the middle of a battle?"

Rain Bear glanced down at the frightened boy. What man in his right mind would place his only son at risk?

Ecan added in a bored tone, "You may kill us, or respect Matron Weedis's wishes and grant us permission to attend the sacred rites at War Gods Village." He tilted his head, eyes narrowing. "What kind of message would that send, hmm? Killing the Starwatcher on his way to conduct one of the most sacred rituals in your calendar?"

The refugees began shouting, *"Kill him. . . . Kill them all!"*

Rain Bear lifted a hand, and the angry voices dwindled. "We will allow you to pass, Starwatcher." The crowd roared. "We will even send a party of warriors to make certain you arrive at War Gods Village in safety." He smiled. "After all, it is a sacred ceremony. We would want nothing to jeopardize it."

Rain Bear turned and, one by one, singled out several warriors. They trotted forward, following his signals to surround Ecan's party. He could sense the humiliation and anger boiling up within Evening Star. She perplexed him, and just looking at her, he could see her trembling with hatred and desperation.

The Starwatcher watched suspiciously, as if trying to read what might lie between them. Layers upon layers, that was how his mind worked. "That is very kind of you. Now, if you do not object, we will be on our way. I'm sure your villagers wish us to leave as much as we do."

Rain Bear stepped close to Ecan. "Please do *not* make me regret this. If anything were to happen to mar the Moon Ceremonial, I would take it as a *personal* affront."

The threat in his voice was clear for all to hear.

Ecan nodded obligingly. "It is my great respect for you that has brought me here today."

"Then perhaps you have a dose of wisdom in addition to audacity." He turned to the lead warrior. "Running Cat, collect their weapons."

"What?" Ecan stiffened.

White Stone shouted, "We will not surrender our arms!" His warriors crouched in a defensive circle, gripping weapons in sweaty hands.

Rain Bear looked straight at Ecan. "You claim to be on a peaceful mission. If that is true, you will not need arms. And, regardless, I will not allow you to enter Matron Weedis's village with armed warriors.

We will keep your weapons here. You may retrieve them after the ceremonial."

Ecan's jaw clenched. His warriors shot panicked looks back and forth, waiting for his instructions. "You will leave us defenseless. What if we are attacked on the trail?"

"My warriors will protect you with their lives." Rain Bear looked at Running Cat, and the muscular young man squared his shoulders. "Do you understand?"

"Yes, my Chief," Running Cat said. "But I will need at least two tens of warriors to protect them."

"Call upon as many men as you require."

"And if we *refuse*!" Ecan declared hotly.

"You may deal with them." Rain Bear waved at the angry refugees.

While Running Cat trotted through the crowd, speaking to warriors, Ecan's angry gaze turned on Evening Star. She stood stiffly, looking as if about to explode.

Talon leaned sideways and whispered, "Let me send some of my warriors along."

In a low voice, Rain Bear replied, "If something happens, I want them to blame us. Not you. Your clan has suffered enough."

Talon's bushy brows pulled together. "Very well, but you won't mind if a party of my warriors follows yours up the trail, will you?"

"No, if you will give me your word that they will make no trouble."

"It is given."

Running Cat trotted back through the shifting crowd with a large party of warriors. He walked straight to White Stone and said, "War Chief, order your men to lay down their weapons."

White Stone gritted his teeth, measured the hungry faces of the people encircling him, and turned his hot eyes on Rain Bear. They traded looks; then White Stone growled, "Put down your weapons!"

His warriors pulled war clubs, stilettos, and knives from their belts and placed them on top of their casting spears. The little boy removed a crude stone knife from his belt and laid it down with the rest. Rain Bear saw a button nose sniffing from inside the pack. The boy did carry a puppy.

Running Cat turned to Rain Bear. "Shall we escort them up the trail now, my Chief?"

"Yes. Detail a runner to go ahead and tell Matron Weedis you are coming."

Running Cat nodded and used his spear to gesture to Ecan. "You may proceed, Starwatcher."

Ecan's lips curled into an unpleasant smile. He gripped the boy's hand again and gave Evening Star a final promissory glance as he passed.

Villagers followed in a flood, shouting curses, waving fists and weapons. In a matter of heartbeats, the area around Rain Bear was virtually empty.

Pitch said, "Thank the Spirits. I don't think I've taken a breath since he arrived."

"I don't think any of us has," Rain Bear said.

Evening Star said with quiet urgency, "I told you the truth. He's going to attack you."

"Just your presence in the village might have made him change his mind," Rain Bear interrupted. "Let us wait and see."

Her blue eyes glittered. "That's not wise. Kill him while you can."

"No. Not yet."

Talon said, "Well, if you will permit me, I must organize a party of warriors to follow yours. Great Chief, I'll meet you back here in a finger of time, and we will go look at that body."

Rain Bear nodded, and Talon trotted off toward his camp.

The last of the angry villagers rounded the bend in the trail and disappeared, but their hostile voices continued to float through the forest like a foul miasma. The only people left sitting around the campfires were the very old and the very young. Even the wounded had managed to pull themselves to their feet to join the mob following in Ecan's wake.

Roe struggled to pull Pitch's good arm over her shoulders. "Father, could you help me get Pitch to our lodge?"

"Here, let me support him." She moved out of the way, and Rain Bear draped Pitch's good arm over his shoulders and hauled him to his feet. "Walk slowly, Pitch. We don't wish to break open that wound."

Glancing back up the trail, Rain Bear remembered the expression on Ecan's face: knowing, smug. Why? What had happened here? Somehow it had all gone just the way Ecan had hoped it would.

Fifteen

Snowbear clamped his left hand over his belly wound and used his right to quietly push aside a fir bough; he eased past, and the wolf tails on his blood-streaked moccasins whispered against the brush. When he released the bough, it bounced and swayed, stirring the thick mist that eddied through the trees.

Curse that Pitch and his sharp stiletto! The man was a Singer! A lousy holy man. How had he done this?

He turned around.

"I know you're behind me, witch! I can't see you, but I know you're there! Face me!"

When only the mist moved in response, he let out a breath and staggered up the trail.

"Think. Think!" he whispered to himself. "Do you want to die?"

This was the trail to War Gods Village, wasn't it? Only one trail led from the shore up the mountain. He had seen it when he'd first started running, but in the fog, it looked different.

His punctured guts twisted, and he gasped. "This must be the way! Just . . . keep going."

He stumbled toward a section of the trail lined with twisted alders and wind-smoothed rocks. In the swirling mist, the blocks of basalt resembled a stairway cut into the mountainside. He stepped onto the first stone, then the second. As he continued up the trail, he thought he heard a voice call his name.

Snowbear whirled and tripped over a tree root. As he careened forward, gray ropes of bloody intestines wormed through his belly wound. The scent almost gagged him. He pushed them back inside, only to have black blood gush out to drench his groin and legs. He forced himself to take deep breaths.

"Who's there?"

A phantom, spun of ice and fog, glittered on his backtrail.

"Is that you, witch? Show yourself! I'm not afraid of you!"

From old habit, his hand went to his belt where he kept his atlatl tied—only to find it gone. Had he dropped it when Pitch stabbed him? His strength was failing. His legs had started to shake so badly he could barely keep standing.

"If you kill me, you'll never know who hired me!" he cried. "Have you thought of that?"

He blinked at the black haze that ate into his vision. Why hadn't she killed him?

Snowbear boldly waved his spear. "You probably think it was Ecan, don't you? He doesn't have the courage of a grouse! He wouldn't dare try to kill the likes of you, witch!"

Silver sparkled to his left, and Snowbear spun so quickly he almost toppled to the forest floor. He glared wide-eyed at the fog. Wind Woman had strengthened, blowing the mist into strange, eerie shapes.

"Are there two of you?" he shouted. "Stop hiding! Face me like warriors!"

A flock of gray jays hunched in the firs, their feathers fluffed out for warmth. They watched him with bright, glistening eyes.

Then—at the very edge of his vision—he saw her.

She walked out of the mist like a black ghost, her cape billowing around her tall, slender body. A waist-length red braid draped her shoulder, and a war club hung from her belt. Her dress, the color of fresh blood, flashed beneath her cape.

Let's Dance! The words hung on the still air. But had he really heard them? Or were his ears deceiving him?

"Go on!" he shouted. "Kill me! Get it over with. *You'll never know who sent me!*"

Dzoo must have moved. Her war club was now in her hand. The terrifying thing was that Snowbear hadn't seen her pull it from her belt. He felt as if, for several instants, he'd fallen into a dark hole in the world and only just reemerged into the light. A chill tingled the back of his neck. People said that just with a look, she could make a man's soul slip from his body.

His gaze locked on her eyes, but he saw only an emotionless calm, centuries deep.

"Don't you wish to ask me anything?" he shouted. "Did you just come to watch me die?"

Feel the Dance? Her image wavered, almost disappeared, and he wondered if she was really there at all.

Snowbear started laughing. Great belly laughs that forced his insides against his hand with such force intestines squirmed between his fingers.

"He is more Powerful than you will ever be, witch! If you kill me, Coyote's Spirit Helpers will creep up from the underworlds and squeeze your heart until it bursts!"

The spear whistled as it cut through the air. It struck him in the back with the force of a fist. Snowbear slammed face-first onto the rocks. As he fought to roll to his side, his guts slithered out like dying worms. They lay on the snow, slowly writhing. To his amazement, he could feel them growing cold.

The vision of Dzoo dissolved into a tall and muscular warrior. The man trotted to Snowbear, kicked the spear from his hand, and stared down. Snowbear could see every blood vessel pulsing.

Dogrib! Blessed Ancestors, I'm dead.

More warriors ran up, but Snowbear's gaze remained on the legendary young man who had fought so valiantly in tens of battles.

"Do you know him?" a man asked from behind Snowbear.

Dogrib scrutinized Snowbear's face, then shook his head. "No. But he's definitely one of the Wolf Tails. Look at his moccasins."

Snowbear's head trembled.

Dogrib knelt beside him, gripped his chin, and forced Snowbear to look at him. "Where's Dzoo? Her tracks vanished halfway up the trail. What did you do with her?"

Dogrib's mouth kept moving, but Snowbear couldn't hear his words. A glittering silence had descended.

Warm fingers touched his throat.

Snowbear saw his precious spear point pendant swinging before his eyes. Dogrib wanted to make certain he saw it, for it swung there for what seemed an eternity before his enemy ripped it from Snowbear's neck and cast it as far out into the mist as he could.

Cold filtered through Snowbear's arms and legs, numbing them. Finally it seeped into his face. As his vision went gray, he realized Dzoo was looking at him from across time and space. The last thing he saw was her two luminous eyes pulsing with bright bloody trails. . . .

Cimmis sat in his usual place in the Council Lodge, behind Old Woman East. His attention had begun to wander a hand of time ago. The session was dragging on forever, and he could have cared less about who would occupy which lodges at Wasp Village. His gaze drifted absently over the lodge. The largest structure in Fire Village, it spread ten body lengths across and was decorated with exquisitely painted hides and beautifully woven sea-grass blankets dotted with shell beads. On either side of the door stood lineage poles the height of a tall man. The lines of descent had been masterfully carved, one for each of the four clans. He swore that every time he sat here, the eyes of Cougar and Bear stared right back at him.

Old Woman North tapped the hearthstones with her walking stick and said, "Old Woman South and her family should occupy the lodge closest to Mother Ocean. The sand will make it easier for her to walk."

Old Woman South smiled in agreement. She had bad knees. Walking across pebbles was agony for her.

Old Woman East raised a hand and said, "My son wishes that lodge! He will be the one who gathers crabs and fishes for us. He should have that lodge!"

Cimmis held his tongue. Who would squabble over such things when tomorrow or the next day the world might tumble down around them? More than anything, this kind of idiocy demonstrated how far the North Wind People had fallen.

He shut it out, seeing the afterimage of dentalium shells ringing Old Woman East's neck as he closed his eyes. What wealth, and most of it came through Rain Bear and Sandy Point Village. Ecan should have been there by now.

A faint smile crossed his lips as he speculated on how that meeting had gone. One of the joys of his brilliance was concocting schemes such as this. If it worked out one way, Ecan was already dead, his body mutilated and desecrated on the way to one of the Raven People's most holy ceremonies. If so, Cimmis was well rid of Ecan and his constant trouble. Further, Rain Bear and the peace coalition would take a serious blow to their prestige. The recriminations for Ecan's murder would destroy any chance that Rain Bear might have to create an alliance among the squabbling Raven clans.

If it worked out the other way, Ecan would be allowed to pass, and carry out his plan. That way, too, would discredit Rain Bear. The rival clans would blame him for allowing Ecan to pass and commit his evil deed. Better, one of the Raven People's pillars of faith would be cracked at worst, broken at best. The symbology was masterful.

Then, a moon from now, when he was no longer necessary, no one would raise an eyebrow to discover Ecan's murdered body lying in his new lodge at Wasp Village. His death would obviously be blamed on some Raven assassin, the result of what Ecan had done to their ceremonial.

Perfect symmetry, balance, and poise in politics. Cimmis reveled in it.

Hushed voices sounded beyond the lodge, and the Council went silent.

A woman called, "Kstawl, daughter of Chief Cimmis, would speak with him!"

Cimmis sighed and clapped his hands to his knees. "Forgive me. I'll return as soon as I can."

He hurried to the door and stepped outside into the gray veil of dusk. High up on Fire Mountain a whirlwind careened back and forth, whipping the red cinders into the air where the hot soil had melted yesterday's snow.

Kstawl wrung her hands and said, "Please come, Father. It's Mother. She's—she's biting at me like a dog and foaming at the mouth! I don't know what to do!"

Politics had symmetry; his life didn't. He hurried after his daughter, heedless of the staring slaves.

Cimmis sat on the floor, Astcat limp across his lap. As Kstawl anxiously worried her way around the lodge, firelight cast her shadow in huge relief against the walls and painted shields. The faces of Killer Whale and Wolf seemed to recede when she crossed in front of them, only to leap out again as she passed.

He dipped his fingers in the water cup and dribbled it into Astcat's lax mouth.

"Swallow, my wife. Please, swallow."

He tenderly massaged her throat, but she didn't respond. She'd suffered a seizure at dusk and had been shaking periodically for the past hand of time as though her soul hovered somewhere high above and was preparing to leave for good.

Blessed Song Maker, is she dying this time?

Though he'd been trying to prepare himself for such an event, he hadn't done a very good job. At the thought she might die, his heart had begun to pound so hard he thought it might burst his ribs.

Kstawl gathered the cooking bags she needed to prepare a soup of dried onions, pink fawn lily bulbs, and rice root. Astcat's favorite. Cimmis hoped the rich, sweet smell would draw her soul back.

He rocked Astcat in his arms, and his soul continued to shred. Was she trying to take him with her to the House of Air? He'd seen it happen to people who loved each other more than life. Within a few days of one's death, the other followed.

Cimmis buried his face in her gray hair and whispered, "Come back, my wife. Just for a short time. There are things I must do here before I can go with you."

Kstawl looked expectantly toward the door, and Cimmis lifted his head.

A voice from outside called, "I announce the arrival of Old Woman North. She would speak with Chief Cimmis."

Kstawl turned to him, and he nodded.

She walked to the door flap and pulled it back. "Please enter, Old Woman North."

The ancient woman's walking stick appeared first, followed by her shriveled face. Wind Woman had teased her thin gray hair around her head, turning it into a spiky mass of tangles. She wore an elaborately painted cape that bore the mythological images of the War Gods, Song Maker, and Old Woman Underneath Us, who held up the world.

Old Woman North's faded eyes glanced from Astcat to Cimmis, and her mouth puckered. "A runner just arrived," she said in her hoarse dictatorial voice. "Ecan's party has arrived safely at War Gods Village. I thought you would wish to know in case we must prepare for an attack."

"An attack?" he asked in surprise.

"The Raven People are wild animals, Cimmis. Wolves with fangs. As it is, they need no reason to tear out our throats, but our plan will drive them into an insane rage."

"Elder, I assure you, they will be far more concerned with where *we* are going to attack next."

"Is that so?" she said tartly.

"Having second thoughts, are you? I would hope not. It's too late—even the fastest runner can't get there in time to stop *your* orders."

She studied him through faded eyes. "Yes, well, if you had been present at the Council for the entire meeting, you might know that our faith in both the plan and the Starwatcher is undiminished."

Cimmis gently slipped from beneath Astcat and tucked a rolled hide under her head. Before he rose, he smoothed his fingers down her cheek to let her know he was coming back soon.

Cimmis straightened his knee-length blue shirt and bowed respectfully. "Forgive me for leaving the Council meeting so abruptly, but as you see, I was needed here."

She glanced at Astcat. "I think it could be argued that you would have done more good in the Council meeting, Chief Cimmis."

Cimmis clenched his fists at his sides—better there than around the old woman's neck. "That may be, Elder, but if Ecan has arrived at War Gods Village, there is little I can do until we know the outcome. If he is successful—"

"Of course he will be successful," she interrupted. "We must think about what comes after. What do we do next?"

"Next?"

The deep lines around Old Woman North's eyes tightened. "If you had been in Council, you would understand that question."

"I will return this instant if you wish me to."

"The Council is over. We made our decision without you."

"What decision, Elder?"

"I had a vision. I waited until the end of the Council to speak of it."

What? Another one?

"A vision?" Cimmis said.

"This morning just before I woke. We must leave for Wasp Village in eight days."

"Eight days!" he said in shock. "But that is not wise, Elder! Please reconsider. After Ecan's attacks, the Raven People will be waiting for a chance to murder us all."

"There is safety in numbers. We'll all go at once—one procession encircled by our warriors. Wasp Village will be our fortress."

The old hag had decided she would be the new leader of the Council, had she? Well, he'd see about that. "Elder, it would be safer to send a few people at a time. A large party is too convenient a target."

"In addition," she decreed, "we decided that we will intensify our raids on Raven villages. The attacks will serve as a diversion while we are readying ourselves, and then while we are traveling to Wasp Village."

Cimmis just stared at her in disbelief. "Matron, that means dividing our forces. We'll have warriors running around like ruffed grouse in the fall. You can't just—"

"My vision was *true*, Cimmis. I have *seen* our success. Or do you mock the revelations given by the gods?" Her gaze returned to Astcat, who lay on her side staring at nothing. Old Woman North studied her empty eyes for several long moments before asking, "How long has her soul been gone?"

"Since dusk. She—she had a seizure that shook her soul loose, but I'm sure it will return."

Old Woman North shoved the door flap aside with her walking stick. Before she ducked out, she said, "I think the next time you tell the Council you are speaking Matron Astcat's words, we will wonder about that, Cimmis."

Then she was gone.

In a barely audible voice, he said, "Kstawl, you may leave."

He had to be alone with Astcat, to think, to talk with her.

"But, Father, I haven't finished the soup."

"I'll prepare the soup! Just go!"

Kstawl grabbed her cape and rushed out into the gusting night wind.

Cimmis stood like a statue, staring at the beautiful, stylized image of Killer Whale, trying to calm himself. Didn't the old woman realize . . .

From behind him, a soft, weary voice said, "You mustn't get . . . so angry . . . my husband. It makes your eyes bulge like Flying Squirrel's."

"Astcat!" He saw her smiling at him.

He bent and gathered her in his arms, hugging her tightly. "Are you well? I've been so worried."

"Old Woman North is right," she whispered, and nuzzled her forehead against his cheek.

"What do you mean?" He gazed down into her sleepy eyes. "Right about what? The visions she's spouting are nonsense that defy—"

"The Raven People *will* attack this place if they can. We deserve it after the recent Council decisions. We should prepare for the possibility—then, we must leave. Find a more defensible place to live."

Cimmis hugged her more tightly. "They want to move to Wasp Village. Did you hear that?"

She gave him an exhausted smile. "Yes. But Wasp Village is not defensible."

"I tried to tell them. They wouldn't listen. Old Woman North has convinced them these visions are guiding our people. But they make no sense."

"Tell them again. They *must* listen." She twined a hand in his shirt. "If our people gather there, the Raven People will only have to circle the village to starve us out. We don't have enough canoes, so escape by sea will be impossible."

"I'll tell them. Tomorrow morning." As he stroked her gray hair, she closed her eyes and leaned into his touch. "Will you stay with me tonight? Please, try to stay, Astcat. I need you."

She clutched his arm with no more strength than a baby's fingers. "The Dream keeps calling me back."

"Dream? What Dream?"

"Oh, it's . . . curious. I'm hovering high above Gull Inlet, watching a terrible battle, and I'm afraid."

"Afraid of what?"

She smiled again, and his heart ached. Just looking into her alert eyes eased his fears. "I don't know. I always wake before the end of the battle. But I think"—her hand trembled as it tightened on his arm—"I think I'm afraid I'll never see you again."

He kissed her. "Well, I'm here now. Forget about the Dream. I'm tired of hearing about Dreams. Are you hungry?"

"Yes."

"Let me get the soup started." He started to rise.

"Wait," she said soothingly. "Be calm, my husband. Talk with me for a time; then start the soup."

He smiled down at her. "As you wish."

"I have suddenly come to value the time I have with you. Let's make the most of it."

"Gladly."

Sixteen

A thick bank of clouds had moved in off the ocean, and occasional flurries of snow fell; but in the gaps between, the Star People sparkled like tiny torches. Rain Bear took a deep breath and let it out in a rush. It hung before him as he approached Roe's lodge. On all sides refugees huddled over fires before makeshift lodges, eating whatever food they had scrounged, their voices dire.

He slowed before Pitch's lodge and cleared his throat. "Roe? Pitch? May I come?"

"Yes, Father."

Rain Bear ducked beneath the flap and entered the warm confines of the lodge. In the firelight he could see Pitch against one wall. He looked strained and gaunt. Not that there was much to him to begin with. Roe smiled at him as she removed his grandson, Stonecrop, from her left breast. The little boy had milk smeared around his mouth. His round brown eyes rolled Rain Bear's way, and he let out an excited squeal.

As in most Raven People lodges, a man could only stand bent over. On the walls brightly painted hides hung, and tied bags of dried foods rested in round baskets.

Stonecrop shrieked in sheer joy and crawled toward Rain Bear when Roe placed him on the split pole matting. Rain Bear held his arms out, smiled, and sat down to allow the round-faced little boy to crawl into his lap.

"How are you, my grandson?"

Stonecrop's tiny fists waved; he grinned up toothlessly.

"He's been a terror since Pitch got home," Roe told him as she wiped her wet nipple and straightened her red-and-black dress. She wore her hair up in a coiled braid pinned by rabbit-bone skewers that emphasized her narrow face. She was growing into such a beautiful woman. In so many ways she reminded him of Tlikit. "Stonecrop missed Pitch so much, he won't let him rest."

Where he sat propped against a rolled buffalohide, Pitch smiled weakly. His skin was sweaty, gleaming in the light. Roe turned toward him, and he grimaced as she unwound the bloody cedar-bark-and-moss bandage. He swallowed dryly.

"How's his fever?"

"Very high. I've been forcing him to drink willow bark tea, but it hasn't done much good."

"Has the wound soured yet?"

Roe gently pulled the last of the soiled bandage away so that Rain Bear could see for himself. The puncture had festered. Like an eye, the dark scab stared out from a yellowish puffy iris surrounded by inflamed skin. By morning, Pitch's upper arm would be swollen twice normal size.

Roe asked, "Has Dogrib returned yet?"

"I just finished speaking with him. He killed the man you wounded, Pitch—and he was definitely one of the Wolf Tails."

"Wolf Tail?" Roe shot a worried look his way. "But, they work for Cimmis, don't they? Does that mean that Coyote is Cimmis? Or one of his warriors?"

"Maybe."

"Cimmis?" Face drawn with pain, Pitch asked, "But why would he attack us, Rain Bear? Dzoo and I are just Healers, trying to save a few lives."

"He knows Dzoo is our strength. The refugees trust her. Killing her would be a blow to their spirit. That is reason enough."

Roe reached into the water, squeezed out a handful of seaweed cloth, and began gently washing the wound. Pitch ground his teeth against the pain.

"What about Dzoo? Did Dogrib find her?"

"No." Rain Bear glanced down at Stonecrop, who had grabbed hold of his cape laces and was struggling with the perplexing task of untying them. "Nor did he find her body, which means she's probably alive."

Roe rinsed the cloth in the bowl and dabbed at the wound again.

Pitch gasped, his body tensing as she worked the scab loose and blood-clotted pus leaked out in watery yellow streamers.

Roe pinched her nose against the stench and added, "Maybe she went straight to War Gods Village. She needs to fast and pray—to purify herself before the Moon Ceremonial tomorrow."

Pitch writhed beneath his hide. "Yes. I'm sure that's it." He shuddered as Roe carefully squeezed the wound to drain it. "She's . . . she's very strict about these things. But something . . ."

"Yes?" Rain Bear asked as he dangled a lace in front of Stonecrop.

Pitch was gasping, struggling to keep the thought. "Something was bothering her. As if she knew something terrible, and would not tell. She said things, cryptic things. They left me unnerved."

"Such as?"

"Such as our world was in danger. But she never said how. She's a mysterious woman to start with, but to my thinking, she was even more strange on the journey here. Not that I could blame her after what happened."

Rain Bear heard familiar steps outside.

"We brought the matron, Chief, as you ordered," Hornet called. "May we come?"

Rain Bear turned to Pitch and Roe. "I hope you do not object. I asked Matron Evening Star to speak with you tonight. Perhaps she can make sense of what happened at Antler Spoon's village, and on the trail home."

Pitch nodded, looking relieved as Roe blotted at his wound. "I will be grateful if she can."

"Come," Rain Bear called.

Evening Star ducked into the lodge, and Rain Bear glimpsed Wolf Spider and Hornet as they took up positions on either side of the flap. She smiled uncertainly at Roe, her eyes narrowing as she took in the condition of the wound in Pitch's arm. He had his eyes closed.

Rain Bear experienced a leap of the heart at the sight of her, and cuddled Stonecrop before he slid back to make room for her beside him.

Ten tens of generations of women in her family had ruled the North Wind People. The dignity of her former status still showed in her movements, the elegant wave of her hand, the regal way she tilted her head. By Raven's shadow, had there ever been such a beautiful woman?

She sat down on the mat and gazed serenely around the lodge. She'd braided her long red hair. It hung down the front of her sea-grass cape.

Stonecrop squealed in delight at the sight of her.

An almost unbearable longing filled her eyes. "Hello," she whispered. "Who are you?"

"This is my grandson, Stonecrop."

"Hello, Stonecrop."

Evening Star dug around in her bag and pulled out two small clumps of herbs. "I took the liberty of making poultices for Pitch's wound." She handed them to Roe. "I hope that was all right."

"Are you a Healer?" Roe asked hesitantly.

"My mother was. I learned a few things from her."

Roe lifted the poultices to her nose. "Umm, I smell sagebrush leaves, willow bark, and . . . something else. A flower."

"Coneflower petals."

Roe's eyes widened in surprise. "Coneflowers? Where do you get them? When we can find them, they cost us a fortune in blankets and hides."

"My mother sends—used to send," she corrected herself painfully, "traders far to the east for them."

Roe smelled them again. "How long should I soak them?"

"Just a short while, but keep them damp while they're on Pitch's arm. You want the juices to sink into his wound."

Roe crossed the lodge in a hunched position, put both poultices in a wooden bowl, and poured water over them from a bladder. While they soaked, she pulled shredded cedar bark from a hide bag to make a new bandage.

Pitch shifted against the rolled buffalohide, and a groan escaped his lips.

Roe asked, "What's happening in the camps? Is there still talk of slaughtering Ecan at the Moon Ceremonial tomorrow?"

Rain Bear sighed. "Not as much. I just came from a meeting with the other chiefs. At the moment, the last thing they want is another fight. Their clans have been through too much in recent moons." The lines between his brows pinched together. "I just pray the villagers will abide by that decision. People are angry and desperate. On top of everything else, the attack on Pitch and Dzoo is like flicking embers on a pot full of pine sap. If one lights, it will be a very hot fire."

Rain Bear glanced at Evening Star. She was studying him with bright blue eyes. "Which is why I asked Matron Evening Star to come here tonight. Perhaps her counsel can help us avoid future fires."

Roe carried the poultice bowl and the clean strips of woven cedar bark and knelt at Pitch's side. As she wound the bark around the poultices, water squeezed out, soaking the wound.

Pitch's eyes widened. "Wretched gods! That burns!"

"Of course it does," Roe muttered. "That's how you know the Spirits are alive."

He slumped against the hides, completely drained.

Roe sank down beside him and turned to Rain Bear. "What else did the chiefs say, Father? Did you discuss joining forces under one leader?"

"We did."

She caught the tone in his voice, and being her mother's daughter and quick of mind, gave him a tired smile before nodding. "I was afraid of that."

"What's wrong?" Pitch's gaze darted between Rain Bear and Roe. "What are you talking about?"

Rain Bear gave Roe a sheepish glance and told Pitch, "I'll tell you when I know more."

Evening Star bowed her head, catching the undercurrents.

Truth was, Rain Bear didn't wish to discuss it at all. Doing so would just lead to questions he had no answers for: How many warriors would he have? What were the circumstances that would demand he act? How many chiefs would support him? Could he keep the clans allied despite old blood feuds? What was the ultimate goal of the alliance? Just to stop the attacks, or to break completely the North Wind People's ability to make war? Or was it something even more decisive?

He needed time to work out the details and to come to terms in his own mind where this might take him, his clan, and his people.

Rain Bear's gaze dropped to his grandson, and his heart warmed. The little boy had curled up in his lap and was on the verge of going to sleep. His mouth was open, a tiny pink tongue just visible inside.

"I hate to ask this of you now, Pitch, but we have to know what happened out there."

Pitch let out a weary breath, as though preparing himself. "What is it you wish to know?"

"Did anyone see this man who calls himself 'Coyote?'"

"*Coyote?*" Evening Star started, turning her eyes toward Pitch.

Rain Bear turned to her. "Do you know him?"

"I know *of* him. Even Kenada talked about him in whispers. The word is he's some sort of sorcerer or witch. That Cimmis has had dealings with him, but only on moonless nights, and outside the palisade. The rumor is that even Cimmis has never seen his face. I can't be certain if he actually exists, or if he's a story."

Pitch said, "He tried to buy Dzoo's life from Antler Spoon and Broken Sun."

Evening Star considered that, her expression thoughtful. "Did anyone see him?"

"Dzoo said she watched him for some time."

"Dzoo actually saw him?" Evening Star mused thoughtfully.

Rain Bear forced himself to look at Pitch instead of Evening Star. He was acutely aware that Roe was watching him, a frown on her forehead. He made himself say, "For some time? What does that mean?"

Pitch weakly shook his head. "She told me he smelled like the moss that grows at the base of the lava cliff above Fire Village."

Rain Bear frowned. "Dzoo was that close and let him live? What did she say he looked like?"

"Tall, broad of shoulder, and he wears an ancient coyote mask. Something on his chest catches the light, perhaps a fluted spear point, or shell decoration. No one knows."

Rain Bear peered at the fire. Struggling yellow tongues of flame licked around the wood. He needed all of his concentration, but he remained achingly aware of Evening Star beside him. He could just catch her faint scent, a sweet musk that teased him. "Was he dressed like one of the Wolf Tails?"

Pitch tried to shrug and winced. "The . . . the Wolf Tails don't wear masks, do they?"

Evening Star noted, "The most adept assassins wear masks. It is a sign of their status. Kenada reputedly kept a badger mask in a cedar box in his lodge."

Rain Bear's right hand involuntarily clenched into a fist, as though tightening around the handle of his war club. "Pitch, you said you thought Dzoo knew the man. Recognized him?"

"I think so."

"But she didn't mention a name?"

He shook his head.

Rain Bear pulled the bag of obsidian fetishes from his belt pouch. They clicked together. "Matron, Coyote offered these in exchange for Dzoo." He poured them out into his palm, where they glittered in the firelight. "Have you ever seen anything like them? Who makes fetishes like this?"

"Blessed gods," Evening Star whispered. When she reached out to touch them, her fingers brushed Rain Bear's palm, and a tingle went through him. "They're exquisite. I don't know anyone in the North Wind villages who has the skill to knap these. And believe me, if he existed, I would know of him. Every clan elder would be vying for his work."

Rain Bear poured them back into the bag and tossed it onto the hides at Pitch's feet. "Why does he want Dzoo? To force her to do his bidding? Is it something she owns?"

Evening Star shook her head. "If he wanted any of her belongings, he could just kill her, search her body, and take whatever he wished. It sounds like he ordered his warriors to take her alive."

Roe added another branch to the fire, and sparks flitted and crackled as the wood caught. As she sank back onto the hides at Pitch's side, she said, "Perhaps he just wants her, Father." She glanced curiously at Evening Star, sitting so close to him. Gods, was it that obvious?

Evening Star, however, seemed oblivious; she smoothed her hand over Stonecrop's fine black hair. The little boy smiled in his sleep. "Coyote would not be the first man to desperately want a woman. Especially a woman of Dzoo's beauty and reputation."

Rain Bear muttered in assent. Faces appeared and disappeared on the fabric of his souls, men he had known who would have killed to possess the woman of their dreams. Some of them had indeed killed—or been killed—in that pursuit.

Rain Bear added, "A man desires most that which he has touched."

Pitch's expression made it look as if the very act of breathing hurt. He squeezed his eyes closed for a few instants. "Coyote went to Broken Sun and ordered him to turn Dzoo over, but chief Antler Spoon was too afraid to go through with it."

"That's why he gave Coyote the sick woman who resembled Dzoo?"

"Dear gods," Evening Star whispered. "Was he mad? Didn't he realize Coyote would find out he'd been tricked?"

Rain Bear said, "What became of the sick woman?"

Pitch wet his lips. "Coyote killed her—and he did terrible things, Rain Bear. Cut out her eyes . . . her breasts."

Rain Bear glanced at the bag. "Antler Spoon is a fool. He should have gone to Dzoo the instant Coyote contacted him."

Pitch's thin face had gone pale. He peered at Roe with fever-bright eyes. "They'll never do anything like this again. Dzoo . . . she has already seen to that."

Evening Star's full lips twitched. "In a way that was most convincing, I will wager."

"She convinced me," Pitch whispered. "Not that I'd have ever crossed her to start with."

"Is there anything else we should know?" Rain Bear asked.

Pitch gestured weakly. "She said that in the end, she and Coyote will Dance together. Does that mean anything to you?"

Evening Star stiffened. "Then, she thinks she must face him?"

Pitch gave her a blank look. "That was my impression."

Evening Star nodded as if to herself. "That, more than anything, leads me to believe that Coyote is real. Which sends shivers down my spine."

"Well." Rain Bear gently lifted Stonecrop from his lap and handed the boy to Roe. "We should be going. I'm sorry I had to disturb you tonight, Pitch. I know you're weary and hurting."

Pitch nodded, face going slack.

Rain Bear bent to kiss Roe's cheek, then ducked out the entryway into the cold white light of the Star People. Wolf Spider and Hornet straightened. Evening Star remained inside, talking with Roe about the poultices.

Rain Bear motioned for the guards to walk a few paces away. In a low voice he asked, "Has anyone tried to get close to her?"

Wolf Spider nodded, and strands of shoulder-length black hair slipped over his round face and turned-up nose. He was the older of the two guards, two tens and two summers. "Yes, my Chief. One of her kinsmen came to see her this morning, just before Roe arrived. You said we should use our own judgment, so we asked Evening Star if she wished to see him. She did."

"Who was he?"

Hornet stepped closer. At nine and ten summers, he had the look of a much older man. He wore his long hair in a bun at the base of his skull. "He'd just arrived from Tortoise Shell Village. He said he wished to offer his respects. He seemed harmless. Evening Star spoke with him briefly, and he left."

"What did they discuss? Did you hear their conversation?"

"They spoke about Matron Naida. The man offered his condolences, and asked when Evening Star would assume her duties as the new clan matron."

"What did she answer?"

"She told him that with the current Council, and Chief Cimmis's opposition, she did not know if that was possible, but that she would consider it."

Evening Star ducked out of the lodge. As she walked forward, her long braid swayed and glinted like polished red obsidian.

Rain Bear whispered, "As more refugees flood in, more people will wish to see her. Be cautious. The best assassins are the ones who look harmless."

Wolf Spider and Hornet nodded simultaneously, and Wolf Spider said, "Upon my life's debt to you, he'll have to kill us first."

Rain Bear matched Evening Star's step as she approached, and led the way toward their lodges.

Wolf Spider and Hornet flanked them.

Evening Star didn't say a word until they'd made five tens of paces. "You think Coyote is one of the North Wind People, don't you?"

"I think Coyote is Ecan."

"It's possible, but I don't think so."

Firelit lodges crowded the meadow, and the soft sounds of voices drifted on the wind. He noted the positions of the guards where they stood in the trees or crouched behind boulders, almost unseen.

"Who else would be bold enough to try to buy Dzoo's life? And who else could afford such a wealth of obsidian fetishes?"

She gazed up at him with those stunning blue eyes. "Someone who wants to devour her soul, to dominate her and turn her to his evil purposes."

He almost missed a step. "Or someone who fears her?"

She tugged her cape closed at the throat and hesitated before she answered, "Fears her because she might be the only Healer Powerful enough to destroy him? Perhaps. But I think his desire is more, that it is a thing driven by lust and obsession." She smiled bitterly. "It is only recently that I have come to understand how that can motivate a man."

"Is it possible that Ecan just recently discovered the witch and his fetishes? Perhaps from the rumors you heard? Maybe even through Kenada?"

"Very possible, but don't be too hasty. There are other North Wind elders who would be more than happy to have a witch on their side."

He considered that, thinking of Old Woman North and the stories of her endless visions that seemed to make less and less sense.

"Your daughter is unsure of what to make of me."

"How so? Your status among us should be apparent."

She lowered her voice. "I think she is more concerned about our relationship."

"Our . . . ?" He struggled to keep both his voice and heart in check. "No, I'm sure you're mistaken. If Roe were concerned, she would simply—"

Hornet shouted *"Halt!"* and trotted forward, his spear lifted, preparing to cast. Someone moved in the dark trees ahead.

Rain Bear pulled Evening Star behind him, shielding her with his own body. "Who's there?"

An old man wandered the dark shadows cast by the trees, hands held high. Gray hair and stringy beard blew about his oblong face, but nothing could hide the Power that lived in his dark eyes. In a reedy voice he cried out, "Pray the gods, do not kill me yet. At least until I have warmed my bones. Then you may skewer me like a pack-rat in a berry basket." He paused before adding, "Chief Rain Bear"—he bowed respectfully—"I come in peace."

Evening Star cried, "Rides-the-Wind?"

Hornet backpedaled hurriedly.

Rain Bear gaped. *"Rides-the-Wind? The Soul Keeper?"*

The old man squinted as though he couldn't see their faces in the darkness; then he strode forward in a ragged swirl of hides and enveloped Evening Star in his arms. "I'm so glad to find you safe. When I heard you'd escaped, I feared the worst."

Hornet swung around to face Rain Bear and hissed, "How did he get past our guards? He should have been stopped!"

"Yes, yes. For now, find someone to clean out the storage lodge behind mine—most of the food's been eaten anyway—then send a runner to my daughter asking her to bring food, blankets, and anything else she thinks might help."

"But Great Chief," Hornet protested, "he's the most Powerful of all the North Wind Seers."

"Yes, and now he's here." *The gods alone know why.*

As Hornet hurried away, Rain Bear turned to find the old man's glittering eyes fastened on him like a falcon's on a field mouse.

"I'm here, Chief Rain Bear," he said calmly, "because you need me."

Seventeen

Pitch was sitting up when he drifted off to sleep. His head lolled on his lax neck. He jerked back—and pain shot through his abused arm, burned across his shoulder, and hammered his fatigued and fevered brain.

At his pained cry, Roe asked, "Pitch? Are you all right?"

He blinked, seeing her across from him where she wiped Stonecrop's bottom with dried moss. She held the gurgling little boy by the ankles as she swabbed, then threw the soiled moss into the fire, where it smoked, caught, and began to burn.

"Just trying to get comfortable," he lied. There was no such thing when a man's arm was raging and fever laced his mind with floating visions. Even now he could hear the faint cries of Coyote's fetishes, and wondered at the malignant Power that filled them.

"Would you like another cup of tea? It will help to keep you warm during the night."

"Please. I've been dying of thirst all evening."

Roe dipped a wooden cup into the tea bag and brought it over.

Pitch took it and, for an instant, saw his reflection in the dark liquid. His beaked nose made him resemble a bird of prey. The mellow tang of dried cranberries rose. He took a long drink and rested the cup on the buffalohide covering his belly.

"There's something I didn't tell Rain Bear."

"What?"

"I'm not sure what it means . . . if it means anything." The teacup trembled in his hand.

She watched him silently, waiting for him to find the words.

"When I first touched the obsidian fetishes, I heard a voice."

She frowned and slid closer to him. "A voice?"

"Yes."

"Whose voice?"

Wind Woman's chill fingers reached through the entryway and stroked Pitch's body. He set his tea down and tugged the buffalohide up to cover his naked chest. "I don't know. A man's."

Roe filled a wooden cup for herself and rested it on her drawn-up knee. For several moments, her gaze fixed on their son. "Did the voice sound like anyone you know?"

"No."

She turned toward the bag that lay like a painted egg in the dark brown buffalo hair. "Why would a man's voice be in the fetishes?"

Gods, why hadn't Rain Bear taken them with him? Pitch looked at the bag, and he swore he could *feel* the obsidian creatures moving beneath the leather, as though waking from a long sleep.

"It's as if someone breathed his soul into one of those fetishes, Roe."

She watched him carefully. "Witches steal souls and breathe them into objects. Is that what you think happened? This man was captured by a witch?"

"I don't . . . I need to speak with Dzoo about it. She has more experience with these things. She is closer to Power."

"Dzoo will be occupied for a few days at the Moon Ceremonial."

Stonecrop let out a small cry, and Roe tucked the hides around him where he nestled in his bed. The infant made an annoyed sound, then fell right back to sleep.

As Pitch watched her, fever rippled his vision; it was like seeing the lodge from underwater. His body, hot and burning, felt as if it floated up off the floor. The fetishes whispered to him from inside their bag. His gaze riveted on the leather, and the red coyote tracks seemed to Dance across the dark surface.

"What's wrong?" Roe asked.

Pitch tipped his head, trying to hear better, and whispered, "I hear him. He's weeping. As though . . ."

"As though what?"

The voice sounded pathetic, desperate. "I don't know. I . . . I need to find a holy person. Surely if I can't speak with Dzoo, there's someone in the village who will understand what . . . who . . . is calling."

"Roe!" someone shouted from beyond the door.

"Yes?"

"Chief Rain Bear has sent for you! Someone has arrived. It's the Soul Keeper Rides-the-Wind, can you imagine?"

An image flashed in Pitch's mind, as if he could see the old man's sharp eyes burning into his very soul. Was it his imagination, or did he hear the fetishes whispering greedily?

Tsauz sleeps wrapped in a warm blanket made from a dall sheep's hide. One side is covered with the bristly thick hair, the other, closest to his skin, is painted with a single peering eye. Despite the quiet night, the Dream tightens its grip. . . .

Twisting spirals! One of yellow-white light, the other of smoky darkness. They meet and wrap, twisting around and around, as if in a Dance.

Tsauz watches them turning, writhing, as Power drums in the distance. From the surrounding haze, he can sense Mother's presence, her fire-blackened face just beyond his perception, her melt-glassy hair, streaking her charred scalp.

"Are you ready, boy?" a voice asks from the darkness.

"Mother? Is that you?" But the voice doesn't sound like Mother's. It is deeper, hollow, as though echoing from over a great distance.

"You are like Halibut," the voice tells him, "about to be yanked from the safety of the depths. Can you breathe outside of your familiar water? Or will you lay flopping, gasping, your eyes protruding from your head while your heart slows? Will your flesh become dry and cracked?"

"I don't understand!"

A low rumbling begins in the distance, and the twin strands of fire-yellow and char-gray wind ever more tightly about each other like spun cord. Fire and soot, they wind into a stiff pillar that reaches high into the night sky.

"If you wish to speak to me, you will have to ride the lightning, boy!" The voice booms now.

Fear, palpable, beats and claws inside him like a frightened and trapped animal.

"Seek me, if you are brave enough. I will tell you how to save your world."

As if pulled tight, the rope of fire and smoke bursts into a whirlwind of chaos. From the middle of it, a single great eye stares into Tsauz's frightened soul. The gaze is painful, and he tries to cower, only to feel a stab of light, like a lance, burning him away, searing, charring, and he is dying. Dying in fire, the way Mother—

A hard hand clamped over Tsauz's mouth.

The familiar scents of the lodge swelled in his nose: the grassy odor of the sleeping mats, musty leather, the smoke of the fire. He tried to scream as he was dragged from the warm hides, *"What—"*

"Hush!" Father ordered, "We must leave now."

Tsauz nodded, and Father released him. Tsauz could hear Father moving, his clothing rasping, and then moccasins slapped onto his chest. "Put them on. Hurry!"

He fingered the familiar leather and bent to pull them over his cold feet. "Why, Father? What's wrong? Isn't it still dark?"

"Be quiet!"

Tsauz heard Father ease his way to the lodge flap. He seemed to be listening to the sounds of War Gods Village: snoring and coughing. A baby whimpered.

"Where's your cape, my son?"

"Here, Father!" Tsauz groped and found it where he'd left it.

"Put it on. We have to go!"

Tsauz swung the painted deerhide cape around his neck and rose uncertainly to his feet. "What's happening?"

Father's fingers dug into Tsauz's shoulders, his voice as brittle as a dry fish bone. "Listen to me! You must do exactly as I say. Don't think about it. *Just do it.* Do you understand?"

Tsauz nodded.

"Come with me." Father grabbed Tsauz's hand and tugged him out of the lodge into the cold darkness.

"Father, where's Runner? Runner? Runner, come!"

Father's hard hand clapped over his mouth. "I said *quiet!* He's probably sniffing around the trees. Forget about him."

Tsauz tripped over a stone and fell. Father jerked him to his feet.

In the process, Father's hand slipped off his mouth. "Father? Runner is my only—"

"Don't make a sound. *Not another word!*"

He held tight to Tsauz's hand and forced him to run as fast as he could. Every time Tsauz tripped, Father hauled him to his feet, hurting his shoulder, and they ran again. The strong scent of fir pitch and whale oil came to his nose. Tsauz took a deep breath. His people used the mixture to make fires that burned hot and fast.

The footing grew treacherous as Father dragged Tsauz onto steep terrain. Rocks kept turning underfoot, and Father literally jerked him along. Tsauz bit his lip, aware that Father's terse breathing boded ill should he speak. Fear began to beat bright within him.

Father shoved Tsauz down on a cold slab of rock and ordered, "Slide back. This is a small rock shelter."

Tsauz backed awkwardly into the wet and gritty womb. Cold stone bit into his back. The tight hole was just big enough to hold him. He stared blindly at Father, waiting for him to slide in, too. There didn't seem to be enough room. "Father, is this big enough for both of us?"

"I want you to stay here. I have to return to the village."

"Please find Runner for me. He's so little: he wouldn't have gone far." Tsauz reached out and grabbed a handful of Father's cape. "Please! He'll be so frightened without me."

"Yes! Yes! Now, listen to me. *Don't move.*" Father spun around. He stopped breathing, listening to the winter night. Then he whispered, "I'll be back for you as soon as I can."

"No, please!" Tsauz started to crawl out of the rock shelter. Father's hard hand pushed him back as Tsauz whimpered, "Please, don't leave me! Tell me what's happening? Where's Runner?"

Father shoved him so hard his head cracked on the rock. Tsauz stifled the cry of pain, knowing it would only make Father madder.

"Warriors are coming, Tsauz! Do not move. I have to fight, but I'm coming back for you, I promise!" A pause. "Now, don't move. I'm covering your hole."

The rock made a hollow knocking sound as Father settled it into place. The grinding and clunking continued as Father placed other rocks over the opening. Tsauz could feel the cold radiating from the rock. He reached out, running his fingers over the gritty surface.

"My son," Father whispered. "No matter what happens, I need you to know how much I love you. Never, never forget."

"I won't, Father." Sobs pulled at Tsauz's windpipe.

Father's steps sounded as he hurried back across the unstable hillside.

Then silence settled.

Too terrified to breathe, Tsauz sat perfectly still, listening for Father's steps.

"Runner?" he whined softly.

You are like Halibut, about to be yanked from the safety of the depths. Can you breathe outside of your familiar water?

The words echoed in Tsauz's memory.

Eighteen

Where she hunched over the glowing coals of a dying campfire, Dzoo waited. She had spread her cloak out like a conical tent to capture the heat. She could feel the warm smoke from the red embers rising along her skin, cleansing. She enjoyed the sensation as the heat nibbled along her thighs, across her vulva, and up her abdomen. It slipped along the curve of her breasts, massaging her nipples and trickling around her sides.

She leaned her head back to stare up between the shadowed branches of the fir trees. Scattered patches of Star People twinkled against the blackness.

The faint clatter of spears carried on the heavy night air. Dzoo felt the future fall into place. Visions spun inside her, like glimpses of oblivion. Phantoms grimaced, men screamed, and fires touched the edges of her soul.

She filled her lungs with the crystal scent of the night. Rising smoke leaked past her cloak to filter through her gleaming hair.

Somewhere in the distance, a faint shout rang out.

Are you ready? she asked herself, threw back her cloak, and filled her lungs with the smoky odor rising from her warm flesh. Her skin tingled as she raised her arms to the night sky, and her loose hair spilled over her naked body.

"There is no way back now. Let us Sing the first notes of the new Song."

The low hum was born deep in her throat. Then, she extended her slim leg, pointed her toe, and took a quick step. With each twist and bend, the Dance possessed her. Ducking and swirling, she pirouetted around the red gleam of the fire, a thing of the forest, Powered by visions of blood, fire, and Death.

A woman's high-pitched scream shredded the darkness. Tsauz started, banging his head on the close confines of his rocky hiding place. Whimpers of fear caught in his throat where he huddled, cold and afraid.

People began to shriek and wail. Shouts of rage carried to his hidden niche. Then feet crunched in the snow, rocks clattered, and people cursed as they panted in the darkness. Tsauz heard the fires roar to life long before he caught the first faint whiff of smoke. Within moments it settled around him, thick, choking. He could barely breathe.

"Run, you filthy Raven dogs! Run!" a man cried.

The hollow smack of a club striking a skull made Tsauz wince as if from a physical blow. A woman screamed so close she had to be almost on top of him. An infant began wailing.

"No, not my baby! Let him go! He's done nothing to you!"

With a sickly smacking sound, the infant's squalls were ended. The woman whimpered, only to be silenced by another smacking impact.

"Filthy Raven bitch," the man muttered.

Tsauz's heart hammered like a trapped squirrel's.

When he finally gasped for air, he pulled his cape over his nose to keep from coughing.

A small group of people raced past, and he heard the frantic whispers of women and children. Someone must have fallen.

A woman pleaded. "Get up! Get up!"

The other people kept running.

More feet rushed up the slope. Heavy breathing. The hissing of spears. The woman screamed. A child shrieked. When something slapped flesh, the child's shriek muted into a gurgling rattle.

"Come over here!" a triumphant man shouted.

"My baby!" the woman shrilled. "You killed my baby!"

"Make a sound and I'll spatter your brains across the snow! Lie down!" Clothing rustled against the distant screams. "You're going to enjoy this."

The woman wept and made choking sounds.

Tsauz heard the man grunt, and say, "I love a tight woman." The woman's breathing was ragged, as if torn from her throat. The man grunted, "Yes, yes, yes." A pause, and his voice lowered. "This is how it will be, Dzoo. Feel me? Feel my love for you?" Then his breath seemed to catch, and he groaned, sighing, "Gods, yes. All these years, I've waited for you."

The woman's weeping grew louder.

"Dzoo," the man's gruff voice whispered.

A sharp whistle carried in the night.

"Over here. I'm coming." The gruff voice was followed by the rasping of clothing. "Too bad, bitch. If you'd lived, my seed might have grown to greatness in you."

A snapping impact silenced the whimpering, and Tsauz heard an explosive exhalation.

"Where are you? It's black as soot out here," a distant man called.

"Don't shout at me," the gruff voice replied in annoyance. Wood clattered as if weapons were picked up. "What do you want?"

The second voice was closer now. "We're supposed to drag the wounded to the pillars. What's this? She died with her dress up over her head?"

"Shut up."

Arms flopped against rocks, thumping.

The second warrior said, "Why are we dragging them to the pillars? Wouldn't it be easier to just shove them over the cliffs?"

"Of course, but the Starwatcher told us to rope them to the pillars."

The Starwatcher? Father? Is he close by? Tsauz listened hard for his father's distinctive steps, but didn't hear them.

"Why rope them to the pillars?"

"He thinks it will serve as a warning to those who find them. Now, come on—the sooner this is done, the sooner we can get out of here."

Dragging sounds . . . Then a tiny moan was followed by a smacking blow. "Ecan wants them—"

A sob worked its way up Tsauz's throat. Too late, he clamped a hand to his mouth.

"—where all can see."

The gruff voice said, "What was that?"

"I didn't hear anything," the second warrior said. "Where did it come from?"

Tsauz held his breath.

"Maybe I missed one." Tsauz heard the scuffing of a moccasin as it dragged on stone just beyond his hole. Had Father placed the rocks right? Could the gruff warrior see that they had been moved?

"It's dark as First Woman's cave out here," the second replied. "Forget it. We'll search at first light. If anyone got away, we'll get them."

A foot settled on the rock in front of Tsauz's face. He heard the stone shift, grinding like the rending of the earth.

Gruff Voice grunted. "I suppose."

The foot withdrew. Feet crunched the snow; a soft whispering was accompanied by juddering thumps as bodies were dragged up the slope toward the War God pillars.

When he could no longer hear them, Tsauz shoved the rocks away from his shelter and charged across the rocky slope in blind panic, tripping, falling, hauling himself to his feet, and running again. Ferns slapped him across the face, fir branches raked his cheeks, and vines tangled around his feet.

"He—he heard me! He heard me! He'll come back!"

In his mad flight he tripped and fell on a warm body. Scrambling to regain his feet, Tsauz planted his hand full into the dead man's ruined head. His fingers sank through wet blood, broken bone, and spongy brains.

The yellow gleam of dawn tinted the snowflakes that whirled over the mist-shrouded mountaintop where War Gods Village smoldered in ruins.

War Chief White Stone trotted down the slope from the War God pillars toward Ecan. The Starwatcher stood in the village plaza below, his white-caped body wavering in and out of the fog.

"We followed your orders," White Stone said as he bowed. "As we speak, a warrior stands at the pillars to send the signal of our victory to Chief Cimmis. Now let us leave this place. I do not wish to be here when Rain Bear discovers what we've done."

Ecan stared at the wreckage surrounding him, a gloating expression on his handsome face. Snow and fog had damped most of the flames, but charred hides smoldered in piles around the blackened lodge frames. Overturned baskets, gut bag containers, and clothing scattered the ground. A child's doll, made in the shape of Killer Whale, lay torn in half and mud-smeared.

"Beautiful, isn't it?" Ecan asked softly.

"It is but one more ruined village, Starwatcher. The stench is the same." He shot Ecan a measuring look. "But this time we have kicked the wasp's nest."

"And they shall swarm, I assure you." He reached out, and one by one he closed his fingers as if grasping something out of the air. "We are tightening our grip on their souls. Can you hear them, War Chief? Their screams are drifting on the wind, echoing in the ears of each survivor. Ecan, the Starwatcher, strikes terror into their hearts." He drew a deep breath. "Their pitiful bleats are a soothing elixir to my soul."

"Starwatcher, each moment we linger is one less we have to avoid Rain Bear's warriors when he discovers this atrocity."

"Atrocity?" Ecan opened his grip, blew across his palm, and indicated the village. "This is divine retribution, War Chief. Powers are at work here that you cannot understand. We are remaking our world, weaving it into something new."

"Yes, Starwatcher. Now, please allow me to assemble our warriors."

"When I say." Ecan gave him a flat stare. "And not a moment before."

"But, Starwatcher—"

"I wish to savor this." Ecan pursed his lips. "And I must see the matron before we leave."

White Stone hesitated. "Why? She's dead."

Ecan turned and gave White Stone a look that would have withered Cimmis himself. In a terse voice, he commanded, "Just make sure I am safe while I carry out my duties, War Chief."

"Of course, Starwatcher, but we have tied her corpse to the stone. It will take time to walk up there."

"I wish to present her head to our most valiant warrior in gratitude for his service."

White Stone secretly prayed he would not be chosen as the "most valiant warrior." In the past cycle, he'd been awarded the head too often. For the moment, he just wanted to be making tracks away from this place. He could feel anger building in the air around him, as if the wrath of the Raven People were thickening with the storm.

"But I thought we were just supposed to take the heads of her husband and son? Cimmis said nothing about Matron Weedis." White Stone had wrapped the men's heads in several layers of cloth and stuffed them in a pack he'd found in the wreckage. With his luck, they'd leak down his back as he trotted home.

"No," Ecan answered. "The matron defied us. I wish to make an example of her."

"If you must do this, please hurry. It will take us two hands of time to get down to the trail. The fog will shield most of the smoke, but if Rain Bear suspects what we've done—"

"I will take her head; then I will fetch my son, and we will go."

"Your son?" a velvet voice called from a swirling pocket of mist.

White Stone pivoted and grabbed for the war ax tucked in his belt. "Who's there? Show yourself!"

The eerie mist spun, then seemed to part before her as she gracefully walked toward them. Tall and willowy, a long red dress clung to the decidedly female body visible beneath the buffalo cape. Her hood was up, and wisps of waist-length red hair fluttered over her chest. Beneath the hood, though, White Stone saw only shadows.

She walked directly to Ecan, and when she pulled back her hood and lifted her beautiful face, her black eyes seemed to drain the light from the world, sucking it down into endless darkness. She leaned forward and whispered, *"A man who mocks the gods pays a terrible price. Your son is gone."*

"Dzoo." Ecan stood paralyzed, eyes locked with hers.

A terrible smile curled Dzoo's lips, and Ecan reacted as if bludgeoned.

He stumbled back, grabbed White Stone by the arm, and hissed, "Quickly. Find Tsauz!"

The smell would haunt him: coppery blood, the sour tang of entrails, the pungent odor of feces. The wet breeze carried its burden to Tsauz's quivering nostrils.

Not more than ten paces from where he hid in the tall ferns, someone crept furtively through the dead. A half-dazed moan broke her lips. That, and the light step, led Tsauz to conclude it was a woman. She moved slowly, as if mindless of the warriors racing around her or the groans coming from the pillars. Tsauz puzzled at the sounds as she shifted heavy limp objects. Some gurgled; others hissed or made flatulent sounds. The woman whispered under her breath, grunted, and wept as another body flopped wetly onto the stone.

Mist blew over his face. He shivered so hard his teeth chattered. Was he freezing to death?

Where's Father?

The woman let out a small terrible cry, and he heard her fall to her knees. "Wake up now, baby," she wept. "It's morning. We have to wake up."

Tsauz's fingers knotted and flexed and knotted again.

Warriors ran by calling, "Tsauz? Tsauz!"

He opened his mouth to call back, but no sound came out. He opened it wider—and tried to force air from his lungs.

Tears streamed down his face, but his throat remained frozen.

Nineteen

*R*ain Bear?"

He jerked awake to see pale blue light falling through the smoke hole in the lodge roof. Long black hair spread over his chest as he sat up and pawed it out of the way.

Footsteps, coming fast up the trail.

He grabbed his war club, shoved out of his bedding, and lunged outside wearing only his loincloth. A few people had risen. Breakfast fires sparkled across the meadow. Frost glistened on the slender lodgepole pines. Dogrib ran toward him with his white hair blowing around his pink face.

"What is it? What's happened?"

Dogrib extended an arm. "There's smoke rising above War Gods Village."

Rain Bear swung around to look.

Black oily smoke rose through the layer of clouds that cloaked the mountaintop. Not the smoke of ritual feast preparations, but the smoke of burning lodges.

Evening Star ducked out of her lodge ten paces away and looked around, a frown on her fine brow. Long red waves of unruly hair fell down the front of her cape. "What's wrong?"

Rain Bear ignored her, but gripped Dogrib's arm. "Find Talon and Sleeper. Tell them to rouse their warriors."

"Understood." Dogrib left at a run.

Rain Bear turned to Evening Star's guards, Wolf Spider and Hornet. "While I'm gone, let no one come near her! Do you understand? It's the perfect opportunity for an assassin to sneak in."

"No one will get by us, Chief," Wolf Spider called, and slapped his war club in emphasis.

The North Wind elder Rides-the-Wind threw back his lodge flap, and his dark eyes lifted to War Gods Mountain. Thick gray brows pulled down over his flat nose. Very quietly, he said, "If you hurry, Rain Bear, you'll catch them at the fork in the trail."

A faint sliver of gold marked the place on the western horizon where Raven had flown the sun to sink into Mother Ocean's belly. Drifting Cloud People shimmered and winked.

"I can't believe they did this!" Dogrib raged. Blood splotched his buckskin cape and long shirt from where he had cradled victims while he checked for signs of life. "They have desecrated War Gods Village! And we did nothing! *Nothing!* We promised to *protect* these people!"

Rain Bear stood beside Dogrib just below the twin pillars of rock and stared down the narrow ridge, over the smoldering village, to the ocean beyond. "For the moment, we wait."

The rich purple gleam of dusk flashed in Dogrib's angry blue eyes. "Wait?" he hissed. "For what? I say we track them down! We stalk them like the vermin they are! One by one, we catch them, stake them down, and cut pieces from their bodies as they wail their souls into oblivion!"

Rain Bear lifted a clenched fist and glared. "I know! I understand your anger, but this is *my* fault, War Chief. I could have killed him when he entered our village. Do you understand? *I let him go!*"

He closed his eyes, a sick pain in his heart. *Evening Star told me to kill him. But he had his son! His son, by Raven! What sort of man would risk a young blind boy?*

He watched a petite woman's body being dragged up the slope by two older women. Her head hung, swinging loosely as her long black hair tumbled in the muck. Her sightless eyes were gray, half-lidded, her mouth agape in a loose, soundless scream. Her sea-grass cape had been ripped away. In an effort at modesty, the women had tried to cover her, but the glistening stains on her pubis, as well as the bites on her one exposed nipple, gave witness to what her last moments must have been like.

Rain Bear wavered on his feet, a tingling lightness in his gut. All he wanted was to sink to the ground, put his head in his hands, and weep.

They had pulled most of the corpses down from the pillars and carried them to the north side of the mountain, but much remained to be done. They still had to search the collapsed lodges but couldn't until the embers cooled.

Dogrib gripped the shaft of his spear and glowered down into the valley. "This is not like Ecan. Lying so that he could do this within days of one of our most important ceremonies! It's insane!"

Rain Bear tipped his head back to the wounded sky. "It's as Rides-the-Wind said. He's shown us that he's not afraid of us . . . or the gods."

"Then we must teach him different." Murder lit Dogrib's eyes.

"Yes, my friend. And no, don't look at me that way. I will unleash you, but when the time is right. When we can hurt them in a way they've never been hurt before." Rain Bear's heart felt empty as he watched Roe and Evening Star pull a decapitated body across the ground toward the plaza. Wind Woman's breath was redolent with the stench of burning human flesh and the coppery tang of blood.

Rain Bear steeled himself. "What about Dzoo? Has anyone found her body?"

"No, but many of the victims were badly burned. Roe searches every corpse, looking for her fluted spear point, a shred of her clothing."

Rain Bear could see the tiny flame of hope that flickered in Dogrib's eyes. "If she's here, Roe will find her. Pitch is going to try to come up this afternoon to help her hunt."

"My Chief?" Dogrib shifted. "Do you think Dzoo escaped?"

Rain Bear's eyes traced the shapes of the Cloud People. "They may have captured her. If Ecan is this Coyote, and given the things Pitch told me . . ."

Dogrib narrowed his odd blue eyes. "I'm not certain which is worse: death, or her fate as Ecan's captive."

Rain Bear studied Dogrib from the corner of his eye. "If he's got her, we *will* get her back. I promise you. For right now, however, she may actually be exactly where we need her most."

Dogrib's gaze fixed on something over Rain Bear's shoulder.

Rain Bear turned to find War Chief Talon trudging up the hill toward them. Wind Woman tormented the hem of his hide cape and whipped white hair around his wrinkled face. His expression boded ill.

Talon called, "Just as you said, Great Chief. We caught Ecan's rearguard at the fork in the trail. I killed four, took two alive. The rearguard fought well enough to let the others get away. Sleeper took a small party to track them."

"How many escaped?"

"Maybe ten. Maybe more." Talon shoved loose hair away from his sharp old eyes. "There's another thing you should know."

"What is that?"

"They definitely took a woman captive. We found her tracks at the head of the party. She was shuffling along between two warriors."

Rain Bear held Talon's gaze. "Dzoo is missing."

"Dzoo?" The old chief's eyes widened. Then a sour smile came to his lips. "If they took Dzoo, may the gods show them mercy."

"I know her step. I'll have the answer for us soon enough, my chiefs." Dogrib loped off down the trail.

Rain Bear considered for a moment. "Ecan didn't do this without approval from the Council. Cimmis, however, is no one's fool. He knows that he plays a very delicate game. He hopes to frighten us into submission, to demonstrate his strength in a way that will ensure the delivery of tribute, even if it means starving our own people in the process. He wants to push us to the edge, but not over it. So, even if the Council ordered her execution, I doubt that Cimmis would carry it out. He knows that coupled with the desecration of the Moon Ceremonial and the raids, Dzoo's execution would incite rebellion among the slaves. It would drive the Raven People into a frenzy of hatred that would overwhelm his people."

Talon chewed on that for a moment as he watched Evening Star carrying a little boy's limp body. The child's skull had been smashed, and some of his brains hung from the wound. "I'm surprised to see her here."

"She warned us, Talon." Rain Bear glanced around at the smoldering wreckage and then watched Evening Star gently place the little boy's body in the growing line of corpses.

My fault. All my fault.

"In the past, I have acted as a peace chief should. I have sought accommodation and the ways to maintain the peace." He glared into Talon's eyes. "By taking Ecan's word, *I* killed these people! I will not rest until I have destroyed the Council and trod upon Cimmis's headless corpse."

Talon gave him a bitter smile. "Then I am yours, Rain Bear. If Dogrib is your right arm, I am your left."

Rain Bear nodded. "Thank you. I would like to speak with the two warriors you captured."

"I'll have them brought here immediately." Talon looked around at the dead that scattered the slope. Scavenger birds fluttered over the corpses. "My people are outraged, Rain Bear. They want every person in Fire Village dead."

Rain Bear clutched his cape closed beneath his chin and stared up at the twin pillars. Were the hero twins looking down upon the carnage and thinking the same? Or had they sided with the North Wind People?

"We are after the Council and Cimmis and those who work for them, Talon. Just remember that it's not all the North Wind People who have done this." He started down the slope toward where his daughter worked.

Talon trotted after him. "No one has said that, Rain Bear!"

"Not yet, but they will."

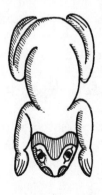

Twenty

War Chief White Stone leaned toward the fire and rubbed his nervous hands together. He had lost six of his warriors. Four were reported dead; two were thought to have been captured. Three wounded men slept rolled in blankets beside a crackling fire. One, Cedar Bark, would probably be dead by morning. The moans that punctuated their disturbed sleep mixed hauntingly with Wind Woman's shrill voice in the trees.

Ecan paced on the opposite side of the fire, hands clasped behind his back, tread slow and measured, as though time was his to command. His magnificent white cape and jewelry flashed with his slightest movement.

Ten paces away, Dzoo sat with her bound hands propped on her knees. The hood of her cape was thrown back. Long red hair fluttered around her beautiful face. With large black eyes that might have been openings to a nightmare, she followed Ecan's every move.

White Stone glanced at the guards behind her and tried to swallow the nervous lump in his throat. Wind Scorpion had volunteered for the duty when the others held back. He was a cunning old dog whom nothing seemed to frighten. His fathomless eyes were fixed on Dzoo. Two more guards stood on the high points watching their back trail. Was that enough to protect them?

White Stone returned to the uncomfortable topic at hand.

"Blessed Starwatcher, I assure you I did everything I could to protect your son!"

"Don't you dare attempt to assure me of anything!" Ecan held up a stern hand to stop White Stone's defense. In the fire light his pointed face and beadlike green eyes resembled a weasel's. "You are the one who talked me into taking my son. You said Matron Weedis would let down her guard if she saw me enter her village holding my son's hand." The vein in Ecan's neck throbbed. "You *guaranteed* my son's safety."

White Stone gaped, having said no such thing in this lifetime or any other. "But, Starwatcher—"

Sweat trickled from White Stone's armpits down his sides. "I personally searched every possible hiding place. You saw me! I did everything I could to find the boy."

Dzoo smiled—and White Stone's flesh crawled. What was it about her eyes? Something dark and inhuman.

Ecan had his back to her. Lucky for him.

White Stone raised his hands, imploring. "I will find your son, Starwatcher. I give you my oath. I'll return to search for him tomorrow."

"Do you know what they will do to my boy if they capture him?" Ecan's mouth quivered with lethal intent.

White Stone nodded. "Yes, I think so."

"They will cut my little Tsauz apart and bring me a piece at a time. With each ear, or hand, they will send word that Tsauz lives. Only at the end will they include a demand, and by then I will do anything, give them anything, say anything." He stared hard into White Stone's eyes. *"Do you understand me, War Chief?"*

The words hung in the air.

Dzoo tilted her head, and her full lips parted, as if hungry for White Stone's answer.

White Stone wondered when he had ever felt this miserable. "Yes, I understand." He glanced warily at Dzoo. "We have our own captive, Starwatcher. Never forget that."

Dzoo laughed—a deep-throated sound, more growl than amusement—and the forest seemed to burst to life as every sleeping warrior lunged to his feet and reached for his weapons.

Ecan turned to glare at her.

When their eyes met, the very air seemed to sizzle and pop.

Dzoo leaned forward and whispered, *"In the end, Starwatcher, your soul will howl in darkness."*

Ecan's expression remained cool, aloof. He just stared at her.

White Stone reached up to finger the polished fluted point that hung at his throat, wondering if even that amulet would protect his soul.

Lost in thoughts, Evening Star walked down the narrow trail, stepping over moss-encrusted deadfall, twisted roots, and occasional stones that protruded from the winding way. Overhead interlocking fir boughs muted the evening light, turning the forest floor into a gloomy dark place that mirrored her wounded soul. Only when faint traces of breeze stirred in the damp darkness did she catch a breath of the moldy duff and loam. The rest of the time, the stench of death rose from her dress, hands, and hair. Each of the corpses she'd carried had leaked fluid onto her.

She had thrown herself into the cleanup like a slave woman. The others had shied from the more horribly mutilated corpses. Those she tackled herself, as if by her diligence she could personally atone for the actions of her people.

The children had been the worst. *Why,* her soul wailed, *do they murder the children?*

She couldn't help but be aware of the mixture of emotions aimed at her by the Raven People: Some barely hid their loathing; others were pensive as they watched her through dark, questioning eyes; and there were those few who nodded, as if it were only appropriate that she deal with the horror of her people's decisions.

Meanwhile, her guards prowled like silent mountain lions behind and to either side of her. They had become her shadows, following discreetly as she carried the corpses, laid them out, and used a fouled bit of matting to clean their cold dead flesh in preparation for the funerary rites.

What am I doing here? She huddled in the midst of a people who didn't want her, hated her, in fact.

I should go. Tomorrow, just after sunset. Rain Bear needed all of his people for the coming trial, and she was tying up two of his young warriors each day.

Yes, that was the right decision. Pack her belongings and creep out tomorrow, just after dark. No one would know her destination, or which trail to follow in pursuit. She would have a full night's travel before she went to ground for the day. By traveling at night, she could make her way far to the south. There among some amiable people, she could find a place for herself. Not as a matron of the North Wind People, but as a simple woman competent at certain tasks. A woman who was willing to work could always find a place. She was still young and strong. She could bear a man enough children in return for a place to sleep.

You would do that? the voice of her soul demanded. *Submit yourself to some hunter whose language you can't even speak? Live like a slave in the dirt?*

She took a deep breath, and couldn't help but gag on the odors rising from the gore clinging to her dress, hands, and hair.

Yes, after the last two moons, after this day, the meaning of life had changed. Illusions no longer burdened her. These days she needed only food, water, shelter, and a semblance of security.

The trail switchbacked down into a narrow cut, choked with willow, raspberries, currants, and chokecherry bushes. There, under an overhang, water dashed into a small pool before burbling down the rock-choked streambed toward the ocean.

Placing her spattered moccasins with care, she descended the last of the slope and stopped short. In the gloom she could see the man crouching on a flat stone that jutted out over the water. At first glance she thought him sick from the hang of his head and the loose drape of his muscular shoulders. Then she caught the spasm that ran through him and instinctively knew it for what it was.

Too late to turn back now, and in a moment her guards would catch sight of him. She reached out and stepped full on a fallen branch, snapping it loudly. Then she hesitated and mimicked a sneeze.

The man's reaction was instantaneous. He shot a quick glance over his shoulder, and in that instant she recognized Rain Bear. For a lightning instant she stared into his swollen eyes before he averted his face, bent down, and cupped up water from the pool, splashing it into his face.

By the time her guards eased down the incline, Rain Bear looked like a man just finishing his ablutions.

"Chief Rain Bear?" she greeted, feigning surprise. "I did not mean to intrude."

"No, it's quite all right. Come, Matron. After your day, you need the water more than I do." He reached for his war shirt, used it to wipe his face dry, and stood. She watched him pull the damp hide over his head and down his muscular body. More than once that wide-shouldered frame had intruded into her imagination. It had

Danced at the edge of her fantasies as she imagined what it would be like to be touched by him, to feel that warm strength pressed against her. In her Dreams she had allowed herself to run her fingers over his thick chest only once before she banished it as impossibility.

She turned, feeling oddly shy after witnessing his vulnerability. "Hornet? I would speak to the chief in private."

"Yes, Matron," Hornet called, and waved his opposite back.

She picked her way down to the slab of rock and studied Rain Bear. He sought to look everywhere but into her eyes.

"What is it?" she asked. "Can I help?"

He smiled wistfully. "Can you conjure the dead? Breathe them back to life?" He made an open gesture. "Can you fly back in time far enough to convince me to split Ecan's skull before he reaches War Gods Village?"

At last she understood. The model of strength she had watched all day had been dying inside. "He did this. Not you. If you are guilty of anything it was acting with decency and honor."

His voice took on a bitter twist. "A mistake I'll never make again, Matron."

She reached out, saw the blood and offal on her hand, and hesitated to touch him. "Don't become like them."

The pain behind his eyes stung her. "If I had listened to you, none of this would have happened. Those people would be alive today."

"I was wrong, Rain Bear. There was more at stake than I understood," she countered. "If you'd killed him, it would have given Cimmis a reason to hunt you down and kill you. With you dead, no one could stand against him. You are the one man alive who can rally the Raven People against the Council."

"Those people died—"

"Yes, and in doing so they have become the binding that will tie the Raven clans together. But only if you are there to weave that knot."

She couldn't decipher the look he was giving her. Some mixture of hurt and hope, despair and rage. For long moments they stood thus, each searching the other for resolution.

In a low voice, he finally said, "But for the presence of his son, I would have killed him that day."

"Then the boy was the key to the Raven People's future. And it's the future that you must face. Your people need to be shaped and molded. The story is told that when you came to this land, it was as a few scattered clans, loosely affiliated, and then only by your language. Canoe load by canoe load, you drifted down from the north, hunting, and moving on. Is that what you wish to be forever?"

"We can no longer be subject to the North Wind People's caprice," he countered.

"No, you cannot." She turned away then, stung by her circumstances. "The North Wind People . . . Song Maker help us, what have we become? We're like the great firs, so tall we scrape the clouds, ancient and towering; but cut into our thick trunk, and you'll find a fungal rot. Massive as we might look from the outside, we cannot survive the coming wind." She looked down at the dried blood that coated her fingers.

"Assuming I can create this new alliance of which you speak, what of you, Matron?"

"I believe I shall leave tomorrow night, Chief. Slip away with your help, and vanish. Perhaps somewhere to the south is a land where my daughter's ghost doesn't wail in my dreams. A place where I can forget Ecan and Kenada, and the way their bodies felt against mine."

He stepped to her. An odd thrill leapt at his touch, at the strength in his hands as he rested them on her shoulders. "Stay," he whispered.

"Stay?" she echoed, trying to understand the quiver that ran through her.

"I am going to need your counsel."

"You will have plenty of counselors."

He hesitated. "Why did you warn me you were close just now?"

She blinked, surprised. "I—I didn't want your warriors to see you."

"What difference did it make to you?

She considered and found no answer. "Everyone should be allowed a moment of privacy to weep for the dead."

"And for themselves," he added as he took a breath. "You have a sense about you, Matron. I would have done well to have listened more carefully to you. Stay. Help me. Not just for my people, but for yours."

She swallowed against the sudden sense of falling she felt down in her gut. She gave him a quick nod. His hands tightened on her shoulders as he drew her to him, brushed his lips across her forehead, and stepped back. In the descending darkness, she couldn't see his expression, but her forehead tingled as if afire.

Snow fell silently through the firs and dusted Ecan's small camp. It settled on the sleeping forms of warriors who lay wrapped in hides and bark blankets. It drifted down onto the packs lying about, and sizzled as it touched the hot ashes in the smoldering fires.

The warrior known as Hunter sat guarding the prisoner, Dzoo. Flakes began to dot his hair, giving it a gray look where he sat before a small fire. He pulled up his hood and went back to sharpening his deer-bone stiletto. He'd broken the tip during the War Gods Village fight. The weapon made a soft zizzing sound as he drew it back and forth across a piece of sandstone.

Every now and then, he shot a glance at Red Dog, his companion on guard duty this night. The old warrior sat cross-legged two paces away, eating a long strip of elk jerky. He had a puzzled expression on his battered face. He chewed and gave Dzoo a perplexed squint. Red Dog's nose had been broken in the past, but it hadn't healed well. It had a bend in it that made people stare. This night he wore a tattered deerhide cape with patches of missing hair. He swallowed and twitched his lips thoughtfully.

"What are you looking at?" Hunter asked.

Red Dog cocked his head, clearly lying when he said, "Nothing. I was just thinking about Mica."

"What about him?"

"This is the third time in six moons he's been selected as 'most valiant warrior.' "

"Well," Hunter growled, "for all the stomach you showed at War Gods Village, I don't think you're in danger of being awarded the head."

"I was too busy packing weapons to Ecan. What kind of a fool surrenders his weapons just before a battle, anyway?"

"Rain Bear demanded it." Hunter tapped the side of his head with the stiletto. "It's strategy, planning. Things you're too dumb to do." But he glanced over at the rolled figures around Mica's fire. Earlier that evening, and with great ceremony, Mica had roasted the head, cracked the base of the skull open, and spooned out the old woman's brains.

Red Dog finally muttered, "I'm glad I'm never selected as most valiant warrior. I don't have the stomach for brain."

"Few warriors do. Most carry the heads home and give them to their slaves to clean before hanging them on the wall. I think Mica really believes he's going to get smarter. He's ambitious enough to wipe Ecan's ass twice a day as it is."

Red Dog's worried gaze was fixed on Dzoo again.

"Yes?" Hunter prompted.

"I wish Wind Scorpion hadn't given us this detail. If he wants to watch her, he should do it himself. Me, I don't like being this close to her."

"Nothing scares Wind Scorpion."

Red Dog ripped off another hunk of jerky and slurred, "White Shtone says he's going back to shearch for the boy tomorrow. Will you go with him?"

"Only if ordered," Hunter answered, and leaned back against the old stump. "But if he asks for volunteers, I'll tuck my tail between my legs and run straight home to Fire Village. If Tsauz is still alive— and that's a big if—Rain Bear has him by now."

Red Dog narrowed an eye. "What do you mean 'if'?"

"It was dark." Hunter lowered his voice to a hoarse whisper. "People were running, screaming. I killed three different kids. You know, they just ran by in the darkness and smack, you bash their brains out. Now, if Tsauz came running up to some warrior, bawling like an orphaned elk calf, well, you know . . ."

Red Dog grunted.

"And if he's alive?"

"Rain Bear will use him as bait. Whoever goes with White Stone is a dead man."

Red Dog used his teeth to rip off another chunk of jerky before examining their prisoner again.

Dzoo sat on a log, bound hands in her lap. Snow coated her buffalo cape. In the past four hands of time she hadn't so much as blinked, shifted, or made a sound.

"Do you think she's breathing?" Red Dog asked.

Hunter rolled his stiletto to sharpen the opposite side. "If she were dead, she would have fallen over by now."

Red Dog lowered his jerky to his lap. "I haven't seen her take a breath. The snow's not even melting on her hands."

Hunter blew the ground bone from his sharpening stone and gave Red Dog a reproachful look. "You've seen three tens of summers; that's ten more than I have. You ought to know by now that a determined warrior is a lot more dangerous than a sleeping woman."

Red Dog wet his lips. "Maybe she's Soul Flying. I've heard that Soul Flyers often look dead."

"Soul Flying," Hunter grumbled under his breath. "The way she's bound, that's the only part of her that could move."

Red Dog's burly shoulders hunched as he leaned toward Hunter to whisper, "I thought I saw something earlier."

Annoyed, Hunter asked, "What?"

"Well, I'm not sure. It was tiny, Dancing around her, spinning like a child's top."

"Windblown snow."

"This windblown snow had rocks in its fists and was covered with thick red hair."

"For something you *thought* you saw, you saw it pretty clearly."

"And it had antlers." He held his fingers spread over the head. "Just like a deer's."

Hunter set his sharpening stone aside. "You're telling me you saw one of the Noisy Ones?"

The story was told among the North Wind People that the Noisy Ones were miniature creatures covered with hair. In the day they were invisible and could throw rocks with great accuracy and kill people. Holy people said that the Noisy Ones walked the thin thread of light that separated life and death, light and dark. Hunter believed none of this. He leveled all of his disdain into a hard glare.

"I've heard stories that the Noisy Ones are her Spirit Helpers."

"So you thought . . . what? The Noisy Ones had come to free her?"

Red Dog swallowed, big-eyed. "Doesn't that worry you?"

Hunter threw up his hands. "If she really had Powerful Spirit Helpers like that, you and I would already be dead, and she would be on her way to Rain Bear."

Red Dog considered that. He tore off another bite of jerky and, around the mass, said, "Maybe the Noisy Ones are waiting for something."

Hunter pointed his stiletto at Red Dog's bent nose. "The next time I have to stand guard, I'm. . . . Oh, never mind."

Red Dog's bushy brows lowered. Time passed before he added, "You've heard the stories about Dzoo? About when she was a child?"

"What stories?"

"White Stone told me that a terrible priest among the Striped Dart People saw her fly into his village on wings like Owl's. Dzoo could send her souls flying at the age of four summers! That's why the old priest sent a war party to steal her away."

"Stories change over time, Red Dog. Who knows what really happened?"

Red Dog looked at Hunter askance. "She's got a small soapstone bowl in her pouch. White Stone said she uses it to see long-dead people."

Hunter wiped the stiletto on his hide pants and tested the sharpened tip on his thumb. "Did Mica tell you that Ecan forced him to examine that pack?"

"You mean Ecan was afraid to look inside the pack himself?"

"Apparently."

"And?"

Hunter made an airy gesture with his stiletto. "He found the soap-stone bowl and six leather bags."

"What was in the bags? Witch pellets? Evil charms?"

Witches shot enchanted pellets into their victims to cause illness or death. The area around Hunter's heart started to itch. He scratched it and answered, "Mica said three of the bags contained dirt. Another had twigs and bark. Yet another was filled with bird droppings. And the last apparently had bat dung in it."

"Bird droppings and bat dung?" Red Dog said as though disappointed.

"Mica claimed he had to open two outer bags before he got to the tiny inner bags with the dirt and droppings."

"She triple-bagged droppings?"

"Yes," Hunter said in a scary hiss, "as if she's afraid they might get out."

Red Dog's brows lowered. "You know, truly, someone should take that pack away and burn it."

Hunter shrugged. "Ecan peered into each bag that Mica opened. He said everything looked harmless."

"Dirt and droppings," Red Dog mumbled. Gray-streaked black tangles framed his round face. He shifted uncomfortably before saying, "Doesn't it worry you that Ecan wouldn't touch the bags himself?"

"He's a Starwatcher. He would have known if she'd carried anything dangerous, like Spirit plants or witch amulets."

Red Dog crossed his arms. "Her pack should be destroyed. Just in case."

Hunter waved a hand. "Fine. Reach over, take it away from her, and throw it in the fire."

The furrows in Red Dog's forehead deepened. "Me? This is Dzoo we're talking about. If it were up to me, I'd untie her, dust her off, give her everything I own, and set her free." He rubbed his chin with the back of his hand. "Then I'd pray like I've never prayed before."

"You are such an old fool!" Hunter got to his feet, stiletto in hand, and boldly walked toward the prisoner.

Red Dog looked like he was going to throw up.

Hunter circled her. Snow coated her hood and cape and shimmered in the firelight. "Woman? Are you alive? Or just off somewhere Soul Flying? Can you hear me?"

Nothing.

Red Dog hissed, "See, I told you. She's dead."

Hunter used the tip of his stiletto to poke the woman in the shoulder. She might have been clay.

Hunter bent down, whispering, "Hey, camp bitch, you want a man to share his heat with you? I could be talked into warming you up."

Red Dog warned, "I wouldn't be doing that!"

Hunter grinned at Red Dog, jabbed her again with his stiletto, and cooed, "I could warm you with something a lot stiffer than—"

She moved.

Red Dog leaped to his feet and shouted, "Blessed Ancestors, she's alive!"

Hunter spun too quickly, tripped over his own feet, and tumbled to the ground a handsbreadth from her feet.

Dzoo fixed Hunter with shimmering black eyes that seemed to burn out of the blackness inside her hood.

"Careful, warrior," she said in a soft deadly voice. "Or I'll take you with me the next time I visit the Land of the Dead."

Hunter was so busy scrambling away in terror that he didn't see the triumphant gaze Red Dog was giving him.

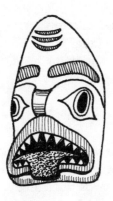

Twenty-one

Night lay cold upon the tree-timbered slopes. The breeze blowing in off the ocean carried the cool moist air of a coming storm. A spotted owl hooted in the shadows, its call wavering among the dark branches of fir and hemlock.

"There's someone out there," Chert whispered, and tiptoed to one side of the tree he hid behind. He glanced over the brow of the low hill to examine the starlit slope. The old burn was grassed over, dotted with saplings and brambles. From his vantage, Chert could just see Ecan's camp. Hide-wrapped warriors lay among the trees far below, their shapes dark and quiet. "Did you hear it?"

"What?" Split Head whispered as he came up behind Chert. He'd gotten his name two summers ago when a thrown war ax had glanced off his skull. A long, hairless gash marked the spot. "I don't hear anything."

Chert put a finger to his lips and listened. No sounds came from the enemy camp. War Chief Sleeper maintained strict rules as they shadowed Ecan's party. They couldn't speak above a whisper, couldn't move about unnecessarily. Instead, they slipped along quietly, seeking some opportunity that would allow their small party to strike, to rescue Dzoo, or perhaps kill Ecan himself. To date, no such opportunity had presented itself.

Curiously shaped rock outcrops fringed Ecan's camp. They resembled crouching monsters. The only sound Chert could hear was his own shallow breathing.

Split Head used a bone stiletto to poke Chert's shoulder. "What did you hear? Someone talking?"

"No, it was rocks." He shook his head. "Or maybe gravel rolling. As though beneath a foot."

"Pack rat?"

"Maybe, but it sounded heavier."

"Probably a badger."

They both stood listening for a while longer, then Split Head whispered, "I'd better return to my post on the hilltop. If you see anything? If one of the guards nods off . . ."

"I'll send immediate word." Chert watched as Split Head started back up the rocky slope.

In the past three moons Sleeper had personally killed four warriors for disobeying orders. Two of those had left their posts for brief periods.

No one argued with Sleeper's punishments. According to the story, a sentinel had fallen asleep, and three tens of Ecan's warriors had sneaked in, burned Deer Meadow Village to the ground, and killed scores. When Sleeper had been elected war chief, he had vowed such a thing would never happen to his people again.

Vigilance had to be maintained.

As Chert returned his attention to the camp below, he heard Split Head stumble and hissed over his shoulder, "Watch your step. All of these rocks are loose. If you—"

The impact sent Chert reeling forward. For a moment he couldn't comprehend. Had Split Head struck him from behind? In that instant, the jarring of the impact became a violent pain that burned through his chest. He could feel the thing wiggling, vibrating inside him. When he looked down, a dark point jutted from his chest. He grasped the spearhead with his hands, feeling the slick blood. The force of his grip sent a shiver through the spear that his punctured lungs and heart could feel.

With one hand, he tried to grab on to a boulder to steady himself, missed the rock, and fell. He landed on his side with his arms flailing. Down the slope, Split Head's body lay like a twisted bark doll.

He tried to fill his lungs to scream, but his mouth only gasped emptily for air.

Near one of the sandstone outcrops, eyes glinted: silver flashes in the starlight. A dog's eyes? As the animal lifted its head, dark pointed ears appeared. But they didn't twitch, didn't move at all. Dead ears.

Then they were gone. Only the quivering of a winter-bare branch marked the presence.

An instant later, Sleeper scrambled down the slope with three men following closely behind him.

The war chief's cape seemed to spread like protective wings as he dropped to his knees. "Where did he go, Chert? Did you see him?"

Chert's mouth had gone as dry as dust. "Just . . . eyes . . . ears . . . there." He weakly tipped his chin and whispered, "Coyote."

Sleeper waved to the outcrop. "Crater, take Kit Fox. Go."

The warriors scrambled in pursuit.

Chert stared at Sleeper. He'd never understood why the man had never married. He had rugged, chiseled features, and his gray temples sparkled. He'd come to Deer Meadow Village two summers ago, and many women had offered themselves to him. Matron Red Kestrel said his heart still bled over the deaths of his family, but . . .

"Sorry," Chert managed to whisper before blood came bubbling up his throat, shutting off his air.

Sleeper clasped Chert's hand in a hard warrior's grip. "It's not your fault. Somehow they've discovered us. The fault is mine."

A warm floating sensation filled Chert. He might have been a feather, rising into the air.

Sleeper drew Chert's hand to his chest and held it.

Chert looked at the Star People until they became fixed white dots. . . .

The storm blew down from the northwest, dull and gray. Streamers of cloud bunched against the cliffs and shredded into misty fingers that drifted through the trees. During the night snow had turned into a cold rain that whispered as it fell on Sandy Point Village. Somehow it was colder. The chill seemed to suck the heat out of the fires, and even snuggling deep into the robes didn't help.

So it was that a shivering Rain Bear threw back his bedding, crawled over to his door, and looked out at the predawn village. Through the graying light he could make out new rivulets that ran down the trails and melted the patches of snow. A soft melody of raindrops pattered on his roof.

He turned a longing gaze on Evening Star's small lodge. Hornet stood by her door, head bowed under a thickly greased hide.

"He looks as miserable as I feel," Rain Bear muttered, and blew to see his breath mist white in front of him. His chilly sleep had been haunted with the knowledge that Evening Star slept so close, yet so far away. In his half-wakened fantasy, her smooth body had molded against his. Warm and soft, she had wrapped herself around him, her legs locking behind his knees; her blue eyes burned into his. The moment his hard penis slid into her warm sheath, his loins had exploded in a tingling rush that brought him wide awake.

How long had it been since any Dream woman but Tlikit had done that to him?

Rain Bear hooked his door hanging on a peg and sank down to brace his back against the frame. Cool wind Danced with the rain, and swept patterns over the village. It brought him the scents of wet earth and conifers. People had trickled in from the trails, shouting about the atrocity at War Gods Village, for much of the night. Whimpers still seeped from a few lodges beyond the screening of trees that separated him from the rest of the village.

Today, people were in shock, overcome by grief. Tomorrow, their hearts would be kindling the fires of revenge.

He could not allow petty attacks against the North Wind People. It would keep the enemy on alert and rapidly deplete his forces. They had to save their strength, build it for one fierce blow.

Five paces away, Rides-the-Wind threw back his lodge flap and crawled out. He wore a woven spruce-root hat and cape that shed the rain. The old man shivered and walked back under the trees to relieve himself. When he tottered back, he stopped, thoughtful gaze fixed on Evening Star's lodge. He stood a long while, just looking.

Thinking what? Rain Bear wondered. Surely she didn't fill the old man's Dreams the same way she filled his. Longing grew within him as the Dream replayed in his memory. His lips still burned from the fleeting contact with her skin the night before.

Their three lodges sat in a triangle around the firepit. Rain Bear had originally selected the spot because a fifty-hand-tall cliff rose behind his lodge. He'd thought the cliff would make it harder for some sneaky North Wind warrior to creep up on him in the night. It would never have occurred to him that he might some day purposely surround himself with North Wind People.

An odd turn of events.

Rain Bear pulled his rain cape and conical hat from the pegs on the bark wall, then grabbed a handful of dry kindling from the woodpile beside his door. He used two sticks to lever a glowing coal from his fire and eased out into the morning.

Rides-the-Wind turned. His gray hair and long beard blew around his oblong face. "Are you feeling well, Chief?"

"I didn't wake you, did I?"

"All those despairing sighs and deep exhalations . . . Why would they wake anyone?"

Gods! How many of his Dreams had the old man been able to interpret? Rain Bear sheepishly knelt beside the firepit and used a stick to scrape away the wet ash as he crouched over the smoldering coal. "Forgive me. I've been thinking about the next two days."

"Ah, that explains it," Rides-the-Wind murmured.

Rain Bear arranged the dry kindling over the coal and blew. It didn't take long for the wood to catch. Flames crackled up. Rain Bear gradually added larger branches until he had enough fire to beat the drizzle.

"How many warriors did Sleeper take to track Dzoo?" Rides-the-Wind asked.

"Ten."

"Will that be enough?"

"Ten is all we could spare, Elder. Our hands were full at War Gods Village."

Rides-the-Wind's expression turned somber. "Well, you will probably be able to recruit from the people who come for the Moon Ceremonial."

"Possibly." *I'd better.*

The rain eased a little, falling in a light mist around them. Rain Bear gazed out at Mother Ocean. Through gaps in the trees he could see waves crashing upon the shore and gulls running before the surf.

The old man extended his bony hands to the flames. "People should start arriving this morning. That will give you a full day to gather forces before the Moon Ceremonial."

"If they stay long enough, Elder. We have nothing to feed them. We sent all of our stored food to Cimmis to pay the tribute we owed. Since the refugees started pouring in, we've been eating half rations."

Rain Bear wiped his wet hands on his black leggings and stood. Elder Rides-the-Wind stood a good head taller than he, but was half as wide. He resembled an ancient wind-gnarled stick with thick gray hair.

"May I offer you some advice?" Rides-the-Wind peered curiously at Rain Bear.

"Your counsel is welcome anytime, Elder."

"Have you thought about what motivates Ecan?"

Rain Bear smiled humorlessly. "I've thought of little else. He seems intent upon destroying our people. Some of the things he did to the bodies of the dead before he ordered them bound to the pillars . . ." He shook his head. "Well, unbelievable."

"I suspect they were no more terrible than what the Raven People did to his parents when he'd seen six summers. I understand that the sight of their bodies was most hideous. As I recall, the Raven People justified the mutilations by saying his parents were witches."

Rain Bear's mouth tightened. "One hurt does not heal another."

"Yes, true, but those who are hurting rarely understand that." Rides-the-Wind gestured to the lodges that filled the meadow. Somewhere, far out in the trees, a man wept. "Not only that, Ecan is just following orders."

"I know." Rain Bear bowed his head.

A gust of wind almost blew off Rides-the-Wind's hat. He clamped it to his head, and said, "The Four Old Women can look into the future as well as you can, Rain Bear. What do you see ahead?"

"More hatred."

"Perhaps they do, too. Perhaps they think if they can make you fear them enough, hate them enough, you will hesitate to strike out at North Wind villages. Brutality now might win them some breathing space."

Rain Bear blinked against the rain. "Do you believe that?"

Rides-the-Wind gazed at the fir branches that dipped and swayed. "I believe we are all one, Rain Bear. Your life, the lives of tens of creatures unseen, living beneath the rocks, or in the highest treetops, is One Life. When we kill the other, we kill ourselves. There is only Life."

Rain Bear pulled the brim of his hat down over his eyes. "Was that a yes or a no?"

The old man smiled. "A no. I don't believe that murdering Raven People will make you hesitate. But my beliefs won't help you much, I'm afraid."

A stick broke in the fire, and sparks exploded. As they whirled upward into the rain, they winked out like tiny torches snuffed in the ocean.

Rain Bear tossed another branch onto the flames. "Well, I agree with you."

Rain dripped into the old man's long gray beard, forming a glistening net of drops. It shimmered when he turned to squarely face Rain Bear.

"Do you know why I'm here?" Rides-the-Wind asked.

Rain Bear gestured uncertainly. "No. Not really."

"Power brought me." He nodded to Evening Star's lodge. "As it brought her."

Rain Bear made no reply as he rubbed the toe of his moccasin over a wet hearthstone.

As though irritated, Rides-the-Wind braced his walking stick in front of him and gripped the slippery knob in a tight fist. Firelight ran up the wet shaft like honey. "You are about to accept the most difficult challenge any man ever has."

"What challenge?"

"The decisions you make in the next few days will touch thousands of lives as yet unborn." The old man's eyes seemed to burn. "So, how will you choose?"

"Choose what, Elder?"

A faint smile twisted the old man's lips. "That is what I have come here to see."

Twenty-two

Pitch walked slowly across the village, conserving his strength. Every time he planted his left foot, pain stabbed his wounded shoulder. News of the attack on War Gods Village had panicked the clans. Warriors had been dispatched to the perimeters, leaving only women, children, and the elderly to sit around their evening fires and whisper about what might come next.

After days of snow and rain, cold damp drafts seeped through the forest, penetrating every garment. To make matters worse, soaked wood, when it burned at all, belched blue smoke but not much heat. Pitch couldn't seem to get warm.

Because he was a young Singer, people turned strained and frightened faces toward him as he passed, mutely asking him why this was happening, what they had done to deserve such punishments from the gods.

Pitch tried to smile reassuringly, but they knew as well as he that something was coming. Too many villages had been destroyed. Too many people needed food. Summer had lasted longer than anyone could remember. Mother Ocean was rising. Everyone saw it. Many of the lesser rock formations near the shore had drowned last cycle. The beach was being eaten away.

The trail ran through a heavily forested area and emerged at the edge of the sea cliff where—less than five tens of body lengths away—silver waves washed the rocky littoral. He paused for a moment. Canoes dotted the water between the beach and the outlying islands. He could see fishermen casting nets in the vain hope of adding to the dwindling larders. As he watched, the calm roar of the Mother's voice soothed him. Two gray-headed elders hunched over a small fire down near the water, and a group of young women watched several children playing chase. They ran up and down the shore, laughing. The firelight cast their huge shadows across the ocean like those of giants.

Rides-the-Wind sat on a rocky ledge overlooking the water. A tan sea-grass blanket draped his shoulders.

Pitch ground his teeth, refusing to move. Why on earth had he thought the old man might help him? He belonged to the North Wind People, and had no obligation to any paltry Healer-in-the-Making . . .

"Stop babbling to yourself and come join me," Rides-the-Wind called without turning. "I've been expecting you for days."

Pitch looked to see if there was anyone else standing close by. "Are—are you talking to me?"

"Of course I'm talking to you."

He hesitantly walked forward. "Babbling? I wasn't speaking out loud. Was I?"

"Are you going to sit, or not?" The elder pointed to the ledge.

Pitch eased down onto the damp gray stone and winced. "Forgive me, Elder. I hope you do not consider my presence an intrusion."

"An intrusion is only made by someone obsessed with his own needs, young Singer. Is that why you've come? To have me assuage your personal needs?"

"No, Elder." Pitch took a breath to fortify his courage. "Dzoo and I had trouble at Antler Spoon's village."

"Yes, I heard."

Rides-the-Wind frowned at the bald eagles perched on one of the dead firs that jutted up along the shoreline; their white heads glinted like beacons. They always flocked to Sandy Point Village during the Sits Down Moon.

Pitch was forming his question when Rides-the-Wind asked, "Are you going up to care for the dead in War Gods Village?"

"As soon as I've spoken with you."

Rides-the-Wind gestured to the sling on Pitch's arm. "Are you sure you're well enough?"

"I'll be all right. Since there is no one else, I have to be. I just hope I have the strength to Sing the sacred Songs."

A faint smile tugged at Rides-the-Wind's wrinkled lips, and his dark eyes turned luminous. "If you need, I would be honored to help you. As a youth I made a full study of your rituals and Songs."

"You did?"

The old man shrugged. "All of my life I have been fascinated by the ways that lead to the One Life. Each is a path that takes the traveler past different sights and experiences. In the end, however, the destination is still the same."

They stared at each other in silence, each measuring the other.

Pitch tried to think of something to say that wouldn't sound trite, or embarrass him.

Rides-the-Wind turned his attention to the eagles. "Why don't you tell me about the obsidian fetishes?"

Pitch's eyes widened. "Did Rain Bear tell you?"

"Of course not. What? Do you think you're the only one who can hear their cries? I started hearing them the day before I arrived here." He held out a skeletal hand. "Let me see them."

Pitch reached into his belt pouch, drew out the fetish bag, and placed it on the old man's palm. "When you open it, you'll see—"

Rides-the-Wind held the bag to his ear and closed his eyes. For a long time, he did not move.

The eagles began shrieking. One flapped into the air; then another lifted off. In a few heartbeats, the entire flock was airborne, shrieking and flapping through the purple dusk.

Rides-the-Wind opened his eyes. "I hear many voices, Singer. Some young, some old. Some male, some female."

"Many voices?"

Rides-the-Wind gave him a bland look. "Yes. Why?"

"Well, I . . . I only hear one voice."

"Have you held the bag to your ear?"

Pitch shook his head warily.

"Does his Power frighten you so much? Listen, and learn. He is dangerous, this witch, but the voices will not harm you. And surely you're not afraid to listen to the dead?"

"Witch?" Pitch whispered. "The dead?"

"Of course." Rides-the-Wind handed the fetish bag to Pitch. "Hold it to your ear and *listen*."

Pitch's fingers tingled as he held the soft leather against his ear. Within moments, the flesh of his face began to crawl. He still only heard one voice clearly, but behind the man's wrenching cries, he thought he made out the faint din of other voices. "Who are they, Elder?"

"I haven't the slightest idea. Who do you think they are?"

Pitch placed the bag on the ledge between them and rubbed his hand on his cape. His fingers burned and tingled as if bitten by wood ants. "If you're right, and the voices belong to dead people, they could be my ancestors."

Rides-the-Wind's gray brows lowered. "That's possible, but that's not what has you so worried, is it?"

"No," he said through a long exhalation. "I hear a man's voice calling to me, begging me for help. How can I help if we're hearing the voices of the dead?"

Rides-the-Wind tugged feebly at the sea-grass blanket over his shoulders. "The question is, dead when? Life is a great circle, Pitch. If you're standing in the middle, birth and death are the same distance from you. What you see depends upon which direction you look. Are you hearing someone who has already died, or someone who will die and have his soul locked into the fetish sometime in the future? Do you hear words, or just cries?"

"Just cries." Pitch clenched his fist in his lap. "Why is he crying? He sounds so terrified and lonely, it wounds my heart."

Rides-the-Wind's gaze followed the bald eagles. A few had landed again. They were preening, plucking at their feathers, combing their wings with their beaks. Out on the water, a whale blew. Water fountained twenty hands into the air. Immediately the fishermen began pulling in their nets, scrambling for paddles. Across the silver waves, they started in pursuit.

In a fierce whisper, Pitch asked, "Has this man already been witched, Rides-the-Wind? Or *will* he be witched? Will someone steal his soul and breathe it into one of those fetishes?"

"You begin to understand." Rides-the-Wind reached for the bag again. He poured the fetishes out into his palm, where they glittered wildly. The largest was a black obsidian eagle with its wings spread. The flaking had been done with such deliberation that the scars looked like feathers ready to catch the wind. A coiled snake had been chipped out of red-brown obsidian, the flakes taken off in a pattern like scales. It glared with tiny polished jasper eyes inset in the triangular head. "He is a master flint knapper, isn't he? Do you know which fetish holds the voice?"

"No. I only touched them once—and then just for a short time. The maker's Power is almost overwhelming."

As Rides-the-Wind studied the stones the purple gleam of dusk flowed into his deep wrinkles and threw an odd tracery of shadows over his face. "In all of my life, I haven't encountered a witch like this one," the old man said. "I've felt him for several moons now, caught the faintest whiff of his Power on the night wind. Sensed his presence at the edge of my soul. He has a great hunger, Pitch. He wants to devour, control, and terrify." He paused, frowning. "And he has come at a time of great danger to us. Why now? Is he part of the pattern?"

"I think he is here for Dzoo."

The stones clinked musically as Rides-the-Wind shoved them back in the bag and laid it on the ledge between them. "He tried to buy Dzoo's life with them?"

"Yes. Antler Spoon called him Coyote. They say he wears an ancient coyote mask, and I think he wears a large shining spear point pendant. Something that catches the light."

"Coyote?"

Pitch swallowed hard, thinking about poor Sweet Grass. *Skinned wings.* His voice quaked when he answered, "Yes."

"Did Dzoo speculate about his identity?"

"She thought he might be one of the North Wind People. She said he may have been born in Fire Village."

"I would like to speak with her. Together, perhaps we—"

"Dogrib found her tracks yesterday. She was taken by Ecan's warriors."

Rides-the-Wind bowed his old head and massaged his brow. "Unforeseen, that. Together she and I could have stopped this. A switching of Power, shifting the weave of life around us." He sighed. "But for good or ill?"

Pitch leaned forward. "Dogrib doesn't think they'll kill her. He said—"

"Kill *her*?" Rides-the-Wind inquired in a curious voice. "Blessed Spirits, Pitch, the fools have no idea what they've done. Depending on what they try to do to her, Dzoo might be tempted to make her own sack of fetishes. And if she does, may the gods help them."

Twenty-three

Rain Bear tugged his cape closed over his chest and sighed. From his perch on a flat boulder near the War Gods pillars, the distant ocean looked glorious, shimmering like an undulating blanket of liquid silver.

He'd spent all day going from one refugee camp to the next, speaking with the elders, coordinating with war chiefs, counting his warriors once, twice, again. The Raven People had the numbers, but they were unskilled. The North Wind People had trained warriors, men and women who'd spent their lives learning how to kill. He had fishermen, woodworkers, sea-grass weavers, and hunters. They had the passion for the moment, but would they hold when the spears began to fly and their friends were killed before their eyes?

Rain Bear shifted his gaze away from the island-dotted vista to watch Evening Star as she walked up the trail toward him. Luxurious red hair blew around her beautiful face, and her leather dress molded to her hips with each step in a manner that brought teasing images to his masculine thoughts. She was tall for a woman, but looked small striding between Hornet and Wolf Spider.

"Any sign of the boy yet?" Evening Star asked as she neared Rain Bear.

"No, and we've searched everywhere."

Evening Star slid onto the boulder beside him, and Rain Bear awkwardly glanced at the guards. Wolf Spider and Hornet pretended not to notice. Both young warriors had their elkhide hoods up. He couldn't see their faces, but he felt their interest. Wolf Spider's head kept turning his way. Was Evening Star oblivious to the effect she had on men? Having her close was like a Spirit plant surging through his veins.

"Didn't one of the villagers say he'd seen the boy?" She tucked a windblown lock of hair behind her ear.

"Yes, an old man named Black Rock." Rain Bear forced himself to study the rough terrain before him. "But it makes no sense. The boy's blind! How can he still be hidden? *Why* would he still be hiding? Hunger alone should have driven him out by now."

She studied him with those knowing blue eyes. "Terror, Chief, can be a persuasive motivator."

On the crest of the ridge to their right, tufts of fog curled around the gods. Massive and dark, the pillars really did resemble headless human bodies.

Her hair tugged loose from where she'd tucked it behind her ear and blew around until it tangled with her eyelashes. Rain Bear lifted a hand to brush it away. Then caught himself. It had been instinct . . . but it shocked him. Did he long to touch her so much? His hand hovered in front of her face for several instants before he withdrew it.

"Forgive me," he said.

"In another time and place, I would have been glad." Kindness filled her eyes as she attended to the wayward lock.

She turned to the distant ocean. "Is Pitch well enough to prepare the bodies of the dead?"

"He says he is. I'm not so sure. He's still fevered. Apparently, Rides-the-Wind offered to help, but Pitch considers it to be his responsibility."

A deep rumble of Thunderbirds came from somewhere out in the fog.

Evening Star said, "Rain Bear, if you were a frightened little boy, where would you hide?"

Rain Bear's gaze drifted over the steep rocky slopes. "During the attack, I suppose I'd hide in the rocks. After the attack, I'd return to the burned village and search every lodge looking for my father."

"He must have known the lodges were filled with dead people."

At death, the soul seeped out with the last breath, but it remained close to the body, not certain where to go or what to do until it was ritually prepared. Often the soul thought it was still alive and tried to speak with the living. Evening Star was right. Only a very foolish or desperate boy would dare risk having a lonely ghost tap him on the shoulder and start asking questions.

"And he's blind," he reminded her. "Maybe he's afraid to leave his hiding place for fear he might fall, or get lost?"

"That could be."

He looked down at the distant shoreline and could see the wide swath of muddy water that hemmed the beach. As the Ice Giants melted, more and more freshwater flooded the drainages and poured into the sea. The mud had already destroyed most of their shellfish beds and killed the algae and seaweed they used to gather. They could still trade for such items, but how long would that last? The mud dissipated as it flowed southward along the coast, but it still did damage.

Wind Woman swept the hair away from Evening Star's face. She tipped her chin up and closed her eyes, as though concentrating on the scent of the sea. "Two moons ago, when my village was destroyed, my baby was in my arms. I could hear my husband screaming behind me, ordering me to run. But there were too many of them; escape was cut off. Before it was over, my husband was killed before my eyes, and my daughter's screams haunted my ears. The only thing I knew for certain was that I was alone—truly alone for the first time in my life." She drew up her knees and propped her arms upon them. "That's how Tsauz is feeling now. No one, especially a child, should ever have to feel that way."

"We'll keep looking."

She rested her chin on her arms. "What is happening to us, Great Chief? Why are we doing this to ourselves?"

"Perhaps this is an age of madness, a shifting, a transition?"

She tilted her head to peer into his eyes. "Your people are still coming for the ceremonial tomorrow. They'll be packed shoulder to shoulder on this narrow mountaintop. If anyone finds the boy, he'll be torn to pieces."

"We'll find him before then." He hesitated. "Evening Star, what do you think Cimmis is planning?"

She straightened on the rock and turned to peer directly into his eyes. "I can tell you this: He did not attack War Gods Village just because Matron Weedis refused to pay the tribute she owed."

"Why else would he have attacked?

"It was meant to force you into a corner and discourage you from striking back."

Rain Bear's gaze drifted over the burned lodges below. Every time he looked at them, he imagined his own village in charred ruins, strewn with dead bodies. He could almost hear Cimmis whispering, *"Do you want Sandy Point Village to look like this? If you attack, I promise you it will."*

He asked, "If we capture Tsauz, what will Ecan do?"

As dusk turned to night, the warriors who stood guard began to light campfires. Orange dots glittered to life on the surrounding hills.

"Ecan is not a fool." She shivered, and Rain Bear wondered if it was from cold, or the strain of discussing Ecan. "He'll be crafty."

"Will he negotiate?"

"You mean will he agree to spare your village in return for his son's life?" Her delicate red brows pinched. "He might, but only as a diversion."

"A diversion?"

"Something to keep you busy while his personal assassins get in place." Gently, she said, "He'll try to kill your family, Rain Bear. Pick off your daughter first, or maybe your grandson, then your most trusted aides. Finally, they'll murder the village elders. Sooner or later, you will understand that it's cheaper to return the boy unharmed."

A cold wave seemed to flow out of his chest into his fingers and toes. "Perhaps I should kill the boy when we find him."

"If you can . . . you should."

It was the way she'd whispered the words. Utterly serious, as though she knew from experience. "Why do you say that?"

"Ecan will be betting that no matter what he's done to you, you can't kill an innocent child. He'll be counting on that. So you must decide now, before you find him, can you kill an innocent boy?"

Sunlight shone from her shell earrings and twinkled in her hair.

Rain Bear slid off the flat rock and walked a few paces away. Hornet and Wolf Spider watched him, faces expressionless.

Kill a blind boy? How? He wasn't that sort of man. And if he didn't kill the child? Suppose one of Talon's elders was murdered: He would demand that the boy be killed to punish Ecan. Rain Bear would then have to refuse. That would set one village against another. People would take sides. If they had managed to build an alliance, it would crumble to dust before his eyes.

He ran a hand through his long black hair. "Matron, I cannot tell you how grateful I am that you are here."

Evening Star gave him a weak smile. Very softly, she said, "You may not be, once you realize that *I* pose the same dilemma for you."

"You? Why?"

She climbed down off the rock. "Please, come with me. I have an idea about how to find Tsauz. We must speak with the orphans. Surely one of them noticed a strange child during the battle. Let's ask if they saw where he was hiding."

"I will never use you as a hostage."

"Won't you?" She looked at him from the corner of her eye. "I am Cimmis's niece. Though he may not care about me, there are other North Wind elders who do. So tell me, where do your loyalties lie, Rain Bear?"

Midday

*A*re *you afraid?"*

I listen to the seagulls crying on the river bank. There must be ten tens of them perched on the wind-smoothed rocks around us. Occasionally, they get into fights. One squeals and another flaps. Tomorrow, the children will run along the bank, searching for feathers and wisps of down to sew onto their clothing.

"No," I say. "I'm not afraid."

The old Soul Keeper shifts, as though that is the wrong answer, as though standing on the edge of Death, I should be afraid. "Fear is good, Chief. Don't shy away from it."

"Courage is better," I whisper.

I was a war chief for many summers. I have seen men lying prostrate on the battlefield, wounded and dying, screaming in fear. They terrified everyone around them. I have also seen men and women who did not cry out. Warriors in the truest sense, boldly standing up to Death, pulling it into them like a lover. They gave their friends strength.

I long for that kind of bravery.

It will not be easy to attain. My injuries are severe. The pain is already beyond imagining. Every time I breathe, broken fragments of rib restrict my lungs. I'm suffocating, slowly but surely.

"Do not crave courage so desperately," he says. "It is only when we are frightened that the gods know we love them."

I wheeze as I cautiously take a breath. "You tie fear and love together . . . like the severed ends of a grass cord."

"The cord was never severed."

I wonder about that. "Opposite ends, then."

"If you like."

"Any god," *I say defiantly,* "who requires that I feel . . . fear . . . to know that I love him . . . is cruel . . . A vindictive child masquerading as a god."

"Is he?" *he whispers, and I catch him looking up at the cottonwoods where eagles float as though weightless.* "If a dying man cries out for mercy—should he hate the gods for making him cry out? Or thank them?"

"That depends upon whether or not . . . they grant him mercy."

He expels an annoyed breath. "Seeking mercy is always good."

"Like fear?"

"Yes."

"Why?"

"Because men who do not seek mercy have no need of gods."

"My point exactly."

He leans over me, pulls the blanket up to cover my throat, and says, "They do not need gods, because they believe they *are* gods."

Twenty-four

That morning Hunter was on guard duty. He reached for another crab claw and sat back to watch the sun rise above the mountains. It shot rays of light like beams across the chilly winter sky. From his position on the hill above Wasp Village, he could look out across the round bark lodges to Mother Ocean. The water had just started to turn a pale pink. The waves glistened like the insides of abalone shells. He watched, a procession of canoes crest the lazy breakers as fishermen paddled out in the endless quest for fish and sea mammals.

Several small Raven People villages had located in the fertile valley, and shrines, studded with their Spirit Boards, perched on every hilltop. Dark lines of worshippers encircled them, waiting to offer their morning prayers to Raven.

In contrast he could hear Wasp Village's Starwatcher, her voice wavering as she stood beside Ecan and Sang the story of Old Woman Above. The morning ceremonies were a reminder of the differences between the people.

How could the Raven People have gotten it so wrong? Everyone knew that Old Woman Above carried the sun across the sky on her back. But somehow, the story had begun to circulate that instead, Raven had stolen the sun from a box in Old Woman Above's house and that he *flew* it across the sky each day. Nonsense!

He cracked the crab claw with his teeth and sucked the sweet meat out. While he chewed it, he smiled at the impossibility. Below him, in Wasp Village, the children had picked up the Song:

Old Woman Above lives in the sky with her granddaughter. Her
*   granddaughter. Her granddaughter.*
Every morning she leaves her house carrying the sun in a basket. A
*   basket. A basket.*
She comes home late at night with a backache. A backache. A bad
*   backache.*
Her granddaughter rubs it with duck oil. Duck oil. Duck oil.
But the oil is almost used up. Up. Up.
When it runs out Old Woman Above will die. Die. Die.
The world would come to an end. End, end, end.

The last words were called quickly, like a drumbeat.

Hunter chuckled. Some people worried about such curious things: the End of the World? He was far more concerned with where his next meal was coming from.

He sucked another crab claw and chewed the meat with his eyes closed. Delicious. The crabs had been boiled with ferns and had a wonderful tang. The matron of Wasp Village, Round Hoof, had truly seen to the comfort of Ecan's warriors. Hunter had slept in a lodge, on a soft stack of hides. Then, before dawn, slaves had delivered a basket of crabs and a big bowl of boiled seal. Both had tasted especially good after the long days on the war trail.

A group of young women walked out of one of the lodges carrying baskets. Their laughter rode the breeze as they fell into line and marched happily toward the central plaza fire.

The shape of Wasp Village was dictated by the long ridge on which it sat. The plaza lay between two lines of lodges that seemed to clutch the rocky ridgetop where it jutted out in a small peninsula. Trails led down the steep slopes to the wave-scrubbed rock and then to the beach.

He fingered his chin as he chewed. Rumors were circulating that the Council wanted to move the North Wind elders here, that they wanted to abandon Fire Village for the more defensible Wasp Village.

"They're crazy," he muttered. Sure, Wasp Village was easier to defend. Any approach by land was restricted to the ridge's narrow neck. And the steep trails leading down to the beach could be held by a handful of warriors. Assuming, of course, that Wasp Village had any warning of approaching danger.

To his left, more lodges—quarters for the slaves—sat atop a low bluff. They had shaded from blue to salmon with the dawn. Slaves climbed up the hill from the spring with water-filled bladders propped on their hips.

Hunter finished his crabs and wiped his hands on grease-streaked buckskin leggings.

Ecan, having finished the morning ceremonies, stood beside Matron Round Hoof outside her lodge. As always, he looked regal. He'd pulled his hair away from his face and coiled it into a bun at the back of his head. The style accentuated the sharp angles of his handsome face. He waved his hands emphatically, and even across the distance Hunter could see her expression of distaste.

Hunter laughed. Round Hoof had a fuzz of white hair clinging to her age-spotted scalp and a nose like a squashed beetle. In all the time he'd known her, he'd never seen her smile. She always wore a dour, vaguely threatening expression. The more Ecan talked, the more Round Hoof scowled. If only she would—

"Hunter?" a voice called.

He turned to see skinny Thunder Boy climbing the hill. The youth had an odd, melon-shaped skull and wasn't known for being particularly intelligent. His shoulder-length black hair flopped around his chin.

"What is it?"

Thunder Boy trotted toward him. "Deer Killer wants you to come immediately."

"Deer Killer?" Hunter rose and quickly strode down the hill. "He's supposed to be keeping an eye on the witch."

Thunder Boy said, "He sent me to get you. Something's wrong with Dzoo."

"What?"

Thunder Boy gave him a blank look. "I don't know."

"Go tell Wind Scorpion. He's supposed to be in charge."

"He's not around."

"He's never around! The coward."

Hunter picked up his weapons and followed Thunder Boy down through the trees to the village. It had been such a nice, peaceful morning. Now the breakfast he'd so enjoyed churned in his stomach as he hurried toward the lodge where they'd imprisoned Dzoo.

Ecan, with his guard, Black Stone, behind him, was still arguing with Round Hoof. The Starwatcher shifted to study him. Hunter tried to act nonchalant, but Ecan seemed to sense something amiss. The Starwatcher's gaze might have been a physical thing as it burned through Hunter's back.

Dzoo's lodge sat on the farthest point above where rolling surf crashed on black rocks. From this height, Hunter could see a scalloped line of sea foam and glittering shells that marked the night's high tide.

"Thunder Boy? Guards are supposed to be standing outside her lodge. Where's Deer Killer?"

"Inside, I think."

"Inside?" Ecan had threatened to roast Hunter's liver if any of his warriors so much as laid a finger on the woman. He'd figured that ordering them to stay outside would alleviate some of their natural male desires. What they didn't have to stare at, they couldn't want.

Hunter stalked to the door. "Deer Killer?"

A pathetic voice answered, "In here, Hunter."

Hunter ducked beneath the flap and had to push himself between five warriors crowded near the door. One held a guttering torch that cast a dim light over the dark interior. Deer Killer looked like a whipped puppy. Meeting Hunter's eyes he swallowed hard.

With a glance, Hunter reassured himself that the figure standing in the back was Dzoo. Her clothes were still on, she was obviously alive, so why was Deer Hunter looking as if his guts had gone to water? "Is there a problem?"

The other warriors faded away—except Deer Killer, who stood with his jaw clenched and his spear clutched in a death grip. Damp strands of long black hair framed his thin face.

"Hunter"—he wet his lips—"I don't know how this could have happened. I swear we have been here every moment! No one passed us!"

"What's wrong?"

Deer Killer gestured toward the far side of the lodge. "See for yourself."

Hunter shoved him out of the way. "Give me that torch."

Deer Killer pulled it away from the man who held it and thrust it into Hunter's hand.

In the flickering light Dzoo had her head tipped back, as though studying something on the domed roof. Her long red braid hung down the back of her rumpled dress. In the torch's gleam, her beautiful face looked eerie, inhuman, as though carved from translucent chalcedony.

"Witch?" Hunter lifted the torch higher. To his right, he saw her pack and cape, and a small bowl sitting on the floor.

She turned so slowly it was hard to see her move. Then she whispered in sibilant and totally incomprehensible words.

"Witch, I don't understand. If that's the language of the Striped Dart People, I don't know it. Speak to me like a human being!"

Her black gaze drifted aimlessly over the bare walls, then came to rest on Hunter. As her gaze sucked at his, he swore his heart tried to scramble out of his chest.

Deer Killer whispered, "I give you my oath, Hunter, I did not abandon my post, not even for an instant!"

Hunter swung around. "I don't see the problem. Dzoo's here, she's alive, and—"

"Her *ropes*, Hunter. They're gone!"

Hunter whirled to look. He hadn't even noticed. He'd bound her himself, but she stood with her hands free at her sides. Bloody wounds encircled her ankles and wrists.

"Who untied her?" Hunter demanded.

Deer Killer shook his head, and the warriors behind him began to mutter, "Not me." "I didn't do it." "I wouldn't touch her for all the—"

Deer Killer said, "I stood right here all night!"

"You stupid fool!" Hunter gestured to two of the milling warriors. "Get in there and retie her. Do it right!"

"But, Hunter, she's a witch. What if she uses her Powers to change me into a woman, or a wolf spider or—"

"Get over there, or by the Blessed Ones, you'll rue the day you were made a man!" Hunter stuffed the torch into Thunder Boy's hand. "Go on!"

Deer Killer edged across the lodge as though walking through a sea of rattlesnakes.

Hunter muttered, "I tied her up like I've never tied anyone before. I pulled the ropes so tightly her ankles and wrists bled. Then I used a third rope to tie her ankles and wrists together behind her back. She was trussed up like a dog over a spit! If she got loose, it was because you were as negligent as a— What's the matter?"

Deer Killer looked around the bare beaten floor. "Where are the ropes?"

Hunter's brows lowered. "They must be here. Where else could they be?"

"I tell you, there are no ropes here. And I don't see any loose dirt where she might have buried them."

One of the warriors snickered, and Hunter glared at him. "The rest of you, go gather your things! We will be on the road to Fire Village shortly."

Hunter turned back to glare at Deer Killer. "Am I the only one here with wits? Give me that torch!"

Thunder Boy held it out in a trembling fist.

Hunter tugged it away. "I'm surrounded by idiots!"

"She hasn't blinked since we got here," Deer Killer said. "I've heard people say she looks into that bowl to send her souls flying."

"Just find the ropes!" Hunter walked across the lodge, hit her pack with a fist, then lifted and threw her buffalo cape against the wall. Finally, he leaned over the bowl. He froze when he saw someone looking back, then realized it was his own reflection. He dumped it out onto the dirt. "It's just water, you brainless rabbit."

"But . . ." Deer Killer cautiously looked around. "Where are the ropes? If she just untied herself and took a drink from that bowl, where—"

"Have you considered that she might have stuffed them into her clothes?" Hunter bravely stalked over to stand in front of Dzoo. He looked her over carefully, trying to see a bulge beneath her dress where she might have hidden them.

"Find them," Hunter said. "She might use them to strangle you the next time you sleep through your duty." He motioned. "Search her."

Deer Killer hesitated. "Me? Search her? A witch? What if she . . . she . . ."

"*What's going on?*" Ecan's deep voice called from beyond the lodge flap. The white hem of Ecan's cape brushed the sand like gossamer wings as he ducked through the door. A faint hissing filled the air as he came forward. Wind Scorpion, returned from wherever he had been, walked behind him, his pinched expression reminding Hunter of a starved fox's.

"Starwatcher," Hunter said, and bowed. "We don't know how it happened, but our prisoner managed to untie herself in the night, and we can't find her ropes."

Ecan glared into Hunter's eyes for so long and with such deliberation Hunter knew the Starwatcher must be contemplating exactly how to murder him.

Ecan quietly took the torch from Hunter's hand and ordered, "Get out of my way."

Hunter stepped to the side, and Ecan fixed on Dzoo.

Hunter exchanged a glance with Deer Killer. The warrior had his hand on his belted knife and looked like he longed to slit his own throat before Ecan could order it done. Wind Scorpion was watching Dzoo through narrowed eyes, a slight smile on his lips, as if in anticipation.

Ecan gracefully walked across the lodge. "Dzoo?"

She didn't move.

Ecan's brows lowered. "There are tears on her cheeks. What happened in here? Did you harm her?"

"No, Starwatcher!" Hunter flapped his arms helplessly.

Deer Killer shook his head vigorously, but Wind Scorpion just stared at Dzoo as if seeing her for the first time.

Ecan watched a single tear trace a silver line down Dzoo's cheek, then said, "*Find* the ropes. Retie her hands. Leave her feet unbound. We will be on the trail in less than half a hand of time." He lifted a finger and pointed. "You, Hunter, search her for the ropes."

He ground his teeth before saying, "W-why can't you do it, Starwatcher? You have great Spirit Power. I am just a common warrior."

Ecan's eyes blazed.

Wind Scorpion said, "I'll do it."

He knelt before Dzoo and spread his huge hands, but couldn't seem to force his fingers to make the actual contact.

"What's wrong?" Ecan said.

"Nothing, it's just . . . just . . ." A fierce shiver ran through Wind Scorpion's body; then his fingers moved lightly up and down her legs, almost caressing, searching for anything amiss. He patted down her back and ran his hands over her arms. He took a deep breath as he faced her, avoiding her eyes, and still shaking, let his fingers trace the curves of her breasts and belly. Finally, he stood up. "She has . . . Gods! She has no ropes, Starwatcher."

Hunter watched in awe as Wind Scorpion burst for the door on wobbling legs, his body shaking so violently that he looked sick.

By Old Woman Above, what kind of Power did the witch have, anyway? Wind Scorpion had always set Hunter's teeth on edge. There was something about him—a dangerous presence about the man—that made Hunter's skin crawl. And Dzoo had turned him into a quivering wreck?

As Ecan turned to Hunter, his cape swirled in the torchlight. "What happened to the ropes?"

Deer Killer hissed, "Maybe she changed herself into a bird last night and carried them far away before she dropped them? I've heard that she—"

"And maybe I'll fry your heart for breakfast because you took them!" Ecan shouted.

"Me?" Deer Killer cried.

"Just tie her up!" Ecan shouted as he swept past Deer Killer and ducked out into the morning.

Hunter waited until he was gone; then he forced himself to breathe for ten heartbeats before saying, "Remove your belt. Use it to tie her hands. And tie them well!"

In the end Hunter had to do it himself. He ducked out of the lodge as the first rays of sunlight bathed the village. To his surprise, Wind Scorpion crouched to one side, his back bent. He held his hands cupped before him, his head down as he sniffed at them as though to catch the faintest of scents. His sweat smelled pungent.

"Are you all right?"

Wind Scorpion stared vacantly at Wasp Village, then whispered, "She wasn't crying until Ecan entered the lodge, was she?"

"No." Hunter gave the old warrior an askance look. "But then I feel the same way when he enters my lodge."

Wind Scorpion rubbed his forehead. "I pray she didn't stuff those ropes . . . She is so much more than I thought she was."

Twenty-five

The young warrior called Kit Fox stood off to the side, his knees shaking as he watched Sleeper examine Crater's bloody body. The man lay on his back, blood running from his nose and mouth. Crater's eyes were wide open, staring blankly at the orange gleam of dawn that sheathed the hills.

They had made camp in the trees on a bench above Wasp Valley. From that vantage point, they had been able to see the fires in Wasp Village where it jutted out into the sea. Now, as the morning sun brightened, they could make out several small villages of Raven People, as well as the slave quarters that served Wasp Village. Finding Crater had been a surprise that shocked each of the remaining warriors to the core.

"His skull is cracked," Sleeper said. "He was struck from behind."

"But I heard nothing, War Chief!" Kit Fox blurted. "I only got a glimpse. The light was bad!" He hesitated. "It . . . it looked . . ."

"Yes, go on."

Kit Fox winced, fearing the war chief's reaction. "It looked like a huge coyote. The head, the ears . . ."

Sleeper's hide cape flapped around his long legs as he stood. He searched the faces of the four remaining warriors. When they'd left War Gods Village, they'd been ten. They were being picked off one by one by an assassin who made no sounds and left no footprints. Panic sparkled in each man's eyes.

They'd expected to be the hunters, waiting for an opportunity to kill Ecan, not the prey.

In the beautiful valley below, Ecan's warriors moved along the trails that encircled Wasp Village. Could one man be doing this? One of Ecan's warriors? Why send one man when he could simply turn his entire war party loose to hunt them down? And more to the point, after all the care they had taken to reach this place, how had the killer located them? It was enough to send shivers through the most hardened of veterans.

Sleeper frowned at the corpse. "When it's fully light, we'll try to track him down. We'll find him. I swear it!"

The warriors glanced uneasily back and forth. A quick look was all that it took to see their flagging courage. If he pushed, they'd break and run.

Sleeper walked a few paces away, and his gaze moved over the leafless alders, as though imagining every dark branch where a man might hide. A magnificent vista of dawn-tinted hills veined by dark drainages stretched before them. He looked eastward up Wasp Valley toward the rolling base of Fire Mountain, two days' run away.

Through gritted teeth, Sleeper hissed, "Very well, Ecan, you and your mysterious Coyote win this time. But we're coming for you. You just wait and see. When we do, I'm going to have a hand in bringing you down."

He turned to his men. "Come. We're going back to report to Chief Goldenrod."

Dogrib and five guards surrounded Pitch and Roe, monitoring the crowd and giving them the privacy they needed for the ritual preparations. Pitch supervised while Roe pulled up the edges of the worn hide and deftly stitched it closed around the headless body of Matron Weedis's son, Flying Squirrel.

People clambered over the mountaintop, and more kept coming. Many of them had been traveling for days or even moons, by foot or canoe, to get here for the ceremonial. Despite the devastated village around them, the War God pillars still stood tall and massive—and that's what they'd really come to see.

As Roe sewed, Pitch felt ill. Horror was such a powerful weapon. Every person who looked upon a headless body quaked deep down in his soul. Didn't Cimmis realize that horror engendered wrath the likes of which none of them had ever experienced before? Even Roe, ordinarily a calm-minded woman, had her teeth clenched; it set her jaw at an odd angle.

"Are you all right?" Pitch gently asked and reached out with his good hand to touch her long red hair.

She looked up. "I want every one of them dead, Pitch."

He let his hand fall. "Your lineage is North Wind."

"The Council declared my mother Outcast when she fell in love with Father. I will make certain, when the time comes, that Stonecrop is adopted into Father's clan. That way he never has to suffer because of my mother's blood."

As though embarrassed by the vehemence in her voice, she lowered her gaze and continued working the bone needle through the hide. The young man's neck gradually disappeared as Roe sewed the shroud closed.

When she'd finished, Pitch straightened and stretched his aching back muscles. The pain in his shoulder wound had grown fiery.

Roe eased his shirt down to study his bandage. "Oh, Pitch, it's bleeding. Let's stop for a while."

"No." Pitch gestured to Matron Weedis's headless body a few hands away. "I want to finish the Healer's purification first. Then I'll rest. I promise."

Pitch rose and led the way to Matron Weedis. As he crouched by her side, Dogrib stepped forward, moving around in front of them as if to form their personal barricade. His long white hair glistened in the afternoon light. No matter how many times Pitch looked at Dogrib, he felt awe at the man's snowy white hair and pink skin.

Roe tenderly touched Matron Weedis's withered arm. "She was a great woman. A fine Healer. I'll miss her."

Pitch removed a small paint bowl from his waist pack. "If you will paint rain on her legs, I'll paint stars on her arms."

Roe dipped her forefinger into the bowl and carefully painted wavy red lines down Matron Weedis's skinny legs.

"Take your time," Pitch said. "We want Gutginsa, who guards the entry to the House of Air, to know that she is truly one of the North Wind People, a relative of the Star People."

Roe's brows lowered. "What do you think would happen if we sent her soul to the Underwater House where the Raven People go? Would her ghost come back to harm us?"

Pitch tilted his head uncertainly. If the Council ever discovered that he'd Sung one of the North Wind People to the Underwater House, they would leave no stone unturned until they found Pitch and killed his entire family. Sending a dead person's soul to the wrong afterworld ensured it would be shunned and abused for eternity.

Pitch said, "I don't think we have the right to decide, Roe. All of her life, she has expected to go live in the House of Air with her relatives. We should respect her wishes."

Roe petted Matron Weedis's arm. "Yes, you're right. It's just that I would like to spend time with her in the afterlife. I'm sorry we will be in different houses."

"That's the way it has always been. They have their places, and we have ours."

Pitch finished the stars on the matron's arms and awkwardly removed a coil of twine and six feathers from his pack. "Here are the feathers."

Roe reached over and pulled his obsidian knife from his belt. She cut the twine into several lengths and replaced the knife in its sheath.

As she tied a feather to Weedis's thumb, Pitch said, "These feathers will give her the ability to fly through the three Above Worlds, and finally to the House of Air."

Dogrib glanced over his shoulder and said, "I don't know why anyone would wish to turn into a star. Spending eternity in darkness sounds depressing to me."

Pitch smiled as Roe tied feathers around the matron's ankles and wrists and then slipped a length of twine beneath her back and tied the last feather over her heart."

Pitch said, "When Sister Moon rises between the stone bodies of the war gods tonight, these seed feathers will sprout, and in a blink her whole body will be covered with feathers. She will have soft gray wings, just like Mourning Dove who gave the feathers, and she will soar away to the first Above World."

When they'd finished, Pitch touched Roe. "We must now care for our own souls. Follow me. Do as I do."

They pulled their clothing off and stood naked in the cold. Roe looked beautiful, perfect. In comparison, Pitch looked as skinny as a drowned pack rat, with trickles of watery blood running down his thin arm from the bandage.

Pitch led her to the fire, where a large basket of shredded cedar bark sat. He sprinkled a fistful over the fire and as the purifying smoke rose, said, "Make sure you scoop the smoke over every part of you, to wash away any evil Spirits who have been attracted by the smell of death."

As the fragrant smoke bathed him, Pitch felt better. He reached for a clean knee-length shirt and dress that lay folded on the ground.

He handed Roe the beautiful leather dress covered with circlets of shell.

Roe slipped it on and smoothed it over her hips. Pitch stared at her with longing before reaching to stroke her hair.

"Before you put your shirt on, Pitch, let me tend your wound."

He nodded wearily and tossed their old clothes onto the flames. "We must not couple for three days."

Dogrib's head jerked up in horror. "That doesn't include me, does it?"

"It does. And the other warriors in your group as well."

"Are you joking?" Dogrib gaped in alarm.

"No women for three days."

"Blessed Ancestors, why not?"

"It's a final precaution against roaming evil. If some malingering Spirit sees you coupling, it might take the opportunity to sneak into your penis and live there. Once there, the Spirits eat away at the flesh, leaving a mangled, shriveled-up—"

"I understand!" Dogrib's knees seemed to turn inward, and the muscles in his legs tightened. "Why didn't you tell me that before we started? Algae is expecting me tonight."

"Well, just explain to her."

Roe added, "She'll understand. Women are naturally predisposed to distrust a man's penis—let alone one festering with pus."

Dogrib walked away with his shoulders hunched, as if something were bothering him.

The moss-covered stones that lined the trail to War Gods Village looked like bright green fur balls. White Stone stepped around them as he led Red Dog up the trail to War Gods Village. From their position, near the crest of the mountain, White Stone could gaze out to the ocean. The late-afternoon gleam painted an orange swath across the slate blue water. He could see the islands in the distance. Some of the islands he had camped upon as a boy had vanished in his lifetime. His favorite, Little Snake Island, was now awash, visible only as a break in the irregular line of swells.

It was the first time he truly understood that the sea level really was rising. It made the stories of the world changing suddenly and brutally real. His heart skipped.

"I don't think this is very wise, War Chief," Red Dog whispered, and stepped around a mossy boulder. "Wouldn't it be smarter to wait until the bulk of the crowd passes before we go to the village?"

"We are trying to look like worshippers," White Stone answered, annoyed. "Keep moving."

White Stone shouldered his way through the crowd. Every refugee for a half moon's walk had to be there. It astonished him. They packed the burned village and filled the narrow trail that followed the spine of the mountain. He turned and could see a serpentine line of people all the way down to the far shore. It didn't seem to matter to them that they had to tramp through the charred wreckage of lodges, or that the sickeningly sweet scent of burned human bodies clung to the air. They all wished to be as close to the sacred pillars as possible.

Yes, the end of the world, indeed.

Like many of the faithful, White Stone and Red Dog had painted their faces in elaborate designs. Red Dog had yellow circles around his eyes, and one half of his face was black, the other white, symbolizing Sister Moon at midcycle. White Stone had chosen to paint his entire face white, then place red and black dots on his forehead and cheeks. The dots represented the Star People who would guard Sister Moon's ascent that night. Few people would recognize them beneath the heavy paint, but they also wore their hoods up to help shield their faces.

Red Dog slowed to allow White Stone to catch up, and whispered, "Rain Bear is taking no chances."

Warriors stood on every high point, on cliffs and boulders; they even perched in the tops of trees. Others worked through the crowd, their red headbands marking them as ceremonial guards. Spears and war clubs filled their hands, and bone stilettos hung from their belts.

"We deceived him once," White Stone murmured. "It won't happen again."

"But why didn't he just cancel the Moon Ceremonial?"

"How could he? Many of these people have been walking for days. If they'd arrived and discovered the ritual canceled there would have been an uproar."

White Stone watched two shapely young women walk by. Both carried infants in their arms and had war clubs hanging from their belts.

The taller woman glared at the charred remains of Matron Weedis's lodge and said, "I pray the gods tear their testicles out of their sacks for what they did here."

"And feed them to the village dogs," the other woman added. "The filthy murderers."

The hatred made White Stone's gut squirm. He waited until they passed, then whispered, "Keep your head down."

"I will," Red Dog managed through gritted teeth, "but Blessed Spirits, if we're discovered, promise you'll kill me before the women can get ahold of me."

They moved into the plaza with the crowd, and White Stone noticed the clothing. He saw faded red capes and holey yellow moccasins, beaded headbands with more than half the beads missing, and old rabbit-fur shawls that looked mangy. No exotic stones or shells sparkled.

"These poor desperate people have worn their best, but it's worse than the slaves wear in Fire Village."

Red Dog grunted and whispered, "Makes you wonder what those old women in the Council think these people are hoarding, doesn't it?"

Evening Star stood on the far side of the plaza and was speaking to an elderly woman. What a stunning beauty she was. Her waist-length hair had been freshly washed and hung over her elkhide cape in thick red waves. She looked pale, weary, and completely enchanting. From the moment he'd first seen her, White Stone had thought her the most attractive woman on earth. What a shame that she'd ended up as Ecan's toy.

"Let's work our way up the slope," he said as a reminder they had a job to do.

White Stone eased through the sea of people and ascended the trail beyond. He climbed onto a rock and stood looking down upon the gathering.

Red Dog climbed next to him. As the crowd eddied, people moved to within a few hands of them. Were they safe here, at the edge? Did the distance and face paint grant them anonymity?

Four rows of people encircled the plaza. Children sat in front, closest to the fire; a boy and girl appeared to be having fights with carved wooden dolls. Behind them, a row of elders sat on hides; then men and women stood behind the elders. Finally, a row of warriors kept watch over the plaza.

The ceremonial would not begin until sunset. That gave White Stone time to just watch. He studied the children sitting around the plaza. He didn't see Tsauz, but he noticed several children kneeling at the northeastern corner of the village with a big man. His movements were familiar.

"Is that Rain Bear?" He gestured with his chin. Back when Rain Bear had been a warrior in Fire Village, he and Red Dog had been friends.

Red Dog examined the man's elkhide cape and long black braid. "He moves like Rain Bear, but I can't tell. What's he doing? Can you see?"

White Stone climbed higher into the rocks to get a better view of the plaza. "It's him."

Rain Bear put an arm around one little boy's back and pointed to a line of dead dogs that lay on the ground. The boy gestured to several and spoke to Rain Bear, as though identifying them. Another child, a girl with long black hair, stepped forward, crying, and petted one of the animals. Rain Bear smoothed her hair and said something to her. She nodded and ran away.

"What's he doing?" Red Dog repeated.

"The children are telling him about the dogs that were killed during the battle."

"Why?"

White Stone rubbed his jaw. "I don't know."

Two guards with red headbands walked to within a body's length of White Stone.

"*When* we catch them, Lynx," the first man said, "I plan to stake White Stone to the ground, slit open his belly, and boil his guts while he's still alive."

White Stone pulled his hood lower and turned away slightly, as though concentrating on the pillars up the slope.

Lynx grinned. "You will have to beat me to it. I plan to cut out his kidneys a little piece at a time and eat them before his eyes. I saw a warrior do that to one of the Cougar People once. It was amazing. Using a white-hot stone to sear the blood vessels, he kept him alive for three days."

The first guard grunted and scanned the crowd. His gaze fixed on Red Dog. White Stone's heart felt squeezed. After what seemed an eternity, the two guards moved on.

"Come on," Red Dog whispered. "Let's go higher. I don't like being this close."

Rain Bear glanced at Evening Star, then pointed to a black puppy with a white face. It wasn't dead, but would be soon. Someone had shoved a spear through its belly. Dirt crusted the blood-caked entrails protruding from the wound. "What about this dog, Wood Quill?"

The little girl twisted the end of her long braid and studied the dog with glistening eyes. "I don't know this puppy. He didn't live here."

Rain Bear patted her back. "Sunfeather told me the same thing. I thank you. You can go back to your grandfather now."

Wood Quill turned and dashed away through the crowd. When she'd shouldered her way into the ring of elders, she climbed into an old man's lap.

Rain Bear gazed at the western horizon. Raven had almost finished flying the sun to the sea. Barely a hand of time remained before Sister Moon's appearance.

A memory floated, that of a little boy with a pack on his back, and the button nose of a puppy barely visible from within. He gently picked up the black puppy with the white face. The beautiful little dog had a pointed nose and spotted ears. It whimpered softly.

Rain Bear petted him. "I know," he said as he carried the puppy through the plaza and down the trail away from the burned lodges. "I promise I will end this pain for you. Very soon."

Twenty-six

"T sauz?" Rain Bear called. "Tsauz, if you can hear me, I found your puppy!"

Rain Bear carried the dog down the trail away from the burned lodges. All day long, Evening Star had walked the mountaintop with the children, hunting for Ecan's son. They hadn't found a single track.

Rain Bear held the little dog close, wondering who had speared it and why. In the heat of battle, a warrior might kill a dog that leaped for his throat, but he wouldn't waste a spear thrust on a puppy—and none of Ecan's warriors had stayed long enough after the fight to prepare a meal, so he doubted the little dog had been targeted for food.

Not only that . . . Rain Bear fingered the dark red paint that encircled the wound. It had come off the spear. The few times he'd seen ground cedar-bark paint, it had been on special ritual tools, consecrated for killing witches. Ordinary warriors wouldn't touch such things.

Five or six people in Fire Village used cedar-bark paint—Cimmis, the clan elders, and Ecan.

He took the trail through the burned guard post. In the past ten hands of time, snow and ash had been trampled into the mud until they'd formed a dark slimy wallow. The mud sucked at his moccasins as he walked through. Just beyond the smoldering lodge, he stopped and studied the rocks that rimmed the mountain trail.

"Tsauz? I'm here! Can you hear me?"

Rain Bear gently placed the puppy on a stone with his nose pointed to the north and his furry tail stretched out straight behind him. The puppy whimpered.

Rain Bear stroked his side, and called, "Your little black-and-white puppy is right on the edge of the cliff! He was speared during the battle. He's dying, Tsauz. If you wish to say good-bye to him, do it now. I promise it is safe for you to come for your friend."

The guard on the point to Rain Bear's left turned. Rain Bear lifted a hand, motioning him to silence. The man lifted a hand in return.

An enormous crowd had gathered on the mountain slope between the burned village and the War God pillars, but here, lower on the mountain, and within sight of the charred bodies, he stood alone.

Rain Bear walked to the cliff and crouched down. The bitter fumes of burned wood and scorched hides stung his nose.

Near the pillars, people began Singing the Death Song.

Rain Bear swiveled to look. As Pitch led the procession up the slope at a slow, resolute pace, eight people followed him, carrying the North Wind People's burial shrouds on their shoulders. Matron Weedis and her son would soon be on their way to the first of the Above Worlds.

Rain Bear propped his war club on his knees and stared out at the ocean. The tide was coming in. The waves had grown violent, battering the shore. He sighed and concentrated on the weariness that numbed his body. He hadn't slept all the way through a night for three moons. It felt good to just sit and watch the water.

Movement caught his eye.

He sat perfectly still as the boy crawled up from the ledges beneath the cliff and used his hands to feel his way. He had his mouth open, and tears coated his young face. Crying without making a sound.

"Runner?" the boy whispered.

The puppy lifted his head, whimpering through the pain in its little body. When he glimpsed Tsauz, his tail thumped the stone.

Tsauz hurried, patting the ground until he felt the dog's pointed nose; then he pulled the puppy into his arms.

"I'm sorry, Runner," he sobbed. "I'm so sorry. I should have hunted for you. I knew I should have. I was just scared."

He kissed the puppy's icy ears and held him close. The puppy's tail wagged again, and Tsauz sobbed against Runner's furry neck.

Rain Bear waited patiently, his heart heavy at the sight. What kind of creatures were humans that here, in the shadow of terrible atrocity, one little boy could bear so much love for a dog?

"I made something for you," Tsauz whispered, and drew a prayer stick and six eagle feathers from his belt. "I heard your souls calling to me."

The sky had turned a pale shade of lavender, and it blushed color into the feathers, making them look like sculpted amethyst.

One by one, Tsauz tucked the eagle feathers into Runner's ears and slipped two between the toes of his front feet, then two in the toes of his back feet.

Rain Bear had never seen the ritual performed for a dog before. The boy was making certain that Runner could find his way to the North Wind People's afterlife in the sky. He must have seen his father preparing the dead for the journey.

"I'm sorry I don't know the Songs, Runner. But when I get home, I will find a Singer to Sing for you. I promise." Tears flooded his cheeks.

Tsauz gently rested Runner on the stone, then got on his knees and turned toward the pillars. Sister Moon remained hidden, but her gleam cast a bright silver halo around the stone bodies of the twin war gods. Could the boy see it?

Tsauz held the prayer stick to his lips and breathed his prayer into the wood: "Blessed Ancestors, please protect Runner. He's been a good friend to me." He placed the stick on Runner's side and choked out, "I love you, Runner. If you see Father in the Above Worlds, please tell him I'm all right."

Rain Bear softly said, "Your father is both alive and well, Tsauz."

Tsauz whirled around, and his blind eyes searched for Rain Bear's voice. His expression twisted with a powerful mixture of fear and hope. He wet his lips, as though afraid to speak, but he said, "Where is he? Where's my father?"

Rain Bear slowly walked down the rocky trail. At the sound of his approaching steps, Tsauz started to shake. *"Where's my father?"*

"By now, he should almost be back to Fire Village."

"Who are you?"

When Rain Bear hesitated, Tsauz let out a muffled shriek, jumped to his feet, and ran.

"No, Tsauz! Don't run!"

Rain Bear pounded after the boy.

Tsauz charged headlong over the edge of the cliff. His feet

churned air; then his body somersaulted down the steep incline like a thrown rock, striking boulders and old tree stumps. New saplings slapped him in the face and raked at his arms and legs. When he hit a huge fir tree, it knocked the wind out of him.

Rain Bear lunged down the slope after him, ordering, "Lie still! Don't move. I'm not going to hurt you!"

The boy screamed, stumbled to his feet, and careened down the slope again.

Rain Bear caught up with him and grabbed Tsauz's flailing arm.

"No, no!" Tsauz lashed out, striking Rain Bear with his fists. "Let me go! *Let me go!*"

"Stop it! Listen to me!" He knelt in front of Tsauz and grabbed both his arms, holding them tight. "I'm not going to hurt you. Do you hear me? I won't hurt you!"

Dogrib and two other warriors skidded down the slope and surrounded them.

Rain Bear held up a hand to tell them to stay back.

Tsauz cried, "You're going to kill me! You're my enemy!"

"Tsauz, please, I'm not your enemy. I wish to help you."

"Then let me *go home!*" The last word turned into a wail.

"I will . . . when it's safe. But for now, please listen to me. I am Rain Bear, chief of Sandy Point Village. After you've eaten and warmed yourself before the fire, we will talk about how to get you home."

The boy's eyes widened at Rain Bear's name.

Rain Bear said, "Do you remember me?"

Tsauz swallowed hard and nodded.

"Good. I'm going to give you my oath, Tsauz, that I will not harm you. Nor will I allow anyone to harm you. Do you understand what a chief's oath means?"

In a very small voice, he answered, "Yes," and clutched Rain Bear's cape tightly. "Please take me home."

Rain Bear motioned for the warriors to back away and said, "I will, but first I'm going to lead you up to the village and get you a warm blanket and a plate of food; then we will talk if you wish, or you can sleep and we will talk tomorrow. Is that acceptable?"

Tsauz tipped his face up, nervously wet his lips, and whimpered, "Yes, but . . . could I hold Runner? Please. He's hurt. He needs me."

Rain Bear looked at Dogrib. "Bring the puppy to Tsauz. And be gentle. He's dying."

"Yes, my Chief."

Dogrib trotted away.

Tsauz kept his fist twined in Rain Bear's cape as they started back up the steep slope.

Hallowed gods," White Stone said to Red Dog. "He has the boy."

Red Dog spun around to look, and the entire crowd seemed to spin with him. Voices rose, wondering what was happening, asking who the boy was.

It took only instants before the name "Tsauz" hissed through the ceremonial.

Rain Bear removed his cape and slipped it around Tsauz's narrow shoulders. The boy shivered as though the sudden warmth tingled his souls. Rain Bear was speaking to him. White Stone could see his lips moving, but Tsauz didn't answer; he just clutched the limp body of his puppy in his arms as they climbed the trail.

Red Dog said, "There's nothing we can do now. Let's get out of here! If we try to take the boy, we'll have ten tens of warriors on our backs beating our brains out with war clubs."

Red Dog was right, but if they returned without the boy, Ecan might very well order them gutted.

"Let us watch for a time longer," White Stone said. "We may yet have our chance."

"Don't forget those women," Red Dog reminded.

Gasps of awe went up, and the crowd turned back to the pillars.

A sliver of Sister Moon's face appeared between the pillars, and light flowed down the mountain in a glistening silver wave. White Stone's face slackened. The huge dark bodies of the war gods seemed to be guarding Sister Moon as she rose into the evening sky. From all the surrounding high points, signal fires blazed to life, telling people in distant areas that here, at the edge of their world, Sister Moon stood shoulder to shoulder with the War Gods. For these few precious moments, everything was right and good. The gods had not abandoned them.

White Stone could not take his eyes from the sight. Across the slope, people reached out to the person closest to them, touching hands or embracing loved ones. He turned to say something to Red Dog, but found the old warrior gazing down the slope at Rain Bear and the boy.

Tsauz had stopped dead in his tracks. The long shadows cast by the pillars resembled arms, holding the boy. His upturned face glowed radiantly in the moonglow.

"Look how Sister Moon favors him," Red Dog whispered. "She seems to be shining directly on him!"

Stunned voices rose. People pointed at Tsauz.

White Stone said, "Dressed in Rain Bear's cape, he looks like a young war god himself, doesn't he?"

Red Dog ground his teeth for a time before responding, "Yes, which means they will be watching him like Eagle does Mouse, expecting him to do something gloriously surprising. Which means we'll never be able to get close to him." He glanced around, eyes fixing on the two young women with war clubs. "Let's leave, War Chief! While we still have the chance."

People descended the mountain trail, slowly at first, then faster, as though each wished to be the first to touch the favored child. It became a mad rush. As Red Dog and White Stone watched, a wall of humanity coalesced around Tsauz. The boy pressed closer to Rain Bear, who drew his war club and used it to shove people back.

White Stone murmured, "You're right. We've lost him. Let's go."

"You go first," Red Dog said. "I will follow in a short while. It will be better if they do not see us leave together."

"Yes, all right. I'll meet you in the alder grove at the foot of the mountain."

Red Dog nodded.

White Stone eased away through the crowd, a tickling fear in his guts.

"*Run!*" a voice called from deep in his imagination.

But he wouldn't. He wasn't that brave.

Twenty-seven

The deep blue of dawn dappled Dzoo's face, waking her, but she didn't open her eyes. She lay on the sand, her bound hands in front of her. A few steps away, near the spring, men talked in low voices. She smelled smoke, but there was something else in the air: a cold dark scent, like the air from a deep cave that never sees light.

Coyote? Is that you? I've felt your hunger pulling at the edges of my soul.

Someone breathed.

Dzoo opened her eyes. The talking ceased.

Four men crouched around a small fire with cups of tea in their hands, staring at her. Ecan sat on a blanket to her right. Across the dark hills, campfires sparkled and blinked as tens of warriors passed in front of them. Dzoo examined the positions of the sentinels.

Ecan propped his elbows on his knees and bent toward her. He had coiled his long black hair into a bun on the left side of his head and pinned it in place with an ornately carved deer-bone pin. Shell and polished bone beads flashed around his throat, and rings glittered on every finger. He wore his usual long white cape and knee-high moccasins decorated with wolf tails. She thought him a handsome man, with his firm nose and green eyes the color of rain-soaked leaves.

In a soft voice, he said, "I finally remember you."

Dzoo tested the bindings on her wrists. The sea-grass cord had eaten into her flesh, leaving raw bloody sores.

The Starwatcher smiled. "I'll never forget the night the tattooed warriors ran into Fire Village, killed your parents, and took you. I recall every detail. We were celebrating the Spring Deer Hunt."

Long-ago images flitted across Dzoo's soul: Old Man Spots sprinkling Fire Village's plaza with sacred seashells . . . the boom of the drum, slow, patient, leading the gods into the flickering firelight . . . six of them, masked figures with antlers, swaying and dipping, their feet pounding out the heartbeat of the world . . . then, out in the darkness beyond the plaza, hideously painted warriors rising up with spears . . .

Fire Village—the bright myth of her childhood. One that had gone boneless, empty, after a few lonely summers among the Striped Dart People on the great grassy plains to the far east.

"The muscular warrior," Ecan said thoughtfully, "the one with the stars on his cheeks, swung you up under his arm and ran away with you."

Dzoo's heart ached for Pearl Oyster. Hoarsely, she answered, "I remember that night, too. You Danced ahead of me in line, and not very well as I recall. You were always clumsy, Ecan."

The corners of his mouth barely turned up. "Are the stories true? Did they take you to the Daybreak Land where the barbarian Striped Dart People live?"

"They did. But do not call them barbarians, Starwatcher. Doing so implies a superiority you do not have." Dzoo sat up and forced her bound legs out in front of her. "Were I you, Ecan, I would be asking questions about tomorrow, not yesterday. I would want to know about the partner you are Dancing with."

"What partner is that?"

She narrowed her eyes. "Don't you feel his cool breath upon your cheek? Isn't that feathery touch in your stomach a warning?"

"Of what?"

"That you are Dancing with Death, Starwatcher. It will finish winding itself around you very soon now. Are you prepared?"

Wind Woman caught the edges of the hide he sat upon and flipped them around his moccasins. "Were I you, I wouldn't speak that way. You'll terrify my warriors. They have already begged me to kill you."

"Then do it," she said tiredly. "My presence no longer matters. Your son was the missing piece. The future is cast, Starwatcher. Oddly, it was you who tossed the final gaming piece. You didn't kill him, you know."

"Kill who? My son?"

"The puppy. It was dark; you only wounded him. Your cruelty has cost you the future. Rain Bear has your son, and he is well on the way to destroying you."

His composure strained. She saw it in the way the lines around his eyes deepened. "What do you mean?"

"I mean you have lost your son forever. You will never see the boy smile at you again. Never share those moments you had always looked forward to. Caress the corpses of your Dreams, Starwatcher; they are about to rise and dissipate like smoke."

He didn't look like he was breathing, but he bluffly said, "Do you think Rain Bear values your life so little?"

"He will not exchange the boy for me."

He leaned closer, as though speaking for her ears alone, and the dark green wells of his eyes glistened. "It will be interesting to see what it will take. Will a single lock of your hair work? Or will it require your right arm? Perhaps a circlet from your skull?"

Dzoo didn't even try to control her laughter.

"You find that amusing?"

When she caught her breath, she added, "Yes. I used to think you were a clever adversary."

"And why don't you now?"

"If you torture me, send a piece of my body to Rain Bear, you will solidify the Raven alliance. What they may not do for him, they will for me."

The rich scent of baking codfish drifted from the warriors' fire. Her empty stomach knotted. On the horizon the last Star People glimmered.

He watched her thoughtfully. "That's all the more reason to kill you immediately, as my warriors wish."

"Before you do that, perhaps you should ask your chief, Cimmis, if *he* wishes me dead. In fact, while you're at it, ask him if he wishes to exchange the famed Healer, Dzoo, for a measly boy. Go ahead, Dead Man, ask."

The muscles beneath Ecan's left eye began to quiver. He stared at her for a long time.

When his warriors started whispering, he got to his feet and walked a short distance away. He seemed to be studying the guard silhouetted on the hilltop to the east. Soft yellow light painted the horizon behind the man.

For over a finger of time, Ecan stood rigid, staring eastward as if he could see all the way to Cimmis in Fire Village.

When he walked back, he dropped to his knees less than a handsbreadth from Dzoo. His eyes had gone cold. "They say brave men

lower their voices when they speak your name, Dzoo. I think that by
the time this is over, you will lower yours when you speak *my* name."

Dzoo leaned toward him and whispered, "I have learned a truth
that you have not, Ecan: Love and Death are the most intimate companions of all. Their eyes are forever locked, because neither dares
look away. *That* is the only thing I fear."

He frowned, as though confused, then rose and stalked toward the
campfire. As he neared the warriors, they leapt to their feet, expecting orders, but Ecan passed without a word.

His warriors muttered to each other, then gradually sat down
again and picked up their conversations.

Dzoo curled onto her side to watch.

He stood alone in the dawn, his fists balled and trembling at his
sides.

Evening Star dipped a cloth in a bowl of warm water and continued
washing the scratches that covered Tsauz's face. The dead puppy lay
across the boy's lap, its dull eyes half closed. Tsauz's shoulder-length
black hair, unwashed for days, hung around his oval face in a stringy
mass. His blind eyes kept jerking toward different locations in the
forest when the guards moved. Rain Bear had assigned no less than
thirty men to surround the boy.

"Is that better, Tsauz?" she asked in the cultured voice of a North
Wind matron.

His fingers sank deeper into the dead puppy's fur, but he said
nothing.

They had just finished the trek down the mountain to Sandy Point
Village after the ceremonial. People had packed the trail; each one
wanted to be close to Tsauz—most for the purpose of killing him.
Others, who had witnessed the Blessing of the Moon that had fallen
on the boy, had the glazed eyes of desperate worshippers. Several
fights had broken out when people leaped for the boy and the guards
had to beat them back.

Evening Star thanked the Spirits that the storms had passed over,
leaving a clear starry sky, but the temperature barely hovered around
freezing. Every breath she exhaled frosted in the cold air.

Roe sat across the fire from them. She had been gradually adding
wood to keep the blaze going. Her infant son, Stonecrop, slept at her
feet, his body wrapped in a bundle of blankets. Five paces away,

Rain Bear, Dogrib, and Pitch stood talking. Their gazes kept straying to the camps. All around Sandy Point Village and down along the beach people lay rolled in blankets and hides. A few fires glimmered against the darkness.

Food was becoming a concern. The fishermen had managed to kill a whale and tow its carcass in to shore. It had taken the edge off, but it wasn't enough. In addition to the fights on the way down, they'd heard grumbles about how little food they'd had at the ceremonial.

"Tsauz," Roe gently asked, "why don't you let me take Runner and lay him by the fire where he'll be warm?"

"No!" He held tight to the dead puppy.

Evening Star exchanged a worried glance with Roe, but said, "Don't you think you should get some sleep? It will be morning soon. You've been up all night."

"I'm not tired."

A handsome boy, he had full lips and large dark eyes. In fact, he looked a great deal like his father. She had to wonder: Did that extend to his soul as well?

"What about his head?" Roe asked. "Father said he took some hard knocks on the fall down the mountain."

"With everything else, I haven't had the luxury of really examining it yet."

"Let me do that." Roe stood, and long red hair flowed around her as she walked around the fire and knelt beside Tsauz.

"Tsauz, tell me when this hurts." She tenderly combed the boy's dirty hair with her fingers, then began to probe his skull for injuries.

Tsauz sat perfectly still.

Roe's brow furrowed. "He has one really large lump on the back of his head, and a few smaller ones."

Evening Star finished washing a deep puncture wound on Tsauz's throat—he must have struck a branch as he rolled down the mountain—and dropped her cloth into the bowl. At least his face and arms were clean. They'd also given him a clean shirt and moccasins to wear. The brown knee-length leather shirt looked tawdry compared to the fine black-and-white hide shirt he'd been wearing, but it was the best they could do.

"Let me feel," Evening Star said. "Where are they?"

Roe touched each, and while Evening Star examined them, she watched Tsauz's face. His eyes tightened a little when she touched the large lump at the rear of his head, but other than that, he seemed oblivious.

Roe waved a hand in front of Tsauz's eyes. "How long has he been blind?"

"Since my mother died," Tsauz answered, and pulled Runner against his stomach. Evening Star hoped he wouldn't squeeze so hard it would tear the sutures where they'd sewed the puppy's insides in.

Evening Star stroked his arm. "What happened? Did you injure your eyes?"

"No, I . . ." He paused as though trying to decide what he could safely say. "My mother died . . . and I stopped seeing."

Evening Star sat back. "Were you there when it happened, Tsauz?"

He wet his lips. "Before Red Dog dragged me out of the lodge I saw her with her hair on fire."

As though the boy's words had painted perfect pictures, her soul could see it all happening: the fire, the screams, the desperation on his mother's face.

"I'm sorry, Tsauz."

Tsauz hugged his dead puppy.

Stonecrop stirred at their voices and began crying.

Roe said, "If you don't need me any longer, I think I will take Stonecrop back to our lodge, feed him, and put him to sleep."

"I'm sorry I kept you so long."

Roe smiled absently, gingerly picked up Stonecrop, and got to her feet. "I will see you both later. A pleasant evening to you."

"And to you."

Roe started up the firelit trail, and Pitch called, "Wait, Roe. I'm coming." He clutched his wounded arm to his chest and hurried to catch her.

Rain Bear and Dogrib spoke for a time longer; then Dogrib headed for his lodge. Rain Bear walked over and crouched opposite Evening Star. In the firelight, she could see the lines that pulled tight at the corners of his dark eyes. He held his hands out to the flames.

"How is the boy?" he asked.

"He'll be all right. Won't you, Tsauz?"

Rain Bear chewed his lower lip, fatigue reflected in his face.

Rides-the-Wind appeared out of the darkness and leaned against the dark smoky trunk of a fir. He had the hood of his tattered cape pulled up, but his eyes gleamed in the shadows.

"Why don't you get some rest?" Rain Bear said. "I'll let Tsauz sleep in my lodge tonight."

"Word will travel fast. You know that, don't you? You should expect 'visitors' soon."

He exhaled hard and nodded. His long black braid hung over his left shoulder. There was something about the vulnerability in his eyes that made her long to hold him.

"I've posted guards around the perimeter of the village and on every high point," he told her. "If they see anything suspicious, they will warn us."

"There won't be anything suspicious. I assure you they'll leave their wolf tails at home."

Tsauz's eyes widened suddenly. Evening Star watched him. He obviously knew who she meant.

Rain Bear drew up a knee and rested a fist upon it while he scrutinized the boy. "A single man will be difficult to defend against. In this mass of humanity, who will notice one more stranger?"

Tsauz blinked, probably understanding more than they thought.

When Rain Bear looked at her she saw the desperation that lived in those dark depths. One man, bearing the weight of his people and hers on his shoulders. How did he manage?

Carefully, he said, "If it looks like the emissary might fail, I'm sure he will have instructions to kill our hostage."

Evening Star smoothed her hand over Tsauz's hair. "I can't believe his father would—"

"No." Rain Bear shook his head. "I don't think his father would. But Cimmis and the Council are another thing entirely."

Tsauz clutched Runner's cold fur.

"Blessed Ancestors," Evening Star whispered. She shifted to sit cross-legged, and her cape fell around her in firelit folds. He had obviously been doing a good deal of thinking since they'd talked.

"Cimmis and the Council will do whatever they must to maintain their authority."

"But, why kill . . . ?"

Her uncle was shrewd and ruthless; it should have occurred to her that he might kill Ecan's son.

Rain Bear's eyes remained on the boy for a time before he said, "It would deny us leverage."

Against Ecan. Yes, of course.

"If he thinks for one instant that Cimmis . . . It might start a war between the North Wind clans."

Rain Bear frowned at Tsauz.

The boy seemed to sense it; he shivered and petted Runner. In a voice just above a whisper, he said, "I want my f-father. Please take me to my father."

Rain Bear said, "We will, Tsauz. For the moment, however, there are a great many obstacles to overcome before we can."

Tsauz's chest spasmed, and he couldn't seem to catch his breath. "I want to go now! *Take me now!*"

It was an order. He was, of course, accustomed to giving them— he was one of the elite in Fire Village. Almost everyone bowed to his needs. Just as they had bowed to her needs only a short time ago.

Evening Star said, "Tsauz, we are all tired after the Moon Ceremonial. I think we should finish this discussion when we are rested."

She put a hand on the boy's arm, and he flinched. "Please, come with me. I'll take you to Rain Bear's lodge."

Tsauz rose on shaking knees and clutched Runner to his chest.

"It isn't far."

"You're Evening Star?" he asked softly. "Matron Evening Star?"

"I am."

"What are you doing with *them*?"

She considered the responses she could have given, and finally told him the truth. "I'm trying to save myself, Tsauz. And in so doing, trying to save our people, too."

"From what?"

"From ourselves."

He let out a deep-throated roar and wrenched his hand from her fingers.

"Fine. All right." She stepped back. "Can you walk at my side? I'll tell you if there's something you might trip on."

He nodded, and she slowly guided him to Rain Bear's lodge at the foot of the gray basalt cliff.

She glanced at Rides-the-Wind. He had his wise old eyes focused on the boy.

Evening Star said, "The door to Rain Bear's lodge is right in front of you, Tsauz. I'm going to pull the hanging back."

He held Runner with one hand and felt for the doorframe with the other. When she pulled the hanging back, he entered the lodge.

Evening Star followed.

It was clean, everything in its place, though the chief seemed to have few belongings. A woodpile was stacked near the door, and three baskets sat near his bedding hides in the rear. She noted the two polished spears and a war club. Leaning beside the door, opposite the woodpile, stood a fishing pole and fishing spear. Two extra buffalohides lay rolled near the fire, probably to sit on. She guided Tsauz toward them.

"Let's make you a bed near the fire. You'll be warmer there."

He shook off the hand she placed on his shoulder and used his toes to feel the way.

"Keep going, Tsauz." She walked at his side until they were a pace from the flames. "That's far enough. Let me spread out the hides for you."

She spread one hide, and said, "All right."

He gently put Runner down, and sat, nervously twisting his hands in his lap. As she unrolled the bedding, he said, "They're going to kill me, aren't they?"

"They will have to go through Rain Bear first." She tried to force assurance into her voice and wondered if the little boy heard through it.

Twenty-eight

Tsauz curled onto his side and pulled his dead puppy against him. Evening Star draped the other buffalohide on top of him, the hair side in, to keep him warm.

"You are about six hands from the fire, Tsauz, so you must not roll into the coals."

The whimper caught in his throat. He closed his eyes. He could see better when his eyes were closed. Twinkles of firelight danced on the backs of his eyelids.

"I'm going to go fetch more wood for the fire. But I'll be right back."

He heard her duck outside.

Sticks clattered.

Tsauz whispered, "It's all right, Runner. We're all right."

He knew he should try to run, but he longed to sleep. He'd hurt himself when he'd fallen down the mountainside. Besides, he didn't know where Rain Bear had gone. He was probably right outside. Even if he weren't, there were many other warriors who'd catch him before he got away.

Cold air blew in through the lodge flap as Wind Woman played in the fir branches outside.

Evening Star returned and placed more wood on the coals. In almost no time, sparks popped and flames licked up around the tinder.

Evening Star said, "Sleep well, Tsauz. You'll feel better this afternoon."

"Are you . . ." He hesitated and heard her turn.

"What is it?"

"Are you my father's slave? The matron he brought home from Obsidian Cliff Village?"

Her cape rustled as though the question disturbed her. "I was. I escaped."

"People said you killed my uncle Kenada." A huge black bubble of pain welled in his chest. Uncle Kenada had always been kind to him, bringing him gifts from War Walks, running races with him. "Did you?"

"Yes."

"You slit his throat with his own knife?"

The way she moved, he thought she might have nodded. "I did." A pause. "Do you know why?"

Tsauz closed his eyes and hugged Runner's cold body. He whispered, "You're Rain Bear's woman now, aren't you?"

"No. He granted me sanctuary, that's all."

"He treats you like you're his woman."

He had heard in Rain Bear's voice a softness he used with no one else, including his own daughter. Evening Star must be his woman. Why would she deny it?

"I counsel him when he asks me to. That's all."

The unexpected sob caught him off guard. "You *are* his woman! He will listen to you. Please, *please* tell him to let me go home!"

She knelt beside him, and he smelled the scents of wood smoke and wet leather that clung to her. "I will do everything I can to help get you home, but it's going to take time. Do you understand? I can't do it right away. It's too dangerous."

Tsauz snuggled his face into the buffalohide and cried.

Evening Star petted his hair. "There are warriors everywhere. By noon today, they will know you are here. The trails will be filled with people who want to hurt you. We must be cautious."

"I know! I heard the people calling me names on the trail!" He whimpered and tried to look at her. "I'm your enemy!"

He heard her sigh. "No, Tsauz. You are not my enemy. You are just a boy who got lost in a battle. A boy caught between two warring forces. We just want to keep you safe."

"But my father is your enemy."

Evening Star hesitated. "He is that. But he is also my distant cousin, Tsauz, as you are. As relatives I don't wish to hurt either of you."

She sounded like she meant it, but Father's words whispered in his head: *Any of them would love to harm you, and . . . and I couldn't stand that.*

Tsauz tucked his face beneath the hide and stared at the darkness where Runner rested. He wished so hard he could make him come alive again.

"Cousin, no matter what, you must promise me that you will not try to run away. Rain Bear's oath is the only thing standing between you and death. Do you understand?"

He swallowed hard. "I promise I won't try to run away."

"Thank you, Tsauz." Evening Star rose and left the lodge.

She spoke with Rain Bear; then an old man coughed, and his steps crunched on gravel. The elder walked slowly, as though each step hurt. Breath wheezed in and out of his lungs. He stopped near Rain Bear's lodge and coughed again. Was there another lodge nearby? The old man's lodge?

Tsauz's paternal granduncle had lived in the lodge right next to theirs in Fire Village. Tsauz had seen him every day until he died six moons ago. Father had gotten up one morning and gone to check on Granduncle and found him dead in his hides. He hadn't suffered. He hadn't even been sick. Father said the gods must have loved Granduncle very much to be so kind.

Tsauz petted Runner's cold ears. Every time he breathed, it felt as though he had broken wings beating a hole inside him.

"I'm all right, Runner," he whispered. "Don't worry about me."

The old man said, "Hurts, doesn't it?"

Tsauz went quiet.

"I said, it hurts, doesn't it?" He had a rough voice that sounded familiar.

Tsauz whispered, "What?"

"That hole inside you."

Tsauz lay still.

"It's supposed to hurt. Don't fear it. That's the gateway, Tsauz. If you take just a few more steps through the darkness, you'll pass into a bright warm place."

Tsauz twisted to look in the direction of the door. "How do you know my name?"

"Someday everyone will know it. I'm just a little ahead of them, that's all."

Leather rustled, like a door hanging being thrown back. When the old man coughed again, it sounded muted. He must have gone inside.

"What's your name?" Tsauz asked.

"Go to sleep, boy. I need rest as much as you do. We'll talk in the morning."

Tsauz held on to Runner's right foot, warming it with his hand, and watched as crimson threads of light played behind his eyelids.

They're going to kill me. Just like they killed you, Runner.

Rain Bear nodded to the guards before he slipped into his lodge and shrugged out of his cape. As he hooked it on the peg by the door, he looked around. The boy rested beneath a buffalohide near the fire. He had his head covered up, but he moved slightly when he heard Rain Bear's footsteps.

The soothing scent of burning alder filled the lodge.

Rain Bear inhaled a deep breath and sat down on his bedding to remove his moccasins and leggings. The boy's sightless eyes peeked out from beneath the hide.

"Sleep, Tsauz. You must be at least as tired as I am, and I'm exhausted."

Tsauz raised his head. In a hateful voice, he said, "Why did you kill my puppy? He was too small to have hurt anybody."

"The spear in Runner's belly was not a Raven spear."

Tsauz blinked. "Not a . . . ?"

"It was a North Wind spear." Rain Bear pulled his leggings off and set them aside. "Most likely a beautiful thing, covered with red paint."

Tsauz stared blindly at the roof, but he seemed to be thinking. After several moments, he fearfully asked, "Was it cedar-bark paint?"

"Probably."

"Oh," the boy said in a weak voice.

Rain Bear untied his moccasin laces and removed them. Though he thought he knew the answer, he gently asked, "Do you know whose spear it was?"

"My father's."

"Why would your father kill your puppy?"

"I don't know. . . . He—he might have worried about Runner making noise, maybe barking during the battle." He sounded soulsick. "But I wouldn't have let him."

Tsauz's hands moved beneath the hides, probably petting the dead puppy.

Rain Bear stretched out atop his hides and heaved a tired breath.

The sensation of lying down was so wonderful, he felt like he was floating. He closed his eyes and let the sweetness of rest filter through him. "I'm sorry, Tsauz. Sometimes people do things that just don't make sense."

As he drifted off to sleep, soft, barely audible whimpers filled the lodge.

Twenty-nine

Afternoon sunlight broke through the clouds and fell across the forest in pale glittering streaks. Changing shafts of light played soundless patterns across Sandy Point Village. People, exhausted from the ceremonies, mostly slept or lounged around.

Rain Bear was half surprised when he found Tsauz still sleeping, but as he flipped off his covers, the boy awakened.

Dragging the dead dog, the boy followed him out into the trees to attend—under the eyes of the guards—to nature. Then Rain Bear led him back to the fire that vigilant guards had kindled in front of his lodge.

"Right there, Tsauz—that's the sitting mat."

Rain Bear helped the blind boy to sit down, and Tsauz rested his dead puppy in his lap. The little dog's belly had begun to bloat, and foul smells were leaking past the stitches Roe had used to sew up the dog's sides. Soon, they'd have to take it away, before the evil Spirits began to leak out.

Rain Bear just prayed he wouldn't be the one who had to do it.

He gave the boy a thorough inspection. Despite a solid night of sleep, Tsauz looked haggard. The scratches covering his face had swollen and turned red. Smudges darkened the flesh beneath his blind eyes.

"Roe started lunch a hand of time ago," Rain Bear said, "but I still have to make tea."

Tsauz brushed shoulder-length black hair behind his ears and clamped his lower lip between his teeth as though awaiting something terrible.

"It shouldn't take long."

Rain Bear went around the fire to where the tea basket hung on the tripod. Roe had already filled it with water and tea. He just needed to boil the water. As he reached for the whalebone tongs resting at the base of the tripod, he looked around the village. Crowds had begun to gather in the plaza and in every opening in the forest. There had to be more than two times ten tens of people camped around Sandy Point Village.

Rain Bear used the whalebone tongs to pluck three hot rocks from the fire. As he dropped each into the tea basket, steam gushed upward in a white cloud, and with it the sweet scents of birch sap and fireweed leaves.

A basket of pemmican—buffalo intestines stuffed with a mixture of blueberries, venison, and fat—rested in the ashes. They'd made it last summer when the blueberries ripened. He'd hoped they wouldn't have to use it until spring, but spring was still another three moons away. They needed it now.

"How are you this afternoon, Tsauz? Did you sleep well?"

Tsauz glanced up from beneath long lashes but didn't answer.

"I'm sure you must be hungry. Did you eat anything before we found you?"

Tsauz shook his head.

"Then you must be starving. Evening Star took half of our pemmican to exchange for Roe's seaweed cakes. She'll be back soon; then we'll eat."

He poked the sizzling lengths of pemmican with a stick while he absently listened to the conversations that filled the valley. Because people had been up half the night, they'd slept half the day. Many were just rising.

One of the newly arrived chiefs—Bluegrass—was walking straight for him. The old man was accompanied by a small band of his warriors. As they approached, they fixed their eyes on Tsauz.

"Great Chief," Bluegrass greeted, his thin-lidded eyes still on the boy. "I wish to thank you for your work in making the Moon Ceremonial as pleasant as it was . . . considering the circumstances."

"Thank you for coming, Chief. We face desperate times and appreciate your support."

Bluegrass remained fixed on Tsauz. "So, are the rumors true? Is that Ecan's son?"

"He is. His name is Tsauz." Rain Bear noticed that Tsauz had recognized Bluegrass's tone. "He's under my protection for the moment."

"What are you going to do with him?"

"Treat him like the guest he is."

Bluegrass lowered his voice. "If you wish to see future cooperation from me or my people, you will kill the little weasel. The sooner, the better. Me, I want a piece of him. Maybe just his hand. Something I can send to his father. Compliments of the visit he paid to my village. A reminder of the way he treated my daughter when she was his *guest*." His face worked, pain and grief mixing. "Ecan deserves it after what he did to our villages."

"Ecan deserves it, yes. What has the boy done to you?"

"Don't stand in my way, Great Chief. I'm not alone in my desires. And if you wish to build this alliance we've been hearing about, you'll need friends."

The old man stalked off wearing a thunderous expression. He'd be back. Meanwhile, he'd be going from camp to camp, speaking with the other chiefs, rallying his support.

The color had washed out of Tsauz's face. His sightless brown eyes were holes of fear. He seemed to be having trouble swallowing, the way he would if his mouth were too dry.

Perhaps more ominous, Rain Bear could see unknown warriors standing just beyond the ring of guards he'd posted. They were three deep now. They'd made no hostile moves, but they stood with their spears or clubs propped on their shoulders, as though awaiting instructions from their chiefs.

Rain Bear kept his eyes on the warriors, and in a low voice asked, "How old are you?"

"T-ten summers."

Rain Bear braced his arms across his knees and considered his words. "I wish to speak with you honestly. I know you are not yet a man, but I must treat you as one."

Tsauz's blind eyes widened.

"I need to tell you things that I would not tell a boy."

"What?"

"The truth, Tsauz. Is that bad?"

"No. I—I want to hear the truth."

"I'm glad. You see . . . we may be in trouble."

"Trouble?" His blind eyes widened. "Then, you will give me to Bluegrass?"

"No." He frowned. "I gave you my promise."

"Father gave me his promise."

"I cannot speak for your father. Only for myself. For now, this is what you must know: Let me start with the North Wind People first. I know you understood much of what we were speaking about last night."

Tsauz blinked as though uncertain how to answer. "You mean about the Wolf Tails?"

"Yes."

Almost against his will, Rain Bear's gaze lifted, searching for a familiar face, for someone he had seen at Fire Village. He had to spot the assassin and kill him before he could get close. Many of the warriors he'd once known in Fire Village were on the run, preferring life in the bush to following the Council's insane orders. How would he know if the familiar face was a friend, or a killer in disguise? The best way for Cimmis to succeed would be to send someone Rain Bear had known and trusted.

"They'll be coming for you, Tsauz."

Tsauz nervously petted Runner.

"They will try to rescue you, but I can't let them do that."

Tears filled Tsauz's eyes. "You told me you would let me go home. When it was safe. You promised! Why can't I go home with the Wolf Tails?"

"Keep your voice down." Every warrior within a hundred paces had turned to stare at them. "There are people close by that I do not wish to overhear us."

Tsauz whispered, "You said you'd take me home!"

"I *will*. When this is over. But for now, you are the only leverage I have against your father. Do you understand?"

"My father?"

"Tsauz, I must convince your father that if he does not help me, I will hurt you. I won't. I promise you. But I must make him believe that I will."

Tsauz's chin trembled. "But you'll have to hurt me if my father doesn't. To prove to him that you're serious."

"No." When Rain Bear shook his head, his long black braid fell over his shoulder. "That's just a risk I'll have to take."

Tsauz didn't seem to be breathing.

Rain Bear continued. "You will be guarded at all times—but only by warriors I trust with my life. Warriors who will—"

Tsauz interrupted. "What if the Wolf Tails can't rescue me and they try to kill me? That's what you meant last night, wasn't it? When you said that Chief Cimmis and the Council would do anything to maintain authority? Can your warriors protect me from the Wolf Tails?"

Rain Bear slowly straightened. "I think so, but I'm not sure. The Wolf Tails are very skilled assassins. If the stories are true, they have managed to kill a number of people who were well guarded. I can only tell you that my warriors will give their lives to protect you."

Tsauz anxiously toyed with Runner's front paw. "It won't make any difference. If they have orders to kill me, they'll kill me."

Strained laughter burst from the trees, and Tsauz spun to stare blindly.

Rain Bear glanced at the two warriors who, not so playfully, shoved each other. "What makes you say that?"

"Matron Gispaw believed that all the warriors guarding her were loyal, but two of them were Wolf Tails. They answered only to Cimmis."

Carefully, so as not to sound too eager, Rain Bear asked, "Do you know which two?"

"No, and I—I'm not sure I would tell you if I did."

Rain Bear nodded. Firs swayed and whispered in the wind. "That's fair. But at some point, you may wish to tell me. You see, from what I have been able to gather, Cimmis selected the best warriors in Fire Village to serve as Wolf Tails. I have been gone for a time, but I think I still know who those warriors are. Do you see why you may wish to tell me?"

Tsauz's eyes darted over nothing. "Because you may know their faces when they come here?"

"Yes."

"But maybe they can rescue me and take me home."

"I won't let them, Tsauz."

The boy obviously longed to shout or cry, but did neither. He sat straight, his young face rigid. "Will you tell me the truth about Cimmis? There's something I must know."

"If I can, I will."

"Why would he order the Wolf Tails to kill me?" His voice broke. "I—I don't understand that part."

Rain Bear leaned forward and propped his elbows on his knees. "Cimmis will rightly fear that I may be able to use you to get to your father, Tsauz. And if I can force your father to help me, I may be able to kill Cimmis."

Astonished, he whispered, "Is that what you wish to do? Kill Chief Cimmis?"

"I do."

"Why?"

Rain Bear picked up the stick and turned over the lengths of pemmican. Fat sizzled inside the gut wrapping. "Cimmis has ordered many of our people tortured and killed. At War Gods Village you learned firsthand what he does. You heard the screams; smelled the death of elders, women, and children like you on the wind. He has done this to more villages than you have fingers. It must stop, Tsauz. We just want to live in peace with the North Wind People."

"But we need you to bring us food."

"We can't find enough food to feed our own villages. You heard the people last night along the trail."

"You're hungry?"

The boy seemed surprised by that. Had his father told him they were withholding tribute out of spite?

"Many of our children and elders died last cycle. Pitch and Dzoo tried to Heal them, but they couldn't. No one really knows why the fevers came, but the fact that they were hungry couldn't have helped."

"Cimmis says you are just hoarding food so you can starve us. Because—because we are better than you! And you hate us!"

Rain Bear tossed his stick into the fire and watched the flames eat into the bark. "Some Raven People hate you. And some of the North Wind hate us. I don't. My wife was one of the North Wind People, and I loved her very much. Roe is one of the North Wind People, as is Evening Star. So was Matron Weedis and so many others that the Council has ordered Cimmis and your father to kill."

The boy just sat on the log, breathing hard.

Rides-the-Wind stepped out of his lodge. The bright afternoon light glinted in his thick gray hair and beard. He wore a knee-length tan shirt beneath his deerhide cape. "Pleasant afternoon to you, Chief."

"And to you, Elder. Are you feeling rested today?"

Rides-the-Wind picked up the worn walking stick propped against his lodge. "Much better."

Rain Bear gestured to the woven bark mat beside the fire. "Please join us. Tea is almost ready."

As Rides-the-Wind walked toward the fire, he noticed the concentric circles of warriors. His gaze took in the wide variety of clan markers on their capes, and his steps faltered for a brief instant. Then his gray brows lowered, and he continued toward the fire.

When he got close, Rain Bear rose and took his arm, gently supporting Rides-the-Wind while he sat down on the mat next to Tsauz.

Rides-the-Wind quietly observed, "It appears that you're surrounded, Chief. What do you plan to do about it?"

Rain Bear smiled. "Have lunch. As soon as Evening Star returns.

She went to Roe's lodge to exchange our pemmican for some of Roe's seaweed cakes."

Rides-the-Wind gave him a knowing look. "Is it safe for her to wander the village like that?"

"She is well guarded."

"If you say so." Rides-the-Wind tugged his cape over his moccasins to keep his feet warm, and shivered.

"Cold?" Rain Bear rushed to take off his cape to give to the old man.

"Keep your cape. It's not the weather. It's their faces." He gestured to the warriors.

"Don't let them concern you, Rides-the-Wind."

"Rides-the-Wind!" Tsauz shouted. He swung around, and his mouth fell open. "Rides-the-Wind, the Soul Keeper?"

The old man's eyes glinted. "The same. Do you remember me?"

Tsauz stammered, "Yes, I—I do. You used to come to Fire Village often. You trained the greatest Dreamers and Healers who have ever walked among our people." Awe filled Tsauz's voice. "My father told me that he would have given anything to have been trained by you!"

Rides-the-Wind's skeletal fingers groped to close an opening that Wind Woman had teased open in his cape. "I don't recall your father asking for me."

"His grandmother wouldn't allow it. She said you were too dangerous."

"Well, I'm sorry to hear that. I would have enjoyed training your father."

Tsauz's face lit up. "You would?"

"Of course. Your father has abilities he barely realizes. Not as many as you do, but enough to sting a man's interest."

Tsauz blinked. "Me?"

"You."

Rain Bear lifted a curious eyebrow at the content of their talk, then reached for the nest of wooden cups near the hearthstones. "Have a hot cup of tea. You'll feel stronger." He dipped the first one full and handed it to Rides-the-Wind.

Rides-the-Wind cradled his cup and sniffed the aroma. "Um, fireweed leaves and sweet sap. One of my favorites."

Rain Bear said, "Would you like a cup, Tsauz?"

"Yes. I thank you."

Rain Bear lifted Tsauz's hand and put the cup in it. The boy's stomach growled as he gulped it down. He drank the entire cup in four swallows.

Rain Bear reached for the cup again. "Let me refill that. I didn't realize you were so thirsty."

He refilled the cup, put it in the boy's hands again, and saw Evening Star coming up the trail, flanked by Hornet and Wolf Spider. She carried a basket. Long hair fell from her hood and fluttered over her cape. She smiled back when she saw him, and suddenly his day brightened. The sunlight was stronger and warmer. The colors of the world blazed.

Low conversations broke out among the warriors. Most eyed her with curiosity. Some with malevolent intent.

"Did you get the cakes?" he called.

She nodded. "Yes."

Evening Star knelt on the mat between Tsauz and Rain Bear and, as she unwrapped the cakes, said, "A pleasant afternoon to you, Elder. Are you well?"

"Better, thank you for asking." His gray hair fell around his oblong face like a curtain woven of spiderwebs.

"Pitch has been worried about you."

He made a light gesture. "Well, he needn't be. There are many circles left for me to explore."

The old man's piercing gaze landed on Tsauz.

"What do you mean?" Rain Bear asked.

Rides-the-Wind made a light gesture. "I mean life is a series of circles within circles, never ending. If a man faithfully walks the spiral to the center, and doesn't fall off, he will eventually find the solution."

Evening Star gave him a curious look. "Is that an answer?"

The old Soul Keeper smiled. "It is the only answer, Matron. Apparently you haven't found the question yet." He turned to the boy. "Tsauz, I have heard that your father uses beautiful obsidian fetishes in his Healing ceremonies. Does he make them himself?"

Rain Bear's heart rate increased. He met Evening Star's wide eyes. *The obsidian fetishes Coyote paid for Dzoo's life? Did Ecan get them from Coyote?* Gods, did the old man know who Coyote was?

Tsauz put down his cup and wiped his hands on his leggings. "I don't know where he gets them. He just brings bags of them home from his trips. I think he Trades for them."

"Hmm," Rides-the-Wind said, and smiled. "Well, if you ever remember the maker's name, or the place where he gets them, I hope you will tell me. My hands have grown too stiff to knap out fetishes, or anything else for that matter."

The tea bag swung when Evening Star reached down to refill her cup.

Tsauz suddenly asked, "Who attacked War Gods Village?"

Rain Bear stared at the boy. How could he not know? "You were there, Tsauz. We tracked your father's party after he left War Gods Village. We killed four, and captured two more. You would have known the captives, Red Sleep and Wet Hand. They told us that they warred for Cimmis."

A swallow went down Tsauz's throat. In an agonized voice, he said, "My father couldn't have known about it, Rain Bear. He was surprised by the attack. He jerked me out of my hides and dragged me up the hill to hide me; then he went back to fight them!"

Rain Bear fingered his cup while he contemplated that unlikely scenario. "Tsauz, I—"

"Why would Chief Cimmis send Father and me to War Gods Village and then attack it without telling us?"

Rides-the-Wind let out a soft pained sound as he shifted on the mat to rub his knees, muttering, "Circles within circles."

Rain Bear said, "I don't know, Tsauz." He glanced at Evening Star, who glared back, expression hard.

Tsauz stammered, "P-Perhaps Chief Cimmis couldn't get word to us. We had been on the trail for half a moon. We wouldn't have—"

"This was a well-planned attack, Tsauz. Whoever was behind it had been thinking about it for some time. They knew enough to use the Moon Ceremonial to lull Matron Weedis's suspicions. As they lulled mine."

Rain Bear could see thoughts forming behind the boy's dark eyes.

Finally, Tsauz said, "But the chief is supposed to consult with his Starwatcher. He always has before. Father would have told him not to do it. I'm sure of it!"

Both Rain Bear and Evening Star turned to peer at Rides-the-Wind, wondering when he would comment. He stroked his gray beard and frowned out at the warriors. Voices had started to rise.

Rain Bear turned around to look at the commotion. Three men stalked up the trail. Bluegrass was in the lead. Guards with spears flanked them.

Evening Star said, "I will take Tsauz to my lodge. If you need us, that's where we'll be. Come along, Tsauz."

He picked up the dead puppy and stood. This time he allowed her to take his hand. She led him to her lodge, and they disappeared inside. Hornet and Wolf Spider took up their positions outside her door.

Rain Bear rose to his feet. Softly, he said, "Circles within circles, Elder?"

Rides-the-Wind kept his eyes on the ground but answered, "Perhaps, Great Chief, you have found the question."

He gestured at the approaching chiefs. "Right now I think I need answers more than I need another question."

The old man smiled. "Ah, then you begin to understand the teacher's dilemma. You know the answer, but haven't the foggiest idea how to make your students believe it."

Thirty

A dark blue wall of Cloud People pushed over Fire Mountain. Dzoo studied it as she shuffled up the steep trail that led around the outside of Sea Lion Village's palisade. Ecan's warriors marched in front and behind her. Everyone had their gazes fixed on the village, looking through the slats in the gaping palisade to the lodges within.

She remembered this place, had played here as a child. Then the village had contained over five tens of lodges, though only a few people had actually lived here, mostly Dreamers and caretakers. The rest of the lodges held caches of dried food, tool stone, and seashells.

The Holy trails that covered their mountainous land angled off in every direction, intersecting each other, sometimes running parallel, but they all converged at Sea Lion Village. It was the spiritual crossroads to the House of Air. All lost souls began their journey here.

As they rounded the eastern end of the rickety palisade, a gray-haired acolyte dressed in a drab brown tunic hobbled out of the interior carrying a basket that brimmed with bones. He nodded as he passed. She watched him continue to a small mound of sun-bleached human bone. It gleamed in the light, cracked, flaking, and rain washed. Thick green grass grew out of the tangle. Over the years, quite a pile of it had built up. Here and there, a battered skull stared out, the empty eyes questioning, the braincases nothing more than the perfect place for mice to build their homes. She looked back over her shoulder as the acolyte carefully placed the bones onto the pile.

The North Wind People varied in their tastes. Some wanted to be buried close to where they'd lived. Others found it worthwhile to have their bones prepared, and to send tribute to the Holy people who lived here in return for having their souls prayed over, separated from the bones, and sent to the House of Air.

Dzoo tilted her head and listened to the old man's lilting voice calling the Star People to come and carry the soul to the road of light that led to the first of the Above Worlds.

"Are we traveling on to Fire Village?" she asked.

Warriors glanced at her, but no one answered. Far ahead, Ecan's white cape flashed in the sunlight as the Starwatcher led them up the trail.

"Are we going on to Fire Village?" she asked, louder.

Exhausted from days of traveling without food, Dzoo tripped over a rock, stumbled, and almost fell before she caught herself.

"Don't fall, witch!" young Hunter said from behind. "I don't want to have to pick you up."

She glanced over her shoulder, aware her vision was swimming. Was that his soul she saw—a loose yellowish blur around his body? Must have been. He looked suddenly frightened, and stopped dead in his tracks to lift his spear. In the slanting sunlight, his haunted expression turned stony. Black hair whipped around his face. Fearfully, he called, "Wind Scorpion!"

The old warrior trotted up, predatory gaze on first Hunter, and then her. "Careful, Hunter. If you're helping her up, she might snag your soul and pull it from your body."

Wind Scorpion gave her a look that sliced like freshly struck obsidian before he trotted past.

Hunter gave him an evil glance and veered wide around Dzoo, gesturing with his spear. "Walk, witch."

She walked, fixing her gaze onto Wind Scorpion's wide back. She squinted, trying to catch a glimpse of his soul. Her toe caught, and she broke contact as she flailed for balance. She turned her attention to her feet, aware she hadn't the energy for both tasks. She'd caught a glimpse, but of what?

The sensation had been of emptiness, as if the man were nothing more than a shell.

"Gods," she mumbled. "It's the hunger. I'm tired. So . . . tired."

Fire Mountain rose before her like a gigantic cone with a snow-covered, chopped-off top. Her hazy vision focused on the cliff just above the tree line. Was that the Fire Village palisade wall?

She shook her head. Maybe it wasn't even there. For three hands of time, she'd been seeing things. Sometimes just faces. Other times, she saw glimpses of the future. Pearl Oyster had come to speak with her. She thought he was trying to warn her about something. She'd seen him reach out to touch her; then he'd vanished like mist on a hot day. . . .

She stumbled again.

Hunter glared at her. "What's wrong?"

She could feel her soul growing lighter, thinning like smoke in the wind. A pink tornado formed in the air before her. Round and round it went, Dancing and bouncing.

Hunter's gaze jerked to the point on the trail where she seemed to be looking, then jerked back to her. "What's *wrong?* Do you see something."

The Noisy One, her Spirit Helper, solidified in the cold-spawned glitter, his arms moving like blades of grass underwater, sweeping up and down.

"Empty out your heart, Dzoo. Drain your soul onto the path to prepare the way."

"Prepare it for whom?" she asked, the words barely audible even to her.

"Our purpose is the boy."

"Which boy?"

"The bloody boy."

"Ecan's son?"

Hunter circled warily, his spear thrust forward. "Who are you talking to, witch?"

Dzoo couldn't feel the ground. She might have been flying, rather than walking.

The Noisy One floated just ahead of her.

"You are almost home," he whispered. *"Like a winged seed coming to ground. But beware. You are being hunted. He is close . . . and, oh, so Powerful. I don't know if you can beat him."*

The Noisy One raised his hands to Brother Sky, and lightning flashed through the approaching Cloud People. Warriors spun to look. Whispers broke out.

"Witch!" Hunter shouted. "Did you do that?"

With the next brilliant flash, the Noisy One's face shattered and blew away like tumbling snowflakes.

"You had better keep walking, witch, or I'll—"

Dzoo staggered, blinked, and pressed her bound hands to her forehead. The vision had been burned into her soul: a tall young man, muscular, his head back, arms raised to the blinding sun.

Blood had trickled down his bronzed, sweat-slicked skin. Every muscle rippled on his naked body—a picture of male perfection. Then she saw his face. The nose was thin, aquiline, the jaw strong, slightly bearded. Wide cheeks caught the light. But where knowing and Powerful eyes should have been, dull stones filled the hollow orbits in his skull. As if he felt her presence, he turned his head, staring straight at her. The sensation was as if her soul were being sucked from her body.

Dzoo blinked and gasped, aware of the jouncing sensation. A terrible headache hammered through her skull. She forced her eyes open and saw Hunter. At first he appeared to be hanging upside down against the sky. As she fought to make sense of it, she realized that she was being carried on a sort of litter.

"Are you awake, witch?" Hunter asked.

"Yes." She sat up and put her hand to her head.

Deer Killer carried the front poles. He kept glancing uneasily over his shoulder, taking her measure.

"What happened?"

"You collapsed," Hunter sneered. "Dropped flat as a soaked cloth. Were it up to me, I'd have just cracked your skull and left you."

Deer Killer added, "The Starwatcher told us to carry you. But I'd rather you walked."

"Hurry up!" Wind Scorpion bellowed from behind. "We're almost there."

"I can walk," Dzoo said softly, the image of the stone-eyed man hovering like a bat in the back of her soul.

She felt stiff as she swung out of the makeshift litter they'd made of coats and poles. She stood on unsteady feet, but the headache began to recede.

"Make time, witch!" Hunter growled. "We're falling behind, and I, for one, don't want to be the center of Ecan's wrath again."

She filled her lungs with the cool air and forced herself into the continuing climb. As she got her bearings, she recognized the village cupped by the brow of the ridge before them like a barnacle.

The twenty-hand-tall palisade of upright poles surrounding Salmon Village had been built since the last time she'd been here. People began to trickle out the front gate to stare at her. They wore beautiful clothing—shirts made of finely tanned mink and marten hides, capes of eagle feathers. The finest dyes had been used to create geometric designs on the clothing. She had forgotten the brilliant purples, yellows, and shades of crimson manufactured by the North Wind artisans.

Ecan dropped back to walk at her side. "Just pass. Don't speak."

Dzoo smiled, turning her head to call, "Beware the blood-streaked man! He has stones for eyes."

People started, stiffening, frowning, as they puzzled over her words. Confusion and worry grew bright in their eyes.

Ecan gaped in disbelief, then raised his hand to strike her. It wavered in the air, quivering like a stressed sapling before he lowered it. "You take dangerous chances."

He stamped ahead. Perhaps he had second thoughts; for he dropped back once more to parallel her course. She cataloged the furtive glances he cast her way, wondering how long it would take.

"What blood-streaked man? What were you talking about?"

"You needn't worry. You won't live long enough to stare into his stony eyes."

"Ah, yes, my impending death again." He pointed to the path that led around the base of the palisade. "Come on. The sooner we arrive, the sooner you can sleep."

As they curved around Salmon Village and climbed higher up the mountain trail, the Fire Village palisade came into view.

"I had forgotten," she whispered in awe.

"Forgotten what?"

"The paintings."

They had been painted on hides stretched over the corduroy of the palisade wall. The bodies of the gods winked and flashed, as though encrusted with fallen stars. To create the effect, the artisans glued bits of crushed shell to the surface of the paintings of Gutginsa, Old Woman Above, Ogre, Killer Whale, Sea Cow, and Wolf.

"I'd forgotten their beauty."

For many summers after she'd arrived at the squalid lodges of the Striped Dart People, dreams of Fire Village had kept her alive. How could she have forgotten?

Her gaze moved to the gate, where two warriors leaned against the palisade. Just inside, her mother's lodge had stood to the right. Was it still there?

Ecan's eyes had an anticipatory gleam. "You are almost home."

Dzoo gazed at the towering lava cliff behind Fire Village. In the afternoon light its shadow cut upward, darkening the mountain. She could feel Power—but it was faint. Shreds crept from the lava and the high snow-patched cinder cone where once it had been a flood. What had happened here? Why had the Power fled? Dzoo concentrated on pulling the shreds around her like a protective cloak.

She asked, "Who killed it? Was it you, Starwatcher?"

"Killed what?"

"The Power. It used to run across my skin like rubbed fox fur."

His eyes tightened. "Cimmis told me the Power vanished when his daughter, Tlikit, decided to run away with Rain Bear."

It was strange to hear someone say her name. Cimmis had declared Tlikit Outcast, dead, and ordered that her name be forgotten. It was a crime to speak it.

"This is not Tlikit's work, Starwatcher." She cocked her head, raising her hands to the air. "No, I think the slow rot of human souls has led to this."

The guards stepped back, and hands still up, Dzoo walked through the gate into the village. Brown-cloaked slaves stood everywhere, watching her. In an instant, someone recognized her, and the word "Dzoo!" was whispered from person to person.

As she remembered, the bark lodges made a perfect circle around the central Council Lodge. Paintings decorated every wall. As she neared a painting of Buffalo Above, it occurred to her that the artist had mixed crushed obsidian with his paint to create the god's shimmering hair. The white eyes must contain crushed clamshells; they glittered as though alive.

Her mother's lodge still stood just inside the gate. It looked smaller than she remembered. Someone had converted it to storage.

A tall man ducked out of the last lodge near the lava cliff. She remembered it as belonging to Astcat, the matron. The tall man shielded his eyes to look in their direction. A gossamer blue cape billowed around him.

"Is that Cimmis?"

Apprehension strained Ecan's face. "That's him."

Another man, shorter and fatter, ducked through the door hanging behind the chief. "Cimmis and the leader of the Big Tail Clan, Tudab. Prepare yourself, witch. Cimmis ordered me to take no captives."

"Then perhaps I will be able to watch you die sooner than I had anticipated. I would enjoy that."

"I wasn't worried about me, Dzoo." He straightened his long white cape. "Hunter! Deer Killer! Keep an eye on the prisoner while I make my report"—he shot a final glance at Dzoo—"and see if our chief wants this worthless woman alive . . . or dead."

Thirty-one

After each of the chiefs had entered his lodge, Rain Bear took a moment to ensure that the guards obeyed him and stayed at least fifty hands away. They did—but no one looked happy about it. Two men stood grumbling in front of Evening Star's lodge, giving steely-eyed glances to Hornet and Wolf Spider, who returned them stare for stare.

He let the hanging fall. As it swung, bars and streaks of gold flashed over the faces of the men seated around his fire. Bluegrass, the oldest, had seen perhaps five tens of summers. A few stubborn white hairs clung to his bald head. Black Mountain, Talon's chief, was next oldest, around three tens and five summers. He had shoulder-length graying black hair, a bulbous nose, and deep wrinkles. Goldenrod, Sleeper's chief from Deer Meadow Village, was the youngest. He'd seen fewer summers than Rain Bear: two tens and six. They made a strange group.

Without waiting for them to speak, Rain Bear asked, "Do all of you want me to kill the boy? Or just Bluegrass?"

Goldenrod shifted to sit cross-legged on the mat, and long black hair fell around his broad shoulders. He extended a hand. "Rain Bear, surely you understand the position you place us in. Most of the people gathered around your village watched Ecan destroy their homes and families."

"They want revenge. Yes, I know." Rain Bear hung his otterhide cape on the peg, straightened his red knee-length shirt, and seated himself across from his guests. "I do not wish to fight over this. If all the chiefs agree that the boy should be executed to punish Ecan, then that is what I will do."

Relieved smiles and nods went around the circle. Black Mountain gave old Bluegrass an unpleasant look. "See? I told you Rain Bear was a reasonable man."

"Well, he wasn't earlier today." Bluegrass glared at Rain Bear. His bald head gleamed in the firelight. "What changed your heart?"

"My heart hasn't changed," Rain Bear replied. "I told you I needed to consult with the elders and other chiefs. Since we spoke, I've been trying to speak with as many as I can." That was a fanciful lie. "Not everyone agrees about the boy. Several of my own clan elders don't want him killed. They believe it's possible to use him as leverage against Ecan."

"I want him *dead!*" Bluegrass shouted. "His father tortured my wife and son to death before my eyes!"

"Bluegrass!" Goldenrod held up both hands in a *please stop this* gesture. "We can all make similar claims, but I would like to hear Rain Bear's words before I decide."

Bluegrass sucked his lips in over toothless gums and angrily flipped his arm at Rain Bear in a motion to continue.

Rain Bear said, "My elders believe that we may be able to use the boy to maneuver Ecan into a position where we can either kill him or pressure him into betraying Cimmis and the Council."

Black Mountain tilted his head skeptically. Soot smudged his bulbous nose. "How?"

"First, we need to decide where our real interests lie. Do we wish to kill Ecan?"

A mingled roar of assenting voices rose.

Rain Bear raised placating hands. "Or try to destroy Cimmis and the Council?"

Another roar.

"Then I suggest," Rain Bear said, "that we do not immediately kill the boy."

"I want him dead!" Bluegrass's elderly face contorted in rage. "I don't just want him dead; I want to slit his belly open and pull out enough of his intestines to roast in a fire while he squeals!"

Rain Bear glanced at Black Mountain and Goldenrod. They both appeared embarrassed by the vehemence. Goldenrod squinted at his moccasins. Black Mountain roughly shoved graying black hair away from his brow.

Rain Bear said, "Killing Ecan will require every skill and tool we have. Shall we destroy our best tool before we've even tried to use it?"

The chiefs started talking at once. Bluegrass shook a fist in Goldenrod's face.

Rain Bear lifted his voice. "And there is another thing I wish you to consider."

The din died down.

Bluegrass gave Rain Bear an evil look.

"By now I think all of you are aware that Ecan took Dzoo captive. If we kill Tsauz, Ecan will kill Dzoo. Is that acceptable to you?"

Bluegrass's withered mouth pinched as though he'd eaten something bitter. "I thought that was just a rumor. You're sure she was taken captive?"

Goldenrod nodded. "My war chief, Sleeper, is tracking the war party. He sent a runner back to say he'd seen Dzoo. She is definitely Ecan's prisoner."

Black Mountain looked at Bluegrass. "I believe she spent several moons at your village two summers ago. Didn't she Heal your sick son?"

Bluegrass clenched his jaw for several moments before expelling an explosive breath. "Yes. And many others in my village. She is worth ten tens of Ecan's sons."

Goldenrod looked around the circle. "If we are to save Dzoo, we cannot kill Ecan's son. At least not right away. I say that later, when Dzoo is safe, we let Bluegrass roast his guts. Who knows? By then, perhaps Ecan will be ours and he can listen along with the rest of us."

Bluegrass twisted on his mat as though ants had crawled into his cape. "For now, I agree."

Black Mountain nodded. "As do I."

Rain Bear bowed his head. "Good. There are other things I wish you to know."

Bluegrass craned his neck to look up. "Now what?"

Rain Bear gazed across the smoldering fire at Bluegrass. "When my daughter was cleaning the boy's wounds last night, she noticed . . . injuries."

"From rolling down the mountain when you were chasing him?" Bluegrass asked.

Rain Bear shook his head. "No, these were old bruises, yellow and purple." He let that sink in.

Bluegrass cocked his head. "You mean Ecan beats the boy?"

"That was Roe's suggestion. Either Ecan or someone else."

"I've heard this before," Black Mountain said, "from Traders."

"As have I," Goldenrod added. "Just after Ecan's wife died in that suspicious fire, I heard that he beat the boy nearly to death."

Bluegrass jerked a nod. "And that he kicked the boy's puppy to death. But what difference does it make?"

Rain Bear shrugged. "It's just something to think about. Ecan beats the boy, and when the battle at War Gods Village grew difficult, he abandoned his blind son and fled."

"More reasons to hate Ecan." Black Mountain drew up a knee and laced his fingers around it. "But I'm not certain it has a bearing on our decisions."

"It tells us something about the value he places on his son's life," Bluegrass said. "The boy may not be as useful a tool as we think."

"True," Rain Bear agreed in a mild voice. "It also means that killing the boy may not *hurt* Ecan as much as we imagine."

"For the sake of the gods, Rain Bear," Bluegrass exhaled the words in a rush and waved a hand. "You never wish to kill anyone. No matter how deserving! In Raven's name, why did we vote you to lead the war party?"

Rain Bear's brows lifted. "As I recall, Bluegrass, you voted against me."

"Yes, but I was outvoted. So there we have it. At least we are all agreed that we must kill Ecan, correct?"

Everyone, including Rain Bear, nodded.

"And Cimmis, if we can, yes?"

"Of course. If we can find an opportunity."

"Anything else, Rain Bear?" Goldenrod asked expectantly.

"Not for the moment." He glanced around. "But I would like for each of you to follow out anything suspicious. We have the boy, and Cimmis knows it. If he can kill the boy before we can use him . . ."

Bluegrass's nose wiggled as he thought about it. "He could take any advantage away from us. That foul sea slug! If he's going to kill our captive, he's going to have to get past me first!"

Goldenrod and Black Mountain were watching him curiously.

"Very well." Bluegrass tottered as he rose to his feet. "Notify me when you wish to next meet in council."

"We will."

Bluegrass walked to the door and stepped out into the bright afternoon sunlight. People instantly began calling questions.

Goldenrod chuckled, rose to his feet, and asked, "Are we finished, Great Chief?"

"Unless you have something else to discuss," Rain Bear said.

Goldenrod shook his head, and Black Mountain said, "I have nothing more." He got up and propped his hands on his hips. "We'll be waiting to hear from you, Rain Bear."

"I will be calling on you soon."

Cimmis lifted a hand to shield his eyes against the afternoon glare of the sun, and frowned at the large group of warriors who walked in through the Salmon Village gate. Several villagers ran out of the palisade gates and followed in the wake of the war party, shouting questions, hugging friends who'd been away. Ecan led the procession. Cimmis knew the Starwatcher by his long white cape. Oddly, he didn't see Ecan's boy. A woman—apparently a captive—accompanied the party.

"Ecan!" Cimmis clenched a fist. "Gutginsa strike him! Look at that! He's brought a woman! I didn't want him slowed down by captives. His need to shove his rod into her sheath might have killed them all."

"Wait, my Chief. Let's hear his story." Wind Woman tousled Tudab's thick black hair, blowing it over his face.

Cimmis said, "The Starwatcher has a bad habit of 'interpreting' my orders to his own benefit."

"Sometimes a man must make quick decisions out on the war trail."

"I spent ten and eight summers as a warrior and never had to 'explain' my actions, Clan Leader. I never disobeyed an order, never 'interpreted' an order. I just did what was expected of me."

Tudab put a hand on Cimmis's shoulder, trying to ease his mood. "We know your record, my Chief. Your complete dedication to the orders of the Council are what have placed you in such an important position. You lead by your example. You, Cimmis, are the Council's strong right arm."

Tudab, if you only knew. Where Astcat's thoughts were the strong heartwood of our people, Old Woman North's head might be filled with punk for all the sense I get out of it.

Tudab asked, "How many did we lose?"

"If that's all of them, too many."

"Some may have been captured. Perhaps we can arrange a Trade to get them back."

"If any of our warriors were captured, they're already dead."

Tudab, a gentle little man, grimaced as though disturbed by the thought. "Is that what you would have done, my Chief?"

"Keeping captives costs too much, Tudab. You have to feed them; warriors must guard them. You never know when one will get desperate and jump for the closest guard's throat. It's safer to question them and kill them."

Cimmis could see them more clearly now. At least three had been wounded. Two limped, and one man cradled an arm to his chest. "I do not understand why White Stone sent no more messages after the battle. He should have sent one message a day telling us the status of the war party. I will have to speak with my war chief. Apparently, he does not understand his duties."

Tudab frowned. "I don't see White Stone. Perhaps he was killed in the fighting."

"Then my wrath will fall on Ecan. *He* should have sent the messages if White Stone couldn't."

Immediately after the battle, a message had been sent, signaling their victory. With White Stone dead, Ecan should have sent additional messages. Perhaps the captive had dulled his wits with her body. The thought of Ecan and his women was disturbing. Cimmis remained irritated by the mess Ecan and Kenada had made of Matron Evening Star's captivity. They were to break and humiliate her as an example to the others, not turn her into a heroine for every malcontent within a moon's journey.

Tudab interrupted his thoughts. "I just hope that our attack has dampened the Raven People's ardor for war."

"It has enflamed their hatred, Tudab, not dampened it." *That's your beloved Council at work, you dolt. Without Astcat's guidance, they're sending us down the trail of eventual disaster.*

Wind Woman flapped Tudab's cape around his pudgy body as he turned to Cimmis. "I don't understand. I thought we attacked War Gods Village to break the Raven People's will. You said we were going to teach them they cannot hide from us. If they refuse to offer tribute, we can kill them anywhere and any time."

"That's what I said, but the Four Old Women had other reasons." Cimmis studied Ecan's captive. He thought he knew her, but couldn't place her face. Red Hair? Gods, that wasn't Evening Star, was it? No, this one was older, more . . . what? Stately?

"What reasons?"

A cold sprinkling of rain began to patter on the lodge roofs and on the back of Cimmis's neck. He tugged up his hood. Tudab stood patiently awaiting an answer.

"Rain Bear's forces grow by the day," Cimmis said. "If we cannot force him to attack us soon with small war parties that we can eliminate, his forces will eventually move like a giant wave of locusts, destroying everything in their path. The Council is afraid the Raven People will wipe the North Wind People from the face of Our Mother Earth."

Tudab's mouth opened. Cimmis could see his coated tongue inside. Finally, he blurted, "Blessed gods, Cimmis! Have you spoken with the matron about this?"

"As you know, she's been . . . away," Cimmis said uncomfortably. "Besides, we will know soon enough. Rain Bear dislikes war, but when he must fight, he is swift to action."

As his leather door hanging waffled in the wind, he caught glimpses of Astcat lying inside beneath a mound of hides. Kstawl knelt beside her.

His heart ached. She had been progressively growing worse. Every time she woke after being "away," she begged Cimmis to tell her what had been going on.

Ecan's group reached the central plaza fire, and the Starwatcher strode forward, his long white cape billowing around his tall body. How did he keep it so clean while on the trail?

The captive's gaze lingered on the painted lodges.

"What's she looking at?" Tudab asked.

"The paintings, I think."

Then her eyes turned on Cimmis. His heart leaped. He couldn't see her face—the sun was behind her and she had her hood up—but something about the way she held herself touched his memories.

People throughout the village continued to whisper with excitement and move about uneasily.

Then it struck Cimmis. He whispered, "Blessed gods. That's Dzoo."

"What?" Tudab spun around. Fear widened his eyes. "How do you know?"

"Once you've known Dzoo, you never forget."

Tudab studied the slaves huddled together in the plaza. "If that is indeed Dzoo, my Chief, we may have a problem. Many of our slaves are Raven People, and she is one of their greatest heroes."

"It's her all right—and the slaves will be the least of our problems."

"Then perhaps we should kill her immediately, before she creates dissent."

In the plaza Ecan gestured to his warriors, and they prodded Dzoo toward the dank lodge where they kept captives and disobedient slaves. Cimmis shook his head in amazement. Even after days on the trail, she moved with uncommon grace; she might have been floating across the ground.

"Tell Lion Girl I wish her to personally take care of Dzoo, and inform Ecan I want to see him immediately."

"Yes, my Chief."

Tudab bowed and waddled down the hill toward Ecan as fast as he could.

Thirty-two

Cimmis watched as Dzoo stopped in front of the opening to the captives' lodge. She stood perfectly still, her head down. The hair on the back of his arms stood on end. It was as though he could feel her soul moving about the village, touching things. Ecan pulled the door hanging back for her, but before she stepped into the lodge she turned to meet Cimmis's gaze. Long red hair fluttered around her beautiful face. She smiled at him.

It was the kind of smile an enemy warrior gave you just before he slit your throat.

A guard bravely prodded her arm with his spear, and she ducked down into the lodge.

"There's a . . . a traitor," Astcat weakly said.

"My wife? Are you awake?" Cimmis hurried into his lodge.

Astcat lay on her side, her jaw slack, eyes focused on nothing. Gray hair framed her wrinkled face.

"Ecan has returned," Cimmis said as he strode across to kneel at her side, "but you do not need to concern yourself with that. Try to sleep."

Kstawl said, "I think her soul is coming back, Father. In the past hand of time, she's awakened twice."

Cimmis stroked her damp gray hair.

"What did you say?" Astcat blinked at the lodge, as if not certain where she was.

"I said Ecan is back."

"Ecan?" Astcat blinked at the painted shields. "How many warriors did we lose?"

"I don't know yet. I've sent for him."

Astcat wiped at the saliva that had run from her open mouth down her chin. "How long was I away?"

"Two days, my wife, but nothing important has happened."

Cimmis couldn't let anyone know how bad she had gotten. The Council would demand she be removed as matron of the North Wind People. They would order that another female from her lineage be installed in her place. Kstawl was the likely choice, but her three and ten summers had not prepared her for leadership.

"My Chief?" Ecan called from beyond the lodge flap.

"Enter, Starwatcher." Cimmis rose to his feet.

Ecan entered and bowed to Cimmis before striding forward. "Good news, Great Chief! We have—"

"I said *no* captives, Starwatcher. Do you take my orders so lightly?"

Ecan's handsome face tensed. Wind Woman had teased hair loose from his bun and left it hanging around his face. "No, my Chief, I do not." He untied the laces of his white cape as though they were choking him and let it fall open, revealing the beautiful red, yellow, and black shirt beneath. "This is no ordinary captive. I thought you would find her more valuable alive than dead."

"You have brought the most dangerous woman alive into my village. Are you trying to destroy us? Do you think the Raven People will just sit by and allow us to harm their precious heroine?"

"Please, my Chief, I believe that she will be a very powerful tool we can use against our enemies. If we can force Dzoo to witch—"

"Dzoo?" Astcat's eyes widened. "You captured *Dzoo*?"

Ecan bowed to Astcat. "Yes, Matron. We found her at War Gods Village."

Astcat lifted her head. "Asin's daughter?"

"Yes, Matron. Do you remember her?"

"Oh, yes." Astcat stared with such vacancy Cimmis feared her soul might have slipped loose again. But she asked, "Has she said anything, Starwatcher?"

"Mostly nonsense about the future. She collapsed on the trail this morning. We had to bear her most of the way."

Astcat's eyes cleared. "What did she say?"

Ecan made a dismissive gesture. "Something about a blood-streaked man with stones for eyes."

Astcat's frown deepened as if she didn't understand. "You must tell me if she says anything else. Anything at all."

"Yes, Matron."

Cimmis could tell that Ecan was lying. He would deal with that later, when it wouldn't upset Astcat. "What was she doing at War Gods Village?"

"I assume she came for the Moon Ceremonial."

"I always expected her to become Starwatcher." Astcat smiled in a dreamy way.

"Everyone did. She had more Power at the age of four summers"—he glanced at Ecan through heavy-lidded eyes—"than most Starwatchers do when they've seen five tens of summers."

Cimmis vividly remembered Dzoo sitting in the plaza with her clan's sacred Dolphin Bundle in her lap. She would speak, then hold it to her ear and nod, hearing the Spirit inside. Dzoo had terrified every other child in Fire Village. And many of the adults. Especially him.

Astcat whispered, "Yes, we were alike, the two of us."

"Were you?" Ecan inquired impatiently. "My Chief, I must tell you—"

Cimmis turned to Astcat. "In what way were you alike, my wife?"

Astcat's smile faded, and her eyes went vacant. Spittle trickled from the corner of her mouth.

Cimmis gently wiped it away with his sleeve. "She's probably remembering her youth. You see, at the age of nine summers, Astcat was chosen by the North Wind elders to be the Starwatcher in Fire Village."

"So I have heard," Ecan said with a nod. "Our matron was a very Powerful child." He looked at Cimmis. "But, my Chief, we must discuss—"

Astcat laughed suddenly and shouted, "Dzoo used to run with the Noisy Ones! I saw her once, spinning around, trying to fling them off her skirt."

"I remember you telling me," Cimmis said in an affectionate voice. "She spun around so fast that all the Noisy Ones flew into the air and turned into butterflies."

"Yes." Astcat's voice wavered. "I . . . saw it."

Cimmis tucked the hides around Astcat and stroked her gray hair. "Sleep now. I'll tell you everything later."

He gently extricated his hand and stood up. "How many warriors did we lose?"

"Over the past two moons, we've lost two tens and three. Two were captured during the War Gods Village battle."

"Captured?"

Ecan propped his hands on his hips. "War Chief Talon ambushed us at the base of War Gods Mountain. We had to sacrifice a few to get away."

"And was my war chief one of them?"

"White Stone remained behind."

"Why?"

Ecan's perfect mouth hardened. "Rain Bear's warriors were crawling all over the mountain, and I—I lost my son. I don't know what happened. But after the battle, we were hunting down every last one of the North Wind People, to kill them, as you ordered, and my son must have . . ."

Astcat started weeping and whispered things that Cimmis couldn't hear, tender things.

He touched Ecan's arm. "Come, let us speak outside. I don't wish to upset her further."

He ducked beneath his door hanging, and Ecan stepped out into the cold beside him. A triumphant crowd had gathered around the returning warriors. The afternoon echoed with laughter and the rhyming work songs the slaves used to occupy themselves. In the distance, a keening arose as wives, girlfriends, and children learned of the death of their men. Dogs barked at the commotion.

"Before the battle," Ecan continued, "I hid Tsauz in a pile of rocks, but he wasn't there when we went to find him. I think he may have been captured."

"Then consider him dead, Ecan." Which saddened Cimmis; he'd genuinely liked the boy. Using him to allay Rain Bear's fears had been a stroke of brilliance. The gamble had been that Rain Bear, known for his leniency, would allow the war party to pass. Then, later, when blame had to be assigned, it would fall on Rain Bear's shoulders, further weakening his position and splintering the Raven People. Time would tell if that goal had been achieved.

Ecan's jaw muscles squirmed as he ground his teeth. Then he said, "It's possible—I'll grant that—but we searched for several hands of time looking for any sign. We found nothing. Nothing!"

Cimmis pinned him with hard eyes. "So you stayed longer than necessary. You risked, and lost, our warriors' lives searching for a little boy?"

"No longer than necessary! We searched for Tsauz while we were fulfilling your orders to hunt down the last of the North Wind People."

"Didn't it occur to you that the villagers might have found him and beaten him to death? Perhaps you just did not recognize your son."

"None of the dead wore his clothes. I think it is more likely that he was taken captive."

"If Rain Bear captured him, he's dead."

"Not necessarily," Ecan rushed to say. "Rain Bear may think he can use my son against me."

Cimmis turned. The vein in Ecan's temple throbbed. The man's heart was beating as quickly as a trapped rabbit's, desperation in his eyes.

"Use him in what way?"

"Perhaps to convince me . . ." He swallowed hard.

Cimmis gazed out at the veils of windblown rain that blew across the mountain. Thunderbirds rumbled high up near the cone. "Then let us pray that a runner appears today to tell us your son is dead. That way you will not be tempted to betray me, and I will not be tempted to kill you before you have the chance."

Ecan stepped back, aghast. "I would *not* betray you, my Chief! No matter what Rain Bear offered me."

Against Cimmis's will, his gaze strayed to his swaying door flap, where he glimpsed Astcat. "Don't lie to me. I *know* what men will do to protect the people they love."

Late Afternoon

Gutginsa guards the door to the House of Air. The journey to get there is long and arduous. There are many villages in the Above Worlds, each about a moon apart, through which the soul must fly. The Spirits who live there set traps and snares to try to catch unwary souls, which they eat."

My breath rattles in my lungs. I manage to suck in enough air to say, "I know all this. Is there . . . a reason . . . you feel you must tell me . . . the old stories?"

"I want to make certain you understand them."

He pauses, and I manage to lift my eyelids long enough to glimpse him gazing down at the river, or perhaps at the seagulls that flutter over the deep green water. The scent is powerful this afternoon, rich and earthy.

"Now listen carefully."

I sigh and nod.

"At the end of the flight, there is one final test. Gutginsa waits at the door to the House of Air, holding a living spear with the head of a serpent. He points his spear at each soul that arrives, because the serpent can tell good souls from evil souls. If the person has done very bad things in his life, Gutginsa's spear flies from his hand and punctures the heart of the evil soul, killing it. But if the person has been compassionate just once in his life, Gutginsa's spear hesitates."

I can feel my lungs flutter, like a bird's wings preparing to take flight. I have to force them to settle down before I can say, "Then the soul . . . has a chance to explain."

"Yes, that's right. It may do no good, but it may also be your redemption."

I whisper, "I always thought . . . Gutginsa's spear . . . was too generous."

"Ah," he breathes, and I feel his cape sway as he lifts his arm in some gesture. "Then you miss the point. You see, the desire to explain is everything. It is the very heart of deliverance."

I think about that. I suppose every soul must, at some point, realize that it needs to be redeemed, or redemption is impossible.

I smile. "I want . . . to explain."

His gnarled old fingers touch my arm. "I know. I'm praying very hard that you have the chance."

Thirty-three

Dzoo leaned back against the damp bark wall, listening to the rain fall outside. It spattered in front of the lodge door and trickled across the plaza. The Thunderbirds grumbled unhappily as they passed over Fire Village.

As the downpour increased, the villagers moved inside the lodges, but she could still hear them. In the lodge to the right of hers, a warrior told glorious tales of the battles he'd seen in the past two moons. Wooden bowls clacked, as though his wife served supper while he spoke. Occasionally, a little boy stopped him to ask a question.

Across the plaza, in the Council Lodge, women spoke. She couldn't make out the words, but their voices sounded weary and worried.

The Four Old Women. They should be worried.

Dzoo stared at the faint filament of gray that outlined the door on the other side of the lodge. Guards stood outside. Now and then, she heard them move.

She was alone.

She found it a curious sensation.

No one needed her. There were no wounded or sick to care for. The grieving didn't beg her for guidance. For the first time in moons she had only herself to think of.

She pushed back her buffalohide hood and examined her prison.

A smoke hole had been cut in the roof, but there was no fire hearth. Not even a ring of stones.

"Perfect," she murmured, and laughed softly.

A filth-encrusted bark container—for bodily wastes—rested near the door. Prisoners could only sit and stare at the blackness and worry about their futures.

Dzoo leaned her head back, closed her eyes, and conjured the image of the blood-streaked young man. Again she looked into his two stone eyes and felt her soul sway. She clung to that moment, feeling the few tendrils of Power slipping around her.

Feet sucked at the mud outside.

Ecan said, "Has she tried to escape?"

One of the guards responded, "I don't think she's even moved, Starwatcher."

Ecan flipped the door hanging aside and ducked into the lodge carrying a leather sack. He wore a woven bark rain hat and cape. "I thought you might be hungry."

She studied him as droplets of water sprinkled the dirt floor. "That surprises me."

"What does?"

"That the needs of another would occur to you."

Ecan roughly tossed the sack to the floor in front of her. Carved shell and bone jewelry flashed from his arms and ankles. Beneath the cape he wore a beautiful knee-length buckskin shirt dyed red, black, and white. Designs of Killer Whale, made from polished stone beads, winked in the faint light. He'd obviously bathed. His hair hung down his back in a long damp braid.

He paced before the door curtain. "You'll find a water sack and several seaweed cakes in the bag. Enjoy them or starve; I don't care."

Dzoo opened the bag. She pulled out the elk-bladder water sack first and took four swallows. Trickles ran down her chin and dripped onto her cape. After days of almost no food or water, she had to ration it or her stomach would rebel. She set the water aside and reached for the seaweed cakes. They'd been wrapped in thick layers of bark to keep them warm. She gave Ecan a wary look. Why this strange kindness?

He kept pacing.

Dzoo took a bite of the cake and chewed it slowly. It tasted salty and delicious.

Grimly, he said, "You are fortunate. Both Chief Cimmis and Matron Astcat remember you. I think if you offer to help them overcome the present crisis with the Raven People they might be inclined to spare your life."

Dzoo watched him as she chewed. She hadn't noticed before: raindrops coated his pointed face. "Why would I do that?"

"Cimmis has ways of making people do as he wishes, Dzoo. I wouldn't toy with him if I were you. Staking a person down, cutting a slit in his belly, and pulling out a length of intestines to roast in a hot fire is currently considered the most gruesome manner of—"

Dzoo laughed softly.

Ecan stalked across the room and knelt in front of her. He smelled fragrant, like cedar bark. Did his slaves store his clothing in a cedar box? "Your lack of humility is liable to get you killed before I can—"

"What?" she asked. "Use me for your own purposes?"

Ecan hesitated; then, as though it had just occurred to him, he touched the hem of her buffalo cape. "If I thought I could use you, Dzoo, believe me, I would." He moved his fingers tenderly over her cape. It was an intimate gesture, like stroking a lover's hand.

Dzoo leaned toward him and whispered, "Go ahead. Take me here in the dirt. A man's soul is never as vulnerable as when he is panting atop a woman. After you lay spent, I shall have more of you than just your seed."

Ecan stared at her, but drew back his hand. "Will you help me, or not?"

"What would you have me do? Witch your enemies? Or give your son wings so he can fly back to you?"

"Both."

Dzoo wiped the crumbs from her fingers onto her leather leggings. "Are you really surprised that Cimmis isn't already organizing a war party to run down the mountain and bring your son back?"

Ecan smiled. "Not exactly. Apparently, Cimmis fears I will betray him to get my son back."

Dzoo drew her knees up and braced her arms atop them. She finished her cake and reached for another. "Perhaps we have something in common after all."

Ecan's handsome face turned stony. "Don't even think it, Dzoo. He would kill me in less than a heartbeat if he even suspected I might do something like that."

"Then you must work very hard to keep his trust."

Ecan glanced at the door and listened for movement, afraid they'd been overheard. In the plaza, someone laughed. The guards shifted. One of them murmured something he couldn't hear.

Dzoo whispered, "You look like you just met Gutginsa's spear, Starwatcher."

His green eyes narrowed. "I believe Gutginsa's spear is pointed at us now, in this world. Not after we die. I believe it more today than I ever have."

He turned suddenly, and a thin sliver of light glinted on his water-slick rain hat. Before he exited into the pale gray gleam, he gripped the use-polished doorframe. "You understand, don't you, that I will do whatever I must to save my son?"

"You even lie to yourself, Ecan. You will do whatever you must to save yourself."

"That, too."

He pulled the curtain back, but just stood in the entry. Around his tall body, she saw the rain-soaked plaza and part of the large Council Lodge. Smoke curled from the roof.

Dzoo leaned back, waiting.

Ecan stared coldly at Dzoo as the rain began to slow.

She looked at him with those stunning midnight eyes, and he wondered if she was drinking his soul. Long red hair streamed over the front of her cape. Every move she made, every word she spoke, had a dangerous, sensual quality. She was at once frightening and frail, a combination that drew him like a wolf to a rabbit burrow. She had begun their game of dog and rabbit.

But he would finish it.

He stepped outside, where Wind Scorpion waited beside Horned Serpent. "Guard?" He motioned to Horned Serpent.

Horned Serpent trotted over and bowed. He had his brown hair tucked up beneath his rain hat. "Yes, Starwatcher?"

"Keep a close watch. Let no one pass. She is very Powerful, and she—"

"Oh, I know, Starwatcher. I have heard stories about her strange gods." The youth wiped rain from his broad cheeks.

"Stories? What stories?"

"Well . . ." He glanced at Ecan, then at the door hanging. "It is said that while she was a girl, the Striped Dart People taught her how to fly, and at night her soul takes the form of a bird and soars into the Underwater House to sit on the branches of a great tree hidden deep inside the Cave of First Woman. While there, she speaks with strange half-human half-buffalo men and drinks the blood of dead children."

"For the sake of . . . ," Ecan said in exasperation. "Just let no one pass, Horned Serpent. We can't stop her from visiting the Underwater House if she wishes, but we can stop someone from trying to rescue her."

The warrior nodded vigorously. "Yes, Starwatcher. As you order. I promise to guard her with my life."

Wind Scorpion stepped forward, an eyebrow lifted. "Starwatcher, if you would prefer, I would be more than happy to stay here. The witch's wiles don't scare me."

Ecan saw the faintest flicker in the grizzled warrior's eyes, and shook his head. "No, I want you with me. I trust you like no one else."

Wind Scorpion nodded, the slightest quiver at the corners of his mouth.

Ecan stalked away from the captive's quarters. Nothing was working out as he had anticipated. By Gutginsa, why? What had he done to affect his fate this way?

The slaves still out working—pounding octopus meat on stone slabs, smoking fish on racks over the plaza fire—watched him pass in silence. Rain glistened on their hats and capes. None would dare speak to him unless spoken to first. Instead they covered their faces when he neared—especially the young women—and nodded respectfully. Only other North Wind People met his eyes, but even they did so with trepidation.

Ecan walked up the slope to his lodge, which stood just inside the palisade at the base of the lava cliff. He threw aside the leather door hanging and ducked inside. Wind Scorpion took up his position outside the door.

Home. He experienced a sudden sense of relief. Three body lengths across, the vaulted ceiling rose two body lengths over his head. Baskets filled with fragrant Healing herbs lined the walls. Skulls hung on the roof poles, four tens and four of them. They watched him from empty sockets, hollow with the memory of their death and his victory over them.

When no one could see, he leaned heavily against the wall and glared down at the flickering fire a slave had kindled in the hearth. Panic threatened to engulf him.

He clenched his fists and looked up at the skulls. Soot blackened the curved surfaces of the braincases, brow ridges, sockets, and jaws. As the warmth of the fire rose, heat wavered around them, and their fixed grins began to deepen, as though trying to tell him something.

In the wake of the panic, a slow-burning anger stirred deep in his veins.

"Yes, my precious gods, give me rage," he whispered. "It will wipe away everything else."

The need to kill was almost overpowering. He turned, calling, "Wind Scorpion! Go and find me a girl. Someone young, untouched by another man. Someone that no one will miss. Do you understand?"

"Yes, Starwatcher."

Ecan listened as the man's steps faded, and then he turned his attention to the things he suddenly wished he could avoid.

His bedding hides lay rolled on the far right, next to his son's. Baskets stuffed with toys sat atop Tsauz's hides, and his tiny spear leaned beside Ecan's near the door.

Ecan reached for it and smoothed his fingers down the wood. He could feel Tsauz in every nick and scrape. His son's smile lived in these walls, these toys.

His fault. All of it.

If he hadn't agreed to White Stone's plan . . .

"Enough!" He balled a fist and slammed it into the lodgepole. *"Stop this!"*

A tripod with a tea bag hung near the flames, scenting the air with the tart fragrance of dried cranberries.

As he bent down for a wooden cup, reaction to the strain set in, and he began to shake. He stared at the blood welling on his skinned knuckles.

He got up again and started walking, shedding jewelry and garments as he went. Shell bracelets and rings slipped from his hands and bounced across the floor as if alive. When he pulled his shirt over his head and violently threw it at the wall, the garment fluttered down like a many-colored feather. Sweat glistened on his naked chest. He tried to unlace his moccasins, but his fingers could not seem to find the knots.

White Stone and Red Dog had not returned yet, and he thanked the gods for the reprieve. Every instant White Stone was still out looking for Tsauz, he could hope the boy lived. But if they returned with news that Tsauz . . . that his son . . .

"Dear gods, not today. I couldn't stand it."

His dreams had been tortured. Every time he started to fall asleep, he heard Tsauz shout, *"No, Father, please! Please, don't leave me!"*

He reached for his son's bedding, crumpling it in his fingers as he pulled it to his chest, buried his face in it, and wept.

Thirty-four

White Stone pulled off his drenched cape as they entered Fire Village's palisade gate and exchanged pleasantries with the guards. He glanced at Red Dog. The old warrior looked as exhausted as White Stone felt. His graying black hair stuck to his furrowed forehead in wet locks. Mud spattered his bare legs, and his skin was threaded by red welts from branches, briars, and snags. They'd run straight up the mountain, eating and drinking as they went.

Two days before, they had rounded a bend in a patch of thick timber—and collided head-on with Sleeper's warriors, who were headed the other way. In the melee that followed, White Stone had yelled, "Run!" and he and Red Dog had burst through, beating feet as they'd never run before.

Sleeper's warriors had chased them the entire way. White Stone and Red Dog had used every trick known to them, doubling back, leaping off the trail, splashing up or down streams, then climbing out through tree branches to keep from leaving signs of their passage. Sometimes they stayed just beyond spear range. At others, it had seemed inconceivable that Sleeper's warriors could have followed the convoluted path they'd taken. Then they would magically appear several hands of time later, still dogging their trail.

White Stone made a face as he ran his hands down his trembling legs.

"Red Dog, I want you to stand guard while I speak with Ecan."

Red Dog scratched his broken nose. "Are you afraid of being overhead, or afraid you might need my protection?"

Annoyed, White Stone ordered, "Just keep watch."

Red Dog grinned, flipped up his hood, and nodded as they plodded wearily toward Ecan's. Rain was falling again, the drops pattering on White Stone's head. At the moment, he couldn't have cared less. The way he felt, everything below his waist might have been made of stone.

White Stone approached Ecan's decorated lodge with a look of dread he knew he couldn't hide. His heart was beating dully as he called, "Starwatcher? War Chief White Stone wishes to speak with you."

He could hear someone scrambling about inside. The rustling of bedding and a low whimper made him look questioningly at Red Dog before he asked, "Starwatcher?"

"Maybe you'd better check," Red Dog muttered.

"Keep watch."

"Yes, War Chief." Red Dog smiled. "Just wake me when you're finished."

White Stone clapped him on the shoulder and ducked into the interior. Larger than most domiciles, Ecan's stretched three body lengths across. His sleeping hides lay against the west wall beneath a row of weapons. A collection of finely flaked stone axes glinted in the light. From poles above stacks of bark boxes and willow baskets hung a row of skulls.

It was said that Ecan fed them powdered seaweed every day when he was home. When he was away, the slaves had instructions to keep them happy with offerings. The story was that Ecan used to abuse them until old Rides-the-Wind told him that if the souls grew unhappy they could destroy the village.

White Stone wasn't sure he believed it, but who wanted to take chances?

The bedding moved again, and White Stone squinted, making out a girl, perhaps nine or ten summers old, cowering under the hides.

"Who are you?"

She swallowed hard, eyes huge with fright, but no sound passed her lips.

"Get out of the Starwatcher's house, now!" White Stone extended a finger toward the door. "This is no place for little imps like you to be playing."

To White Stone's surprise, the little girl bolted from the covers, naked as a seal pup, and shot through the door out into the rain.

"What the . . . ?" Red Dog cried.

"A child was hiding in here."

"You forget where you are," Red Dog replied meaningfully.

White Stone stiffened, understanding crawling through him.

"Greetings, Starwatcher!" Red Dog's coarse voice barked outside. "The war chief is waiting for you."

White Stone made a face and looked toward the door in time to see Red Dog bow as he pulled the lodge flap aside.

Ecan entered like one of the gods. His hair fell in long black waves over his broad shoulders. He hadn't even bothered to put on a rain cape. Walking directly to White Stone, he demanded, "Where is my son?"

"Rain Bear has him."

Color drained from the Starwatcher's face; a quiver pulled at his lip.

White Stone frowned and looked away. He hated weakness in another man, especially someone as brutal as Ecan. "They used the boy's dying dog to lure him out." White Stone turned back. "Did you spear the dog?"

"Of course I did!"

Fatigue made him careless. "Next time you do something that stupid, make sure you kill it."

Ecan's eyes had taken on a weird light; his voice dropped to a hiss. "If I'd let it live Tsauz would have insisted upon taking it with him. I couldn't take the chance that the miserable little cur would give away his hiding place."

"Well, in the end, it worked out just that way."

Ecan ignored the tone in White Stone's voice. "Where did Rain Bear take my son?"

"The last we saw, they were fussing over Tsauz in the plaza during the Moon Ceremonial. We were surrounded by tens of people. We had to leave."

Ecan took a deep breath. Dark blue smudged the flesh beneath his eyes. He looked like he hadn't slept in days.

"How did Tsauz look?"

White Stone lifted a shoulder. "He had scratches and bruises. Most of all, he looked frightened half out of his mind. He kept clutching that whimpering puppy so hard he was squeezing the guts out through the wound in its . . ."

A tremor, the sort icy fingers made on the spine, ran through Ecan. Then he said, "Fear can be endured. Bruises heal."

"Yes."

A frightening glitter filled Ecan's eyes. He glared at White Stone for several heartbeats, maintaining control by sheer force of will.

White Stone, fatigued past good sense, just glared back.

Ecan's dark brows lowered. "What do you think we should do next?"

White Stone shifted in confusion. "Don't you understand what I've been saying? There's nothing more *any* of us can do. If Rain Bear took him to Sandy Point Village, the boy is surrounded by tens of tens of warriors. They'd swat us like flies if we tried to rescue the boy. Unless you can talk the Council into approving a prisoner exchange, there's no hope." He could see by Ecan's eyes that that wasn't about to happen.

"Thank you, War Chief." Ecan turned away. "Please go and report to Cimmis. He's waiting for you."

White Stone stared. "I'll do that; then I must see the families of the warriors who were killed or captured. I'm sure they're—"

"One last thing." Ecan gracefully walked toward him. "I told Cimmis that you stayed behind because of Rain Bear."

The rest remained unspoken.

White Stone picked up his rain cape. As he swung it around his shoulders, he woodenly said, "I *did* stay behind because of Rain Bear. I needed to judge the effects of our strike on War Gods Village. I needed to study his camps and count his warriors. How can we ever hope to crush him if we don't know his weaknesses?"

"I agree, War Chief."

White Stone walked by Ecan and pulled the lodge flap aside, but didn't exit. "Ecan, I share the responsibility for what happened to the boy. Let me know if I—"

"Yes, War Chief," Ecan interrupted. "I will."

White Stone hesitated. "Um, you should know. I heard someone in here. There was a little girl . . ." He indicated the rumpled bedding.

"What?" Ecan glanced up, confused; then his eyes cleared. "Oh, yes. That. Never Mind. Cimmis is waiting in the Council Lodge for your report to him."

White Stone stepped out into the rain. Red Dog met his gaze, and White Stone tilted his head, cueing Red Dog to watch Ecan. "I'll be back soon, Red Dog."

"Yes, War Chief."

Half sick with dread, White Stone plodded wearily toward the Council Lodge.

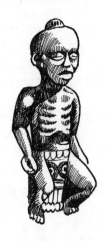

Thirty-five

Red Dog stood in the rain beside the Starwatcher's lodge and watched White Stone slog his way through the downpour toward the Council Lodge. Had he ever been this root-sucking tired before? Fatigue, like a warm fuzziness, weighted his limbs and lay heavily in his guts. His brain felt hot inside his skull despite the cold rain pattering on his bark hat. Still, he tried to peek through the swaying flap at Ecan. The Starwatcher looked like he'd been kicked in the stomach.

After a few more moments, Ecan pulled the leather hanging aside, and Red Dog slid his gaze to the slaves still going about their duties despite the downpour.

"Is everything all right, Starwatcher?" Red Dog asked offhandedly.

Ecan stepped out into the rain. He had the kind of sculpted face that made women stare admiringly.

In a voice laced with irony, Ecan said, "Everything's fine."

Red Dog gave him a quizzical look. "Starwatcher?"

Ecan's eyes resembled shiny green beads. "I wish to hire you to undertake a special mission."

"Really?"

"I will reward you very well."

Red Dog lifted a shoulder. "I'm already wealthy, Starwatcher. When you hired me to burn down the Council Lodge where your wife's family was gathered, I made a fortune."

Ecan clamped Red Dog's wrist. "That was *necessary*, Red Dog.

She was going to set my belongings outside our lodge. I would have lost my son! Her clan would have taken him away from me!"

Red Dog looked down at the Starwatcher's hand—the man had never touched him before. "I just meant I am already rich, Starwatcher."

"This is an important mission, Red Dog. Of course, it must seem as though you are strictly the chief's messenger, but we need an intermediary to work with Rain Bear. Rain Bear knows you. He once trusted you."

The cold grip of fear banished his fatigue. "That was a long time ago, Starwatcher. I guarantee he is no longer under any such illusion."

"You are still the best choice."

"I'd send someone else. Maybe Flying Fish. He's reliable." Red Dog glanced toward Cimmis's lodge. Matron Astcat was staring at him through the doorway. She gazed about warily and crooked a beckoning finger before the door hanging dropped back in place.

Ecan leaned close, his nose within a finger's width of Red Dog's. "You're going. Unless you'd like to tell me the name of the man who makes the fetishes you Trade for. I'd hire him in an instant. He's Powerful, anonymous, and living right in the middle of us."

"By Gutginsa's balls, you're right he's Powerful!" Red Dog agreed, wondering what Astcat wanted. "Powerful enough that I'm not going to cross him. Not even for you, Starwatcher."

Ecan backed away, a satiated smile on his lips. "Then perhaps you wouldn't want it whispered around that you were serving a witch, eh, Red Dog? What's his name? Coyote?"

Red Dog swallowed dryly, the fear coiling in his gut. "Look, I've never so much as seen his face. He wears a mask when we meet. He talks funny, with an accent, to hide his voice."

"A man who *says* he works for a witch, could even *be* the witch."

Red Dog shivered, but forced himself to say, "Or he could be someone like a Starwatcher, wearing a mask, hiding his voice."

Ecan laughed harshly at that. "Stop prattling. You're going, Red Dog. That's all there is to it."

Red Dog took a deep breath, knowing he had no choice. Liaison to a witch or not, Red Dog couldn't afford to cross the Starwatcher. Not yet.

Ecan said, "It means you'll have to run hard to get back by tomorrow night."

"Tomorrow! I just got home!" He had to see Astcat—and from her gesture, it was something furtive.

"It's all downhill, and you're accustomed to running for days straight. You're perfect for the task."

"Perfect for roasting over Rain Bear's coals, you mean. He will eat my liver first."

"Perhaps, but if you survive, you will be the wealthiest man in Fire Village."

Red Dog pulled his wrist away and stole a quick glance at the lodge where he hoped Dzoo was being held. Dzoo, Astcat, Ecan . . . gods, this was getting complicated. "Why don't you tell me what you have in mind; then we'll discuss how much my liver is worth."

Tsauz held the dead puppy as he walked into the meadow between Evening Star and Rides-the-Wind. Scattered clouds passed above to collect in a gray, cottony mass on the volcanic mountains farther to the east. A faint breeze stirred the firs, and a ring of warriors surrounded them.

For Evening Star, the ceremony came as a relief. The dog's corpse was swollen, leaking brown liquid, and downright putrid.

How odd that a child's grief can hold an adult's common sense hostage.

It had been Rides-the-Wind who had had the courage to insist that Tsauz bury the rotting puppy. Fearing the boy might change his mind, Rain Bear had wasted no time preparing a cordon of guards to see them out of Sandy Point Village. People in the surrounding camps had watched in disbelief as the processional wound through their ragged camps. And for what? The burial of a puppy?

To Evening Star's mind, it was either the stuff of legends, or a most ridiculous comedy. She looked around the grassy meadow Rides-the-Wind had picked. Alders, pine, and a ring of birch surrounded the opening.

"How much will I owe you, Elder?" Tsauz asked as he laid the limp corpse on a rock that the Soul Keeper had led him to. I—I don't have anything here with me, but when I get home, I give you my oath I will send you—"

"I don't wish to be paid, Tsauz. I'm just happy you asked me to help you."

Crying, Tsauz said, "I promised him, Elder. I told him I would find someone to Sing his soul to the afterlife." He wiped his cheeks on his sleeve. "Thank you, Elder."

The gratitude in the boy's voice was wrenching. "Let's get started so Runner can be on his way."

Sunlight glimmered on Rides-the-Wind's gnarled hands as he reached into his ritual pack. He pulled out a small white bag and poured powdered seaweed into his palm. It shimmered a pale green.

Rides-the-Wind touched the boy's shoulder. "Can you help me Sing him to the House of Air?"

Tsauz choked out, "Yes."

Rides-the-Wind lifted his voice in the Death Song, and after a few moments, Tsauz's voice, and then Evening Star's, joined his:

In a sacred manner, we send a voice.
  We send a voice.
The path of Gutginsa is our strength.
The path of Gutginsa is our hope.
  A praise we are making.
  A praise we are sending.
In a sacred manner, we send a voice.
Hear us, our North Wind ancestors.
  Come and lead this puppy's soul
  to the entry to the Above Worlds.
In a sacred manner we are sending a voice.
  Come, Blessed Ancestors, take this puppy's
  soul to the House of Air.

The guards sifted through the trees around the meadow, quiet, alert, watching them. It was, perhaps, the first time any of them had heard the North Wind Death Song.

Rides-the-Wind lifted his hands. "The ancestors will find him here, Tsauz, and take his soul flying to the House of Air. Tonight he will be watching over you from high above."

Tsauz looked blankly up at the cloud-packed morning sky where ravens flapped lazily toward the sea, cawing to each other.

"Is it true, Elder, that the dead can fly down to earth and make rainbows?"

Rides-the-Wind smiled and followed Tsauz's gaze. The sky had started turning a deep shade of amber. "I think it's true. They can bring rain and call the Thunderbirds . . . and make rainbows. Why do you ask?"

Tsauz chewed his lip. "I'll be looking for Runner's rainbow, that's all."

Evening Star watched them, her heart heavy. How would a blind boy see a rainbow? She thought of her daughter, and all that the little girl would miss in life. Love, grief, smiles, and laughter. She would never enjoy that lift that came with a young man's smile, or feel the tingle in her pelvis as she shared a man's body. No life would be conceived to grow in her womb, and the tearing pain of childbirth would never be hers. So much was lost when a child died.

Rides-the-Wind stroked Tsauz's dark hair. "You'll see Runner's rainbow. Someday soon, I imagine."

The guards shifted. Several whispered to each other and squinted at their back trail.

Evening Star could feel something happening out there. "Let's go back and eat breakfast. Soul Keeper, would you join us? Rain Bear promised to come for tea once he's finished meeting with the other chiefs."

"I would like that very much." The old man looked at her with a knowing gaze.

At that moment, a warrior loped in from the forest, breathing hard, and called, "Where's Chief Rain Bear?"

"The Council Lodge," Evening Star's guard Hornet answered. "What's happened?"

"We caught one of Ecan's assassins sneaking up on the village!"

Evening Star stiffened. "Elder, please make sure you get the boy back safely."

"What about you?" Rides-the-Wind asked.

A cold shiver went through her. "I know some of the Wolf Tails. Perhaps I can name this one."

Thirty-six

Rain Bear shoved a low branch aside and continued up the trail behind young Feathers. He was just a skinny boy, little more than gangly bones, but his body betrayed the terrible importance of his current position. He was guiding the great chief. No doubt his young friends were going to hear about it over and over.

The fire in the clearing ahead threw long, dancing shadows over the firs and boulders. It made the forest seem alive with translucent wings. As they drew near, Rain Bear saw Dogrib standing with three men. He was binding the middle man's hands behind his back. Two others held his arms in viselike grips.

Rain Bear called, "What have we got? Who is he?"

Dogrib called, "One of Ecan's assassins. We captured him crawling through the boulders on his belly."

"That's a lie!" the man shouted in response, and struggled against Dogrib's hard hands. "I came in peace, openly!"

Rain Bear entered the halo of firelight and recognized the burly form. "Red Dog?"

"Yes. It's me. My friend, I must speak with you!" The dirt on his face had mixed with his sweat and turned to mud in the deep furrows in his forehead. "Rain Bear, get these young wolves off me! You, of all people, know I am no assassin!" He glared at the two warriors holding his muscular arms. They grinned like cougars over a freshly killed carcass.

Rain Bear halted on the opposite side of the fire. Dirty hair had come loose from Red Dog's bun and framed his round face. He appeared on the verge of panic. *Good.*

Rain Bear said, "You came in peace to do what? Try to kill one of us? Or to rescue Ecan's son?" He paused. "Sorry, old friend. Sleeper's warriors beat you back. I have just been in council with Goldenrod. He said they almost had you and White Stone more than once."

Red Dog nervously scanned the faces of the people around him. "I bring you a message from Fire Village."

"From whom?"

"Astcat, matron of the North Wind People."

Red Dog's deerhide cape had large patches of hair missing. Not the usual garb of one of Fire Village's best warriors, but he'd probably shed everything that would tie him to Cimmis.

"Astcat has not attempted to communicate with me in six and ten cycles—not since she made her own daughter Outcast for running away with me. Why now?"

Red Dog sucked in a breath. "I can't tell you, but believe me, you truly do not wish to kill me until I've spoken with you!"

"Go ahead. I'm listening."

Red Dog glanced suspiciously at Dogrib and the rest. "My message is for you alone."

Rain Bear composed his face, deepening the lines as if in great study. "Bind him up like a trussed walrus."

He watched as a length of sturdy rope was located and Red Dog was thoroughly wrapped and secured with doubled knots. Then Rain Bear pulled his war club from his belt and motioned for Dogrib and the other men to back off. "Give us a few moments."

Unhappy with the arrangement, Dogrib said, "As you order, but we'll be close enough to see, if not hear. Should he even look like he's moving against you—"

"I expect you to kill him," Rain Bear calmly said, and thumped his club into his palm. "The fact that he knows that should make our discussions more straightforward."

Red Dog nodded. "I assure you, it will."

Dogrib strode to the edge of the clearing with the other warriors.

Rain Bear took his time walking around the fire toward Red Dog. The grizzled warrior watched him warily.

"All right, *old friend*," Rain Bear said in a low voice. "Tell me what's happening."

Red Dog gave him a foxy smile. "Why on earth am I doing this to myself? Look at me! I'm trussed like a pig, covered in filth! My legs feel like wooden stumps, and I'm so tired I could fall flat on my face."

"It's because you're such a scoundrel, and you know it."

Red Dog grinned like a maniac. "That's it, all right." Then his expression fell. "You have to believe me—I didn't know what was coming at War Gods Village. When you took Ecan's weapons and let him continue, I really thought we were on a peaceful errand." He made a face. "After some of the things I've seen . . . done . . . I don't want to do this anymore."

"What would you do instead?"

He jerked his head westward. "There are islands out there. I could take all of my wealth and sit on a rock, surrounded by the sea. Once a moon, I could palm off one of my trinkets to a fisherman for bringing me food."

"You'd be crazy within five days." Rain Bear crossed his arms. "I know you too well. You enjoy scheming; it's part of your soul. You find a crooked pleasure being in the presence of people who underestimate who and what you are."

"And who and what am I?"

"One of the most clever and remarkable men I've ever known."

Red Dog chuckled at that. "You know, your flattery is worth more than all the North Wind People's silly jewels." He paused. "In all of my life, only two people have seen through to my soul."

"Who's the other one?"

Red Dog shrugged. "I don't know."

"You don't have to lie to me."

"I'm not. I've never seen him in the daylight, and at night, he wears a mask."

"You're joking."

Red Dog's expression turned flat, and his voice dropped to a whisper. "About him? Never."

Rain Bear stiffened. "I don't believe it—someone actually scares you."

"Oh, yes, more than Ecan, Cimmis, or the Council. If they found out I was your agent, they'd just torture me to death in a most grisly fashion." Red Dog's eyes glittered. "He'd steal my soul and lock it screaming and terrified into one of his little chipped fetishes."

Rain Bear cocked his head. "Coyote?"

Red Dog jerked. "You *know* him?"

"He's after Dzoo."

"After her how?"

"We think he wants to possess her."

Red Dog looked uneasily out at the darkness beyond the ring of fire. "I'm supposed to deliver Astcat's message. Then we've got to dicker over Ecan's son. After that, I've got to get back. If Coyote's after Dzoo, she's in real danger."

Do you believe it?" Evening Star's voice held a tremor, and it angered her. Gruffly, she folded her arms and leaned against the dark trunk of a fir. This was either a dream coming true, or the beginning of a nightmare. She'd chafed and stamped when Dogrib wouldn't allow her into the meadow where Rain Bear and Red Dog were talking, and now, in the morning light, as she heard Matron Astcat's terms, she wasn't sure what to think.

Rain Bear crouched before her and studied the ragged people moving around the campfires down the slope. He had a strange look on his face. "It's possible. During her lucid moments, Astcat generally made good decisions. Do you think the Council knows about the offer?"

"I doubt it. Nevertheless, she is the matron of the North Wind People. She has the authority to make offers without their approval. I just don't understand why she would wish to."

"Perhaps it is simply an act of kindness."

She shook her head. "Offering to revoke my slave status and give me a lodge in Fire Village is more than kindness; it's very dangerous. My people would flock to me. Within days, I'd be confirmed as clan matron to succeed my mother. Potentially, if anything happened to Astcat, I would be a viable candidate for matron of the North Wind People. Surely neither she nor Cimmis wishes that."

Rain Bear rubbed his jaw. "Nevertheless she has been ill."

"Yes, but she doesn't want me to follow her. She has a daughter, Kstawl."

He propped his elbows on his knees, and she could see the red sash that belted his tan leather shirt. It accentuated the breadth of his shoulders and the narrowness of his waist. "Kstawl is very young, isn't she?"

"Three and ten summers."

Evening Star slipped her hands beneath her cape and rubbed her cold arms. The walk to the meadow had chilled her to the bone. "It is more likely that all this is a lie. Astcat wants to lure me back so that she can reward Ecan by returning his wayward slave."

Rain Bear grimaced at the ground. Tens of feet had trampled the mud; then it had frozen with the fall of night, leaving a pocked, treacherous surface. "Well, we won't let that happen."

Evening Star's throat suddenly tightened. She lifted a hand to rub it.

Rain Bear stood, and she saw the dread and hope that brimmed in his eyes. "But if there's a chance that you might be able to safely take your position as clan matron . . ."

He let the words hang.

"I can't."

"Answer me truly: If Astcat were dead, and the remaining North Wind People asked you to return as the North Wind matron, would you do it?"

Horrifying images flashed across her soul. She squeezed her eyes closed to avoid them, but they only intensified. People crying, lodges on fire . . . her daughter screaming . . .

"During the attack on my village," she said in a shaky voice, "I tried to plead with Ecan for the lives of the children. I had my two-summers-old daughter in my arms and five more children clinging to my cape. He was polite and understanding. He said of course he wouldn't execute children. I let his warriors take them away to a 'safe' place beyond the burning village. But it wasn't far enough. I . . . I . . . could hear . . ."

"You don't have to tell me this," he murmured.

"Yes, I do. You asked if I could go back to the North Wind People." Tears of anger leaked from her eyes. The memories made her feel empty and alone. "They killed Bright Cloud first. They bound her to a pole and dangled her in a fire. She kept screaming for me. I leaped upon Ecan. . . . His guards clubbed me down." She looked at Rain Bear and found rage in his eyes. "The men who killed my daughter weren't Raven People. I *can't* go back. I *won't*."

Rain Bear reached out and took her hand in a strong grip. "I understand, but if you . . ."

Evening Star stepped into his arms and buried her face in the hide over his broad shoulder. It took him a moment to realize what she'd done. Then he pulled her close.

"Would it help you if I went back?" she asked miserably. "If I went to Fire Village and secretly worked to rally the North Wind People against the Four Old Women?"

He stroked her hair. "Maybe. Think about it for a time. This isn't something you must decide today."

Wolf Spider and Hornet whispered and looked away, as though trying to give them some privacy.

Evening Star let her body melt against Rain Bear's, and a warm, tingling wave ran through her. It felt so soothing to be held by a man again.

He whispered against her hair, "Red Dog said Ecan is desperate to get his boy back. He said Cimmis wasn't concerned."

"Of course not. His assassins are already on their way. What did Ecan offer?"

"Wealth and promises of my personal safety. Mostly promises he can't keep. He will become more amenable as his desperation grows."

Rain Bear peered down into her eyes. It was like standing on a mountaintop in a lightning storm. Every nerve in her body prickled.

"Red Dog is waiting to hear your answer to Matron Astcat's request. Do you want to speak with him? You don't have to."

"Do you trust him?"

"Red Dog? He has no more scruples than a pine marten in a red squirrel's nest. For the moment he's having the time of his life playing at being everyone's spy. It delights him to no end that Ecan and White Stone think he's a dolt. Cimmis—if he ever even looked sideways at him—would think he was just another lazy unwashed warrior. A menial little better than a slave."

"Then why does he stay there?"

"They pay him. He may be the richest man in the world by now. Oh, and the other thing. He worships Dzoo. It's something I don't understand. I can't picture her ever responding to his devotion—or should I call it an obsession? May your Gutginsa have mercy on anyone who harms a hair on her body, because Red Dog, no matter the cost, will kill him."

"Where is he?"

"Dogrib has him in a secret location outside of the camps. He's under heavy guard."

Evening Star reluctantly stepped away from him, and Rain Bear folded his arms over his broad chest, as though to protect his heart. "If you went to Fire Village, it might turn ugly."

"Oh, you have no idea how ugly it might be."

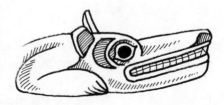

Thirty-seven

Old Woman Above had left her lodge to carry the fiery ball of the sun into the sky. The dawn was so warm, a man did not even need a cape. Tiny pools of water glistened across Fire Village. Only the most sheltered ledges on the black lava cliff gleamed with frosty rimes.

White Stone had been summoned to Cimmis's quarters just after morning prayers. The chief had his square jaw clamped, as though preparing for a hand-to-hand stiletto fight. His gray hair hung loose over his shoulders.

"I don't think you should do this, my Chief," White Stone said as he strode at Cimmis's side. "It's not wise."

"If Rain Bear has shared his thoughts with anyone besides his council, it's Dzoo. If I can get anything out of her, it could make all the difference for us."

"I doubt she'll tell you anything, unless we torture her. After enough pain anyone will talk."

"We're talking about Dzoo. First, I don't think you could ever get her to talk, no matter how much pain you inflicted on her. Second, if word gets out that we're torturing her, not only will it play into Rain Bear's hands, but it might even lead to a revolt among the slaves. Do you understand? She may be the most dangerous woman in the world. Not only will I *not* hurt her, War Chief, I'm going to make her as comfortable as I can."

White Stone gave Cimmis a disbelieving look as he walked away, and shook his head before following. By Gutginsa's bloody spear, didn't Cimmis understand what kind of woman he was dealing with? While on the trail, Red Dog had related some of the stories people told about Dzoo. His warriors had become so frightened, he wasn't sure they'd have had the courage to kill her under a direct order.

He glanced away, thinking. At this time of morning the palisade cast a long shadow that stretched halfway across the village. Slaves crouched around the central fire, pounding lupine root. Their haunted eyes followed Cimmis as he passed. White Stone kept his hand braced upon his belted war ax as a reminder to them. Deer Killer, on guard at Dzoo's door, straightened as they approached. His dark eyes widened. To White Stone's dismay, he always had a startled look when Cimmis came near him.

"Greetings, Deer Killer," Cimmis said. "How is our prisoner?"

"I didn't even hear her move during the night, my Chief."

Cimmis pulled the door hanging back and ducked inside.

White Stone said, "I thought Wind Scorpion was supposed to relieve you at dawn? Where—"

"You fools!" Cimmis shouted, and rushed back into the daylight. *"This lodge is empty!"*

White Stone gave Deer Killer a murderous look.

"I didn't do it, *I swear!*"

White Stone ducked under the hanging. As his eyes adjusted, he saw the bark container on the far side of the circular structure . . . but that was all. "It's impossible! She couldn't have escaped!"

"There she is!" Deer Killer shouted. *"Look! Near Ecan's lodge!"*

White Stone scrambled out. "Where?"

Cimmis stood with a hand up to shield his eyes from the morning glare.

Dzoo stood just to the right of Ecan's lodge, facing the lava cliff. Wind Woman waffled her red dress around her long legs and played with her waist-length braid.

"War Chief!" Deer Killer blurted. "I swear to you I never left my post! Not even for an instant! I . . ." A curious expression slackened his face. "She must have *flown* out. It's the only answer! She changed herself into a bird and soared out through the smoke hole!"

White Stone made a face. Flown indeed!

"Silence!" Cimmis ordered. The slaves had started to stand up and follow their gazes.

In a clipped voice, Cimmis said, "Come with me. Both of you." Then he stalked off across the village with his long gray hair flying.

As White Stone hurried after his chief, he shot a glance over his shoulder at the horrified Deer Killer. "I'll deal with you later. As-suming Cimmis doesn't order your guts boiled first."

When they reached Dzoo, Cimmis slowed, ordering, "Deer Killer, make certain no one comes close enough to overhear my conversa-tion. Including the Starwatcher."

"Of course, my Chief." Deer Killer trotted the two tens of paces to Ecan's lodge and stood, eyes half glazed with fear, shivers racking his body.

White Stone asked, "And me, my Chief?"

The hem of Cimmis's blue knee-length shirt fluttered in the breeze. "Keep your warrior company. Perhaps he has some last re-quests he might wish to make before I deal with him."

He protested, "But, my Chief, what if she attacks you? Before I could get to you, she might—"

Cimmis's dark eyes glittered. "I was a warrior for more summers than you have been alive, White Stone. I can protect myself. Go."

White Stone glanced dubiously at Cimmis's shriveled left arm and backed away to stand beside Deer Killer.

Deer Killer leaned sideways and whispered, "I've never been this terrified in my life! If she could get out of the captives' lodge, there's no place we can hold her. She can fly about as she pleases!"

White Stone glumly watched Cimmis walk toward Dzoo. Just be-yond the palisade, the lava cliff rose like a rough-hewn black wall. She had her chin tipped up, as though studying the old owl nests that bristled in the clefts.

Assuming Deer Killer hadn't dozed off or left his post, how had she managed to escape? "Did you ever find the missing ropes? The ones you used to tie her up in Wasp Village?

"No, War Chief."

"Perhaps she tied them together and used them to climb out of the smoke hole. Did that occur to you?"

Relief made the young warrior's eyes widen. "Blessed gods, do you think so?"

"Maybe." He wondered if Cimmis was going to remember Deer Killer's dereliction, and if so, who would be given the disagreeable task of ending his life?

Dzoo heard him coming. Her vision of the towering black cliff quiv-ered as his feet struck the ground. Heavy feet, pounding out authority.

He didn't speak, just took a stand behind her.

She turned and saw what he had become: tall, lanky, with a square jaw. His long gray hair hung over his broad shoulders like a mantle. His eyes were striking—the eyes of a trapped man who sees no way out.

"So," she said, "you are Chief Cimmis now. It must be difficult for you."

Cimmis's eyes narrowed. She saw him look away, trying not to let her see his fear. *I wonder if he plays this game with every person, every moment of his life.*

He exhaled. "Are you well, Dzoo? My slaves tell me that Lion Girl is ill. Is her replacement, Dance Fly, properly caring for you?"

"Your slave emptied my waste bowls before they spilled onto the floor again. If that's what you mean."

He walked over, close, as though to prove to the people below that he wasn't afraid. The hem of his blue shirt waffled around his leggings. She watched as he gathered the courage to meet her eyes. To his credit, he didn't wince when she stared past into his wounded soul.

"I did not order your capture, Dzoo. But you are here, and I cannot just release you. The other North Wind People would kill me for it. You may be a valuable tool—and these days we must use whatever we have."

"It's too late, Cimmis. The time of the North Wind People is coming to a close."

He stared at her as though uncertain. She knew him so well, could read the tracks on his soul the way a hunter read an elk's trail. She smiled as his warrior's instinct insisted that she was bluffing.

"They can't kill all of us, Dzoo, and I assure you those of us who remain will hunt down every last Raven Person who was involved—"

Her laughter came bubbling up from deep inside.

His shoulder muscles tensed.

She shot a glance at his warriors and leaned toward him to whisper, "If you were wise, Cimmis, you would start shedding every vestige of the North Wind People's way of life: their clothing, their jewelry and mannerisms. Your only hope of survival is to blend into the Raven villages and forget you ever knew anything about your own people."

His jaw hardened. In that instant she could tell that he wanted a way out, but couldn't allow himself to take it. The snare that had entangled him was called obligation.

"Dzoo, has Rain Bear managed to bind the refugees into a fighting force? Will they follow him?"

She said, "It will be difficult to disguise your wife, but it can be done. There are many battle victims who have lost their souls. My advice is to run as fast as you can to the northern Cougar People. If she ever starts talking about who she is, just tell them she is not well. Tell them the evil Chief Cimmis killed her entire family before her eyes. So many suffered the same fate. They will believe you."

His eyes might have been brown chert, hard and shiny. "I can't believe Rain Bear wishes the destruction of his daughter's relatives."

She leaned closer, their faces less than a handsbreadth apart. She watched him lose the battle to pull away, thinking it would shame him before his people. In reply he could only glare.

"Escaping your own people will be the final test. But you know that, don't you? The North Wind People will never forgive you for saving yourself and your wife. They expect both of you to die for them. To provide cover for their escape." She shrugged absently. "I will tell you truly, I have not seen that part."

"But . . . you have seen the rest?"

"Oh, yes."

A swallow went down his throat. "Are you telling me you have seen the end?"

"The end is only a fragment. There is much more to fear."

His teeth ground beneath the thin veneer of flesh.

"If you tell me the entire vision, Dzoo, from start to finish"—he exhaled a shaky breath—"I will set you free."

"Despite the fact that you will die for it?"

He nodded stiffly. "I give you my oath."

"Do you know what it's like to fly, Cimmis?"

"No."

"Before this is over, you will." She gestured to the beaten path that led through the middle of Fire Village. "Shall we go?"

"Go?" He squinted unsurely. "Where?"

She toyed with him like a spider tapping a trapped fly with its leg. "You had my old lodge cleaned out, didn't you? I wish to go home."

She started down the trail. He said nothing, stunned and motionless.

White Stone cried, "Stay where you are, witch!"

Cimmis hurried to catch up.

White Stone started forward, muscles flexing as he gripped his spear at the ready. "What is she doing out here, my Chief? How did she escape?"

Cimmis bluntly told him, "She is moving to her old lodge, War Chief. I want you to escort her."

"Her old lodge?" White Stone gestured in disbelief. "Why?"

Cimmis exploded. "Because *I ordered it*! I had it prepared for her. Tell the guards that she is to move about freely." He shot her a slitted stare. "But if she makes any attempt to get through the palisade, they are to kill her immediately."

White Stone lowered his spear. "I'll tell them, but they won't understand any better than I do."

Dzoo gave White Stone a teasing smile. "The chief wishes me to be comfortable. Ask yourself why."

Cimmis rolled his hands into fists, the muscles in his forearms popping and straining.

White Stone glanced at his chief. "Then you must be willing to tell us about Rain Bear's plans. I am relieved that you've come to your—"

"Rain Bear's plans?" Her laughter was crystalline. "You think Cimmis worries about Rain Bear's plans?"

Cimmis tried to hide his alarm, making his voice louder, more confident. "White Stone, take Dzoo to her old lodge. She'll tell you where it is."

"Yes, my Chief."

Cimmis walked away, slowly, acting as though he had all day to make it back to the safety of his lodge. Every eye in Fire Village watched him.

White Stone grumbled, "Deer Killer, apparently you're going to live to see sunset this day. But if I were you I wouldn't repeat my dereliction of duty. Do you understand?"

"Yes, War Chief." His body was trembling, and Dzoo watched it with a certain glee.

When Cimmis was out of hearing range, White Stone hissed, "I don't know how you got out of the captives' lodge, witch, but I'm taking no chances with you. You'd better be very careful."

She bowed her head and smiled.

As they walked into the lower half of the village, children came racing out from behind a lodge and circled around, shrieking in joy, as barking dogs nipped at their heels. When they noticed White Stone, panic gripped them. Like a flock of spooked birds they retreated to the edges of the plaza to let him pass, eyes like huge dark holes in the world. A strange silence descended.

"It seems, War Chief, that you have a Powerful effect on the small and frail. Would you like to know what the Dead think of you?"

"Just walk, witch."

She studied the painted lodges in awe. The lifelike renderings of Eagle, Killer Whale, Grizzly Bear, and Owl were the product of a people who never had to scramble for a living. "How many North Wind People are left in Fire Village, War Chief?"

"You mean pure North Wind?"

"Yes."

His steps faltered, but he regained his composure quickly. "How many were here when you left?"

"Almost ten tens."

"There may be eight tens now."

Eight tens. "At that rate, the village is losing one a year. In another eight tens of years, there will be no purebloods left."

Water puddles dotted the ground, muddying their moccasins. She watched White Stone as he considered her words; they seemed to be eating at him like a termite in an old log.

"Did Cimmis order all of the other North Wind People killed?"

"Some of them," White Stone admitted, "but there weren't many left to begin with. Six and ten summers ago, when Tlikit fled with her lover, they started leaving. Several have died over the cycles. Astcat begged the North Wind People from the neighboring villages to come and live here. A few did."

"Does it bother you to serve a dying people?"

"I don't understand. You're one of them. A pureblood, but you favor the Raven People."

"Poor War Chief," she whispered. "How lucky you are. You need not look past your orders. I envy the simplicity, if not the quality, of your life."

White Stone's gaze shot involuntarily back up the hill. She could feel his nerves prickling, see it in the set of his shoulders. When she followed his stare, it was to see Ecan standing outside his lodge like a carved statue. His long hair hung loose around his tall body. His eyes might have been coals glowing through a darkness of hatred.

It didn't matter; she was going home. Already she could sense the ghosts of her ancestors, hear the whispers of Power coming from the aged wood and bark of the house where she was born.

As she walked up and placed a hand on the familiar doorway, she heard her mother's ghost crying.

"Yes, Mother. I know. *He* is hunting me."

Thirty-eight

Morning light fell across the ocean, reflecting from the curls of mist that twined along the beach. Rain Bear took another sip from his teacup as he stared out at the islands offshore. Despite the early hour, men were plying nets in the muddy water. Another whale had been harpooned, almost swamping the canoe as it sounded. The hunters had regaled the crowd with the story of their perfect cast—the harpoon skewering the blowhole—and their wild ride while the suffocating whale thrashed.

After the carcass had been towed ashore, people had swarmed it, using large obsidian knives to process the blubber and rich red meat. Not even darkness had slowed them. By torchlight, the whale had been rendered to bone.

Feasting had lasted until well after midnight. And while most of the village still slept, the refugees were up and moving about through the forest.

". . . *today you'll speak . . . Thunderbird.*" Rides-the-Wind's scratchy old voice penetrated his lodge.

Rain Bear cocked his head to listen. Rides-the-Wind had been whispering to Tsauz since long before dawn, preparing him for some task. He'd caught only a few words of the conversation. Something about hunting and magical stones.

He clutched his hot cup and concentrated on the warmth that

penetrated his fingers, trying to will it into the rest of his frozen body. Half of a cod was propped on sticks jammed into the charcoal-black earth and tilted so that the chevrons of meat slowly cooked over the fire's low heat. The odor was sending Rain Bear's stomach into fits.

Evening Star slipped out of her lodge, her face swollen with sleep, her eyes heavy. She glanced at him first thing, smiling as if just for him. She stood, reached for her cloak, and walked off into the forest to attend to her morning needs.

Rides-the-Wind's garrulous voice rose and fell as he regaled Tsauz with some story about Thunderbirds.

Rain Bear was pondering that when Evening Star stepped out of the dew-beaded trees, deposited a scapula comb and something else in her doorway, and walked over to accept the cup of tea he had already brewed for her.

"They're still in there?" She gave him that smile again, and glanced at Rides-the-Wind's lodge.

Rain Bear yawned, watching his breath frost. "I think Tsauz has been adopted. He moved his bedding in with Rides-the-Wind. I heard last night after I returned from the island that the Soul Keeper had volunteered to train the boy."

Evening Star studied the browning cod with hungry eyes. "I hope the boy knows just how lucky he is."

"Lucky?" Rain Bear smiled at the thought. "Half the world wants to kill him as a means of getting back at his father."

She considered. "This story about him going blind after his mother died . . . It seems to me the boy has already paid a terrible price for being Ecan's son."

"Do you believe he just went blind? Just like that? Without being hit in the head, or having his eyes injured?"

Her stare fixed on the distance inside her. "Oh, yes, Great Chief. I myself . . . I just wish I could have gone blind, and deaf, and perhaps mute as well. It's punishment, you see. The desire to atone for failing my daughter, my husband and mother . . . my people."

"Matron, you don't—"

She held up a hand. "Oh, yes I do. And to make sure I punish myself, I will continue to live, see, remember, and hear their screams. Taking the other route and giving up would be too easy."

He let her stew for a moment. "I never knew your husband, but I knew Naida. I wasn't aware that either she or your husband had a reputation for cruelty."

She glanced at him. "Cruelty?"

"Or that they were petty, or even mean for that matter."

"What are you talking about?"

"Just this: If you had died, and your husband had lived, I am to understand you would want him to punish himself for the rest of his life for your death?"

"Absolutely not!"

"Ah," Rain Bear added gently. "Then you would want your mother, had she lived, to blame herself for your death?"

She was giving him a suspicious look now. "If I were dead, and they alive, I would be furious with them for blaming themselves."

"Then what would you want them to do?"

"I'd want them to . . ." It sank in on her then, her expression getting small, her eyes seeing inward.

"To go on with their lives," Rain Bear added with assurance. "As the Naida I knew would want her daughter to do with hers. What about your husband? I've heard he was a good man, kind and thoughtful. Were he here, sitting in my spot, what would he tell you?"

She took a deep breath. "I need to think about this. I just . . ." She shook her head. "I don't know. I'm angry with myself. Confused."

"We're all a little confused."

Her blue eyes burned when she looked up at him. "I'm feeling doubly guilty. That's all. They're dead—their souls barely on the road to the House of Air . . . and all I can think about is you." She gestured. "My husband was a good man. What happened to him was wrong. I just—"

"It was an arranged marriage," Rain Bear pointed out.

She nodded. "We did our duty."

He used a stick to prod the fire where blue smoke spiraled lazily from blackened branches and puffed around the sizzling cod. "If Tlikit had done her duty, she would have pined for the rest of her life, thinking of me. She never let on, never knew that I knew, but until the day she died she believed she had failed her people."

Evening Star might have been staring into the past. "If she had stayed . . ."

"Would the present be different? Perhaps. She might be the North Wind matron in Astcat's place. Or she might have died in childbirth years ago, or been struck by lightning, or killed in a fall. One never knows how life would be different if one had chosen another path. And for every decision, there is a price."

She looked up, puzzled. "Was it worth the price she paid?"

"She thought so." He smiled wistfully. "We balance our lives just like children do when they play on a balancing pole in the forest. On one hand is our duty to our people, or clan, or family, and on the other is our duty to ourselves. Sometimes certain people get both. Other times they have to choose based on what they think right."

"And what should I have chosen, Great Chief?"

"You cannot change the things you've chosen, Evening Star, only the things you choose now, and in the future."

For a long time they stared at the blue smoke rising off the fire. The skin on the backside of the cod had begun to bubble. Rain Bear grinned. "While you wrestle with your choices, I suggest that you do so with a full stomach."

Her expression was thoughtful as Rain Bear removed the succulent meat from the skewers and laid it on a wooden platter.

Pitch, his arm tightly bound to his chest, picked his way through the camp. The night before, Rides-the-Wind had come and drained his wound. The process had entailed a sharpened wooden skewer that Rides-the-Wind had used to reopen the scab. Then he had carefully massaged Pitch's arm, squeezing foul-smelling contents into a small wooden bowl.

Pitch hadn't been aware that the human body could withstand a pain like that. His voice was still raw from the screams. But the fever had broken. Last night, he had been exhausted by the ordeal, relieved that the swelling was down, and overjoyed that the sour smell of the leaking punctures had dissipated. He had actually slept.

As he approached the little triangle of lodges where Rides-the-Wind, Rain Bear, and Evening Star lived, he remembered his reaction to the sight of the blood-clotted pus.

"It's all right," a solicitous Rides-the-Wind had told Roe when Pitch threw up. "He needs to be cleaned, inside and out." The old man had frowned as she carried the wooden bowl out to the roaring bonfire and tossed it into the center of the flames.

The old man had smiled as the corruption was consumed. "You'll heal now, Pitch." He had hesitated, a question in his eyes. "I wonder, would you do something for me tomorrow?"

"Yes, Elder?"

"Tsauz was awakened in the night by Thunderbirds." His eyes began to gleam.

"You want to prepare him to climb the Ladder to the Sky?"

"And I would like your help." The Soul Keeper had looked around. "This isn't the best time or place, Singer, but the boy is being called."

"He's very young. Climbing the Ladder, Elder . . . well, I wasn't sure I was ready when I did it last year."

The old man had only shrugged. "When you are called, Pitch, you are called."

So here he was, still light on his feet, his arm smarting in its sling, as he made his way across the damp morning camp.

The old man ducked outside. His long gray hair and beard shimmered. Tsauz came out behind him. The boy always stood so straight and tall, he reminded Pitch of an alder sapling. He wore the beautiful black-and-white cape he'd been captured in. It had been freshly washed, and the white spirals around the collar made his shoulder-length black hair seem darker.

"Good morning, Soul Keeper," Pitch called.

"How is your arm?"

"Better today. My family and I send our thanks." He glanced at Tsauz, seeing the hesitation, fright, and worry in the boy's eyes. "Have you prepared yourself, Tsauz?"

"I—I think so. Rides-the-Wind had me in a sweat lodge most of yesterday. I stayed up all last night listening for the Thunderbirds and praying."

Rides-the-Wind took Tsauz's hand. "We had best be on our way." He looked out at the gray skies and the shredded bits of misty clouds that clung to the trees. "It's a good day to go hunting."

Pitch fell into line behind them and checked the guards. A shadowy crowd silently flowed through the forest, moving as they moved. "Will the guards interfere?"

Rides-the-Wind shot him a glance. "They are an unwelcome necessity." He turned to Tsauz. "I want you to concentrate on the lightning bolts that woke you in the middle of the night, Tsauz," Rides-the-Wind instructed. "Remember every detail."

Is he ready for this? Pitch wondered as he studied the blind boy. Pitch wasn't sure but that he'd rather go through the ordeal of having his wound drained again rather than face the Ladder to the Sky.

Rides-the-Wind said, "Remembering is like shooting the bolts back at the Thunderbirds, Tsauz. If you're fortunate, you'll hit one and knock him out of the sky."

Tsauz's blind eyes searched for Rides-the-Wind's face. "But . . . won't that make him mad?"

"Certainly. It will make him angry enough to blast you into small pieces, and that's exactly what we want."

"I want my soul to be blasted by a lightning bolt?"

"Absolutely."

Tsauz cast a blind glance over his shoulder to where Pitch walked. The boy's expression was anything but sure.

They took the western trail that climbed steadily toward a series of low foothills. At this time of the morning, the firs whiskering the hills cast oddly shaped shadows.

Rides-the-Wind kept his pace slow and guided Tsauz around the rocks that littered the trail. The scent of damp firs was strong. They passed through a grove of white-barked alders and emerged into a grassy meadow.

Pitch took a moment to appreciate the beauty. The trail wound across the meadow and up over the top of a gray cliff that stood perhaps ten tens of hands in height. Low clouds hovered around the rim rock. In the distance, Mother Ocean's waves rose and fell.

"We'll climb to the top of the cliff and stop," Rides-the-Wind said.

As Old Woman Above carried the sun higher into the morning sky, bright yellow light flooded the cliff, and the clouds shredded into tufts of mist.

"This is high enough?" Pitch wondered as they topped the cliff and the land opened on a small meadow. His eyes fixed on the patches of cloud that blew through the jagged firs across the meadow from them.

Rides-the-Wind lowered himself to a square chunk of stone, breathing hard. The guards shuffled through the forest around them, watching with curious eyes but keeping their distance.

Pitch examined their backtrail. Several of the refugees had followed along behind. They stood with their hands propped on their hips, waiting to see what would happen next. Pitch shook his head. But then, nothing about this situation was normal. If Tsauz succeeded in his hunt—if he managed to climb the Ladder to the Sky, receive his vision, and live through it—it would be the talk of the land. People still whispered about the Blessing he had received during the Moon Ceremonial, and that Rides-the-Wind himself had come for the boy. Mystery and legend were already swirling.

"I'm going to sit here for a while. Pitch, I wish you to help Tsauz with the hunt." Rides-the-Wind waved a skeletal hand.

"Of course, Elder. Has Tsauz been presented with his weapon?"

Rides-the-Wind untied his pack from his belt and pulled out a beautifully polished chert stone. It looked like it had been rolling around in the bottom of a river for tens of cycles.

"This is the most sacred of weapons. It has slain a great many Cloud People. Open your hand, Tsauz." Rides-the-Wind dropped the stone into the boy's palm.

Pitch could see a white zigzag that ran through the center of the red chert.

"Do you see the lightning bolt, Singer?" Rides-the-Wind asked.

"I do," Pitch replied. "The lightning bolt is in the shape of a zigzag, Tsauz, while the stone is the color of blood."

"A lightning bolt?" Tsauz smoothed his fingers over it. "But . . . how did it get in the stone, Elder?"

Rides-the-Wind rested his hands on his knees. "I found that stone in the belly of an ancient monster."

"A monster?" Tsauz whispered in awe.

"Yes, a monster from the Beginning Time who'd been turned to stone."

Roe had been telling little Stonecrop the Beginning Time stories. According to legend, when the North Wind People emerged into this world of light, they found it filled with huge lumbering monsters that wanted to eat them. The twin war gods were given the task of killing the monsters before the North Wind People were all hunted down and devoured. But how did one kill a monster? They had no idea. The stories of their various attempts were numerous and frightening. Time after time they barely escaped with their lives. Finally, fleeing in desperation from a pursuing monster, they climbed a rainbow to escape. Old Woman Above saw them clinging desperately to the rainbow and asked them what they were doing in such a tenuous place, since everyone knows that rainbows eventually fade. They told her of the monsters eating the North Wind People, and touched by their courage, she gave them lightning bolts to cast. Thus the twins climbed down. This time when the monsters attacked they cast the lightning bolts and turned them into stone.

Tsauz tucked the stone to his breast. "Was the lightning bolt frozen in the monster's blood when he was turned to stone?"

"Very good," Rides-the-Wind said in a perfectly normal voice. "That stone is a drop of monster blood with a fragment of lightning bolt inside."

Tsauz's blind eyes riveted on the rock. "Why did you give it to me?" he asked.

Rides-the-Wind pointed a crooked finger at Tsauz's hand. "*It's very Powerful.* Remember that. Pitch, I want you to take Tsauz out into the forest and have him kill one of those Cloud People floating in the trees."

"Kill one of the Cloud People?" Tsauz asked incredulously. "How do I do that?"

"Tsauz, you must throw that stone as hard as you can, or the Cloud Person will live and turn on you." He waggled a crooked finger. "You don't want that to happen. He might kill you . . . and Pitch, too."

Tsauz swallowed hard. "But, Holy Hermit, I don't want to kill one of the Cloud People."

"Do you wish to talk with Thunderbird?"

"Well . . . yes."

"It's the only way you can prove to Thunderbird that you are worthy of speaking with him. After all, Thunderbirds kill Cloud People for breakfast every morning. They think it's easy. You must earn their respect."

The look of terror on Tsauz's face sent a shiver through Pitch. What if the boy failed? If he didn't pass this test, he surely wouldn't survive climbing the Ladder to the Sky.

Rides-the-Wind flicked a hand.

"Now, go on, you two. Go into the forest and start hunting. You must return with a cup of Cloud People blood."

"Blood?" Tsauz wondered. "Cloud People have blood?"

Pitch took Tsauz's hand. "Are you ready to go hunting?"

The boy looked like he longed to run back to the village, but he glumly answered, "I guess I have to."

The guards moved through the trees around them as Pitch led the way forward along the path.

When they'd walked five tens of paces, Tsauz tugged on his hand and hissed, "Wait!"

Pitch stopped. "You don't want to disappoint the North Wind People's most Powerful Soul Keeper, do you?"

Tsauz wet his lips. "No, but . . . I'm scared."

"Well, so am I. If you miss and the Cloud Person turns on us, he'll probably eat me first. I'm bigger."

"Yes, but you can see to run. I can't!"

The boy needed reassurance more than anything. "I'll warn you. I promise."

Clouds twined among the branches like gauzy dreams. "There are a lot of Cloud People hovering around us. I don't think this is going to be too hard. Is the rock ready?"

Grudgingly, Tsauz lifted it.

"Good. Let's sneak into the trees and find a Cloud Person who's looking the other way."

Tsauz whispered, "How will we know he's looking the other way? Have you ever seen a Cloud Person's face?"

"Yes, I have." Pitch smiled. "I've killed one myself."

"You did? Was it hard?"

"It's always hard to kill." Pitch considered the filaments of mist hanging in the air. "One of the great truths is that life and death live within each other. They are like male and female: different, but necessary to each other. They lay intertwined like lovers, forever together, but separate."

Tsauz considered that. "When you killed the Cloud Person, were you afraid?"

"Oh, yes." He knelt before the boy. "Tsauz, listen to me. If you do this thing today, you are going to face the most difficult trial of your life, but I want to ask you a question, something that I think might help."

"All right."

"When you were hiding during the attack on War Gods Village, were you afraid?"

Tsauz swallowed hard, clutching the stone as if it were the most precious possession on earth. He jerked a short nod, his expression betraying shame and reluctance. "I didn't like it," he whispered.

"I'm sure you didn't." Pitch patted his shoulder. "But you know what fear is in a way that few other boys of your age do. As unpleasant as it was, you lived through it, didn't you?"

Tsauz nodded.

"I want you to remember that in the coming days. You will be judged by your courage, and by the way you face your fear. If you can overcome it, you can speak with the Thunderbirds." He patted the boy again. "So, come on. Let's go hunting."

Pitch led Tsauz to a thick copse of leafless alders where tens of sleeping Cloud People clung to the trees like bats. "Cloud People," Pitch whispered. "They're thick in the trees ahead of us. We'll have to approach carefully. Sneak up on them."

Tsauz gripped the rock tightly as he whispered back, "All right. Show me where they are."

Pitch aimed the boy's forefinger at each Cloud Person in the trees. "See, they're everywhere."

Tsauz's eyes flitted over the branches for a long time before he suddenly stiffened and said, "I *do* see something."

"You do?"

"Yes, they look like glittering yellow serpents crawling around behind my eyes. Is that them?"

"Probably. Can you hit one?"

Tsauz lifted the stone, but he didn't cast. He started walking in a small circle, stopping, looking, then walking again.

"What are you doing?" Pitch asked in a hushed voice.

"Trying to decide which one to kill."

The dark clouds that had been hovering out over the ocean had drifted closer. A bruised thunderhead billowed over the top of the trees to his right.

Pitch told him, "More Cloud People are coming."

"Where?"

"Behind you. There's one peeking over the fir trees we just came through."

Tsauz spun on his heel and looked straight at the thunderhead, as though he could see it. With the quickness of a weasel, he flung the stone.

Pitch watched it fly higher and higher; then it started down. It fell through a small tuft of mist and into a leafless alder, making several thunks as it clattered through the branches to the ground.

"I think you missed. But don't worry, we can . . ."

Thunderbird roared so loudly it knocked Tsauz off his feet. As lightning danced over their heads, the entire cliff shuddered. Pitch was just standing there, his mouth gaping, when a massive white bolt crackled from the sky and exploded in a fir to their right. Chunks of wood whipped through the air.

"Look out!"

Pitch crouched over the boy, trying to shield his hurt arm.

"Stay down, Tsauz!"

Then a strange thing happened. The tufts of mist started to rise through the rain, floating into the sky to join the other Cloud People.

All except one.

The smallest tuft of mist—the one that Tsauz's stone had fallen through—melted before his eyes. It spread out, thinned, and settled to the ground.

Pitch whispered, "Tsauz, you got one!"

Tsauz looked up in surprise. "I did?"

"Yes! Come on." He rose and grabbed the boy's hand. "Let's go see what's left."

Pitch led him through the splinters, mangled branches, and bracken to the place where the Cloud Person had fallen.

"Do you see it?" Tsauz asked breathlessly. "What does it look like?"

Pitch cocked his head. A tiny puddle of water lay cupped in a rocky hollow atop a protruding basalt boulder. "Well . . . like a water puddle."

"A water puddle?" Tsauz sounded disappointed.

"Yes, a water puddle, but"—he squinted at it—"it doesn't look ordinary. It has lots of colors flashing through it."

Excited, Tsauz said, "Scoop it up. We'll take it back to Rides-the-Wind. He'll know if it's a Cloud Person's blood!"

Pitch awkwardly untied the cup from his belt and dipped it into the puddle.

Tsauz looked anxiously around the forest.

"What's the matter, Tsauz? Do you see more yellow serpents behind your eyes?"

"No," Tsauz quietly answered. Deep reverence filled his young voice. "They slithered into the sky right after Thunderbird cast his lightning bolt. But . . . I hear something."

"What?"

"It's a—a rhythm. There's a rhythm to the shishing the drops make in the trees. Don't you hear it? It sounds like words."

"Words?"

"Yes." Tsauz nodded. "Words spoken almost too softly to be heard. But I think if I just had the time to listen, I might be able to figure out . . ."

"Yes?"

"I don't know. They're so faint."

"As a Singer, I can tell you that when you're ready to hear, the words will come to you. Meanwhile, we need to get this cup of Cloud People blood back to the Soul Keeper."

Thirty-nine

Rain pattered in the trees as it fell from the brooding clouds. Pitch tucked the cup of Cloud People blood into the boy's hand when they stopped before Rides-the-Wind.

"Elder, Tsauz killed a Cloud Person." He was still trying to come to grips with what he'd seen. When he'd gone through the ritual, he'd thrown a stone through a streamer of mist, too, but it had been nothing like this. No bolt of lightning had blasted a tree. Pitch's little tuft of cloud had drifted away, unlike Tsauz's. No puddle of water had lain below the wounded mist.

Tsauz clutched the cup in both hands as he carefully felt his way forward. *"Rides-the-Wind, look!"*

"Well," the old man said. "I'm surprised to see the two of you alive."

Tsauz halted in front of Rides-the-Wind, breathing hard. "Why?"

"Because I heard Thunderbird. Didn't you realize he was hunting that same cloud? You must have killed it right under his nose to make him that angry."

Huge raindrops splatted on the elder's gray hair and beaded on his hawklike nose as a sense of wonder filled Pitch. He studied the whip-thin boy again. Power was threading around them, light and pulsing, echoing from the falling rain, the winter grass, and the slumbering firs.

Gods! Just who was Tsauz, anyway? What kind of Power lay at his beck and call? Pitch was aware of Rides-the-Wind's knowing gaze.

Tsauz chirped, "But we lived! And we got it!" He held out the cup. "Look!"

The Soul Keeper took the cup and peered into it. Rain stippled the surface. "Yes, you did get him, didn't you? Did you see the thousands of tiny rainbows in the water?"

"Yes! . . . Well, no, but Pitch told me about the colors."

"These aren't just colors. Come here, look."

Tsauz felt his way forward with his moccasins, and Rides-the-Wind put the cup in his hands again.

"Do you see them?"

Tsauz blinked. After a few moments, he said, "I see . . . waves. Black waves. Like looking at a lake at night."

Rides-the-Wind stared curiously at Tsauz. "Are the waves shiny, or murky?"

"Shiny."

"Do they have a voice?"

Pitch flipped up his hood and shifted uneasily. *A voice?*

Tsauz listened to the cup. "I don't hear anything, Elder."

Pitch added softly, "Elder, you should know that Tsauz heard Thunderbird's voice. Right after Thunderbird blasted the tree, he said the raindrops in the forest had a rhythm to them, like words."

Tsauz nodded. "Yes, I thought they were words, but I couldn't make them out. I guess it could have just been the rain."

"It wasn't the rain," Pitch reminded. "You *almost* heard words."

Rides-the-Wind shoved to his feet with a soft, pained grunt. "Well, let's see what Tsauz hears after he's had a sip of Cloud People blood."

Tsauz's head jerked up. "I have to drink Cloud People blood?"

"That's why we went to the trouble to kill a Cloud Person. Tonight, if you succeed in climbing the Ladder to the Sky, you will fly to the Above Worlds. Dead people do it all the time, of course, but to do it while alive, a human needs to have the blood of the Cloud People inside him." He put a hand on Tsauz's shoulder. "First, you must be properly prepared."

Tsauz stood rigid, his eyes wide.

Rides-the-Wind took Tsauz's hand, guiding him down the trail. Over his shoulder, he called, "Pitch? Would you be so kind as to see if you could find my rock?"

"I'd be honored, Elder."

Evening Star listened to the patter of rain on her roof. She had retired to her lodge after sharing Rain Bear's breakfast. He had gone off to another of his endless council sessions as he tried to hammer out an alliance with the other villages and clans.

Now she lay in the darkness, reviewing the words he had spoken. In truth, it wasn't her fault that her village had been taken and her family killed.

It's not your fault. And yes, Rain Bear was correct: Both her husband and mother would have been saddened by her behavior.

"So what are you going to do about it?" she asked herself softly. Her fire had burned down to a bed of red glowing coals; in the gloom she was left alone with herself. She heard the wood and bark of her lodge creak, as if a weight had been placed upon it. Her gaze silently lifted to her sagging roof. The storm had soaked the wood. It might be rain dripping from the trees onto the lodge, or onto the ground.

She sighed, tossing onto her back to stare up at the darkness. Placing a hand to her pelvis, she realized she was cycling. With the death of her daughter and with her captivity, her milk had dried up. It was known that women missed when they were under stress of starvation, hard work, or abuse.

Having passed her moon her loins were coming alive again, and her thoughts took her straight to Rain Bear. She smiled wryly into the darkness. Life had a way of making up for death, didn't it? Here she was, safe, fed, protected, and in the presence of a man who filled her idle moments with fantasy. She watched him, and kept those moments for later so she could recall the way he moved, how he smiled. She liked little things about him: the way he held his shoulders, the lines at the corners of his eyes. That longing in his eyes touched her in particular.

Love or duty? That had been the choice Tlikit had faced, and in the end, she had chosen this man over the needs and demands of her people.

"I have never truly been in love with a man." The simple statement shocked her. She remembered the boys she had liked and teased as a maturing girl. Then, before she could catch her breath, she had suffered through her first cramps, passed her period in the menstrual hut, and been married.

Within the year she was pregnant and slowly accepting more and more of her aging mother's responsibilities. It hadn't even crossed her mind that she might be something else besides the matron of her village.

And now? She reached down to press on the tender spot just inside the swell of her pelvic bone. Just what *did* she want for her future? The wood creaked again, as if the weight were being released. She looked up, puzzled. Then heard the soft rasping of something heavy being dragged away.

Were her guards up to something? She cocked her head, hearing stealthy steps as wet moccasins scuffed the muddy ground outside her lodge.

She crawled across the floor and picked up a piece of firewood to use as a club.

Wind Woman breathed through the lodge flap, and the coals in the firepit flared, casting a fluttering halo of red light over the walls.

A voice hissed, "I know you're alone. I just want to speak with you. Don't be afraid."

Her first impulse was to try to run, but he'd just club her as she ducked out the door, if that's what he'd come for.

Where are my guards?

An obsidian knife blade eased the flap aside, and she glimpsed a face. Then he ducked inside.

He was a thick, rough-looking man. Greasy graying black hair straggled over the front of his brown cape. *A slave's garment.* Despite his dress he acted like anything but a slave. She thought he might even have been of the North Wind People.

He glanced down at the firewood in her hands. "You won't need that."

"Who are you?"

"A messenger."

He squinted in the dim gleam, calmly surveying the lodge. "Did you get the message? The one Red Dog was carrying?"

She swallowed hard, and jerked a quick nod, her fingers tightening on the length of firewood.

"You could be the next matron, you know. People are already starting to talk about it."

"What do you want?"

He squatted on her bedding hides. "I'm not here for your pretty head, if that's what you think. I've been sent for the boy. If you have accepted the high matron's offer, help me smuggle the boy out of here. After that, we'll meet up with a party of warriors, and I'll take the two of you back to Fire Village."

Evening Star glared at him. "Then you must be one of Cimmis's assassins."

A half-contemptuous chuckle came from his lips. "Maybe his best. Where's the boy?"

She lifted an eyebrow, thinking. "Rides-the-Wind took him. He's preparing the boy for some sort of ceremonial."

That caught the grizzled man by surprise. "The Soul Keeper has him?"

"He's training him," she said firmly.

She saw the sudden hesitation, the faint worry his eyes couldn't quite hide. *Why does that news upset him so?*

"Matron, I *need* that boy!"

Evening Star used her chin to indicate her dress—the fine one with the dentalium. It was worth a small fortune. "If you'll forget the boy and leave here, I'll give you that."

He glanced at it, eyes barely flickering as they passed over the garment. "Will you help me, or not?"

Her fingers tightened around the piece of firewood. For a timeless instant, every sound and scent seemed exaggerated; the pattering of the rain on her roof, her shallow breathing, the pungent scent of the fir smoke that drifted through camp like a blue-gray snake. How had he made it this far? Rain Bear had guards everywhere.

"Tsauz is gone."

"Where to?"

"Does it matter? He's not here. Rides-the-Wind took him. You've failed. If you value your life, you'll make a run for it immediately—though I doubt you'll make it out of camp alive."

He smiled and leaned forward. She could see that a large stone gorget, or pendant, hung behind his shirt. "There are so many new arrivals here every day, all I have to do is kill you, and walk out into the crowd."

"And all I have to do is shout an alarm. Besides, I'm getting irritated by your muddy moccasins on my bedding."

He glanced down at his moccasins and smiled. "Truthfully, Matron, I don't have orders yet to kill you, only to learn your answer. If it's yes, I am to get you and the boy out of here. If it's no . . . well, I'll come in the middle of the night next time. When you're fast asleep and lost in your final Dreams." He propped his obsidian knife on his knee with the point aimed at her chest. "Are you going to accept Matron Astcat's offer?"

"I sent my answer with Red Dog. It was for Astcat alone. But you'll know it soon enough. I'm sure the news will run through Fire Village like a molten wave."

His face screwed up, but his eyes resembled little knives, cutting away at her, seeking to slice down to her heart. Somehow, he read the tracks of her soul. "So that's the way of it?" He chuckled softly. "I don't need to kill you, Evening Star. You'll be dead before Sister Moon rises."

He ducked out, and the hanging waffled, letting a cold gust of wind in. Evening Star sat frozen in fear, the length of wood tight in her aching hands. Not until she heard him walk away did she dare breathe.

Her heart jumped again when she heard him speak softly with another man.

Who?

Their voices dwindled as they walked away.

Evening Star got her shaking legs under her and prepared to burst from her lodge to run like a scared rabbit.

A shout split the silence; then feet pounded past her lodge, and enraged screams broke out.

Rain Bear shouted, *"No! Don't kill them! We need them alive!"*

At the sound of his voice, such relief rushed through her that her knees buckled. She sat down hard. The entire camp must have roused. Tens of voices lifted and blended into an indecipherable din. People raced up the trail, shouting, screaming questions.

Rain Bear threw the lodge flap back, his war club in his hand. His dark eyes blazed. "Are you all right?"

"How did he get so close?"

"Evidently by working with Wolf Spider. They killed Hornet. His body is out in the trees at the end of a blood trail. Who was he? What did he want?"

"An assassin. A Wolf Tail. He wanted Ecan's son," she answered in a shaky rush. "Did you catch him?"

"Dogrib's gone after them. They took the trail that leads up toward War Gods Village. We'll get them."

As the reality of how close she'd come to doom sank in, her entire body started to quake.

Rain Bear knelt and touched her hand. "I'm sorry you had to go through that."

"I'm alive." Blood started to rush through her veins like an incoming tide.

His voice came out so soft and tender, she almost didn't recognize it. "Two guards was a mistake. I should have known better."

"Two, ten, it doesn't matter! He was dressed like a slave! He could go anywhere." She balled her fists, muscles tense against the trembling. "You've got to understand. I tried to buy him off. He didn't even look twice when I offered my dress for Tsauz's life."

Rain Bear glanced at the decorated dress. "Interesting."

"And another thing: It was eerie but I've never seen anyone so calm and self-confident. It was as if . . ."

"Yes?"

She glanced at him, puzzled. "He wasn't afraid in the slightest that he'd be caught." She shivered. "Something about him frightens me in a way I've never been frightened before."

"Great Chief?" Dogrib called from outside.

Still shaking, Evening Star followed Rain Bear out into the dusk. In the gray light Dogrib's white hair seemed to glow. She could see his puzzled expression. Behind him, two warriors came dragging a limp body by the armpits, the head lolling, the feet trailing in the mud.

"What's happened, War Chief?" Rain Bear asked, stepping forward.

"You're not going to believe this," Dogrib muttered uneasily. "When it became apparent that we were going to cut them off, the stranger killed Wolf Spider. Split his skull. Then he dove into a patch of bushes beneath the cliff."

Evening Star watched as Rain Bear stepped to where the body hung between the warriors' grip. He bent, caught up a handful of the blood-soaked hair, and lifted the head so that Wolf Spider's face could be seen. The wide eyes, slack features, and gaping mouth looked stunned in death.

"I take it that you surrounded him?" Rain Bear asked.

Dogrib was shifting uneasily from foot to foot, his expression a mix of anguish and disbelief. "A coyote ran out, my Chief. A single, huge coyote. It was so quick we couldn't react, wouldn't have anyway. We thrashed those bushes, sorted through them by hand."

"And?"

"Nothing!" Dogrib cried. "There was nothing there but this!" He held up a small thong from which dangled a perfectly chipped obsidian effigy in the shape of a coyote's head.

Forty

Word of the Wolf Tail spread in ripples through the camps surrounding Sandy Point Village. Although full dark had fallen, people began to collect around the large central fire across from Pitch and Roe's lodge.

Rides-the-Wind led Tsauz down through the trees to watch. He cocked his head, curious as to how the people would respond. He could sense it: Tonight was a turning point, one way or another.

Coyote! The name was whispered from lip to lip. Rides-the-Wind studied the somber faces in the crowd. People's eyes glittered with fear, excitement, and worry. He could hear their anxious voices as they bent their heads and asked, "How did he get past the guards?"

He smiled, his hands on Tsauz's shoulders. *As if guards were any hindrance to a man of his Power.*

How curious, though, that he had come for the boy on this night, of all nights. A turning point. Yes. Rides-the-Wind leaned his head back and sniffed the cool night air. The earthy fragrance of the coming storm mixed with the odor of burning pitch torches. Power laced the air. Coyote knew it. He knew it. Did the tense boy under his grip know it as well? Those blank eyes might have been wells in the boy's soul.

"Coyote came with a message for Matron Evening Star!" Rides-the-Wind heard someone whisper. That, too, was slipping from lip to lip like an eel in the kelp.

A tense silence fell as Rain Bear and Evening Star stepped into the circle of firelight. The great chief took a moment, nodded to Talon, Goldenrod, Bluegrass, and the rest of the elders and chiefs.

It was Evening Star, however, who stepped forward, her expression serious. Every, face—some reflecting hate—turned toward her. The story had circulated that she was working to betray them.

Even from where he stood, Rides-the-Wind could see her body was rigid with tension. He wondered if it was from the strain of her assault, or fear of what she was about to say.

Someone shouted, "Is it true she betrayed us to the Four Old Women of the Council?"

"Is she working with Coyote?" another demanded.

A cacophony of voices rose, shouting accusations, calling her names.

Rain Bear bellowed, "Quiet! You must hear what has occurred!"

The din subsided, and Evening Star stated, "Last night, a messenger came here from Fire Village. The rumors are correct. He *did* bring me an offer from the matron of the North Wind People. Astcat said she would revoke my slave status in exchange for cooperation."

"Go home!" a woman shouted, and waved a fist. "We don't want you here!"

Mutters of assent eddied through the crowd, and expressions turned grim.

Bluegrass cried, "Cooperation? What does that mean? What does she wish you to do?"

Evening Star stood tall and still. "Astcat wants me to convince you to leave these lands. She wants you to travel in small parties, and promises that if you do, she will guarantee you safe passage through the lands of the North Wind People."

A confused babble filled the forest; then an old man stepped forward. "This is my home! My father and mother are buried here, as are two of my children! I'm not leaving!"

Another person yelled, "My ancestors died here. My clan has been here since the beginning. I won't leave!"

Yet another reached down and raised a handful of the damp soil. "Raven gave this ground to us! If Matron Astcat wants to fight Raven, let her!"

"What's Astcat trying to do?" War Chief Talon whispered. "Get rid of the Raven People so the North Wind People can have all the hunting and fishing grounds?"

Dogrib replied, "Surely she's not that foolish."

Tsauz lowered his head to peer sightlessly at the ground.

A tall burly man shoved through the crowd to glare at Evening Star. "I heard that Coyote offered you even more. Will you return to Fire Village as matron?"

"Matron?" someone whispered into the sudden silence.

Evening Star clenched her fists at her sides. "This is what I told Astcat: I would return to Fire Village if, and only if, she disbanded the Council and turned their Starwatcher over to Rain Bear!"

From the darkness beyond the fire, a voice called, "Then you'd all better start running now, because Ecan is coming to kill you!"

Howls of rage broke out, the crowd surging back and forth. Fists were raised, and the cacophony of shouted threats became a roar.

"Are you all right?" Rides-the-Wind bent down to whisper into Tsauz's ear.

"They hate my father."

"We are all filled with passion, Tsauz. Each of us is the master of it, for good or ill. How will you use your passion? For hate, like this? Or to make yourself and your world better?"

Dogrib's eyes narrowed, and he motioned some of his warriors forward in a thin line between Evening Star and the crowd. A slow drizzle had begun.

Tsauz stood rigid, his blind eyes wide and still, digesting all that he heard. Then he lifted his chin. It was a royal gesture, like that of a young ruler about to make a decree. "Elder?"

"Yes?"

"I must speak with Evening Star."

"This is not a good time, Tsauz, but I'll see if I can arrange something for later. Will that be sufficient?"

Tsauz let out a shaky breath. "Yes."

Evening Star had waited out the worst of the crowd's vitriol. She raised her hands, waving until the babble died down. Her voice called loud and clear: "My people! Listen to me!"

"We're *not* your people!" an old woman shrilled.

Rain Bear threw his head back. Rides-the-Wind saw the tendons and veins standing out in his neck as he screamed the most blood-curdling of war cries.

Silence fell over the crowd as Rain Bear's bellow died out. "Listen to her," he said into the awkward silence. "Hear her, as I did."

Evening Star pushed her way forward, passing Dogrib's line of guards as she stalked up to the old woman and shouted, "Yes! You are *my* people—as I am yours!" She whirled, pointing from face to face. "What binds us together is our hatred for the Council! For what they have done to us!" She lifted a clenched fist, her sleeve falling down to reveal a pale arm. "Cut this flesh, and my blood runs as red as yours does! My soul bled as yours did when the Council ordered my family's murder! As they have killed your relatives, sons, and daughters, *they killed mine!*"

She glared at them, pacing from person to person, her anger a burning and brilliant thing. Rides-the-Wind grinned at the authority radiating from her.

"I *killed* Kenada when I could stand no more abuse!" She raised her hands, pale fingers shining in the firelight. "With these hands I *cut his throat!*"

A low muttering of approval passed through the crowd like a lapping wave.

"Coyote," she cried, "offered me the choice of betraying you in return for little Tsauz and the promise of safety!"

Rides-the-Wind felt the boy tense.

"I refused!" Evening Star told them vehemently. "And because I did, he has sworn to kill both me and the boy!"

A muted bellow was born in the press, a rekindling of the old hatred and injustice.

Evening Star thrust her hand out, pointing at Rain Bear. She was standing among them now, one of them. "In poor murdered Hornet's name, I tell you: There is salvation for all of us! To live, we must join forces with Chief Rain Bear, *and break the Council once and for all!*"

Shouts and whistles of approbation broke out, people shaking their torches, howling their support.

Rides-the-Wind watched, fascinated. "She has won them," he noted, more for himself than for Tsauz's benefit.

But the little boy looked up, his blank eyes like pits of pain. "I'm scared, Rides-the-Wind. If I don't stop it, lots of people are going to die."

"You think you can stop this?" he asked carefully.

"I must try." The boy nodded frankly. "I've seen it in a Dream. But if I do, I may die a terrifying death."

Forty-one

Tsauz heard Rides-the-Wind add more wood to the small fire the old man had built in front of his lodge. With the light drizzle, the evening had turned cold and damp. Thick mist blew through the firs, coating his face and hands. Water dripped from the brim of the bark rain hat he wore.

"I'm sure she's coming, Tsauz."

Tsauz twisted his hands in his lap. "But she's late, isn't she?"

"Her meeting with the chiefs probably took longer than she'd thought. That's all."

"What do you think they are discussing?" Tsauz straightened his black-and-white cape. He couldn't seem to keep his fingers still.

"They're probably trying to decide how to stop the assassin."

Tsauz sensed Rides-the-Wind's movement when he leaned toward the tea bag hanging on the tripod over the fire. It creaked as he dipped up a fragrant cup of fir needle tea.

"I could hear behind your voice, Rides-the-Wind. You don't think Coyote can be stopped."

"Not by guards, no." A pause. "Here." Rides-the-Wind tucked the cup into Tsauz's hand. "Drink this. It will soothe your heart."

Tsauz took the cup, smelling peppermint, but didn't drink. He stared blindly in the direction of the trail Evening Star would take when she came home.

"You heard Evening Star. Coyote will be coming to kill me next time. If the guards can't stop him . . ." He had to swallow the rest, unable to state what lingered in his soul like a festering barb.

"Then I will." Rides-the-Wind's voice was barely audible.

"You?"

"This isn't a battle fought by warriors, Tsauz. Coyote will either be defeated by Power, or by his unwholesome appetites. Time will tell. And you're not the only one he's hunting."

"There's Evening Star."

"Yes, that's true. Among others."

Wind Woman gusted through the forest and behind him, Rides-the-Wind's lodge puffed in and out, as though she were taking a deep breath. Tsauz shivered. Every sound affected him like a physical blow.

"Rain Bear doubled your guards, Tsauz."

"Are they still out there? Can you see them?"

Rides-the-Wind pulled Tsauz's left hand away from his cup, took hold of his first finger, and aimed it. "That man's name is Blue Frog. It wouldn't take but a halfhearted toss of a stone to make him really mad." Rides-the-Wind pointed the finger at the next guard. "That is Chases His Foot. He's leaning against a fir trunk, and over there"—he shifted the aim—"that's Elktail. He's a burly giant with shoulders like a buffalo bull. I don't know the names of the others, but this is where they're standing." Rides-the-Wind calmly aimed and pointed Tsauz's finger. When he finished he curled it around the teacup again.

The boy mouthed the words: *Elktail, Blue Frog, Chases His Foot.*

Tsauz's souls had been drifting, as though this were all a Dream: the mist, the guards, and the racket of tens of people coughing and talking at once.

He heard steps coming up the trail; his breathing went shallow. "Is it her?"

"Yes. Evening Star walks at Rain Bear's side."

"Tell me what she looks like," he asked, desperate to picture her behind his eyes.

"She looks tired. Red wisps of hair have come loose from her braid, and fringe her face. Her eyes show the day's strain, but she walks with her shoulders squared. The white concentric circles painted on her deerhide cape blaze as she enters the fire's glow."

"And Rain Bear? Does he look angry?"

"No. Worried. His war club dangles from his hand—and his black braid hangs to the middle of his back. Two new guards walk behind Evening Star."

"Only two?"

"Only two."

Tsauz heard Rides-the-Wind pull out more cups. The odor of the peppermint tea carried on the breeze.

Evening Star said, "A pleasant evening to you, Soul Keeper, and to you, Tsauz." She sat down on the hides on the opposite side of the fire.

Tsauz heard Rain Bear take up a position behind her.

Rides-the-Wind pointed at his fire. "Would you like a hot cup of tea?"

"That sounds wonderful, thank you."

Tsauz heard Rides-the-Wind dip it full and hand it around the fire to her. Evening Star took it; her cape rustled as she leaned forward.

"Tsauz," she said gently, "I imagine you are concerned by what I said earlier."

Tsauz drew himself up and turned to face her. When he spoke, he used the North Wind People's formal dialect, usually reserved for ritual occasions. "Yes, my cousin. I thank you for coming to speak with me."

He could hear the tired smile in her voice. "What did you wish to know?"

Tsauz stammered, "I–I've heard the people in camp whispering all day. They think the assassin really came to kill me, not you. Is that true?"

"Not exactly, Cousin." She hesitated, and Tsauz's face slackened, sensing the worst. "He came hoping that I would side with Astcat, and that I would help him sneak you out of camp. When I told him you were with the Soul Keeper, I could tell that he was most disturbed."

"Tsauz is the center of Power," Rides-the-Wind said. "Coyote has his own goals in all this, and I can tell you now, they aren't the Council's, or Ecan's, or Cimmis's."

"Then what?" Rain Bear asked.

"Power. Pure and simple," Rides-the-Wind replied. "You delude yourself, Great Chief, if you think this is a matter of warriors, battle strategy, and defeating the forces fielded by the North Wind People. If he can't take Tsauz for his own, it will be safer to just kill him."

Tsauz swallowed hard. "Who sent him?"

Evening Star sounded unsure of herself. "I thought Coyote had been sent by the Council."

"He may be acting on his own," Rides-the-Wind said thoughtfully. "There are many people who wish you and the boy dead."

You and the boy.

"Because we are North Wind People?" she asked.

"Many wish us dead for that reason alone, yes."

Rides-the-Wind added, "Cimmis wants Tsauz dead to keep us from using Ecan against him. The Council fears him because he was witness to their attack on War Gods Village. Coyote knows that if Tsauz is not with him, he will be against him. And, of course, if we run out of enemies to worry about, there is always Bluegrass and his followers."

With all the dignity he could muster, Tsauz stared in Evening Star's direction. "My cousin, I wish to"—he tried to think of the right words—"to bargain with you."

Her cape brushed the ground. "Very well, Tsauz. Bargain about what?"

"I know some things. About the North Wind People. I would tell you, if you give me your oath that when the North Wind People turn my father over to Rain Bear, you will promise to let him live."

He had to clamp his jaw to keep it from trembling. He didn't want her to know how frightened he was. Father always said a man could never afford to appear weak before his enemies.

Evening Star sat silently, and then her clothing rustled. Was she turning toward Rain Bear?

Tsauz waited, wondering if Rain Bear had nodded yes, or shaken his head no.

He added, "My cousin, I swear to you, my father has not done the things the Raven People accuse him of doing. He is a good father to me and a good Starwatcher."

"Tsauz," she said softly, "I understand what you are trying to do. He is your father, and your defense of him earns you both honor and respect. It is because of my respect for you, Cousin, that I tell you this: Your father inflicted terrible pain on me and my family. He did things to me that will mark me for the rest of my life. I have witnessed these things, survived them. I tell you not to harm you, or to disagree with you, but so that you may understand that it will take a great deal to make it worth our while to spare your father's life."

"Because the Raven People believe he has killed many of their people?"

"That, too," she said in a low voice. "Before you speak, you must know that if you tell me this thing, I may not think it is worth saving your father. Further, the information you provide must be important enough to the Raven People that they will understand why I bargained with you."

"I understand."

"The final thing you must understand is that I have no real authority here."

Tsauz thought about that. Father had often spoken of the Raven People as an unruly mob; perhaps she truly couldn't guarantee his father's safety. If ten tens of Raven People decided to kill him, could anyone stop them?

Tsauz saw it happen on the fabric of his souls—a sea of people with clubs and axes surrounding Father, beating him . . .

He listened to Evening Star's movements. She lifted her cup to drink, then turned to look at Rain Bear again.

As if a memory, he heard a voice saying, *You must choose now. And when you do, you cannot go back.*

Tsauz took a deep breath. "Cousin, as you have shown me honor in these negotiations, so I will honor you. I will tell you what I know, and in so doing, I call upon you as a kinsman and friend to do your best to protect my father." He raised his head toward where he thought Rain Bear stood. "Chief Rain Bear told me he wanted to kill Chief Cimmis. Is that still true?"

To his surprise, Rain Bear's voice came from behind. "Yes."

"Then you will wish to know that the North Wind People are going to abandon Fire Village. They have been packing in secret."

"What?" Evening Star sucked in a surprised breath.

"They have been packing in secret because they did not wish to give the Raven People time to plan an attack. They are going to move, very soon, to Wasp Village. They will be on the trail and vulnerable for several days."

A crackling sound came from Rain Bear's knees as he squatted behind Tsauz. "When?"

"Very soon, I think."

Evening Star said, "Hallowed Ancestors, it seems inconceivable. The North Wind People have lived on Fire Mountain since the Beginning Time. The gods walk freely there, talking with the elders, guiding them. How can the North Wind People leave?"

"Old Woman North had a vision," Tsauz said. "She said that Wasp Village will be the rebirth of the North Wind People. We will grow bigger and better than we ever were on Fire Mountain."

Evening Star whispered to Rain Bear, "It's possible. She often had visions."

Rain Bear said, "What was the end of the vision, Tsauz? Did she see the North Wind People actually living in Wasp Village?"

Tsauz tried to remember what Father had told him. He shook his head. "I don't think Father told me, or if he did, I don't remember. He did tell me, though, that we must travel at night. The vision said that North Star Woman will lead us."

Rain Bear must have motioned to the guards. Several men trotted in from the forest.

"Yes, Chief?"

Rain Bear said, "Dogrib is in Algae's lodge. Tell him I know he's busy, but I need to see him. Now."

As the warrior ran away, Evening Star kept her gaze on Tsauz. The boy was shaking. Sweat beaded his face and ran down his throat.

He had the kind of spun-silk courage that only the very young could possess: frail and shining, but somehow more powerful than a thunderstorm.

She reached across the fire, taking his hand from the cup he held. "It took remarkable courage to bargain with me, and even more courage to say the things you did. You must never mention to any of the North Wind People what you've just said."

His stricken face looked ashen, his voice little more than a croak when he said, "I know, Cousin. Now I must live with the choice."

"We all live with our choices," Rides-the-Wind agreed.

She withdrew her hand and said, "I thank you, Cousin. I will do what I can to save your father. But do not expect miracles."

"I think I must talk to Rides-the-Wind. Alone please." Like a dutiful child, he rose to his feet.

Rides-the-Wind struggled up beside him. As he clasped Tsauz's hand, Rides-the-Wind said, "If you need us, we'll be awake for a time."

She watched Rides-the-Wind lead the boy into his lodge.

After the door flap fell, Evening Star heard Tsauz say, "Please, I have to fly to the Above Worlds tonight, Rides-the-Wind. I must speak with Thunderbird. I don't think I can wait any longer."

The old Soul Keeper was quiet for a moment; then he said, "Do you understand the importance of what you're asking, Tsauz? What you do tonight may change your life forever. If you are not worthy, you may even be killed."

"I understand, Elder."

"Then come over here by the fire and rest while I send for Pitch."

Wind Woman picked that moment to blast through the village, whipping the trees and churning up old leaves and sand. Several surprised warriors grabbed for their weapons, then laughed.

Evening Star closed her eyes.

She could barely stand to think of what lay ahead.

Forty-two

Rain Bear crouched just inside Rides-the-Wind's door and chafed. He'd barely begun to give orders when Pitch had summoned him away from Dogrib's council of warriors and led him to Rides-the-Wind's. Pitch had insisted it was important. Now that he was here, he was just sitting, and receiving occasional measuring glances from the old Soul Keeper.

A storm was moving in. Icy air gusted against the lodge, rattling the baskets to his right and buffeting the two red ritual capes that hung on the peg just inside the door. Until recently, this had been a storage lodge. Hide bags still hung from the ceiling poles, filled with fragrant herbs: sagewort for sore throats, ground aster root for pinkeye, bluebell for fever and heart trouble. He shivered. To his left, Tsauz lay curled on his side, staring at nothing. The fire in the center of the lodge cast a flickering gleam over his young face.

Rain Bear whispered, "Are you all right, Tsauz?"

He nodded and whispered back, "What are they doing now?"

Rain Bear turned his attention to Rides-the-Wind and Pitch, who sat cross-legged in the rear of the lodge. Both wore long white shirts decorated with leather fringes. The cup of Cloud People blood sat on the hides between them. Four beautifully painted leather bags surrounded the cup. As Rides-the-Wind directed, Pitch picked up a bag and poured something into the cup; then Rides-the-Wind stirred it.

Rain Bear whispered, "They're pouring things into the Cloud Person's blood."

"What things?" Tsauz's blind eyes shimmered orange in the firelight. He had bathed a hand of time ago, and his black hair glistened.

"I can't tell. I'm not sure I'd know even if I were down there and could smell them. They're probably secret ingredients used only by very holy people."

Impressed by the gravity of his voice, Tsauz nodded. "My father won't even let me touch the bags that contain his Healing plants. He says their Spirits will fly up and kill me."

A powerful gust of wind rocked the lodge, and the walls squealed and shuddered.

"That's good, Pitch. Let's start building the spiral ladder," Rides-the-Wind said.

"What ladder?" Tsauz hissed. "The ladder to the sky?"

Rain Bear struggled to keep the impatience out of his voice. "I don't know what they're talking about."

Rides-the-Wind shot him a censoring glare, then got up and duck-walked across the lodge to reach for a coil of ropes. He handed them to Pitch and pointed to the lodge cord. "You remember how to tie them?"

Pitch smiled thoughtfully. "How could I forget? When I climbed Grandfather Vulture's ladder, I thought I was going to fall off and die. I remember everything perfectly."

"Good." Rides-the-Wind picked up the cup of Cloud People blood. "While you're doing that, I'll prepare Tsauz."

Tsauz sat up, eyes huge. His black-and-white shirt coiled around his feet. "Is it time?"

"Almost."

Rides-the-Wind got down on one knee beside the boy and looked him straight in the eyes, as though the boy could look back. "Now listen to me, Tsauz. No matter what happens, you must be strong and brave. Thunderbird values these things. And more importantly, if you show weakness, he might kill you."

"My Spirit Helper might kill me?" Tsauz was rubbing his hands together.

"Oh, generally he doesn't do it on purpose. Thunderbird gets annoyed with you, flips over in midair, and you fall off his back and die."

Pitch was in the process of tying different lengths of rope to the ceiling pole. Since his son-in-law had only one usable hand, Rain

Bear shifted far enough to help him with the knots. Once hung, the short sections of rope swung around like dead snakes.

"H-have you ever known anyone who fell and survived?" Tsauz asked.

"One. A girl . . . many cycles ago. She accidentally screamed when Thunderbird dove after a particularly succulent Cloud Person—she said she just couldn't help it—but it scared Thunderbird. He flew right into a mountain peak and exploded. She lived only because she jumped off at the last instant. The scars from the tree branches she hit on the way down never really healed." Rides-the-Wind put the cup in Tsauz's hand and clamped his fingers around it. "There's one more thing."

Tsauz croaked, "What?"

"You must call out to Thunderbird in his own language. Buffalo do this naturally, but it's harder for humans. Here's what the word 'come' sounds like." Rides-the-Wind formed his mouth in a circle and made a rumbling sound deep in his throat. "Try it."

Tsauz nervously smelled the contents of the cup, appeared to be thinking about it, then attempted to say "come" in Thunderbird. A high-pitched rumble-shriek vibrated his throat.

While he helped loop another knot, Rain Bear's gaze returned to Pitch. He'd started threading feathers into the ropes, pushing the quills through the twining. Vulture feathers. They bobbed and twisted.

Rides-the-Wind looked skeptical. "That was good, Tsauz, but try to make it sound deeper, more like thunder."

Tsauz swallowed hard, lifted his chin, and rumbled again, deeper this time.

It didn't sound like thunder to Rain Bear. It sounded like they both had something stuck in their throats, which perhaps explained why Tsauz looked like he wanted to throw up.

Rides-the-Wind slapped him on the back. "Excellent. Pitch, are you ready?"

Pitch softly answered, "I'm ready, Soul Keeper," and backed away from the ropes. He had a reverent, slightly frightened expression on his thin face. He wore his hair in a bun at the base of his skull, but black strands had come loose and tangled with his eyelashes.

Rain Bear noticed the beads of perspiration on Pitch's skin, the wary dart of his eyes. It wasn't the temperature in the cold lodge, nor was it any lingering fever. *Blessed Spirits, if this is bad enough to make Pitch sweat when I'm freezing half to death . . .*

"Follow me, Tsauz," Rides-the-Wind instructed, and started for the ropes.

Tsauz crawled after him.

"Sit right here on the hide."

Tsauz knelt in front of the dangling ropes. Rides-the-Wind pulled the boy's left hand from the cup of Cloud People blood and let Tsauz touch the different lengths of ropes.

"What are they?" Tsauz asked.

Rides-the-Wind leaned close to Tsauz's ear and whispered, "They are feathered serpents."

Tsauz jerked his hand back. "Why do I have to touch them?"

"Because they form a spiral ladder that soars into the Above Worlds like Grandfather Vulture. In a little while, you will need to climb them."

"But I—I thought Thunderbird would come to get me, and I would climb onto his back and we'd fly away?"

"You must demonstrate your worthiness first. That means you have to climb these ropes into the Above World where he lives. Climb as high as you can. His home is beyond the Cloud People's— almost to the Star People. Thunderbird will be watching. *If* Thunderbird admires your courage, he'll meet you and take you flying."

"What if I can't climb high enough?"

Rides-the-Wind and Pitch exchanged a doomed look that Tsauz couldn't see, but Rain Bear did, and it shivered his very soul.

"Elder?" Tsauz asked, and wet his lips. "How can I speak with Thunderbird if I only know how to say 'come' in his language?"

"If you climb high enough, Tsauz, you will be able to speak with every creature in its own language: deer, elk, Star People, even Thunderbirds. So. Are you brave enough?"

Tsauz replied, "I have to be. I have to ask Thunderbird to save my father."

Rides-the-Wind nodded. "All right, then it's time we went away."

"Went away! What do you mean? You're leaving me?" Tsauz lunged to grab a handful of Rides-the-Wind's white shirt.

Rides-the-Wind pried the boy's fingers off. "This is something you must do alone." He clamped Tsauz's fingers around the cup again. "Now, I want you to drink the Cloud People blood slowly, and when you feel you're ready to climb, grab onto the longest rope. You'll know when you're ready for the next rope, and the next. Each will lead you higher into the Above Worlds."

Rides-the-Wind motioned, and Rain Bear ducked outside into the patchy moonlight. Puffs of cloud made blots against the sky. A short while later, Rides-the-Wind and Pitch filed out. Both men unfolded beautifully painted red ritual capes and draped them around their shoulders.

Rides-the-Wind lifted a hand to Rain Bear. "You may go now. We thank you for your help."

"Outside of tying a couple of knots, I don't know what good I did."

The old eyes were knowing. "You were a witness, Chief. You have just seen the future change. One way, or another."

"Will he be all right in there?"

Rides-the-Wind made a shrugging gesture. "That is up to him and the gods."

Rides-the-Wind gave him a final fierce look before he and Pitch went to take seats before the fire.

Rain Bear rubbed a hand over his face. Go back to Dogrib's? No, he had too many things to do tomorrow. If he didn't get some sleep, what kind of chief would he be?

As he passed Rides-the-Wind's lodge on the way to his, he heard Tsauz calling out to Thunderbird.

A faint smile bent his lips as he checked to see the guards lined out around Evening Star's. He watched her lodge for a long moment, thinking of her, soft and warm in her robes. If only . . . if only.

He sighed, ducked through his doorway, and pulled his war shirt over his head. He scratched, and reached down to pull his thick buffalo robe back—only to have it move under his fingers.

"What?"

"Shhh! Be quiet or the whole camp will know."

"What are you doing?" he whispered.

Evening Star took a halting breath. "I don't want to be alone. Not tonight. Not after Coyote. I just . . . well, I have separate robes to sleep in if it makes you more comfortable."

He frowned into the darkness. "No. It does not."

Her skin was warm against his as he slid in beside her.

Forty-three

Tsauz wrinkled his nose. The Cloud People blood had a moldy smell. He took a tiny sip, and his mouth puckered at the bitter taste.

"I'm trying to come to you, Thunderbird," he whispered. "Please, hear me."

He rumbled the word "come" deep in his throat, and listened.

Nothing happened.

Tsauz took a good drink, choked it down, and reached out to touch the ropes. They didn't feel like serpents. They weren't scaly. They felt like feathers tied to woven bark ropes.

He called again, struggling to make the deep-throated rumble Rides-the-Wind had taught him.

"Thunderbird? Are you listening? Am I saying that right?"

He was probably speaking in badly accented Thunderbird. But Spirit creatures understood things humans did not. He figured Thunderbird didn't really care about accents, and hoped it was a person's heart that mattered.

"I heard them, Thunderbird," he whispered anxiously. "When Evening Star mentioned my father, the Raven People's cheers sounded like growls. If they ever get their hands on him, they'll tear him apart. I know they will."

He exhaled and ran his fingers over the cup. It felt crude. Big chips had been knocked off the wooden lip. They scratched his mouth when he drank again.

"Please help me, Thunderbird."

He tipped his face heavenward. The more Cloud People blood he drank, the more empty he felt—as though his bones were becoming as hollow as a bird's.

He tried again to make the rumble that would call Thunderbird.

Wind Woman sneaked into the lodge and batted the ropes around. They swung against each other, and he heard a strange hissing. It had to be the feathers brushing each other. Didn't it?

He rumbled again. And again.

The last four swallows of blood tasted especially awful. He set the empty cup on the hides.

The hissing came again, louder.

Rain.

It pattered the sand outside. The storm had moved in. Had Thunderbird come with it?

Closing his eyes, he concentrated on calling and calling. . . .

The scent of wet earth filled the lodge. Tsauz reached out to touch the ropes again, and the feathers brushed his hand. They felt cool and soft. What would Father be doing right now? Sitting before the fire in their lodge, thinking about Tsauz?

He missed Father so much it was like a fire in his chest.

A coyote yipped somewhere up on War Gods Mountain, and across the valley, an answering yip echoed. The first coyote yipped again, then howled, and up and down the shore packs of coyotes lifted their voices to join hers. The haunting melody carried on the night.

Coyote. He's going to be coming for me.

Tsauz held on to the rope and called again.

He was so tired. He'd never been this tired in his life. The lodge started to sway. Back and forth, very slowly, as though *Dancing*. He could feel it moving all around him.

Rain began to pour out of the sky. He felt sorry for Pitch and Rides-the-Wind. By now they'd be soaked. Should he call to them? Tell them to come back? They could try again tomorrow, or when it finally warmed up.

"No," he whispered through gritted teeth. "No, I have to do this! If Thunderbird is my Spirit Helper, he may be able to save Father."

Again and again, he made the deep-throated call until his throat felt like it had been sanded.

He could barely stay awake. . . .

A hiss came from the rope, and it twisted in his fingers. Tsauz gasped and instinctively grabbed it with both hands, hanging on for dear life.

Thunderbird roared across the forest, and the lodge shook with such violence that Tsauz went rigid, ready for anything.

"I'm right here, Thunderbird," he whispered. "I'm not afraid!"

The rope coiled around his wrists, tying them together. His heart battered against his ribs with such force, he couldn't breathe.

The next roar of thunder exploded right over Tsauz's head. He cried out when the rope suddenly went stiff, like a dead snake in his hands.

"Oh, gods, what . . ."

"I'm coming, young Singer. Hold on very tight."

With a jerk, the rope soared upward, dragging him with it as it blasted through the roof and flew away into the rainy sky.

After a terrible night of rain, storm, and lightning, a cool morning wind blew out of the south, tousling Ecan's white cape and whirling red volcanic sand across the mountain below. He crouched on the rim of the black lava wall behind Fire Village, watching the dawn-gray trails. Red Dog would be due to return this afternoon. None of the scouts, however, had sent word that they'd seen him. Had something gone wrong in Sandy Point Village? Surely Rain Bear would not have killed a messenger from Fire Village?

Slaves walked up and down the trails carrying packs on their backs or baskets propped on their hips. In the distance, down the mountain, he could see people in the Salmon Village plaza. Their gloriously colored clothing flashed as they moved.

After Matron Gispaw's murder, her daughter, Kaska, had become the town matron. Her first order had been to build an enormous ceremonial lodge where she and a few of her most trusted allies lived—and, no doubt, where they could watch each other's backs. He didn't blame her for being frightened. The Wolf Tails were paid well enough that they could buy off almost any guard.

Dzoo emerged from her lodge, and people scattered like ripples of frightened birds across the Fire Village plaza. He watched her through slitted eyes. Every servant they sent her became seriously ill. Now, wherever she walked, people avoided her.

"Are you ever the clever witch," he mused. "No one has the courage to watch you too closely. Those who do end up vomiting their guts out for days."

She shielded her eyes and gazed out to the west.

Ecan followed her gaze. Someone ran the trail in the distance. Each time his moccasins struck the ground they left a dark dimple in the trail.

Red Dog?

He glanced back at Dzoo, and his pulse began to pound. She couldn't see the runner. The palisade blocked her view. How could she possibly know he was out there?

One of the slaves who'd been scraping hides near the central fire glanced up, noticed her, and froze. She nudged her neighbor, and within moments they had picked up their scrapers and left. Immediately thereafter, the flint knappers grabbed up their tools and scuttled inside. In the space of a dozen heartbeats the only people left outside were Ecan, Dzoo, the guards and a few of the Four Old Women's slaves. They had no choice. They'd been ordered to stay in the plaza, but hushed conversations broke out.

He rose to his feet.

Dzoo's gaze lifted to him.

It was like being struck by lightning. His fists clenched involuntarily.

Her long red hair danced in the sunlight. She wore a clean maroon dress, and her large spear point hung down between her breasts. She smiled, but her eyes remained as inhumanly luminous as polished obsidian beads.

Ecan didn't breathe until she turned away again to look in the direction of the man trotting up the trail. She tilted her head back and closed her eyes. As though she could *feel* him.

Ecan signaled to the guard who stood at the opposite end of the lava cliff.

The young man trotted toward him.

"Yes, Starwatcher?" Hunter bowed. His thin face bore a coat of dust. Dull-eyed, he must have been standing guard all day.

"Find out who that runner is. If it's Red Dog, send him to me immediately."

"Yes, Starwatcher." Hunter bowed and trotted away.

A commotion broke out when Red Dog arrived at the palisade gate. He wore a dirty brown knee-length shirt and a red headband to keep his gray-streaked black hair out of his eyes. Hunter approached him, then turned to point to where Ecan stood on the crest of the lava cliff. Red Dog dusted off his sleeves, said something, and headed around the palisade to the trail that led up over the cliff.

When he'd climbed to within three paces, Ecan called, "Greetings, Red Dog. I pray your journey was uneventful."

"Uneventful?" Red Dog walked toward him. "Sleeper's warriors chased me half the way home. He's canny. You never know where he is or what he's up to. You just catch glimpses of him or his men running behind you."

"At least you're alive."

"Yes, well, once I've eaten and rested, I might agree with you." He mopped his sweating forehead with his brown sleeve. "I presented your offer."

"Yes, and . . . ?"

"Rain Bear said he would not exchange your son for the witch. It seems he didn't believe you could get Dzoo out of Fire Village."

Red Dog had a strange gleam in his eyes that Ecan didn't understand, but it made him nervous. He said, "Then he refused my offer."

"I didn't say that." Red Dog braced his feet, as though he could barely keep standing. "He said he hated dealing with a spineless coward, but he had his own offer to make."

Ecan bristled at the word "coward," but said, "What offer?"

"He wishes to meet with you. Somewhere away from Fire Village. You may bring one guard, and he will bring one—"

"*What?*" he half shouted before he caught himself. "Does he think I'm a fool? Meet him with only one guard? I would never agree to something so ridiculous! Why is it important that we meet?"

"He doesn't believe he can trust your messenger." Red Dog grinned. "But then he doesn't know how much you're paying me."

Ecan would be completely vulnerable. But if Rain Bear actually came as promised, so would he. No, no, it was too dangerous to consider.

"Did you see my son?"

"No." Red Dog shook his head, and his graying black hair fluttered over his muscular shoulders. "The instant I got close to their camp, Dogrib grabbed me and had me trussed up like a deer ready for roasting. I never got inside the village. They kept me hidden in the forest. Which probably saved my life."

Ecan felt suddenly hot. By now, Tsauz would be feeling utterly lost and alone. "Did you hear anyone speaking about my son?"

"Several of Rain Bear's warriors whispered that Tsauz was sleeping in Rides-the-Wind's lodge. They said the crazy old hermit was *teaching* your son."

"Teaching him?"

"That's what they said."

Ecan frowned. "Why would that old fool choose to teach *my* son?

Tens of young Dreamers come to Rides-the-Wind every cycle begging to be taught by him."

Was it some kind of trick? Perhaps a way of turning Ecan's own son against him? "I doubt you heard correctly, Red Dog."

"Oh," Red Dog replied with arched brows, "I heard correctly, but the guards might have been lying. Perhaps they knew I was listening and said it just for my ears. Why would that be? They wished me to tell you, so that you would . . . what? Call down the Sea Eagles to tear the old man apart?"

Ecan couldn't think of a good answer to that. The information about Rides-the-Wind was inconsequential. It wouldn't change his actions one way or the other. So, maybe it was true. Rides-the-Wind the Hermit was teaching his son to be a Dreamer.

Of all the would-be protectors Ecan could imagine, Rides-the-Wind was the only one with the Power to actually keep his son safe. A tiny thread of hope stitched across his chest.

"I'm tired, Starwatcher. I've told you everything important. If there's nothing else, I'd like to go."

"What about the Council's offer?"

"Refused."

Ecan narrowed his eyes, trying to think past Tsauz and his situation. "What does Rain Bear want?"

Red Dog gave him a sly glance, hesitated, and whispered, "The end of Cimmis and the Council." With an offhanded gesture, he added, "If we had different leadership, perhaps there would be peace."

Ecan's heart leapt, but he said, "Before you go, you should know that your friend Mica is dying."

"Mica?" Red Dog grimaced. "What happened? He was fine when I left."

Ecan shrugged. "I wish I knew. White Stone came to me yesterday to tell me they'd found Mica lying on his floor shaking. Every muscle in his body is twitching. I suspect he'll be dead by morning."

Red Dog's brows knit. "Isn't Mica the one who opened the witch's pack right after the battle—"

"Yes."

"But you said the bags were filled with harmless things: bat droppings and dirt!"

Down in the plaza, Dzoo stood in the same place, watching them, her full lips slightly parted as if in anticipation. He said, "Lion Girl and Dance Fly are also ill with the shaking disease."

Red Dog glanced at Dzoo and whispered, "The slaves who were tending Dzoo?"

"Yes."

"Hallowed Ancestors! And the great chief? How is he taking this?"

Ecan smiled grimly. "Cimmis wants to make her happy here. He seems to think she could be a rallying point for the Raven People if she's harmed. He's had her old lodge prepared and ordered his slaves to bring her new clothing and moccasins. He even ordered his personal jewelers to make her pendants and bracelets from the finest polished stones and shells in Fire Village. Oh, and she's free to wander about as she pleases."

Red Dog raised a pensive eyebrow. "*Free!* But that's insane! Doesn't he understand who she is? *What* she is?"

Ecan rubbed his jaw. "Yes, well, apparently we can't keep her locked up anyway. She might as well be free."

Red Dog stared at him. "Excuse me?"

"Depending on which story you believe, she walked through the wall of the captives' lodge one night. Deer Killer was standing guard. He thinks she changed herself into a bird and flew out the smoke hole. White Stone is convinced that she used the 'missing ropes' to climb out."

Red Dog's gaze fixed on Dzoo. "But if she climbed out, why didn't Deer Killer see her? He didn't fall asleep on duty, did he?"

"White Stone believes he did. That's why Deer Killer is standing double shifts."

"I'm surprised he didn't have Deer Killer skinned alive."

"Apparently Cimmis forgot to give the order. There were four other guards posted around Fire Village that night. No one saw Deer Killer fall asleep. No one saw Dzoo escape."

Red Dog tapped his chin. "Why is she still here? If she could get out of the punishment lodge, the village palisade would be like a net bag is to a bowl of water."

Ecan gave him a thoughtful look. "That, my friend is a good question."

"Anything else odd happen while I was gone?"

"Oh, one man said he saw ball lightning around midnight one night." Ecan lifted a hand to demonstrate. "He said it plummeted out of a starry sky, bounced around the roof of Dzoo's lodge, and vanished."

Red Dog instinctively gripped the stiletto on his belt. "Who said that?"

"Deer Killer."

Red Dog relaxed. "Why, imagine that! Deer Killer again. He probably dreamed it when he was asleep on duty."

"I think his fear has gotten in the way of his senses. He also told me he . . ."

Cimmis ducked out of his lodge and walked out into the plaza. He wore a plain knee-length blue war shirt belted at the waist with a braided sea-grass cord. Rather than the ruler of the North Wind People, he appeared to be nothing more than an aging warrior. Ast-cat was sick again, which meant Cimmis rarely left his lodge.

Ecan said, "Come along. He'll wish to see you right away."

When they started down the rocks toward the palisade, Cimmis saw them and stalked for the gate.

They met him at the entry, and Ecan lifted a hand, calling, "Red Dog has returned, my Chief."

Warily, Cimmis asked, "Red Dog, when did you arrive?"

"Just now, my Chief. I was on my way to see you."

"But you stopped to report to Ecan first. Why?" Cimmis wore his gray hair in a single braid. His thin beard flipped in the wind.

Red Dog gave Ecan an uncomfortable look.

Ecan spread his arms in appeasement. "Forgive me, my Chief. I called to Red Dog and distracted him from his duties." He smiled. "If you will excuse me, you have things to discuss." He stepped through the gate, not bothering to look back.

Across the plaza, Dzoo's maroon dress waffled in the wind as she walked toward the four guards who stood near the central fire. They went rigid before shoving each other to see who could get away the quickest. Deer Killer tripped over his own feet and almost fell into the coals before he righted himself. The other guards laughed and scrambled around him.

Ecan called, *"Deer Killer?"*

The young warrior nearly twisted his neck off spinning around to look toward the palisade gate.

Ecan strode purposefully toward him. "When is your guard duty over?"

"At dusk, Starwatcher!"

"Not tonight," Ecan shouted. "I think you should be standing your post until dawn. From the clouds out to the west, we should have rain again. I wouldn't want you to miss it."

"Yes, Starwatcher." At Deer Killer's miserable look, the other guards chuckled.

Dzoo walked straight up to Deer Killer.

The young warrior bravely pulled his shoulders back and faced her, but his knees trembled.

She said something to him.

Deer Killer looked mesmerized, like a rabbit who's just realized he stepped into a snare.

Dzoo leaned closer and spoke again; then she smiled and walked past him. The watching guards scattered, and Deer Killer's hand twined in the fabric over his heart. He looked like he might faint.

Angry, Ecan closed the last of the distance, eyes blazing.

When he got to within ten paces, a powerful gust of wind blasted the mountain, and a tiny tornado of dirt and gravel spun into existence over Fire Village.

The whirlwind descended, gathering speed as it plunged out of the sky. It touched down, whirling coals from the fire, sucking up baskets and mats.

"Run!" someone shouted.

Ecan bellowed, "Halt! Man your posts!"

Deer Killer flinched when the first stone smacked his shoulder. Another banged across a lodge roof and sailed over the edge. Someone down below yipped.

Deer Killer spun around to greet Ecan, but before he could speak, a basket bounced off his arm with a painful crack, and Deer Killer yelled, "What the . . . !"

A split-cedar mat hit him in the back, then a rash of gravel and hot ash almost knocked him senseless.

Deer Killer, an arm up to fend off the wind, shrieked, *"It's her! It's her!"*

Ecan shouted, "Warrior! I order you to halt!"

Deer Killer bellowed, *"Make her stop! She's trying to kill me!"*

The whirlwind flipped back and forth over the plaza, dust and debris in its wake. Then it careened away down the mountain slope, kicking up dust and detritus as it went.

Dzoo seemed untouched where she stood by one of the lodges, watching with large dark eyes. Not even her dress was rippling as the blow passed.

A breathless silence settled over the village.

Ecan focused on the guards who'd fled the wind's wrath. Falling Cedar pawed at a hot coal that burned in a fold of his war shirt. The others cowered, staring wide-eyed up at the sky, and then back at Dzoo.

"If you are not back to your posts by the time I've finished calling out your names, I will assign you as the witch's personal guards, never to leave her side! . . . Black Cod!" Men lunged to obey. "Thunder Boy!"

The warriors assembled in front of him, forming a line with their chests thrown out, their gazes focused anywhere but on Ecan. The wind had left them with eyes slitted, hair whipped around their faces. Falling Cedar's shirt still smoldered.

"I have never witnessed a more cowardly display in my life!" Ecan marched back and forth in front of them. "Deer Killer!"

The young warrior might have been on the point of tears. "Yes, Starwatcher?"

A nasty lump had already risen where the stone had bashed his temple. He seemed a little unsteady on his feet.

"What did the witch tell you before the whirlwind formed?"

Deer Killer squinted in disbelief. "She—she asked me if she knew me!"

"Knew you? Does she?"

"I've been her guard. She should know me."

Ecan's eyes narrowed. "Then she spoke to you again, didn't she?"

"Yes, but she just asked me the same question." Deer Killer's arms flapped helplessly against his sides.

Soft laughter drifted from somewhere high above him.

Ecan turned in time to see Dzoo make a sweeping gesture with her arm, a graceful winglike motion.

The remaining wind stopped. Just stopped. The air might have gone suddenly dead.

Deer Killer gasped, expression ashen. Nor was he alone. The other guards were bug-eyed, jaws locked, throats working as they swallowed dryly.

Ecan slapped Deer Killer with all the force he could manage. The young warrior staggered, stunned, and wiped at his mouth. Blood leaked onto his lips.

For a split instant, Ecan saw anger glitter in the youth's eyes. As quickly, it vanished.

"Forgive me, Starwatcher," Deer Killer whispered.

Ecan turned, glaring at Dzoo. Their eyes met across the distance. "What is she *doing* to us?"

She couldn't have heard, not from that far away; but she threw back her head, and her eerie laughter mocked them all.

Forty-four

As the whirlwind spun through the village and blasted away down the mountainside, Cimmis braced a hand against the wall. In the roar of wind he couldn't hear his own thoughts, but he watched the twister as it played havoc with his village before rattling the palisade, whipping up red cinder, and heading down to lash the trees.

Red Dog brushed gray-streaked black hair from his dark eyes and squinted at Cimmis. "What's going on down there?"

"It has something to do with Dzoo."

Cimmis watched the ensuing drama as Ecan berated his warriors at the central fire.

"Do you think she caused the whirlwind?" Red Dog asked in a hoarse whisper.

"She'll be blamed for every unusual thing that happens in Fire Village."

People were stepping out, staring around uncertainly. Some went looking for items blown away. Here and there the village dogs came slinking back from their hiding places.

"Come," Cimmis said. "Let's talk in my lodge where we won't be overheard." He led the way to his dwelling, pulled his leather door curtain aside, and gestured for Red Dog to enter.

"Yes, my Chief." Red Dog ducked inside.

The fire in the center of the floor cast a ruddy glow over Astcat's slack face where she lay in the rear. Her soul had been gone since dawn. Cimmis had been dribbling water into her mouth to keep her body from drying up.

"You must be tired and thirsty after your run." He went to the fire and dipped a cup of gooseberry flower tea from the bag hanging on the tripod.

Red Dog eagerly took the cup and sniffed the aroma appreciatively. As he crouched opposite Cimmis, he said, "Thirsty but alive. There were moments when I doubted I'd ever see Fire Village again."

"Rain Bear treated you poorly?" Cimmis seated himself on a folded buffalo robe.

"When he realized I was your emissary he gave me food and drink, and provided a warm fire. I was surrounded by two tens of warriors, but comfortable."

As Wind Woman toyed with his door curtain, it swung, and allowed the rays of sunrise to flash across his painted shields. Killer Whale and Eagle seemed to move. Red Dog turned slightly as though he saw it, too.

"All right, tell me everything." Cimmis laced his fingers over one knee. He hadn't slept well since Red Dog left. His visits to the Above Worlds had been tortured. All of his ancestors kept shouting at him, telling him he was being a fool.

"I repeated your words exactly, my Chief. I told Rain Bear that if he did not leave the Raven People and flee, your assassins would quietly kill him and his entire family." Red Dog took a long drink of tea, almost emptied his cup, and looked across at Cimmis. "He did not accept your offer."

"I see."

He'd expected as much. Now everything hinged on the second phase of his plan. His craftiest Wolf Tail would have arrived yesterday. Evening Star and Ecan's boy would be headed his way, or their bodies were being prepared for burial. The advantage fell to Cimmis with either result. If Coyote had managed to extricate them, Cimmis could quietly kill Evening Star and hand the boy to Ecan, obligating the Starwatcher forever. If it went the other way, Ecan would be rabid over the death of his son and willing to do anything to avenge himself on Rain Bear. The final advantage Cimmis accrued was the effect the murders would have on Rain Bear. His followers would know he was powerless to protect them. Perhaps, just perhaps, to save his precious family, he would choose to fade away like the morning mist. If he did, any chance for an alliance among the Raven People would go with him.

Red Dog was watching him as he thought. The old warrior wet his lips and said, "Rain Bear had an offer of his own to make. He said that in memory of Tlikit, if you would secretly send Astcat to him, he would do his best to protect her from the Raven People's wrath."

Cimmis felt a shiver run through him.

Red Dog frowned down into his cup. "He also said he regretted he could no longer do anything to protect you."

"Yes, I'm sure he regrets that very much," he said tartly. Rain Bear had shamed him before the entire village six and ten cycles ago. He could still hear Old Woman East's shouting, *You are the great chief! Your daughter has run off with a slave warrior? How could this have been going on beneath your very eyes?* Of all the things Rain Bear could have offered, this was like a slap to the face.

No, don't think about it. Not yet.

"What was your opinion of the sentiment among the Raven People? How did the attack on War Gods Village affect them?"

Red Dog chuckled. "I would say they're on the verge of scattering like a flock of quail under a hawk's shadow. Like always, each chief is ready to turn on his fellows, each carried away by his petty jealousies." He paused in consideration. "More than that, I'd say that you had them right where you wanted them."

Then perhaps Coyote has already broken their will. He would know soon enough.

Red Dog finished his tea and set the cup on the hard-packed floor.

With a flip of his hand, Cimmis dismissed him. "Go and rest. Food will be provided. I'll send for you when I require your services again."

Red Dog stood. "I'll be waiting, my Chief."

The warrior threw back the curtain to leave, then disappeared with a swishing of the hanging.

Cimmis dropped his head into his hands. His belly ached. For over a sun cycle, he'd been killing his relatives and bullying the Raven People at the Council's behest. He was too worried and tired to do otherwise. Astcat might have been the matron, but Old Woman North wielded the true authority. And he acted in an attempt to forget his own bitterness over Astcat's illness.

He whispered, *"Blessed gods, show me a way out."*

Sunset

*P*owdered dust from the sage flats near the river coats my wrinkled face, and sweat trickles down my neck. The rest of my body is wrapped in hides. I actually feel a little better, more aware. More here.

"You are a good teacher," I whisper.

"There is no such thing as a good teacher. Teachers are of no consequence. They are accidental moments. Vanishing instants. Even to themselves. They must be. If a teacher pretends to offer permanence or truth, he does not give, he takes away."

"But I thought you were teaching me the ultimate truths of existence?"

"Ultimate truths?" He scoffs. "A strange pairing of words. That is the one contradiction that does not lead to enlightenment. Instead, it leads to the darkest depths of human cruelty."

"Then, there are no ultimate truths?"

He pauses. "Have you ever watched water?"

If I but had the strength, I'd give him an annoyed look. What could water possibly have to do with ultimate truth? "I've spent my entire life living on the ocean, you old fool. Of course I've watched water."

"I don't mean looked at it; I mean actively studied. For example, do you know its nature?"

"The nature of water . . . is to be wet." I open one eye.

He's gazing down with a stern expression, as though I'm the first real idiot he's ever seen.

"All right," I say. "What is the nature of water?"

"Water is the softest, most yielding thing in the world. It works very hard to flow over and around. It only splashes against something when it's being tormented and has no choice." His thick gray brows lower. "I suspect you've done a lot of splashing in your time."

"Yes," I answer with a smile. "But I had no choice. The jealous have always tormented me."

He chuckles and shakes his head. From the corner of my eye, I catch movement. I thought we were alone. We're not. Others wander the riverbanks.

The old Soul Keeper says, "What does water seek? Do you know?"

I remember the ocean smoothing the sand. The waves are like a heartbeat. "The earth?"

"In a way, yes; it seeks low places. Every moment is a calm, patient, sinking downward."

"I spent my life climbing upward, Soul Keeper. I always strove to soar with the Comet People. Are you telling me I wasted my life?"

"No, Chief. Nothing is ever wasted. Along with the notion of 'ultimate truth,' that is the great hoax. Every movement, every sound we make, has a purpose. But that purpose is not to soar upward."

"It is to sink downward?"

"Of course. Look at water. It settles among the smallest creatures, tiny insignificant things that dwell beneath grains of sand."

"You think the goal of life is to fraternize with small, low creatures?" I say sarcastically. I want to make up for the comment about water's nature. "That sounds particularly idiotic to me."

"Perhaps—if you're a particular idiot—it does. But it is only when you sink to the lowest place that you find the foundation of things—and others who understand it."

"I see."

"Do you? Do you understand what all this has to do with compassion?"

The old Soul Keeper rises to his feet, and his cape flaps around his tall body.

"Where are you going?" I ask.

"To get you a cup of soup. I think perhaps you're strong enough to eat. While I'm gone, think about compassion and water."

I close my eyes. Out over the lazy river, gulls flutter and squeal, as though the people are throwing them tidbits of food.

Water and compassion. Being soft and yielding. Low places and low creatures. The foundation of things, not lofty ultimate truths. Sinking downward . . .

I am sinking downward. I feel it every instant.

The thought terrifies me.

Forty-five

Astcat propped herself on her walking stick and stared at the darkness behind the swaying door flap. Red Dog had waited until Cimmis had left for the Council lodge before he'd sneaked in. His meeting with her had been short, terse, and as disappointing as the rest of her life. Even though he had left, the pungent scent of his sweat lingered in his wake.

Plots within plots. She had been good at this once, back before her soul had loosened. She had no notion of how long she had been away this time.

Her knees wobbled as she slowly made her way back to the thick stack of hides beside the fire.

Most of their belongings had been packed and sent ahead to Wasp Village. The lodge felt barren. She kept looking for the baskets and bowls that had been sitting in the same spot for many summers and now were missing. The constantly lost sensation left her feeling gutted.

She combed shoulder-length gray hair away from her wrinkled face. The coals made the very air seem awash in blood. Across from her, Killer Whale swam on his shield, his tail swaying slightly. "What do you think I should do? Hmm? Run or fight?"

The red and blue shades of Killer Whale's body had faded. At least she thought they had. Perhaps her soul sickness had affected her eyesight. She strained to think. Blessed Ancestors, she had to think. . . .

She heard ghostly steps outside and thought it might be Red Dog returning. What had he forgotten to tell her? The steps almost weren't there, like snowflakes falling upon the ground.

Astcat stared at the door.

A tall woman lifted the flap and stood silhouetted against the starlight. She had her hood up, but long hair streamed around her familiar form.

"Ah," Astcat whispered, "I've been expecting you for a long time."

"This is a dangerous game you play, Matron, moving around the edges of your husband and the Council. Red Dog carries one secret message for Ecan, another for the Council, and a third for you. It's like playing dice with a grizzly bear."

Astcat bowed her head. How could the woman have discovered . . . But, then this was Dzoo. Perhaps she'd seen it in a Dream, or in the patterns of the future. Perhaps a wood rat had told her while it was carrying grass to its burrow in the rocks. "Of course it's dangerous. But what do you think would happen if I announced tomorrow that I was stepping down?"

Dzoo whispered, "The North Wind People would begin killing each other in the fight over the succession."

"Yes." Astcat nodded soberly. "And if my daughter survives, she'll struggle to find her position. As the new clan matron, the Old Women would bully her, or any other successor, into anything they wish. If I do not step down, Rain Bear will lead the Raven People against us. No matter what I choose, there will be war."

"And if Evening Star returns?"

Astcat anxiously tapped the floor with the head of her walking stick. "You think that's why I invited her back? To declare her matron? Think about this, Dzoo. Once the Raven People have amassed their warriors, how long do you think they will let her rule? How long do you think they will let her *live*?" Tears welled in Astcat's old eyes. "If I were to declare her matron tomorrow, it would be her death sentence."

Wind Woman teased the hood masking Dzoo's face. "She will not accept no matter what you offer."

"She must. She has to. She cares too much. She knows how young my daughter is. I'm sure Evening Star has regretted that her mother ever opposed us. Were it not for Naida's obstinacy, Evening Star would be a village matron now, and on her way to being matron of the North Wind People."

Dzoo placed a hand on one of the lodgepoles and leaned in the entry to whisper, "There is *another* way."

Her face reflected the red gleam of the lodge like a pool of water. "What other way? Give up? Throw myself upon Rain Bear's mercy?"

"I am not the Dreamer you must listen to." Lightning flashed, silhouetting her tall body in the doorway. Dzoo cocked her head. "He has found his wings."

"Who?"

"You will know."

The night sky seemed to darken behind Dzoo as thunder rumbled across the rugged land.

Astcat wiped at the tears that ran down her cheeks. "Why don't you come and sit with me? I haven't had a woman to talk with for a long time—except the old hags in the Council, and they're not much company."

As Dzoo stepped into the lodge, her buffalo cape billowed, blocking the light.

For an instant, Astcat's lodge went as black as the tunnel to the Underwater House.

Pitch yawned and shivered in his wet cape. Thunder rumbled over the mountains. Rain had begun to fall with the morning and softened the lines of the sea and shore. In the murky blue radiance before dawn, the bark lodges resembled a slumbering herd of wet animals. The only people awake—other than he and Rides-the-Wind—were guards. Occasionally, he glimpsed them fighting fatigue as they stalked the forest.

Pitch adjusted his arm. The pain wasn't quite so bad, but the sling had started to cut into his shoulder. Best of all the swelling was down, and he could move his fingers.

Rides-the-Wind lay wrapped in hides to Pitch's right, his gray head propped on his arm. He'd been silently staring at the fire for over a hand of time. A hide bag full of seal meat and onions simmered where it hung from a tripod beside the fire.

"Why don't you try to sleep, Pitch. I'll stay awake."

He shook his head. Wet black hair stuck to his cheeks, making his beaked nose look long and sharp. He'd barely slept in the past day and a half. "I'm all right, Elder. Just worried. Does it always take this long before a Dreamer wakes?"

"It depends on how far he's gone." A pause. "And if he's coming back."

Pitch turned to look at Rides-the-Wind's lodge where Tsauz still Dreamed. Raindrops beaded the roof like tiny glistening shells. The last time he'd checked, the boy lay on his back staring blindly at the ropes swaying above him.

Lightning flashed, strobing the peaks, and thunder rolled through the village.

"How many times have you done this?" Pitch asked. "Helped a young Dreamer to climb Grandfather Vulture's ladder to the Above Worlds?"

A soft shishing could be heard as the rain increased.

"Many times. Two tens, maybe three tens."

"Tsauz is so young. I was surprised you permitted him to try."

"I generally know people's souls, what they're capable of."

"Have you ever been wrong?"

"Yes," he answered softly. "If he survives this, Pitch, he'll become a very Powerful Holy man."

Pitch twisted to look at Rides-the-Wind's lodge again. Off to the right, a faint coil of gray rose through the smoke hole of Rain Bear's lodge. He had seen the furtive shape slip from the doorway just before dawn and watched Evening Star scuttle to her own lodge. Neither he nor anyone else had missed the way she and Rain Bear had started to look at each other. People had begun to say unkind things. And even Roe was unsure if she approved of where this relationship might be going.

Rides-the-Wind indicated his lodge. "Make sure he's all right."

"Yes, Elder."

He quietly walked to the lodge and pulled the flap back. He stared in for a long time, before calling, "Elder? I think you'd better come."

"What's wrong?" Rides-the-Wind sat up in his hides, and long gray hair fell around his shoulders.

"Tsauz is having trouble breathing. It—it sounds like he's suffocating."

Rides-the-Wind walked stiffly across the wet fir needles and knelt before the flap.

Tsauz lay on his back with his knees crooked and his arms spread. The position had drawn his black-and-white cape out like wings. Wet black hair haloed his head. He *was* having trouble breathing. He wheezed and sucked at the air as though he couldn't get enough.

"He's flying very high now," Rides the Wind murmured. "The air is thin up there. Leave him alone and let him concentrate. This is the most dangerous part of the journey."

In a hushed voice, Pitch asked, "Is he riding Thunderbird yet?"

"Oh, yes."

"Why is his hair wet? The hides are dry. Almost no rain blew in."

"Thunderbird may be soaring through rain showers. We won't know until Tsauz comes back to us. Now come, let's go back to our fire."

As Pitch turned to follow, lightning cut a brilliant gash across the sky. It took Thunderbird's voice a few instants to reach them, but when it did, they both jumped and looked up into the rainy sky. Lightning flashed in all directions, creating an eerie luminescent web over the trees.

Pitch walked back and sat on the log, his gaze lost in the faint flickers of fire. Rides-the-Wind returned to his hides.

"Elder?" Pitch asked. "What's it like to ride on Thunderbird's back?"

"Where did you go when you climbed Grandfather Vulture's ladder?"

"For me, the ladder led to the Underwater House. I talked with my dead mother. That was just after I discovered Roe was pregnant with Stonecrop. Mother helped me to understand what made a good father. I have heard the ladder leads each person to a different place."

"Usually, yes."

Pitch caught the tantalizing odor of boiling seal meat as steam drifted his way. Off and on throughout the night, they'd eaten small amounts to keep up their strength.

A massive white bolt of lightning crackled right over their heads. Pitch let out a cry—drowned out by the deafening booming that shook Sandy Point Village. After images burned his eyes.

When the sound trailed away, Pitch saw Rides-the-Wind staring pensively at his lodge.

A low whimper came from inside.

Pitch leaped for the lodge. When he threw back the flap, he found Tsauz standing, hunched over, hands on his knees, shaking like a leaf in a spring gale. Bloody scratches covered his face and hands.

Pitch ducked into the lodge. "Are you all right?"

Tsauz staggered, about to topple face-first to the floor. Pitch steadied him and felt the boy's flesh, like ice. He wrapped him in a section of elkhide and dragged him out to the fire. Tsauz collapsed on the ground like a child who'd been spinning around with his arms out.

"Tsauz? It's Pitch. Can you answer me? Are you all right?"

Rides-the-Wind stepped to the wet pile of wood and tossed more branches onto the fire. Then he bent over the boy, peering intently into his eyes.

Tsauz sucked desperately at the air, filling his lungs, letting it out and filling them again. "We dove through the top of the forest to get here."

"Thunderbird was in a hurry?" Rides-the-Wind asked.

He nodded. "I had to close my eyes. The light was too bright."

Pitch waved a hand in front of the boy's eyes. Nothing. He'd been hoping . . . but it didn't matter. He stroked the boy's hair. "You did well, Tsauz. We're so proud of you."

Rides-the-Wind stopped and surveyed Tsauz with expert old eyes. "Are you hungry?"

The boy wiped his runny nose on his sleeve. "Yes. But I must see Rain Bear first."

"Pitch, these scratches need tending to. Please, fetch my Healer's bag."

Pitch scrambled into Rides-the-Wind's lodge while Rides-the-Wind draped the hide closer around Tsauz's shoulders.

When Pitch returned with the bag, Rides-the-Wind said, "Tsauz, we need you to relax for the moment. When you're warm and we've tended your injuries, we'll send for—"

"I must see Rain Bear now!" His blind eyes widened in terror. "I saw . . . saw all of you . . . and you were *dead*."

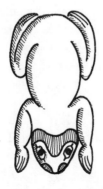

Forty-six

Rain Bear sat across the fire with his teacup braced on his knee. Morning was breaking, sending a shallow light through the camp. It illuminated the low blue wreaths of smoke that hung in flat layers. Every muscle in his body cried out for more sleep, but he forced himself to sip his tea and struggled to come awake.

Little Tsauz sat across the fire, Rides-the-Wind and Pitch flanking him on either side. The boy's dark eyes looked strangely luminous, as though some of Thunderbird's light had suffused his young body. Rides-the-Wind had cleaned and treated his facial wounds, but a few of the deepest cuts across his forehead still oozed blood.

Rain Bear's sleep-hazy mind wasn't capable of rational thought this morning. Instead it kept clinging to memories of Evening Star's body against his. He had never made love with a woman who fit so perfectly against him.

He glanced surreptitiously at her lodge, wondering when she had slipped away last night. Waking without her this morning had left him with a sense of desolation and loss.

He sniffed at the cold, sipped his tea, and forced himself to concentrate on the here and now.

"What happened?" Rain Bear gestured to the boy's wounds.

"He flew through the treetops on Thunderbird's back," Rides-the-Wind answered matter-of-factly. "The branches scratched him."

The branches scratched him? Rain Bear put more faith in good clubs and spears than he did in gods, but he didn't exactly disbelieve.

Pitch handed Rain Bear a bowl of seal meat stew, and he nodded his thanks while he tried to sort this all out. As he stirred the stew, the mingled scents of seaweed and seal encircled his face. He took a bite. Tender and succulent, the seal melted in his mouth. Swallowing, he gestured questioningly. "I'm glad the boy had a vision, but why am I here?"

Tsauz clasped the bowl Pitch inserted into his hands and slowly let out a deep breath. "Chief Rain Bear, I spoke with Thunderbird."

Rides-the-Wind gave the boy an intense look. "Did he meet you at the top of the ladder?"

"No. He grabbed the rope and dragged it away, but he made me climb to the middle while it swung through the air"—his lips parted, as though seeing it all again on the fabric of his soul—"and then we soared away."

Rides-the-Wind leaned forward. A clean dry deerhide rested over his shoulders, but he still shivered periodically, as though the cold night had settled in his bones. "Where did you go?"

"We flew to Fire Village." Steam curled around Tsauz's face as he ate a bite of stew. He chewed it thoughtfully and swallowed. "I saw my father."

That got Rain Bear's attention. He perked up, studying the boy.

Rides-the-Wind asked, "Did you speak with him?"

"Thunderbird wouldn't let me." Grief strained his voice, but his eyes remained clear.

"Then Thunderbird had good reasons. Did you ask him to save your father?"

"Yes."

"What did he say?"

Tsauz lowered his bowl to his lap and fumbled with it. The words were almost too soft to hear. "He told me that I could either save my father, or save all of our peoples. One or the other."

"Did he say why?"

"No."

Rides-the-Wind's gray brows slanted down. "How are you supposed to do that?"

"He wouldn't tell me. He said he'll come back and tell me more later. Right now, he just wanted me to get word to Matron Astcat."

"Word about what?"

Tsauz ran his thumb around the rim of his bowl. "He told me how to stop the war."

Rain Bear's spoon stopped halfway to his mouth. He put it back in his bowl with a clunk. "How?"

Tsauz's blind eyes drifted in his direction. "It's not something for you, Great Chief. Only Matron Astcat and I can stop it."

The hair at the nape of Rain Bear's neck prickled. "Tsauz, I must insist—"

"No, you must not." Rides-the-Wind gave a shake of his finger. "If Tsauz were to betray the trust of his Spirit Helper by revealing the Dream to you, it might anger Thunderbird. We would be worse off than we are now. At least we know there *is* a way to stop the war."

Rain Bear set his half-eaten bowl on a warm hearthstone. "You mean that I'm supposed to trust Tsauz when tens of tens of lives are at stake?"

"Apparently. So let's spend our time thinking about a runner. Who should we send with Tsauz's message?"

"Just a moment!" Rain Bear glared back and forth. "You're asking me to bet the future of my people, clan, family, and warriors on the vision of a ten-winters-old boy?"

Rides-the-Wind gave him a thoughtful appraisal. "Do you remember when we talked about why I came here? I told you that Power brought me here. Just as it brought you, Tsauz, and Evening Star to this place. I told you that you would have to make a choice. Do you trust Tsauz's vision? Or prosecute your war in an attempt to exterminate the North Wind People?"

"I have no wish to exterminate the North Wind People." He scowled at the old man.

In a gentler voice, Rides-the-Wind asked, "What will be the ultimate price of your alliance, Great Chief? What will Bluegrass, Goldenrod, and Talon demand in return for their service?"

Rain Bear started to shake his head, and then a cold realization sank in. Yes, that would be it, wouldn't it? He might start out with the assurance that his forces were only going to break the Council's authority, but once the warfare began, who would keep the pent rage from feeding on a desire for revenge?

"Ah, yes." Rides-the-Wind read his expression. "Where will it end?" He turned back to Pitch. "Let's see. We were talking about a way to get Tsauz's message to Matron Astcat."

Rain Bear was painfully aware of Tsauz. The boy was staring at him with such intensity Rain Bear would have sworn the boy could see him. It went against every fiber in his body, but he said, "Whatever we do must be done immediately. The next time Coyote prowls Sandy Point Village, he'll kill Tsauz."

Pitch's beaked nose caught the gleam of firelight as he glanced uncertainly at his father-in-law. "It has to be someone special, doesn't it? Carrying the message will be dangerous."

"It has to be someone they wouldn't kill right off," Rides-the-Wind said. "Someone important enough that they would listen to him."

"Someone like me."

Rain Bear and Rides-the-Wind turned to Pitch, asking in unison, "You?"

"I'm perfect for it."

Rain Bear placed a hand on Pitch's shoulder. "What about your wound?"

"It's healed enough. The swelling has gone down. I can do this. And, given my wound, I'm surely not intimidating to them."

Rain Bear mused, "Roe isn't going to like this, but if I'm stuck with this lunacy, you're the best choice. Not only that, you're my son-in-law—married to Astcat's granddaughter, for what that's worth."

Rides-the-Wind smoothed his hand over his gray beard. "By sending you, they will know the value we place on Tsauz's vision."

Pitch muttered, "Tell that to the assassins who speared me on the trail home from Antler Spoon's village."

"Yes," Rides-the-Wind said softly. "I've been thinking about that."

Pitch frowned and looked back and forth between them. "But I thought we'd decided Coyote hired them, and Coyote was Ecan."

Rides-the-Wind's eyes glimmered. "If Coyote were Ecan, Evening Star would have recognized him the other night. No, this is someone who can play many roles. Someone smart enough to let other people believe him harmless."

"If Dzoo was right, and he's obsessed with her, why isn't he trying to get her out of Fire Village?"

The old Soul Keeper's smile was anything but friendly. "Oh, he hasn't forgotten her. You see, when I say he's clever, I mean it. How patient he must be, seeing her every day, waiting, knowing that the entire world is about to explode in warfare."

"And in the chaos . . ."

"Exactly."

Rain Bear pinched the bridge of his nose. "We must warn her."

Rides-the-Wind was watching him from the corner of his eye. "Do not worry about Dzoo, Great Chief. She and Coyote are already Dancing and darting. They have locked themselves in a duel. What happens between them is out of your control."

Rain Bear shot him a mistrustful look.

Rides-the-Wind replied, "Why do you think she let Ecan take her to Fire Village in the first place?"

Pitch rose. His red ritual cape swung around his long legs. "Let me get my pack. I'll be ready in moments."

Rides-the-Wind gripped Pitch's free hand as the Singer walked past, and whispered, "Take the obsidian amulets to Dzoo. She may need them."

"Yes, I will." He sprinted away.

Rain Bear studied Tsauz. The boy had his chin up, bravely facing them, but his fingers had twined in his cape and hardened to fists.

What had Tsauz really experienced last night? Had he truly flown with the god, or was he just a very imaginative child? One touched by Power, to be sure, but the boy had been desperate to get a message to his father. *And now I have given him a way to do just that.*

Would the message actually stop the war?

Or start it?

His gaze returned to Rides-the-Wind, and he found the elder staring at him with dark penetrating eyes.

"Quite the unsettling decision, isn't it?" the Soul Keeper asked.

"I was just wishing I was the only one I had to trust."

A grim smile curled the old man's lips. "Then you'd be in real trouble."

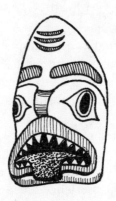

Forty-seven

Ecan ducked out of his lodge, his prayer bag in hand, and looked across the mountain. The gleam of dawn painted the belly of Brother Sky, turning it into an iridescent lavender bowl. At least twenty people already stood on the high points around Fire Village, facing east, toward the mountain peak.

He nodded to the young woman who knelt on a woven sea-grass mat ten paces away and proceeded up the trail toward the eastern palisade gate. Wind Woman blew his long black hair and stirred the wolf tails on his knee-high moccasins. They made a pleasant swishing sound.

North Wind People rarely appeared to offer morning prayers, which he thought foolish. Of course it meant associating with the unwashed rabble, but it was also a powerful symbol. If Matron Astcat were any sort of leader, she would order everyone except North Wind People to stay in at dawn, so that the sun shed its newborn light on North Wind People alone.

As he passed a lodge he glimpsed the knot of slaves bent over a still form. Wind Scorpion stood there, his grizzled face stern, arms crossed resolutely. Ecan had never really liked the man. He was taciturn, quiet, and watched the world through predatory eyes. Cimmis placed a great deal of credence in his skills, sending him constantly on scouting chores.

Ecan stepped over, stopping at his side to see what the commotion was.

"Good morning to you, Starwatcher." Wind Scorpion didn't raise his eyes to Ecan's, but continued to stare suspiciously at the proceedings.

"Warrior." The slaves were busy rubbing Lion Girl's body with mint leaves and crushed fir needles. "So she died, did she?"

Wind Scorpion's lip lifted in a sneer. "I asked Cimmis to let me take the witch out into the forest." He lifted a war club in his bony right hand. "One smack. Right in the back of the head. And she'd never kill another of our people with her potions."

Ecan glanced at the corpse. "It does seem that everyone around her becomes ill, doesn't it?"

"Deer Killer is complaining of a stomachache this morning." Wind Scorpion shook his head. "Ask our chief, will you? See if you can get him to be rid of the witch before we're all as dead as that girl."

"And Dance Fly?"

Slaves usually cared for their own. They dared to call upon Ecan's skills only in the direst of circumstances.

As they had yesterday for Lion Girl and Dance Fly.

When he'd entered the slave lodge, he'd been horrified by the raised wartlike lesions that covered their faces, hands, and legs. They'd been trembling spastically. He'd left willow bark tea and larkspur ointments—both very valuable because they, too, came as tribute—to relieve their pain. Now, seeing how Lion Girl had turned out, he wished he'd saved his precious ointments.

"If Dance Fly isn't dead by midday, it'll be a miracle. She's lost her soul; her breathing is so fast you'd think she'd run for miles." Anger welled in Wind Scorpion's voice. But then, it was known that he consorted with most of the slave women.

"If she dies, the rumors about Dzoo will be flying like bats."

"She's doing this to scare us." Wind Scorpion's war club bounced in his hand. "Just mention it to the great chief, will you, Starwatcher? I'll drag her out of here on the end of a rope. I'm not afraid."

Ecan remembered how Wind Scorpion had been with Hunter on the trail back from War Gods Village. No, he wasn't afraid. Not in the light of day like now. But come nightfall and Dzoo's proximity, and well, it would be another thing.

"I'll mention it," Ecan agreed as he turned back to his duties.

The guard standing at the far northern end of the cliff lifted a hand to him. Ecan couldn't tell if it was Hunter, or that bellyaching fool, Deer Killer. He lifted a hand in return and continued on his way through the palisade.

The cliff rose like a giant midnight wall. Another guard stood two hundred hands above. No, not a guard. Ecan knew White Stone's stance. The war chief always stood with his back straight and legs spread.

White Stone had been acting strangely since Red Dog's return. Sensing that Red Dog carried important messages, he would rightly assume that plans were being laid in secret.

Ecan shrugged it off. He hadn't slept well. Tsauz had wakened him several times in the night, calling out as though he was hurt and needed Ecan. The visions had left him drained and anxious.

He reached the trail that led to the top of the lava cliff and climbed. Footprints disturbed the frost. Anger warmed his veins. He'd given strict orders that no one should ever disturb his morning prayers. . . .

Dzoo leaned over the edge of the cliff above him.

Ecan froze. How had she managed to pass the guard at the palisade gate? Cimmis had ordered her death if she even tried to pass. Now she turned to study him. Inside the frame of her hood, her beautiful face looked pale, like polished chalcedony. Her black eyes shone.

The town had gone quiet. He turned to see people staring, waiting to see what he'd do.

As he stepped off onto the rimrock, her gaze followed him. Just her gaze. She stood three paces away, tall and willowy, silhouetted against the pink sunrise like a dark Earth Spirit.

"A pleasant morning to you, Dzoo," he greeted, and went to stand at the southern point of the rim, where he always offered his prayers. "They were supposed to kill you if you tried to leave the palisade."

"My guard said he was sick this morning."

"Yes. Lion Girl died last night."

"He's good, isn't he?"

Ecan turned his head. "He? Who?"

"The man who killed them."

"People think you killed them."

"Yes. They are supposed to."

He ignored it as another of her ploys. As he loosened the laces of his prayer bag, she moved up behind him, her steps silken.

Ecan's back muscles crawled. He said, "I'm glad you're here. It will give us a chance to speak."

He pulled four small leather pouches—each a different color—from his prayer bag.

As he opened the yellow pouch; he said, "It is considered ordinary courtesy to talk back when—"

"You have no interest in my courtesy."

Her deep voice had a curiously penetrating quality. It seemed to echo inside him. "I saw you enter Matron Astcat's lodge last night. You were there for a long time. It would be worth a great deal to know what you discussed."

He hadn't heard her approach. Barely more than a handsbreadth from his ear, she whispered, *"Your death."*

Annoyed that he'd jumped, Ecan dumped powdered red cedar bark into his hand and as he sprinkled it to the east, Sang, *"Come Old Woman Above, rise and carry the sun across the sky."*

He stuffed the yellow bag back into his pack and jerked open the laces of the red bag. As he poured powdered clamshell to the south, he said, "Is that something you will accomplish, Dzoo?"

She turned to stare up at the mountainside where White Stone was perched. "What will you do now that Rain Bear has rejected your offer?"

Ecan's hand stopped. Shell blew from his fingers in a haze. How could she know?

"You must find another way to recover your son—and soon."

"Or what?"

She paused. "Or he'll kill you."

"Who will?"

She just smiled.

Ecan finished his prayers, sprinkling bitter cherry bark to the west and ground oyster shell to the north. Then he offered his shell-covered hands to Brother Sky, and bent to touch Our Mother Earth, chanting, *"Come Old Woman Above, be on your way to the Dark Place."*

Wind Woman swept the lines of bark and shell together, blending them into a rainbow haze before carrying them away down the mountain. They fell over Fire Village like a glistening mist, blessing it.

"Cimmis's assassin failed. That must make you happy."

Ecan's head jerked around. "What assassin?"

"You didn't know?"

"*What* assassin?"

Her gaze had fixed on the cliff where White Stone stood, as though waiting for something. Waist-length red hair streamed around her hood like long dancing legs. From his angle, he could see the lavender light shining on her turned-up nose and full lips. The rest of her face remained hidden by her hair.

"You really don't know, do you?"

"Is this some trick? A lie designed to make me . . ."

She turned, and Ecan went still. His loins stirred, though he couldn't say why. Something . . . lethal . . . gazed at him from those ebony depths. Something not quite human.

"Your chief sent an assassin to kill your son. He failed. Barely made his escape. A worrisome thing for a man of his skill."

Ecan's heart thundered. "You're lying!"

She didn't even blink.

His hand quaked as he stuffed his blue pouch back into his prayer bag and tied it to his belt. It wasn't that he doubted Cimmis would do something so heinous; he just couldn't fathom why his own spies hadn't informed him. Cimmis would certainly make another attempt.

"When did this happen, Dzoo?"

"Two days ago."

"Did Astcat tell you?"

"Are you ready?" She smiled, and he felt it like the final plunge of an assassin's knife.

"Ready for what? Stop playing games with me."

"It's almost over now." She extended her palm and breathed across it, as though blowing dust to the wind.

"What is?"

"Your life, Starwatcher."

Forty-eight

The news had traveled like a racing wolf. Within a single hand of time, everyone around Sandy Point Village knew that Pitch had left to carry a message to the matron of the North Wind People—a message Thunderbird had given Tsauz in a Dream. Many people, tired from running and heartsick over their losses, rejoiced that Thunderbird had told Tsauz how to stop the war. But there were others— Raven People who'd been looking forward to killing North Wind People—who grumbled around their fires while they crafted enough spears to serve their needs five times over.

Rain Bear's elkhide cape billowed as he and Evening Star slowly continued up the trail toward the hastily arranged meeting place. He had picked an old hunter's storage lodge some distance from the camps. Dogrib's warriors had kicked out the squatters who occupied it and had seen to the refurbishment of the place. Rain Bear hoped they would be away from prying eyes and interference. Guards stood every ten paces, ringing the lodge like hard-eyed statues.

"My Chief, let me examine this place before you enter." Dogrib trotted toward the moss-covered lodge in the trees ahead. Warriors, thicker than the trees themselves, stood around talking, laughing, casting curious glances at each other.

"At least no one has thrown anything pointed in our direction," Evening Star mused wryly.

He shot her a glance from the corner of his eye. "We just got here. There'll be plenty of time for that after the council."

"I love optimists."

He was puzzled by her, and still more than a little off balance by what had occurred that night in his lodge. He hadn't been prepared for the passion of their lovemaking—either for his reaction, or for how she had clung to him as her body tensed and undulated under his.

Nor was that all. Since their coupling she had changed. He'd been surprised by the emergence of a cutting wit and subtle but dry sense of humor. He had heard her laugh, and periodically, a sparkle lit her blue eyes.

A terrible longing grew within him. More than anything, he just wanted time to learn her moods, see her laugh. From somewhere came the memory of Cimmis's offer: He could leave. Take this marvelous woman, load his canoe, and paddle off into the north with his family. They could build a lodge on one of the small islands, fish, pick berries, and live out their lives.

If only . . . if only . . .

Dogrib reemerged from the lodge; his long white hair blazed in the morning's yellow gleam. He waved Rain Bear forward. At that moment the other chiefs emerged from the trees, maintaining the fiction that they had all arrived together.

Rain Bear nodded to this one and that, wondering if the old lodge would hold them all. Before he could enter, Dogrib grasped his arm and whispered, "There is a new war chief here: Brush Wasp. Says he's Gray Owl Clan from Trailing Raspberry Village. I don't believe it."

"Why not?" Rain Bear whispered and glanced at the two guards.

Dogrib's eyes bored into Rain Bear's. "Look at his earrings."

Rain Bear followed the others under the flap into the council.

Nearly two tens of chiefs packed themselves in two concentric circles around the fire. The chiefs formed the inner ring while their war chiefs knelt behind them. Rain Bear knew Brush Wasp instantly. The rough-looking young man sat cross-legged to his right, alone. He had seen perhaps twenty summers, but the battles he'd fought showed on his face. A long scar cut across his forehead, as though someone had almost succeeded in scalping him. He obviously had no chief here. His appearance would have meant little were it not for his earrings. They had been beaten from copper nuggets.

Copper was the property of the North Wind People. The rare nuggets were jealously guarded and only given to Raven servants for the most meritorious of service.

Had Brush Wasp simply forgotten he was wearing them?

The grizzled old Talon nodded as Rain Bear walked around the circle. He and Evening Star took seats beside Goldenrod, Dogrib settling close behind them. They made a stark contrast. Goldenrod was twenty-six and wore his black hair coiled in a stern bun over his right ear. Evening Star, on the other hand, had left her long hair loose. It fell over the shoulders of her elk suede dress in glossy red waves. It seemed that all eyes were upon her.

Goldenrod whispered, "The warriors outside are growing restless."

Rain Bear raised his hands to the assembly. "I pray that the Ancestors will watch over us today and grant us wisdom. We have many decisions to make."

Chief Black Mountain leaned forward. His bulbous nose and shoulder-length graying black hair shone, as though freshly washed. "Let's begin with the boy's 'vision.' We have all heard the stories. It is said that Ecan's son flew on the back of Thunderbird. That Thunderbird told him how to stop the war. Do you believe it?"

Whispers eddied through the lodge. Several chiefs shook their heads in doubt.

Rain Bear looked around the room, meeting each pair of eyes. "Rides-the-Wind believes it; so, too, does Singer Pitch. As to whether I believe it? Honestly, I don't know. I've always placed more faith in the actions of men and women. But I was there for part of it. Something happened to the boy. I watched him prepare, and I saw him after he came out of the lodge. Much of what happened to him cannot be explained. How did a boy inside a lodge get soaked while the rest of the lodge remained dry? How did he get the scratches that he said were from branches?"

"I saw him at the Moon Ceremonial," Talon said reverently. "A shaft of white light fell only on him. He seemed to glow in the night."

"His little dog took a message to the gods," old White Flicker added. "The Soul Keeper himself saw the dog rise like smoke."

Several grunts of assent followed this. Rain Bear said nothing, but wondered at the awe in so many of the chiefs' eyes. They *wanted* to believe.

Black Mountain was among the skeptics. "What was in this vision, Great Chief? What did the boy say? That he can do what? Turn himself into a shaft of white light and burn the Council away, or send his Spirit Dog to rip Ecan's throat out? Or will he simply walk up to Fire Village and order Cimmis to leave us alone?"

Mutters of both assent and dissent rose in response.

Rain Bear spread his hands in a gesture for silence. "I do not know the whole vision. He would not say. I do know, however, that Thunderbird told Tsauz that only the matron of the North Wind People could stop the war. His message was for her alone."

Talon straightened where he sat behind Black Mountain, and his white hair glinted in the firelight. "Then, you do not know what message Pitch carries to Matron Astcat?"

"Tsauz told no one except Pitch."

Disagreeable grumbling broke out.

He shouted above the din, "But Tsauz told us other things you must know! They are the reason I called this council." He lifted his arms again and waited for the din to hush. "Tsauz told us that the North Wind People will be leaving Fire Mountain, abandoning Fire Village, and moving to Wasp Village. They will be on the trail and vulnerable for several days."

"Then this may be our chance!" old Bluegrass shouted. "When?"

Black Mountain twisted around to speak to Talon, then turned back and called, "None of us wish to fight, unless we have to. Have you received an answer from Cimmis? Will he and his wife step down and turn over their Starwatcher to us?"

"We have received no answer. But it no longer matters. If we are to end the North Wind People's attacks, *we must strike in the next few days.*"

Every chief turned to whisper to his war chief, and a rumble of voices filled the lodge.

Goldenrod loudly called, "As you know, my war chief is not here. He and several of our warriors are still out keeping vigil along the trails, so I am hindered by not having his counsel today—but I have serious doubts about all this." He turned to Rain Bear. "You lived in Fire Village for many summers. Chief Cimmis is not a fool, is he?"

"He is not a fool," Rain Bear agreed.

"Then isn't it possible that the boy was left behind at War Gods Village just to give us these words? Perhaps if we attack the North Wind People on the trail to Wasp Village, we will be leading our warriors into an ambush. Perhaps they are not moving at all."

Heads nodded and conversations hushed.

Rain Bear gave them a serious nod. "It's possible. Cimmis would love to crush our forces in a single blow. But I think the boy was telling the truth. Regardless, I believe it is prudent to attack the North Wind People if they leave Fire Mountain."

Brush Wasp clamped his jaw.

Rain Bear noted it, and let his gaze drift around the circle. Many of the chiefs here were new to him. They'd come in for the Moon Ceremonial and had remained to hear this new talk of an alliance.

Bluegrass rose to his knees and propped his hands on his narrow hips. "Would someone please tell me why the boy would reveal this? He has no reason to. We are his enemies. Telling us about the North Wind People's move will endanger the lives of his relatives." He waved a hand in self-deprecation. "This makes no sense to me, but perhaps I am just not seeing as clearly as others in this lodge."

Black Mountain glared across the fire at Rain Bear. "Bluegrass is right. Why would the boy tell us this?"

Evening Star said, "He was bargaining with me."

"Bargaining? With *you*? To what end?" Black Mountain asked.

She answered, "He asked me to help save his father's life."

"Save Ecan!" Bluegrass cracked his walking stick across a hearthstone, and his toothless mouth twisted in rage. "Over the dead bodies of every member of my clan!"

"Hear me out!" Evening Star shouted as the lodge exploded with questions. "If you can attack and win against Cimmis's warriors, you can break the North Wind People once and for all! Isn't that worth sparing the life of one man?"

"No!" Bluegrass struggled to his feet. He had to brace both hands on his walking stick to remain standing while he glowered at the other chiefs in the circle. "How many of you watched your families murdered before your eyes while Ecan stood on a hilltop out of spear range giving orders?"

"I did." A young man to Rain Bear's left rose. His fists clenched at his sides. "My mother was tortured to death while Ecan roasted my father's intestines five paces away! If I have the chance, I'll kill him myself! No matter what agreements you've made, Evening Star! Who are you to say what happens to Ecan?"

Just above a whisper, she answered, "No one."

Bluegrass pounded his walking stick on the floor. "Have you agreed to this, Rain Bear?"

He glanced at Evening Star. She had her head down. Red hair spilled down the front of her cape, glinting in the firelight.

"No," he answered. "I have *not* agreed to it."

A clamor of shouted questions rose. Many people waved their hands, trying to get his attention. He pointed to Bluegrass. "Yes, Elder?"

"I want to know why she's here. Has it occurred to you that she might be playing us like a spider luring bugs into its web? That she and the boy are working together to get us all killed?"

Roars went up from every part of the lodge.

Rain Bear lifted his voice above the din. "I asked her here because I thought she might be able to help us understand the North Wind—"

"Why do you trust her?" Bluegrass spat the words. He wobbled on his walking stick. "She is one of *them!*"

He didn't see who muttered, "He's just thinking with his penis."

People began to stand up, as if preparing to walk out on the meeting.

"Fools!" Evening Star shouted as she stood. Before Rain Bear could react, she had whipped a hafted obsidian knife from her belt pouch and raised her other arm. Her sleeve fell back, revealing her pale forearm.

As the stunned chiefs watched, she slashed the underside of her arm. A thin line of red widened as blood began to leak down her arm.

"I give you my oath!" Her blue eyes were flashing, daring each of them. "The Council, Great Chief Cimmis, and that foul maggot Ecan are my enemies!"

Dropping her knife into her pouch, she wiped at the welling blood until it dripped from her fingers. Then, with a dramatic gesture, she flicked blood into the fire, where it sizzled and hissed.

"With the blood of my body, I seal that oath!" One by one, she glared at them. "I am here because I am *tired* of tribute and raiding. The old ways serve none of us anymore—neither the Raven People nor the North Wind People. The Council is led by the insane. Wolf Tails stalk the North Wind families while North Wind war parties sack Raven villages. And all the while the world grows warmer and the sea levels rise. Mud chokes the beaches and kills the fish." She might have been a trapped cougar the way she looked at them. "Our world is changing. I, for one, am ready to change it more."

"Then why do you plead for Ecan?" Bluegrass demanded. "That's just like the North Wind, forever protecting their own!"

Shouts rose in support.

Evening Star, heedless of the blood dripping down her arm, walked and stood face-to-face with Bluegrass. "Chief, I have as much claim on Ecan as anyone in this room. I'm not the only one here who witnessed the Starwatcher burn my village, kill my mother, boil my husband's intestines while he screamed, and had to hear my daughter killed. I *know* what he does to women, because he kept me for almost two moons!"

She was nose to nose now as her voice dropped. "Unfortunately, I have to be more than just a woman crying for revenge. I have to consider more than just my grief, and rage. I have to be a *leader*. Do you understand?"

"Of course." Bluegrass didn't sound so sure of himself.

"Then you know that to *lead*, you have to think beyond yourself. Beyond this moment when we all cry for revenge! Sometimes you have to make bargains you don't like in order to serve the better interests of your people. Isn't that right, Bluegrass?"

He swallowed hard. "Yes."

"Then you can understand why I gave Tsauz my oath that I would try to save his father in return for his help in destroying the North Wind Council."

The only sound in the lodge was the crackle and hiss of the fire as Evening Star met each chief's eyes. "We have the chance to break the Council and change the way we live. We can only do this if we act together. Sometimes you have to give up a little to receive a lot." She returned to Rain Bear's side.

"Hear, hear!" Black Mountain cried.

Rain Bear rose to his feet. "We must attack together, all of us pooling our warriors and resources, or we will fail."

Goldenrod got up and stood shoulder to shoulder with Rain Bear. "I agree! My warriors will join Rain Bear! Who will fight with us?"

Over a dozen chiefs rose to their feet calling in assent.

Bluegrass slapped his war chief on the shoulder, turned his back to Rain Bear, and headed for the lodge flap. Four others followed him out into the cold morning wind.

Evening Star folded her arms and waited until they'd gone. "Forgive me," she murmured miserably. "I shouldn't have said anything."

Black Mountain gave her a narrow-eyed stare. "Bah! Without you, Bluegrass would have taken half of them out with him." He shot her a grin before he stood to speak with two other chiefs.

Rain Bear glanced at Brush Wasp. He had the unhappiest face Rain Bear had ever seen: a face from which all hope of peace had fled. Etched in every line, resolution battled with despair. He remained seated as the others slowly filtered out into the morning.

Rain Bear called, "I thank you all for coming. Please, go home now and discuss this. The next time we meet, it will be a war council."

As people began to file out, Goldenrod said, "Evening Star is right. Sometimes you give up a little to get a lot more." The tone in his voice wasn't pleasant.

"What do you mean? Only five refused to join us. That's better than I'd hoped for."

"They didn't refuse to join us, Rain Bear. They set themselves up against us. We're going to have to dispatch half our forces to guard our backs while the other half attacks the North Wind People. I'm not sure where the greater threat will lie. In front of us . . . or behind us."

"They need some time to think. They may yet join us, once they understand the stakes."

Goldenrod wasn't convinced. "I pray you're right."

Black Mountain gestured to Goldenrod, who touched Rain Bear's shoulder in a show of support and followed Black Mountain outside.

Brush Wasp waited until the lodge was almost empty before rising and crossing the floor. He bowed to Rain Bear, then knelt in front of Evening Star. "Matron, I must speak with you."

Evening Star frowned. "Yes?"

"I carry important news, Great Matron."

"I am not a great matron."

"Not yet. But you will be."

She cautiously asked, "Who are you?"

Brush Wasp glanced around warily, then whispered, "I am Sand Wasp, war chief to Kaska, matron of Salmon Village."

Rain Bear heard Evening Star gasp.

Sand Wasp continued, "She wishes you to know that the North Wind People will be leaving Fire Village by the dark of the moon in seven days."

Evening Star studied him, as though searching for treachery. "Why would she tell me this?"

"Because her mother was murdered by Chief Cimmis's assassins. She wants him dead. She believes you are her friend." His gaze searched her face. "That's true, isn't it?"

"Tell my cousin that I love her as much today as ever."

"I was sent to determine if you really were working with these people to attack Cimmis. After the things that were said here, I'm sure." He glanced uneasily at Rain Bear. "Can you trust him?"

"I can."

Sand Wasp held her gaze for several moments before he whispered, "Very well. Know this: If you can arrange for an attack on Cimmis, Matron Kaska promises her forces will be at your command."

Evening Star's shoulders tensed. Rain Bear waited anxiously for her response. Another fifty trained warriors . . .

Evening Star said, "What does Kaska think she may gain from this?"

"Cimmis's death."

"Others may be killed, as well. Perhaps Matron Astcat and the

Four Old Women. Does she hope to become the next great matron of the North Wind People?"

Sand Wasp was taken off guard by the accusation. "No. I mean, she does not! In fact, she suggested that perhaps *you* might ascend to that position."

"I cannot accept her offer."

Sand Wasp blinked in surprise. "Why? After seeing you face down that chief, I'm convinced you are more worthy than ever."

"You heard what was said here today. Take it to her. Tell her Rain Bear's intention is to break the North Wind People—not just Cimmis. If she agrees—"

"Wait." Dogrib held out a hand to Rain Bear. "Great Chief, we can't allow him to return to Fire Village. He may be an emissary from Matron Kaska, but he could just as easily be a spy for Cimmis."

Sand Wasp's mouth tightened. He carefully drew back his cape, allowing them to see his hands, then reached into his belt pouch. He pulled out a magnificent spear point pendant. "Matron Kaska sends you her mother's pendant as a token of her loyalty."

He handed it to Evening Star.

Evening Star's fist closed around the precious gift. "Gispaw was a good friend," she whispered, "and a great leader of our people."

Dogrib stepped closer. "Cimmis may have ripped it from her corpse and sent it to you himself! We have no way of knowing if Kaska actually sent it."

Sand Wasp gave Dogrib an evil look.

Rain Bear considered as he tried to read past Sand Wasp's building anger. "I say we fill Sand Wasp's pack with food and let him go."

"What?" Dogrib asked. "Why?"

Rain Bear's gaze remained locked with Sand Wasp's, judging the set of the man's jaw, the fire in his eyes. "Because even if Sand Wasp repeated every word he heard today, it wouldn't change our plans. Nor would it change the Council's. Cimmis already expects us to attack him on the trail to Wasp Village."

Sand Wasp granted him a wary smile of respect. "You are right, Great Chief. He sent White Stone to us several days ago and laid out our defensive strategy." He knelt on the floor, and his cape folded around his moccasins. "I will show you how he plans to defend against your attack."

Dogrib exchanged a look with Rain Bear before he knelt beside Sand Wasp.

"These are the places Cimmis thinks the North Wind People will be vulnerable." Sand Wasp made a dot in the dirt with his finger.

"Fire Mountain." He drew the main trail down the mountain between Fire Village and Wasp Village. "Tomorrow, he will send war parties to begin securing narrow, confined, and dangerous sections along the trail. Scouts will sweep the country for hidden enemy warriors in an attempt to deny you the element of surprise."

He tapped the dirt. "But he still expects you to reach the trail with enough warriors to pose a threat. His best spear throwers will encircle the North Wind People like a great wall as they travel."

Dogrib smoothed a hand over his jaw. "How many warriors does he have at his disposal?"

"He has ten tens of his own and another ten tens from nearby North Wind villages, but five tens of those belong to Matron Kaska."

Dogrib's eyes narrowed as he looked at Rain Bear. "We may be able to glean ten tens of warriors from the camps here, but I suspect it will be more like eight tens, and many of those will be inexperienced youths. We will be badly outnumbered."

"Yes," Rain Bear said quietly, "but there will be a few hands of time where Cimmis's forces are split three ways. That is when we must attack—before they can reunite around the North Wind People."

"That will be tricky." Dogrib tapped the map on the ground. "If we're not *very* careful, we will end up with enemy warriors in front of us—and behind us."

Sand Wasp rose to his feet. "Matron Evening Star, if you have no further need of me, I will leave you to your plans. It will take me two days to get home. Matron Kaska will send a messenger with her answer."

"Go, Sand Wasp. I pray the Star People watch over you."

He bowed to her and left.

"Seven days," she said, and gave Rain Bear a heartrending look.

"We don't have much time." He smiled encouragement to her. "But first, let's attend to that arm. We can't have the next great matron bleed to death from an oath."

Forty-nine

Word had arrived long before Pitch's party could make its way up the trails. Ecan watched his son's messenger as he was borne on a litter up the trail from Salmon Village.

Sunset's soft amber gleam flooded Fire Mountain, turning the men who carried Pitch's litter into wavering shadows. People crowded the trail, calling greetings, shouting questions.

Ecan smoothed his hair. In preparation, he had pulled it away from his face and twisted it into a bun at the rear of his head. The style gave his chiseled features a stark look that he liked.

He shielded his eyes. No less than six warriors bore the litter. Pitch had one arm in a sling, and it left him off balance. Though he gripped the side poles with his good hand, he bounced every time the warriors' feet struck the ground. The party had been traveling for two days to reach Fire Village.

Ecan straightened his long white cape and headed for the gate. As he marched down the trail, Cimmis stepped out of a group of warriors. His blue cape flapped around his tall body.

When Cimmis caught Ecan's eye, he broke away from the warriors and strode toward him. Two guards, Hunter and Deer Killer, followed. Cimmis had his square jaw clamped, and his windblown hair and beard made a snarled gray halo around his face.

"The matron and I will meet with the messenger in the Council Lodge, Starwatcher. We will send for you when we are finished."

"But, my Chief," Ecan said in surprise, "my son sent the messenger. He may—"

"I am aware of who sent the messenger. If Singer Pitch does carry a message for you from your son, I will make certain you have the opportunity to speak with him *after* the matron and I do."

"But that's foolish! I may be able to understand things that no one else can."

Hearing the unbridled anger, Cimmis gave him a narrow-eyed glare, then swept past him and headed toward the Council Lodge. Hunter and Deer Killer stood uneasily to either side. Wind Scorpion leaned on a nearby lodge, his dark eyes missing nothing.

Sharply, Ecan asked, "What are your duties, warriors?"

"The chief ordered us to bring the messenger to him, Starwatcher," Hunter said, squaring his shoulders. "Then he wishes us to stand guard at the entry to make certain they are not disturbed."

"I see."

Deer Killer gave Ecan a half-panicked glance, then fixed his gaze on the gate. He'd coiled his black braids over his ears and secured them with rabbit-bone pins. It made him look like a big-eared bat.

"How's your stomach these days?" Ecan asked slyly.

Deer Killer swallowed hard, placing a hand to it as if it were tender.

The guards standing on either side of the entry shouted the arrival of the messenger.

Ecan said, "I want you to bring the messenger to me immediately after Matron Astcat is finished with him. Do you understand?"

"Of course, Starwatcher."

They fled with unaccustomed swiftness.

As the litter was lowered to the ground, Pitch jumped off and clutched his slung arm, as though in pain. He looked like a skinny boy. Nothing more. His thin face and hooked nose glistened with sweat. He wore a tattered elkhide cape. Ecan's eyes narrowed. So this was Pitch? Rain Bear's son-in-law?

Pitch spoke quietly to the guards. Hunter and Deer Killer escorted him up the trail to the Council Lodge, where he ducked beneath the door flap and disappeared. Hunter and Deer Killer took up positions outside.

Ecan gruffly folded his arms. Odd, he didn't even remember Pitch, though he must have seen him in Rain Bear's camp, which proved how much of an impression the youth had made. He stared at the Council Lodge for a time, then turned.

Dzoo stood behind him—perfectly still, as though not quite real.

"Greetings, witch." He instinctively clenched his fists. Wind Scorpion had a slight smile on his lips, as if expecting something.

Her deep voice had a velvet quality. "Where is the matron?"

Ecan looked up the trail to her lodge. No guards waited to take her to the meeting. "She must already be in the Council Lodge."

Which meant Cimmis had received advance warning from a scout. He had had time to both rouse his wife and escort her to the Council Lodge long before he'd sent runners to notify Ecan.

"What are you doing out here?" he asked.

"Waiting," she whispered, and tipped her chin toward the Council Lodge. "For that."

Cimmis ducked under the door hanging and walked out into the plaza. He looked angry as he paced back and forth with his arms folded tightly across his broad chest. Finally, he stopped short, glancing this way and that until he picked out Wind Scorpion. He summoned the grizzled warrior with an angry gesture.

Ecan would have sworn that Wind Scorpion smiled ironically as he trotted toward the great chief. Smiled? When Cimmis looked as if all the fury on earth was building in that old battered body?

Ecan said, "Now, there's a curious development."

Dzoo's voice was as musical as the wind. "The message Pitch carries is for Astcat alone, but I wasn't sure if she would have the courage to dismiss her husband."

He stared at her. "How do you know this?"

"Do you know what they're discussing in there, Ecan?" Dzoo whispered, as though she didn't wish anyone to overhear them. Her eyes seemed to have no pupils.

"No. Do you?"

She leaned forward to hiss, "They're selling you. It's like the summer solstice market. They'll haggle over price for a short time, and then—"

He cut her off with a gesture and untied his cape laces, opening the front to the wind. He was sweating. "Do you really think I believe your threats?"

Her gaze drifted over Fire Village before she asked, "How is Mica?"

The change of subject left him floundering for an instant. "Dead. But he lasted a lot longer than I thought he would."

Ecan boldly stepped to within a hand's breadth of her, close enough to smell the earthy scent that clung to her hair. "What did you do to them, Dzoo? Some sort of poison? Some strange plant you brought from those buffalo hunters out on the plains?"

She softly laughed, "He's taking them one by one—everyone who was near me. Hunter and Deer Killer will have to be next. Eventually he will have to eliminate White Stone and then . . . you."

Matron Astcat was seated on a log before the fire, her long seashell-covered leather cape spreading around her feet in firelit folds. A walking stick leaned against the log beside her. She wore her gray hair twisted into a bun on top of her head, which accentuated the gaunt lines of her wrinkled face.

"Matron Astcat, I bring a message from Tsauz, son of Starwatcher Ecan," Pitch called formally as he knelt before her.

"Before you deliver the message"—she put a bony hand on his shoulder—"I want you to verify a rumor."

"If I can, Great Matron."

"Two hands of time ago, a Trader passed through here. He said there was a great uproar in your village because Ecan's son had had a Spirit Dream. Is it true?"

"Yes, Great Matron." Pitch nodded, eyes still downcast. "There is indeed an uproar. Our people—"

"I mean about the Spirit Dream. He really did fly on Thunderbird's back?"

Pitch nodded again. "Yes, Great Matron. Rides-the-Wind and I were both witnesses. As a Singer, I have no doubt. The Soul Keeper thinks Tsauz will be a very great Dreamer someday."

She let her hand fall.

Pitch looked up.

She had kind, vulnerable blue eyes. "Then perhaps he is the Dreamer I am supposed to listen to."

Pitch frowned, not sure what she meant.

She smoothed her hands over the cape that covered her knees. "What is the message?"

"Tsauz was told that our peoples are like Eagle and Raven with their taloned feet locked together in a death grip. So long as we fight this way, neither can fly."

"An apt analogy," she whispered absently, her blue eyes distant.

Pitch nerved himself. "Thunderbird told Tsauz that all we can do is spiral ever downward, no matter how hard we beat our wings. He said that even if one of us manages to kill the other, we shall still be locked in the death grip." He winced. "And, in the end, we shall spiral, exhausted, into the waves."

"Neither an eagle nor a raven can swim," she noted.

"No, Matron. In Tsauz's vision, we are swallowed up by the sea. But it does not have to end that way. Tsauz was told a way to stop it."

Her gray brows slanted down. "How?"

"You must make the most painful decision of your life."

"What? Must I forgive my enemies? Surrender my position as matron? Deny my daughter her rightful succession?"

"You must take another husband."

"Another husband?" Matron Astcat's wrinkled mouth hung open in surprise. "Why?"

"Tsauz did not tell me why, Great Matron. Just who."

Astcat straightened. Behind her, firelight fluttered over the bark walls in golden waves. "Who is this man I am supposed to marry?"

"Tsauz, Great Matron. You must marry Tsauz to end the war."

A mixture of anger and disbelief creased her face. "Is this some joke? One of Ecan's charades? I will not marry a ten-summers-old boy!"

Pitch bowed his head and stared at the floor. Tiny flakes of obsidian, the debris from stone toolmaking, had been pressed into the dirt and glittered around her moccasins. "Tsauz said that you do not have to divorce Cimmis; he will be content as a second husband, but Cimmis must step down as chief."

"That's *preposterous*!" she exploded, then consciously lowered her voice. "Force Cimmis to step down and install a boy in his place! Never!"

Pitch continued staring at the floor. "Tsauz also said to tell you that you must marry and announce him as chief quickly . . . or within days you will be crying over Cimmis's dead body, and nothing will stop our peoples from destroying themselves."

She picked up her walking stick and propped her hands on the polished knob. For a long time, she stabbed the stick at anything nearby: the hearthstones, the woodpile, the tripod holding the tea basket.

Finally, she gruffly asked, "You say the Soul Keeper, Rides-the-Wind, believes this Dream?"

Pitch nodded solemnly. "He does."

Matron Astcat made an irritated sound. "Did he send a message to go along with the boy's?"

"No, Great Matron."

"No explanation at all?"

"No."

"The old fool. I suppose he just expects me to do it."

Pitch lifted his eyes. Wan evening light from the smoke hole slanted across her face and shimmered in the last red hairs that threaded her bun. They were the same color as Roe's hair. This was his wife's grandmother, yet they'd never met. He felt oddly as though it were his fault. Perhaps he should have made some attempt to run up the mountain to speak with her before his marriage to Roe. Roe would have hated the idea, but . . .

"Go now." Matron Astcat took a deep breath and let it out slowly before adding, "Send my husband to me."

Ecan spun around when voices rose. A chastened-looking Pitch walked out of the Council Lodge to speak briefly with Cimmis, who immediately ducked back inside.

Hunter used his war club to gesture to Ecan. Pitch marched toward him with Hunter and Deer Killer on his heels.

When Pitch approached, Dzoo's expression softened, as though she was glad to see him.

Ecan stepped deliberately in front of her. "He's coming to speak with me. Back away."

Dzoo only gave him a cold smile.

Pitch strode up and bowed respectfully to Ecan. "Greetings, Starwatcher. I bring a message from your son."

"Yes, what is it?"

"He said to tell you he loves you and is trying very hard to save you."

"Save me? *Me?*" Ecan asked in confusion. "From what?"

Pitch walked around him and embraced Dzoo. She rested her chin on his shoulder and stroked his back, as though comforting him. In a soft voice, she asked, "You told her?"

"I did." Pitch pushed away to meet her gaze. They just looked at each other. Each appeared relieved and happy to see the other.

Ecan frowned. How could she know what message he'd brought?

How can she know any of the things she seems to? Does she truly see the future? Or is there a spy in Fire Village? Someone carrying messages between her and . . .

He suddenly felt weak.

It was the only answer.

Dzoo said to Pitch, "Have they assigned you a lodge?"

"Chief Cimmis told me that after I spoke with you and the Star-watcher, I would be confined to—"

"No. You will stay with me." She glanced at his arm. "I need to see to your wound. Your journey may have harmed it."

He wet his lips nervously and looked around Fire Village. "Will they allow it?"

"Let us hope they do not interfere." She gave Ecan a lethal glance, put her arm through Pitch's, and started leading him toward her lodge. Just loud enough for Ecan to hear, she said, "What of the fetishes? Did you bring them with you?"

"Yes." Pitch touched his belt pouch.

"What fetishes?" Ecan called.

Pitch looked like a boy with his hand caught in the berry basket. "I—I brought something for Dzoo. It's actually hers to begin—"

"Hunter! Remove his belt pouch and bring it to me."

The young warrior trotted forward, untied the hide pouch from Pitch's belt, and handed it to Ecan. He jerked the laces open and pulled out a small leather bag painted with red coyote prints.

In less than three heartbeats, his hand stung, as though being bitten by a thousand tiny ants. Fearfully, he whispered, "Where did you get these?"

"You don't know?" Dzoo asked.

"No!" Ecan hastily tied the bag to his belt and tossed the empty pouch back to Hunter. "Return this."

Pitch stared in shock. "Starwatcher, you can't take that! I'm a messenger! Under the protection of—"

"They do not belong to you, young Healer," he said.

Dzoo challenged as she whispered, "Lift the sack to your ear, Ecan. Tell me what you hear?"

Ecan hesitated, searching her half-lidded expression for some sign of a trick. Pitch had a wide-eyed look, part wary, part fearful. Ecan lifted the sack, and never taking his eyes off Dzoo, listened.

Only the faintest of voices seemed to come from the bag, but voices nonetheless. The rim of his ear began to burn, prickling like his hand. A cold shiver, as if driven by a winter blackness, ran down his spine.

"I heard nothing," he lied.

Dzoo's lips parted, her eyes like the swells on a midnight ocean. "Did you hear your own voice, Starwatcher?"

"My voice? Don't be ridiculous."

She tilted her head, red hair spilling. "Then perhaps he'll just let you die in peace. I thought he would want you, too."

"What are you talking about? He? He who? And why would he want me?"

"I want my bag back," Pitch said stiffly, and extended his hand.

Dzoo's long hair fluttered around her shoulders as she released Pitch's arm and walked toward Ecan. "Do they belong to *you*, Ecan?"

He opened his mouth to respond, but Hunter said, "Starwatcher? The chief is motioning you to the Council Lodge."

Ecan shot a quick glance to confirm that Cimmis was waving. He started up the trail, but his steps faltered when a sudden dark sensation swelled from the bag and filtered through his chest. He looked down.

Whispers. I hear whispers. They're calling my name.

In a series of flashes, he saw dozens of faces: some old, some very young. All had their mouths open: screaming or crying, he couldn't tell. They reached out to him.

"Yes," Dzoo said softly, her voice penetrating past the whispers. "They think you can save them, Ecan. They don't know you, do they? And more important, *you* don't know them."

It required great effort for Ecan to walk all the way to the Council Lodge.

Fifty

Cimmis crouched before the fire that Kstawl had built in their lodge. Worried in a way he hadn't been in years, he laced his hands over one knee and watched Astcat pace near the door. On the way back from the Council Lodge, wind had torn locks of hair loose from her bun; it hung around her face in glistening silver threads. She kept propping her walking stick, staring at the floor, then taking a step, turning, and walking back in the other direction.

"Mother?" Kstawl called from outside, then thrust her head past the hanging. She looked as if some terrible thing were about to befall her. "Old Woman North has convened the Council and demands your presence. She's sending warriors to—"

Astcat turned. "Who is great matron? Me, or that vision-racked old hag?"

Kstawl's mouth worked like a beached salmon's.

From outside, White Stone's voice called, "You are, Great Matron. I will take your regrets to the Council and inform them that you will call them at your convenience."

Kstawl, looking slightly sick to her stomach, withdrew. Cimmis sat stunned, hearing footsteps beating a hasty path away from their lodge.

"As if I didn't have enough to fret about!" Astcat snapped irritably.

"Please, don't drive your soul away."

"Drive my soul away?" She raised her thin arms. "As if that was my only worry!"

"My wife, please, your hold on your soul—"

"My soul will stay where it is for the moment." She closed her eyes, looking pained.

"Why won't you tell me the message? Is it so terrible that you—"

"I need to think about it." She heaved a tired breath and looked at him. Love sparkled in those blue depths. "I wouldn't hurt you for anything in the world. Do you know that?"

"Yes, of course," he said shortly. "What does that have to do with the message from Ecan's son? By Gutginsa, he's just a silly little boy."

As she walked toward him, the seashells on her cape winked in the firelight. "Apparently, that silly little boy has become a Dreamer."

Cimmis shrugged, but dread knotted in his belly. The news must be bad or she wouldn't be using this roundabout way of telling him. "Did he Dream our deaths?"

She stopped in front of him and lowered a hand to stroke his hair. In a tender voice, she said, "Not our deaths . . . yours."

Dzoo slowed as she approached her lodge, turning so the sunlight filled her face. It burned in her red hair and turned her eyes into black pits. She fixed her attention on Hunter and Deer Killer, who walked behind them.

"Of the two of you, only Hunter has a child. A boy." She smiled with deadly earnest. "And you, Deer Killer, you are thinking of marrying New Fawn."

Pitch watched as both warriors swallowed hard and backpedaled. They wore expressions that were a mixture of loathing and horror.

"If you desire to sire children in the future . . ." Her voice dropped. "No, let's say if you would ever even *enjoy* lying with a woman again, you will stay as far from this lodge as you can tonight."

To Pitch's astonishment, the guards almost shook their heads off their shoulders, nodding in agreement.

"Good," Dzoo said simply. "The Singer and I are going to be mixing potions. Try not to breathe the fumes. Some . . . Well, never mind."

Pitch followed her into the lodge, where a fire had burned down to coals. Dzoo indicated a place by the hearth, where a roll of buffalohide made a cushion. "Let me check your wound."

Pitch stopped long enough to glance out the thin slit at the door's side. Both guards were well out of earshot.

"Hungry?" She raised an eyebrow and pointed to a carved wooden bowl beside the hides.

Pitch sat and exhaled in relief. As she dipped stew out and handed it to him, he took inventory of the lodge and related all the events leading up to his departure.

"He's going to be great," Dzoo said thoughtfully after Pitch told her of Tsauz's flight with Thunderbird. "If this coming trial doesn't kill him."

Pitch ate a spoonful of sea lion stew, relishing the rich flavor. In addition to the meat, the stew contained red laver and dried skunk cabbage. It had been a long time since he'd eaten such a meal. But no matter how much he ate, his stomach squealed for more. "Forgive me," he said, and awkwardly repositioned his injured arm. The sling had started to saw into his shoulder. "I know I'm not very pleasant company. The only thing I've had to eat in two days is dried packrat jerky. I'm starving."

"Eat as much as you can hold, Pitch. Meanwhile, let me see that wound."

"No, there are many things I must tell you."

While Dzoo undid the sling, Pitch examined the beautiful painted leather dress she wore—the scarlet color was stunning. Her long red hair tangled with the tiny shell beads that covered the bodice.

Pitch gestured with his horn spoon. "We heard you were locked in the captives' lodge."

"I was."

"Who gave the order to release you?"

"Cimmis, when it became apparent that I wasn't interested in leaving."

"How did they capture you?"

"They didn't. I surrendered to them at War Gods Village." She stared thoughtfully at his wound. "Sometimes, the choices we make condemn us either way."

"Why didn't you warn the people at War Gods Village?"

She stared at him, a terrible pain in her eyes. "I had to choose between Coyote and all those people. To defeat Coyote, I had to be captured, had to be brought here under constant guard."

"He's that dangerous?"

"Stopping him may be more important than defeating the North Wind Council."

Pitch nodded, chewing thoughtfully. "What of Astcat? She wasn't what I expected."

"Astcat is not well."

He swallowed a bite of sea lion and said, "I know she's supposed to have blank spells where her soul flies away, but she seemed fine when I spoke with her. Alert, intent on hearing my words."

"Then she's having a good day. That is not always the case. How did she react?"

"With shock and dismay. But not with the vehemence I was expecting. In my dread, I thought she'd scream and have me thrown out, maybe even order my death."

She studied him thoughtfully. "But you came anyway?"

"It is a matter of Power. How could I have refused?"

On the eastern wall, two sacred bundles hung from the lodgepole. He scooped up his last succulent bite of meat and studied them while he ate. The bundle on the left was decorated with red and yellow circles, imitating the pattern of the Star People in the Wolf Pup constellation. An eye glared from the center of the bundle, black and glistening as though alive. Beside it, Dzoo's Noisy One bundle hung. The miniature face of her Spirit Helper covered the leather. The Noisy One had empty white eyes, a black circle for a mouth, and a squat, hair-covered body. The longer Pitch looked at Dzoo's sacred Power bundles, the more he felt their souls creeping around inside him, testing him to see if he was worthy to touch them, whispering just below his ability to hear.

She followed his gaze. "Ecan had them returned to me. I think he was having bad dreams while they were in his possession."

Pitch set down his empty bowl and wiped his mouth on his sleeve. "Hallowed gods, that was good. Do you eat this way every night?"

"Living here is very much as I recall from my childhood. At dawn and dusk, slaves bring bowls of food, carry away waste bowls, deliver clean clothing, sweep and straighten the lodge. The only thing that's really changed is they know the tribute is running out. They've been stockpiling it for many cycles, but it will be gone soon. Long ago, they wiped out the sparse resources on the mountain. Without tribute, they can't survive here. . . . And the ghosts have changed."

He reached for a seaweed cake. As he ate it, green crumbs trickled down the front of his white shirt. "How so?"

Her gaze fixed on the doorway. The curtain swung gently in the draught that constantly breathed up the mountain slope. "They used to be happy ghosts, going about their days laughing and talking. Now they're frightened. They roam the village at night, crying, screaming the names of people I suspect are long gone." Dzoo turned to look at him. "You'll hear them. Just wait. They wake me every night."

"You often hear things I don't." He finished his cake and wiped his hands on his red leggings. "What about Astcat? If she agrees to this marriage, it will drastically change the balance of Power. Imagine what the other North Wind People will do if she goes through with it."

"I suspect they'll assassinate her."

Pitch ate another cake and studied the doorway. Past the door curtain, he could see one of the guards keeping his distance in the gathering dusk. The man kept shooting owlish glances at Dzoo's lodge, as if he expected grizzly bears to bolt from the door at any instant.

Pitch whispered, "Why do you think Thunderbird told Tsauz this was the only way?"

"It probably is."

"If she marries him, will the Raven People be content? Or do you think they will still demand the deaths of the North Wind People?" His wife and son were North Wind People. Pitch had already begun to plan his family's escape. They would flee southward, perhaps run all the way to the Elderberry People. . . .

Dzoo said, "I can't say."

He brushed at the green crumbs on his shirt. "You know that Evening Star is trying to save Ecan, don't you?"

Dzoo nodded. "Tell me about Evening Star and Rain Bear, Pitch. Are they . . . together?"

He lifted a hand. "I think so."

Dzoo closed her eyes for a moment, as though thanking the gods. "And the fetishes. Why did you bring them?"

Pitch let out a breath. The lodge smelled fragrant, a mixture of roasted sea lion and black seaweed. "Rides-the-Wind wanted me to ask you about one of the fetishes."

"Which one?"

He held up his thumb and forefinger to show her the large size. "It's obsidian—in the shape of a coyote. It took me a long time to determine the one that—"

"Contained the man's voice?"

Pitch went numb. The hair on his arms prickled. "How did you know?"

Dzoo smiled. "I heard his voice the first time I touched the bag."

Filled with dread, Pitch asked, "Why didn't you tell me?"

"Because he was calling to you. You had to hear it for yourself, or it meant nothing."

"Hallowed Ancestors, Dzoo," he said loudly without thinking, then made an effort to lower his voice again. "What does it mean? Who is he? And how did his voice get into the Coyote fetish?"

She shoved long red hair over her shoulder, and the tiny lines around her eyes deepened. "Now you know why I have to hunt down Coyote. He has enough Power to capture souls and imprison them inside those fetishes. I just don't know if it was in the past or in the future."

Pitch sank back against the wall and rubbed his forehead. The orange gleam of the fire fluttered over his hand. "If we knew whose voice that was, maybe we could stop it from happening."

A strange haunted smile touched her lips. "What if he deserves this fate?"

He just stared at her.

She smoothed her fingers over the soft buffalohide she sat upon. "Those fetishes are more than just magical stones. You know that, don't you?"

It felt like an earthquake building in his heart, ready to shake his world apart. "Yes. And?"

Her black eyes flared. "That bag is an army of ghosts for the man who knows how to use it."

Pitch had trouble swallowing. The fire's gleam seemed to close in around him. "Rides-the-Wind thinks he's the most Powerful witch to exist in a long time."

"Very possibly." She ran a hand through her long hair. "I haven't had the chance to ask him."

Fear swelled like a black bubble in Pitch's chest. "Are you saying he's here? In Fire Village?"

Dzoo tilted her head, as though considering. "He is often here. He comes and goes. But he's never far from me for long."

Pitch reached out to touch her hand. "Do you know who he is?"

"Not yet. But I will. When he wears the mask, I can smell damp moss. At other times . . ."

Her voice faded as footsteps crunched the sand outside.

A man gruffly asked, "What are you two fools doing? And why do you both have your hands cupped over your balls? War Chief White Stone wishes to see both of you. I'll stand guard while you're gone."

Dzoo sat up straighter, one elegant eyebrow cocked.

"But, Red Dog," Deer Killer objected, "Ecan told us to stay here until dawn. I'm in enough trouble, I don't wish to—"

"Yes, yes," Red Dog said irritably. "That was before the great chief changed his mind. White Stone has convened a war council around the central fire. That lazy Wind Scorpion is missing, so you are each going to be leading war parties tomorrow."

Whispers broke out, both men asking questions at the same time.

"Don't ask me," Red Dog said. "Go and get your orders straight from the war chief. I wouldn't keep him waiting too long. He's in a foul mood."

The guards grumbled, then pounded away into the dusk.

Dzoo rose to her feet with the silence of Wolf and stared at the doorway.

A few instants passed.

Red Dog ducked his head through the curtain. He gave Pitch a gap-toothed grin that was anything but reassuring. His gray-streaked black hair was pinned back in a bun, which made his broken nose stand out even more. A tattered deerhide cape draped his burly shoulders.

"Tell me quickly," he whispered. "I'm leaving tonight."

Dzoo hissed, "The slaves say that Astcat and the other matrons will lead the group, encircled by the best spear throwers. Cimmis will bring up the rear. He'll be dressed as an ordinary warrior. It won't be easy to spot him. He—"

Someone walked up the trail outside, his steps as soft as spider silk. He carried a torch; its orange gleam edged the door like liquid flame. Red Dog's eyes went wide a second before he ducked back outside, taking up his proper guard position.

The torch's gleam strengthened as the man came closer.

Pitch held his breath, listening.

Ecan's deathly quiet voice called, "Well, well, Red Dog, imagine finding you here."

Pitch rose to his feet, but Dzoo stopped him short when she asked casually, "Tsauz said Ecan would die?"

He frowned. It took him a moment to understand; then he replied, "Poor little boy, he's frightened half to death for his father."

"Why didn't Tsauz ask you to tell Ecan?"

"I—I think he was afraid." Pitch shrugged in mimic. "How does a boy like that tell his father he's going to die?"

"But if Ecan is going to die before he gets to Wasp Village, something must happen on the trail. Is he killed in the fighting?"

Pitch tried to decide what to say next. Outside, an unearthly silence had descended. Ecan's ears must be trained on their voices. "Tsauz didn't tell me, Dzoo."

She lowered her voice and said, "Death has already wrapped its tendrils around Ecan. That cannot be changed. What of Tsauz? Does he survive?"

They continued talking for what seemed a long time, making up this and that.

"You've heard enough," Ecan growled outside. "Get out of here, Red Dog. And don't go spreading their poison, or I'll slice your liver out of your body."

Steps sounded as Red Dog left, followed shortly by the wavering of Ecan's departing torch.

When the same two guards returned to their door, Pitch slumped to the floor, breathing hard. He whispered, "I don't understand. What is—"

Dzoo clenched a fist to order silence. "You must be exhausted, Pitch. Why don't you try to sleep?"

So. Even at a whisper, it was not safe to discuss Red Dog. Pitch's thoughts twined around that fact.

Dzoo paced back and forth in front of the fire, clearly distressed. Firelight sparkled across her beaded dress.

Pitch curled up on the buffalohide, but his heart pounded like a drum at a ceremonial.

"So much at risk," Dzoo whispered to herself.

Fifty-one

T hose were her exact words?" Kaska asked.

"Yes."

She stood beside Sand Wasp outside her lodge in Salmon Village and gazed up at the glittering Star People who arced like a giant wheel around the cone of the mountain.

When she'd been notified that Sand Wasp had returned, she'd risen straight from her husband's arms. She must look it. She was barefoot, and long red hair streamed over her cape. "Do you think Rain Bear can do this?"

Sand Wasp braced his hands on his hips. "With enough warriors, he and Evening Star can do anything, Matron."

The soft hum of conversations radiated around Salmon Village. She could hear children crying and dogs barking. Old Woman Shuffling Feet snored loudly, as she had for as long as Kaska could remember.

It was so hard to imagine anything but this. Where would she go? What would she do? She had taken for granted that her two-summers-old daughter would grow up as she had: beloved and respected, with everyone knowing she would eventually be the matron of Salmon Village. She loathed the idea of telling little Sotic that instead of being one of the most powerful women in their world, she was going to spend the rest of her life in hiding, trying to scratch out a living with her bare hands. Assuming, that is, that a band of bloodthirsty Raven People didn't smack the brains out of her little skull first.

"How many warriors does Rain Bear have?" Kaska asked.

"Ten tens at most. Those are his trained warriors. In addition he has plenty of hunters, fishermen, old men, and boys. They're mad enough to fight, but probably won't stand when they see their best friend shot through the guts with a spear." The long scar that slashed Sand Wasp's forehead gleamed whitely when he turned to her. "If we add our warriors to his, however, we'll even the odds. If not, he will be badly outnumbered."

Wind Woman rushed up the slope, and the hem of Kaska's cape flapped around her legs. Her toes were quickly turning to ice. "What is your advice, War Chief?"

"I cannot advise you, Matron, beyond telling you that joining an alliance of Raven People to make war on North Wind People makes me most uncomfortable."

"A bit like sleeping with a rattlesnake, isn't it?"

"Very much so, Matron."

Kaska smiled wanly. On the night of Gispaw's murder, her mother had told her, *The North Wind People are doomed, my daughter. Leave now. Take your family and run.* Kaska had, of course, vehemently disagreed.

That was two moons ago.

After her mother's murder—and so many others—she had begun to fear that Mother may have been right. If the Raven People didn't kill them, her people would murder each other just for spite.

But Evening Star has joined them. Could Naida's daughter be making such a terrible mistake?

"Tell me how the Raven People reacted to Evening Star speaking in their council."

"She won most of the doubters over, Matron." He smiled in the darkness. "She might have had the support of a couple of the chiefs going in, but when it was over she had even won the respect, if not the hearts, of the dissidents."

"How did she look, act?"

He gave her a piercing glance. "Like a great matron should." A pause. "And I mean no disrespect, but if I were Astcat, let alone Old Woman North, I'd be sending every Wolf Tail I could find to cut her head off."

"That persuasive, was she?"

"Yes, Matron. Even while arguing for Ecan's life."

Kaska took a deep breath. The future was looming before her. In a stroke, she could be destroying her whole family. A loyal Kaska would be worth a great deal to the Council. Her heart ached for Astcat. Then she imagined Evening Star, haunted, hunted, fleeing desperately through the forest . . .

"How would I go about putting our warriors under Rain Bear's command?"

"It won't be easy. They think they're supposed to fight Raven People, not help them." Sand Wasp gave her a somber look. "If we do this, we will have to get word to Rain Bear soon. He must have time to plan how to use our warriors, and we must get our people into position without arousing the suspicions of the great chief, his Starwatcher, or White Stone."

Kaska curled her toes to keep them warm. "I need you here to help me. Can you find someone else to deliver the message to Rain Bear?"

"I can, but it will cost a great deal, Matron. To assure secrecy, we must *buy* a messenger."

"I will pay whatever is necessary. But choose well, Sand Wasp. What little tribute we have left is rapidly disappearing. Make him aware of the consequences if he betrays us."

Sand Wasp stood quietly for a time, then whispered, "What will happen to us if Rain Bear wins, Matron?"

Kaska studied the wealth of sparkling Star People, wondering how her ancestors would answer that. They were probably all glaring down at her this instant, asking how one of Gispaw's children could betray her own people. She prayed with all her heart that her mother could explain it to them.

"The North Wind People will be reborn as something else, Sand Wasp. But for good or ill, I cannot say."

"Where will we go?"

"I suppose we will live at Wasp Village for a time. After that . . . who can say?"

Sand Wasp took a deep breath and whispered, "Know this, Matron. No matter what happens, I am your servant."

Tears sprang to her eyes. She lightly touched his shoulder. "Thank you, my friend. Now, leave me. Find a messenger."

Sand Wasp bowed and left.

Kaska's gaze followed the steep mountain slope up to Fire Village. Even at night, the images of the gods painted on the palisade wall shimmered as though alive.

She walked back to her doorway. Just before she ducked through into her firelit lodge, she murmured, *"Forgive me, my daughter."*

Fifty-two

The air cooled with the coming of night, and the savory tang of the fires and burning alder filled the forest. Rides-the-Wind drew it into his lungs as fingers of breeze stirred.

Rain Bear and four people—Tsauz, Dogrib, Talon, and Evening Star—sat around the great chief's fire.

"If I can pull Matron Kaska's forces into mine on the south"—Talon leaned over the map they had sketched into the charcoal-stained soil near the hearthstones—"it will create an opening to Cimmis's inner circle. Assuming, that is, that Kaska's warriors obey my commands."

Dogrib pointed. "If you can create that opening, I'll rush my forces into the center as quickly as I can." He kept his voice low. "But by the time we get there, his strength will be closing around the North Wind People. No matter how well this goes, it's going to be precarious. One wrong move, one delay, and the battle will fall into chaos, every warrior fighting for himself."

Rain Bear said, "We can't let that happen."

Rides-the-Wind looked out at the ring of guards that encircled them. The warriors stood fifty paces away in the forest, or perched on boulders overlooking the ocean, but their ears were trained on the conversation going on around the fire.

"We must take the boy." Talon shoved age-silvered hair away from his sharp eyes. "We may need him."

"Too dangerous." Evening Star straightened. "The boy should stay here. Tsauz is only valuable to us if he's alive."

"It's no more dangerous for him than it will be for the rest of us, Matron," Talon replied.

Dogrib braced his elbows on his knees. "Talon is right. If our situation grows desperate, we may need to hand Tsauz over to save people we care about."

Tsauz's blank eyes seemed to quiver in their sockets.

Rain Bear leaned sideways to whisper, "It's all right. We're just talking. We haven't made any decisions."

"He must go along," Dogrib said. "What if we cannot free Pitch and Dzoo? Cimmis will certainly use them against us. Tsauz gives us a bargaining piece."

"Cimmis will not bargain for the boy," Evening Star said. "Tsauz will only be useful if we are bargaining with Ecan. Or have you forgotten Coyote's visit not so long ago?"

Rain Bear nodded. "Tsauz is only valuable if we can wring concessions from Ecan. And who is to say he's safer here? At least if he goes with us, he'll be surrounded by friends. Here he's easy prey for the next Wolf Tail who prowls through."

Rides-the-Wind's gaze turned to the pebble-strewn beach where the canoes were drawn up. There, on the landing, refugees walked the shore looking for crabs or anything else that was edible. Beyond the soft whisper of the surf, an odd stillness cloaked the camps.

He propped his walking stick and said, "Perhaps it would be helpful if you asked Tsauz what he thinks."

Tsauz blinked.

Rain Bear's brows lowered, but he said, "Tsauz, should we take you with us?"

Tsauz licked his lips. "If you leave me here, you will have to leave fifty warriors to guard me, won't you?"

"Probably."

He lowered his gaze to assure Rain Bear he meant no disrespect. "You *will* need those warriors in the battle."

"I would rather not risk having you hurt, Tsauz. I promised I would make sure you got home, and I must try to do that."

"I—I would rather go with you."

Evening Star tilted her head. "Why is that?"

"Two reasons: If you do not take me, Cousin, my father will assume I am dead. Second, Coyote will find it harder to kill me when I'm with you."

Dogrib nodded, and his pale hair glinted in the firelight. "Smart boy."

Wind Woman gusted through the forest. Rides-the-Wind shivered and tugged at the deerhide over his shoulders.

Rain Bear exhaled hard. "There is one last thing we must plan for."

"Yes?" Talon asked.

"Kaska may be working with Cimmis."

Evening Star said, "No, she wouldn't. She's not—"

Rain Bear held up a hand to halt her words. "If she is, at a critical point in the battle, her warriors will turn on us."

Dogrib nodded. "It would make a perfect trap."

"I know Kaska. We almost grew up together. She wouldn't do such a thing," Evening Star insisted stubbornly.

"Wouldn't she?" Dogrib asked, "Forgive me, Matron, but you have no idea what pressure the Council might have put upon her. What if Coyote drops in on her every so often to remind her how simple it would be to kill her family? Her warriors are another matter. Will they obey her when she orders them to fight against their chief?"

Evening Star stared at him for a moment, took a deep breath, and nodded. "Yes, you're right, War Chief. We must plan for that eventuality."

Everyone started talking at once, and Tsauz's blind eyes turned to Rides-the-Wind.

He walked over and lowered himself to the mat beside the boy. "What is it, Tsauz?"

Tsauz felt for Rides-the-Wind's ear and pulled it down to his mouth. He whispered, "Thunderbird told me something."

When the boy didn't continue, he asked, "What did he tell you?"

"That Rain Bear doesn't know how to win."

Rides-the-Wind pulled away and looked down at the boy. "Did Thunderbird say how?"

Tsauz swallowed anxiously. "No. I just have to be there. But you can't tell Rain Bear I said so."

"No, of course not," Rides-the-Wind said.

In the distance, over Fire Mountain, thunder rumbled.

Tsauz spun around to look. "Did you hear that?"

The old Soul Keeper said, "I heard. What did Thunderbird say?"

"It's beginning," Tsauz whispered.

Sister Moon had risen into the sky; her gleam flooded the forest, shimmering in the trees and outlining every dark boulder. Shadows fell across the forest floor like a tracery of black lace.

Rain Bear hunkered on a fallen log across from Red Dog and studied his old friend. The silver glow reflected from the thick coating of grime on the battered warrior's face. He smelled dankly of sweat, and his gray-streaked black hair straggled around his face as though he hadn't combed it in days.

Red Dog had pledged his loyalty to Rain Bear over a cycle ago. He'd been badly wounded in a fight with Talon. Dzoo had worked day and night to save his life. Since then Red Dog had periodically passed information about the happenings in Fire Village. Of course, Rain Bear wasn't gullible enough to believe all of it. He knew for a fact that Red Dog played his own game for his own reasons, many of them no doubt unsavory, but he seemed to worship Dzoo. How many times had Rain Bear seen that look of longing in Red Dog's eyes as he watched her from afar?

"Thank Raven it's all downhill from Fire Village. I've never felt so tired." Red Dog sighed. "Kaska needs instructions. What do you want her to do with her warriors?"

Rain Bear outlined the proposed plan of attack. When he finished, he asked, "Do you understand?"

"Yes. You want her people to fall on the rear of the North Wind warriors that are fighting Dogrib."

A weight seemed to lift from Rain Bear's shoulders.

"What have you got for warriors?"

Rain Bear chuckled. "I have a core of eight tens of capable men and a couple of women. The rest are an angry rabble. They're the ones who are unpredictable."

Red Dog said, "Tell me truly, old friend. Are you ready for this?"

Wind Woman swept the forest, and the firs creaked in the wind.

"I'd better be. We set out at dawn. Did you speak with Dzoo?"

"Yes." Red Dog licked his chapped lips and winced as though they hurt. "Dzoo heard the slaves whispering. Cimmis will be dressed as an ordinary warrior—blue war shirt, hide cape. Spotting him is not going to be easy."

"Will he walk with the Four Old Women?"

"No." Red Dog looked bone weary. "He will march in the rear."

Rain Bear frowned. "Why?"

"If you ask me, it's so he can run away if it all goes wrong."

"What does White Stone think of this?"

"He's not happy. He growled to me that since the chief insists upon exposing himself, he can defend himself."

Rain Bear plucked a twig from the ground and twirled it in his calloused fingers. If White Stone had gone so far as to tell his warriors the chief could defend himself . . . he was a very discontented war chief. Could Rain Bear use that?

Red Dog shot a curious look at Rain Bear. "He also told us to expect an attack around Gull Inlet. Anything to that?"

Rain Bear rubbed his jaw with the back of his hand. He hadn't given Gull Inlet more than a passing thought.

"What's at Gull Inlet?"

Red Dog drew the U-shaped inlet in the frost. "The trail turns along the sea cliff like this—and branches here. A wise war chief could use the cliffs to his advantage to box his enemies in and slaughter them like scurrying mice."

"I'll keep that in mind. How soon can you go back?"

Red Dog smoothed a hand over his dirty face. "Ecan knows I'm up to something. If he hasn't already hired someone to kill me, it's just a matter of time."

Rain Bear steeled himself. "I must ask that you go back, my friend."

Red Dog stared at the frosty ground. "Isn't there someone else?"

"My message to Kaska must be delivered by someone she trusts. That leaves you or Sand Wasp."

Red Dog's burly shoulders sagged. He closed his eyes for a few moments. "I can't guarantee I'll make it. The first war parties headed down the mountain trail two days ago. If they catch me coming up from the coast, don't assume I'll be able to talk my way out of it. Do *not* count on Kaska receiving the message I'm carrying."

Rain Bear gave Red Dog a sober look. "Do you have friends among the warriors who guard Kaska?"

"I did when I left. But if Ecan has gotten to them, told them I'm a traitor . . ."

An owl sailed over their heads, and its dark shadow flitted among the branches.

"One way or another, this is almost over. If you and I both live through this, I'll find some way to reward you for the risks. I don't know what or how I—"

"Forget it." Red Dog grinned wearily. "I'm doing this for Dzoo. I wouldn't be here but for her." He shrugged self-consciously. "And, who knows, perhaps someday she will be ready to marry again."

Rain Bear nodded in sudden understanding. Then he tugged

open the laces of his belt pouch and drew out a bag of seaweed cakes. "Here. Roe made these. She flavored them with smoked salmon and hazelnuts."

"Thank you." Red Dog stuffed them in his belt pouch and playfully punched Rain Bear's shoulder.

"You know that if there were anyone else . . ."

"You don't have to say it."

Fifty-three

The village cooking fires blushed color into the towering lava cliff and gave the cold evening air a pungent smoky fragrance.

Ecan hurried along the base of an old lava flow that stuck out of the side of Fire Mountain like a low shoulder. He was just east of Salmon Village, where the trees gave way to a basalt cliff.

He kept glancing over his shoulder as he hurried along the dark trail. Cycles ago chunks of stone had cracked loose from the sheer cliff and tumbled down to create a wind-smoothed garden of boulders. These in turn provided a home for brambles of raspberries, currants, and, where the water seeped, cranberries. As night deepened, the place turned black and foreboding. Angular sections of basalt overhung the trail like monsters bent on hearing his passage.

Paintings covered the rocks. At the tops of the tallest boulders, white spirals glowed in the pale winter moonlight. Lightning bolts zigzagged out from the spirals and punctured the red hearts of wolves and bats.

When the path entered a stand of firs, it became pitch black. He could barely see two paces ahead, and slowed, letting his fingers glide along the porous rocks.

The sweet smell of moss seeped from the cave hidden in the boulders ahead. He placed his feet with care. In summer, the cave provided a cool haven, but in winter, the moisture turned to ice.

Ecan stepped around the last turn. The old lava tube resembled a dark womb cut into the cliff.

He stopped at the mouth of the cave. "Are you here?"

His voice echoed, coming back to him sounding tense and edgy.

No one answered.

"Wind Scorpion sent me."

Nothing.

He ducked inside and blinked at the utter darkness. Though he couldn't see it, he knew the cave stretched three tens of hands across and two tens high. A steady stream of water dripped from the ceiling and splashed into a small pool in the rear.

The scent of moss bathed his face.

Ecan braced his back against the entry. The stone fetishes in the bag tied to his belt clicked with his movements. He could feel them, hear them, whispering with excitement.

Since Dzoo had told him about the assassins Cimmis had sent to kill his boy, he'd been able to think of nothing else. His son's face and laughter filled Ecan's every waking moment. He *had* to do something. No matter how much it cost, or—

Someone breathed in the rear of the cave, near the pool.

Fear tickled the base of Ecan's throat. His hand dropped to the stiletto on his belt. "Show yourself."

A form moved in the darkness, no more than a stirring of shadows.

"Wind Scorpion sent you?" The voice was little more than a hoarse whisper.

"I am—"

"I know who you are, Starwatcher."

A tall body moved forward, gradually changing from a black silhouette to a gray apparition. He wore an obsidian-black cape decorated with red coyote tracks. The head remained deeper in shadow, and at first all Ecan could see were the eyes, gleaming with an unnatural light. As the apparition took another step, Ecan's breath caught in his throat.

It had to be a mask, but in the darkness, he would have sworn he saw a huge coyote's head perched atop a human body.

"Why would Wind Scorpion send you here?" the breathy voice asked.

"I asked if he knew who Cimmis might send to murder my son. He told me that if I came here, I might find someone who would be of service."

A long silence passed. Then the breathy voice took on an eerie sibilance. "I shall have to have a *talk* with this Wind Scorpion."

The shiver of fear ate through Ecan. He was used to inspiring terror, not experiencing it.

The masked figure stopped opposite Ecan and gazed outside at the starlit boulders. "You must be desperate to have called upon me, Starwatcher."

"I *am* desperate."

"What do you want?" The coyote mask with its white teeth, pointed ears, and furred brows shone when he turned.

"I have a job for you."

"Indeed? How will you pay me? My fees are exorbitant."

Ecan took the bag from his belt and held it out to the dark figure. The eyes behind the mask fixed on the bag. "What is it?"

"Open it and look."

The second Coyote's hand touched the bag, he stopped, as if frozen. "Where did you get these?"

"It doesn't matter, but I assure you, they are fetishes of great Power. With them—"

"I *know* what they are!" The voice boomed now, undertones laced with anger. *"Where did you get them!"*

"The Singer, Pitch, had them." Ecan tried to swallow his fear and failed.

"Fascinating."

Ecan waited, locking his knees to kill the weakness in his legs. Coyote remained as he was, still holding the leather sack, his head cocked, as if listening to the voices.

"My son—" Ecan began.

"Yes . . ." The voice seemed to come from far away.

"Will you save his life?"

A pause. "You take great chances, crossing Cimmis this way."

Ecan said nothing.

"I see into your soul, Starwatcher. What else do you want?"

"A small favor."

"Really?" the voice mocked.

"Our people are moving to Wasp Village. Supposedly as a rebirth of our Power."

"But you and I know that is a lie," Coyote added.

"Yes, to survive we need to be closer to the resources in Raven Bay. From there we can exterminate the Raven villages closest to us before raiding villages offshore. But that isn't what concerns me now."

"You want me to kill Cimmis and Astcat."

Ecan shifted. Gods, how did he know?

Coyote continued. "Then, with you as the new chief, and the Council aging and dying, you will be the leader of the North Wind People. Who will be your great matron?"

"Astcat's daughter, Kstawl."

"Who is a child, easily intimidated to do your bidding." Coyote laughed. "How soon do you want them dead?"

"Within days of our arrival at Wasp Village. Not before. It wouldn't be wise to create a hole in our leadership before the village moves."

"You are smart, Starwatcher. But what if the Raven People succeed in defeating Cimmis's forces before you get there?"

"I must take that chance."

"What if I could assure you that Rain Bear's alliance was nothing more than a nuisance? Would that be worth something to you?"

A premonition ran up Ecan's spine. "It would be worth a lot."

"How much?"

"A great deal."

"Ah," the hollow voice breathed out. "When this is all over, I want Rides-the-Wind, Evening Star, Singer Pitch, Rain Bear, and most of all . . . *Dzoo.*"

"Consider them yours."

Coyote chuckled. It sounded like brittle bones rattling in the wind. His black cape seemed to breathe, filling with air and letting it out.

Fifty-four

Astcat stepped out of her lodge and set two packs beside the door. Throughout the day slaves would be collecting the North Wind People's last belongings and carrying them down to the plaza to bundle them up for tomorrow's journey.

On the lava cliff high above, she heard Ecan chanting, *"Come Old Woman Above, be on your way to the Dark Place."*

A veil of ground shell swirled through the cold air and swept down across the village plaza where the slaves cooked breakfast. The sweet aromas of roasted lupine root and boiling oysters rose.

Just as they did every morning, people in brightly colored capes bowed to the east before they slowly returned to the warmth of their lodges. A few stopped to speak to their neighbors.

Watching this familiar ritual made her soul ache. Long moments passed as she tried to remember, to place the sights and sounds deep in her souls. She would never see it again. The North Wind People would be on the trail before dawn tomorrow. This was the last day she would be able to placidly stand and look out over the shining majesty of Fire Village at sunrise.

"A pleasant morning to you, Great Matron," Ecan said as he entered through the gate on his return from the cliff. He had plaited his obsidian-black hair into a single long braid. Shell, polished copper nuggets, bone, and stone jewels flashed on his wrists and around his throat.

"Good morning, Starwatcher. You delivered a beautiful prayer this morning." She looked into his eyes, seeing the cunning gleam of what? Triumph? She had never liked him.

"I see you're ready." He gestured to the packs.

"I'm ready for the trip, Starwatcher. Not for what leaving here will entail."

"Well, if our plan works, it will be the last battle. The Raven People will be broken for good."

Wind Woman whipped her cape about her frail legs. "For good? Do you really think we can deal them such a devastating blow?"

He smiled. "Well, let us say they will be no more trouble during our lifetimes. Everything is being handled. The great chief has left nothing to chance. A signal fire last night informed him that Rain Bear's pathetic alliance is on the move."

Cimmis had been planning this for moons, working out every possible permutation, every last detail of the timing—who was friend, who was foe, who *might* be a foe. But there were so many factors he could not anticipate. Exactly *when* would Rain Bear attack and *where*?

She blinked. *Already on the move?* Why hadn't her husband said something? Or had he, and her soul had been loose, flitting about like a bat when it should have been paying attention?

"Thank you, Starwatcher." She turned to peer about.

"Er, you are more than welcome, Great Matron." He seemed confused over what she would thank him for.

"My husband was sending four warriors to carry some things. Where could they be?"

Ecan glanced at the packs. "Four warriors, for these?"

As she started to speak, she caught herself. By the Spirits of the night, was she that doddering? She took a breath. "Oh, I need not bore you, Starwatcher. I'm sure you have important things to do." She made a shooing gesture with her hands.

Her litter was behind the door. But even if he'd seen it, he wouldn't suspect. No one would. Not even her husband, who thought he had planned for everything.

The first sliver of sun glimmered on the eastern horizon. As Old Woman Above carried the glowing orb through the thin layer of clouds, yellow light lanced across the mountain slopes, falling in golden ribbons on the treetops.

Pitch had been rudely pulled from Dzoo's lodge before he even had the chance to relieve himself. He was prodded past the Council Lodge, and up the path that led to Cimmis's lodge. Slaves watched them pass with wide eyes.

"Where are we going?" Pitch asked the guards as they shoved him from behind.

The younger man prodded him with his spear. "Just keep moving."

Pitch had a sick feeling in the pit of his stomach. From the instant he'd left Sandy Point Village, he'd feared being interrogated by Cimmis, or Ecan, or both. He wondered what it felt like to have someone cut a slit through his abdomen, reach inside his living body, and pull out a length of intestine. He knew that people screamed for hours as loops of their guts were slowly roasted. The sizzling sound was said to drive one mad long before pain and thirst could kill.

They halted before Cimmis's lodge, and the guard announced, "He is here, my Chief."

"Bring him."

One of the guards pulled the door flap aside and gestured for Pitch to duck under. He stood blinking to allow his eyes to adjust to the dim reddish glow cast by the fire. A hissing sound came from the middle of the room. He tried to focus on it, and saw a black form shift.

Cimmis knelt beside the fire with a large basket, a plain wooden bowl, and two dozen spears resting on the floor beside him. He wore a knee-length buckskin shirt, and his gray hair hung loosely about his shoulders.

Cimmis said, "Come over here."

As Pitch walked across the floor, Cimmis removed the lid from the basket, and the hissing grew louder. He reached inside, grabbed at something, and drew out a writhing snake.

Pitch jumped back.

Cimmis held the rattlesnake behind the triangular head, but its long body twisted as it wrapped around Cimmis's arm. The tail made a constant angry shishing.

"Sit down. We must talk."

Pitch forced a swallow down his tight throat and squatted. His hide cape spread across the hard-packed floor.

Cimmis deftly hooked the snake's fangs over the lip of the bowl and worked its jaws to drain the venom. As the fluid trickled out, he said, "Who is the traitor?"

Pitch stared at him. "What traitor?"

"The man who carries messages between Dzoo and Rain Bear. He's very clever. I almost had him twice, but he slipped away."

Cimmis stood and dropped the snake back into the basket. Wild hisses and furious rattling rose. The basket rocked. How many snakes were in there?

"Ecan thinks it's Red Dog."

"I don't know Red Dog."

"No?" Cimmis smiled. "Well, perhaps he goes by another name when he is in your village. He's an old warrior, gray-streaked black hair, bent nose. About this tall." Cimmis held up a hand. "Have you seen him?"

"There are ten tens of refugees there. I can't know them all."

"Yes, I've heard the camps around Sandy Point Village are very large, and more people arrive every day, don't they?"

"They do."

He had the terrible feeling this was all staged, like the spring Kelp Dances. Cimmis knew the answer to every question he asked.

The old chief lifted one of the spears from the floor and dipped the obsidian tip into the poison. "I'm debating which of you to kill."

Confused, Pitch asked, "Who? Me or this mysterious Red Dog?"

"I've already given orders to have Red Dog killed the moment he sets foot inside the palisade. I mean you or Dzoo."

"Why should you kill either of us?"

Cimmis smiled, laid his spear aside to dry, and picked up another. "Because I don't like being betrayed. Killing you sends a message to Rain Bear. Killing Dzoo sends a message to the Raven People."

He dipped the spear and rolled it in the venom.

"Personally, I think it would be far wiser to keep both of us alive. It's a bad decision to kill the messengers—one that, like that snake there, might turn around and bite you unexpectedly. It not only makes people reluctant to talk to you, but it invites retaliation. And someday, Great Chief, you really might want to send an important message."

Cimmis pulled the spear from the bowl and blew on it to dry it faster. The wet tip glittered. All he had to do was plunge that into Pitch's flesh.

Pitch tried to keep his voice reasonable as he continued, "Nor would I kill Dzoo. She is beloved by a great many people, both North Wind and Raven. Harming her might ruin your last chance for peace."

Cimmis nodded. "From the viewpoint of the Raven People, Dzoo is probably a more valuable hostage, but you are Rain Bear's son-in-law. Will he make more concessions to get you back, or Dzoo?"

"Rain Bear? Make concessions?" Pitch laughed.

Cimmis propped his spear on his drawn-up knee, studied the basket, and grabbed out another snake. More hissing could be heard. "I've seen Rain Bear risk an entire war party to rescue one warrior. One friend. He will bargain."

"Then you are wiser to bargain for two rather than one. Any Trader can tell you that."

He gave Pitch a measuring glance. "Here is the choice I must make: As much as I would enjoy killing Dzoo, I know how important you must be to Rain Bear. Even if he doesn't die fighting the next few days, I want to punish him for making this alliance. Your death would do that. He would blame himself."

Yes, he would. Pitch felt his guts sink. With all the courage he could muster, he said, "If you decide to kill one of us, kill me."

Cimmis held the rattlesnake up level with his head. Pitch couldn't help but note the same flat stare in their eyes. "Since you are noble enough to offer yourself in Dzoo's place, I shall kill her. Now for the rest of your life you can blame yourself for not saving her."

Pitch balled his fists, a sensation of panic rising within him as he blurted, "Kill her, and you'll die for it!"

Cimmis gave him a sidelong look as he ran a finger across the writhing snake's head. "Oh, why?"

"Because . . . Because she is under the protection of the witch Coyote!"

Pitch saw the color drain from Cimmis's face. In that moment, the man was truly afraid. He almost dropped the rattlesnake as he replaced it in the basket.

"Go," Cimmis ordered hoarsely.

As Pitch scrambled to his feet and ducked out the door, his legs were charged. The guards stepped in behind him as he blinked in the bright sunlight. A numb sensation began in his head and spread through his limbs. The shaking didn't start until Pitch was halfway down the trail.

Then it struck him like a palsy.

Blessed gods, what have I done?

Fifty-five

Red Dog knelt in the rocks east of Salmon Village, watching people walk back and forth before the firelit palisade. Matron Kaska's lodge stood to the south of the palisade in a nest of interconnected lodges. If he sneaked in they'd certainly assume the worst and kill him as a spy.

He climbed to the top of the lava outcrop. Cold wind stung his face. From this vantage he could see the village clearly. Rather than being circular, like Fire Village, the lodges were arranged in a large square around a central plaza. Several interconnected lodges nestled together on the south. Those were Kaska's.

He scanned the uneven ground between his perch and the palisade and counted seven guards—three along the trail and another four scattered on high points. Which meant there were probably another twenty he couldn't see. There would be many more inside, stationed along the path that led to the matron's.

He stepped down into the dark shadows cast by the boulders. Fifty body lengths away, he spotted a guard on the talus slope. Short and pudgy, the man was turned away, gazing toward Salmon Village.

Voices carried on the cold night air: infants laughing, different strains of conversation, dogs growling. Deep in the belly of the village, someone played a drum. The beautiful rhythm drifted down the mountain like butterfly wings.

"Hallowed Ancestors," he hissed to himself, "this is something only a foaming-mouth dog would do."

He hung his atlatl on his belt and trotted up the trail toward the guard.

The warrior saw him almost immediately and yelled, "Halt! Who are you?"

"A messenger!" Red Dog spread his arms wide. "I carry important information for Matron Kaska!"

"What is your name?"

"Red Dog. From Fire Village." He continued up the low rise to where the guard stood. The man had shoulder-length black hair. He'd seen perhaps eight and ten cycles, but had the wary look of a seasoned warrior. He gestured with his stone-headed war club. "I know you. Walk toward the village. I'll take you to the war chief."

The trail curved to the south of the palisade. Red Dog had to bend his head far back to see the guards who stood looking over the lip of the twenty-hand-tall wall. They watched him pass in silence, their eyes occasionally glinting in the light of the Star People.

The guard took him not to the main gate, but to a smaller side gate he'd never been through before. It opened behind the interconnected lodges where Matron Kaska had her quarters and held her village council sessions.

"Walk to the middle lodge, and remember, since you're not expected, you'll be watched by two tens of guards."

"I understand." Kaska wasn't taking any chances since Gispaw's death.

Red Dog passed through the gate and ducked beneath the door hanging the man indicated. The sight that met his eyes stunned him. He had seen Salmon Village many times from outside, but he'd never been allowed into the matron's lodge. Magnificent painted shields lined the walls. He saw Cougar and Mink, Wolf and Grizzly Bear, and many other sacred animals.

"Walk," the guard ordered.

"Forgive me, it's just that . . . these are the most beautiful shields I have ever seen."

"Yes, they are. The matron painted them herself."

Red Dog glanced over his shoulder at the man and continued walking.

"Go through the rear door."

When he ducked through, he entered another lodge, and a rich fruity scent filled the air. It took him a few moments to identify it: blue paint made from dried blueberries. The painter crushed the berries and mixed them with fat; the sweet fragrance smelled intense.

"Don't move," the guard ordered.

Red Dog heard soft calculated steps and turned to see Sand Wasp coming up behind him. The long scar across his forehead looked oddly pale in the light. He had a dangerous look about him, as though it wouldn't take much to push him to kill.

"Hello, Red Dog. I didn't expect to see you back so soon."

"I've covered so much ground my legs feel like they are made of wood."

Sand Wasp examined Red Dog carefully, noting the atlatl and bone stiletto on his belt.

"Take his weapons."

"Yes, War Chief."

The guard relieved Red Dog of his atlatl and stiletto, then untied his belt pouch and removed it. Finally, he patted Red Dog down. In the process he found the other two stilettos Red Dog kept tucked in his black leggings. He laid them all in a pile beside Sand Wasp's feet.

"Can't you find a pretty young girl to do that?" Red Dog groused. "That way I could enjoy it, too."

"He is ready, War Chief," the guard said as he rose.

Sand Wasp's eyes narrowed. "Thank you, Banded Eagle. You may return to your post. I will conduct the messenger to the matron."

"Yes, War Chief." The guard bowed and marched down the corridor.

Sand Wasp waited until he could no longer hear the man's steps. "Who sent you back so quickly?"

Red Dog whispered, "Rain Bear."

Sand Wasp's gaze bored into Red Dog's as though searching for any hint of treachery.

"Hey, what's wrong with you?" He narrowed an eye. "You hired me!"

Sand Wasp swallowed as if something were stuck in his throat. Then he smiled weakly. "Lies within lies, old friend. Treachery, double-dealing, no wonder I'm not sleeping."

"It will be over soon."

Sand Wasp's eyes were full of promise. "Yes," he said simply as he led Red Dog into the matron's lodge, "it will."

A woman called, "What is it, War Chief?"

"I bring a messenger, Matron."

"You may enter."

Sand Wasp walked up and pulled the door hanging aside.

Red Dog stepped into the lodge, Sand Wasp close behind, and looked around in genuine awe. More painted shields covered the walls, but these were even more extraordinary: glorious half-animal and half-human gods Danced around the walls as though alive. He could almost hear eerie voices coming from their open beaks and muzzles.

"I see you have had a safe, if fast, trip, Red Dog," Kaska greeted.

Their last meeting had been at night beside a spring not far outside the gates. Red Dog had never really seen her up close in the light. A tiny, slender woman with a delicately beautiful face, she looked to have seen perhaps two tens of summers.

"I carry word from Rain Bear, Matron."

"Yes?" She stepped forward, concern in her soft dark eyes. "You saw him? Gave him my message?"

"He wants you to bring up the rear of the procession. Be ready to pull your warriors off near the signal point at Whispering Waters Spring."

Impulsively she reached beneath her cape and smoothed her fingers over her belted stiletto. After what had happened to her mother, he didn't blame her for going armed.

"Is that all?" Kaska asked.

Red Dog carefully laid out Rain Bear's battle plan, squatting to re-create the map Rain Bear had drawn for him. "So, there it is, Matron."

Her red-and-black cape hissed as she walked across the floor. "I thank you for your service, Red Dog. Are you heading back to Rain Bear tonight?"

"No, Matron." He winced as he stood on his aching legs. "I am making one last desperate attempt to rescue Dzoo and the young Singer Pitch."

Her dark eyes fixed on his. "That may be very dangerous. Given that Fire Village is packing for the move, your absence has surely been noted, and commented on."

He gave her a crooked grin. "I have lived for a whole turning of seasons because of *Dzoo-noo-qua*. Now that the pieces are being cast in the final game, I must be there for her."

Kaska placed a small hand on his shoulder. "You need to know that my spies tell me Cimmis has ordered your death."

He gave her a gap-toothed grin. "Then I had better hope I'm not caught before I'm done."

She clapped her hands. "Sand Wasp, provide Red Dog with a bag full of rations. Then have one of our warriors escort him to the trail."

Sand Wasp nodded. "This way."

Red Dog took one last look at the shields—he swore their eyes followed him—before he ducked beneath the hanging.

Once outside, Sand Wasp called, "Banded Eagle?"

The guard instantly ducked under the hanging and ran across the lodge. "Yes, War Chief?"

"Please see that this man is provisioned and escorted back out the side gate."

Banded Eagle bowed. "Yes, War Chief."

Sand Wasp watched Red Dog disappear beneath the far door hanging, then softly said, "He is gone, Matron."

"Come and speak with me."

Sand Wasp entered her lodge and stood stiffly, waiting for orders. Her perfect triangular face had gone tight with worry.

She searched Sand Wasp's face, as if the answers lay there. "What are we going to do? Cimmis has ordered me to have our warriors march near the front of the procession. What excuse can I give for marching in the rear?"

"We leave before dawn tomorrow. He will not wish to alter his plans. Not this close to our departure."

"No," she said softly, and her brows slanted down over her dark eyes.

He could see her thoughts whirling, trying to decide. "This plan of Rain Bear's, is it a good one?"

She nodded, staring down at the squiggles Red Dog had drawn in the dirt. "Well, we are committed, then. May Gutginsa bless us with luck."

Sand Wasp said, "Matron, perhaps it is time—"

"No, not yet," she said softly, and bowed her head. "I'll tell our most trusted warriors when the time is right. But not yet, Sand Wasp. The longer they know, the longer they have for second thoughts. Cimmis and the Council would pay a matron's ransom to anyone who would betray us."

"Yes," Sand Wasp agreed absently, "at least that much."

"I will assign warriors to spread the word just before we reach Whispering Waters Spring."

"Yes, Matron." He stood stiffly, jaw clamped.

"Is that fear I see in your eyes?"

"Yes, Matron. Betrayal is a frightening thing."

Red Dog yawned, barely aware of his breath frosting on the cold air. The night was like charred sap: thick and black. He carefully skirted the trail that led from Salmon Village up the mountain to Fire Village. If guards were out, he had to hope the inky blackness would hide him.

Gods, he was bone-weary, his thoughts thicker than matted buffalo wool. He plodded on, one weary step after another. His hips, knees, and ankles ached. Tomorrow would be the beginning of the end.

He had taken this last trip without the permission of either Cimmis or Ecan. Kaska's warning that Cimmis had ordered him killed hadn't come as a surprise. It was a miracle that he'd gone undiscovered for this long. But how was he going to get past the gates, overcome the guards, and sneak Dzoo and Pitch out?

If only he could clear his head for a moment, shake the terrible need to sleep from his body for one more day.

"There you are, old friend," a familiar voice called from the trees at the side of the trail.

Red Dog stopped, peering into the shadows cast by a lonely stand of firs. "What are you doing out here?"

"Caught me one of Rain Bear's spies. Want to see?"

One of Rain Bear's spies? Which one? And, more to the point, what was he going to do about it? This close to the beginning of the attack, it could mean disaster.

Red Dog stepped into the shadows, blinking in the inky darkness. "I can't see a thing. Let's drag him out onto the trail where—"

The whistling war club came out of nowhere, catching Red Dog full on the side of the head. The blow flashed yellow lightning behind his eyes. He heard as well as felt the bones snapping as his head recoiled from the force.

As his swimming vision cleared, he realized he was on the ground, unable to move.

The last thing he saw was the faint outline of a giant coyote's head against the sky.

"Dzoo is mine, you silly fool. All mine."

The words barely penetrated the ringing in Red Dog's head as his vision faded to gray.

Dusk

*S*oul Keeper?" *I whisper.*

"Yes, I'm here."

I breathe, "I . . . I'm afraid. I don't want . . . to die."

I no longer have the strength to open my eyes, but I know night is falling. The light that filters through my eyelids is dark gray. I'm almost used up. For the past hand of time, I've felt myself going cold inside, like an ember slowly fading to ash.

Wind Woman sweeps across the beach and flaps the Soul Keeper's cape. I listen as he resettles himself.

"There is a very old story," he begins, "about Wolf and Coyote in the Beginning Time."

I take a deep breath and let the words flow around me. There are tens of such stories. Which one does he want me to hear?

"In the Beginning Time, no one died. They ate a plant called the Everlasting Flower that kept them alive. Coyote's brother, Wolf, said, 'I think people should die, but rise after two days.' Coyote disagreed. He said, 'There are too many people in the world. I don't want people to rise. They should die forever.'"

"Coyote . . . won," I say.

"Yes, he did. But when Coyote's only son grew ill, he panicked. Coyote ran like lightning across the world searching for one single blossom from the Everlasting Flower."

My soul must be climbing out of my body, because I do not recall this version of the story. I say, "Did he . . . find it?"

"Oh, yes. Yes, he did." The Soul Keeper's voice is grave. "Magpie told him about a cave where the last flowers grew. Coyote ran hard and fast. The cave sat at the foot of a mountain. When Coyote entered the cave, he heard a buffalo's startled grunt; then the animal moved, and the fetid odor of rot filled the cave. Coyote trotted deeper, and he saw the flowers growing at the edge of a still pool. Bright and silver, like Sister Moon's flesh, they glowed in the darkness.

"As Coyote rushed forward to pluck one of the blossoms, a hideously diseased buffalo stepped out of the shadows. It was all but a skeleton. It could barely stand. Hair hung like filthy rags from its rotting hide.

" 'What happened to you?' Coyote asked.

"Buffalo said, 'Do not pick that blossom.'

" 'But I must. My son will die forever if I don't.'

"Buffalo wobbled toward Coyote on rotten legs. 'I ate those blossoms when I was a calf.'

" 'But how can that be?' Coyote asked. 'You look like you might die at any moment.'

" 'Yes,' said Buffalo in a deep, rumbling voice, 'but I won't. I should have died tens of seasons ago and gone to the House of Air to graze green meadows with my Ancestors. But I am condemned to live in this world. All of my family and friends are long dead. No living buffalo will talk to me. I am a rotting carcass to them. I rot a little more every day, without the hope of death.'

"Coyote backed up a step, his yellow eyes wide. 'Are you saying that the Everlasting Flower grants eternal life, but does not rejuvenate the body?'

"The moldering buffalo nodded. 'It just prevents death.' He hung his massive head and heaved a sigh. 'I pray every day to Buffalo Above to grant me the peace of death, but it never comes. So, I stand here to warn others of the cost of the Everlasting Flower.' "

A smile tugs at the corners of my mouth. If I'd been Coyote, I know very well what I would have done.

I say, "I would have . . . grabbed it . . . and run."

"Yes, I suspect most parents would. But what a supreme act of selfishness—condemning a son to live forever because you cannot bear to lose him. How do you think your son would feel when you died? Do you think he would praise your name? Or curse you?"

I understand the lesson.

Does the old fool think I'm no smarter than a common rock? He's telling me I should stop struggling and look upon Death as salvation.

It is so difficult.

My soul keeps wandering through memories of things I've done. . . . Bad things.

How can I believe that salvation awaits me?

I manage to get enough air to ask, "Will you . . . Keep . . . my soul?"

He does not answer for a time, and I know he must be thinking of what people will say. They will condemn him. Maybe even kill him.

He hesitates before he says, "I have not decided."

A swelling emptiness sucks at me.

Fifty-six

Cimmis stumbled in the night. He bit off a curse as he looked up at the cloudless sky. The stars reminded him of foam on the sea.

Odd, he hadn't had a poetic thought for cycles.

He sniffed the cold air, but only smelled his musty cloak, heavy now with the clinging smoke from the Council Lodge. He had spent the last hand of time in the stifling interior going over the final details with White Stone. Time after time they had sketched the organization plan into the dirt.

He had worked it down to a fine system, the warriors going from lodge to lodge, waking the occupants, sending them down the trail in just the right sequence so that everyone moved in an orderly fashion.

Oh, to be sure, there would be grumbles in the predawn darkness, and people would stumble and fall, but by first light, they would be well on the way to Salmon Village. With any luck at all, by the time Rain Bear beat, flogged, and cajoled his Raven rabble into position, it would be to find nothing left but their tracks.

And Rain Bear could attack all the tracks he wanted.

Unless, of course, he tried to keep his unwieldy force together and surrounded Wasp Village. With starvation on the land, that had as little chance for success as rain falling upward.

Cimmis made a face as a stitch of pain shot through his hip. Gods, and he had to walk for the full day tomorrow. Or at least try to. If his warriors had to carry him, it would shame him.

As he approached the lodge, he stopped, staring thoughtfully at the high domed shape. Tomorrow night, it would be vacant, dark and cold within.

He laid a gentle hand on the bark wall, feeling the moss and lichen that had grown there. Here, he had lived most of his life with Astcat, risen with her to the pinnacle of authority. Inside these walls his daughters had been born. Here, too, their young son had choked on a plum pit and died.

"It is so hard to leave it all behind," he said softly.

"Father?" Kstawl called, worry in her voice.

He bent, wondering what terrible thing had befallen Astcat, and ducked inside.

In the fire's red glow, he could see his daughter waiting by a steaming stew hanging from its tripod. Automatically, he glanced at Astcat's bed, only to find it empty.

"Where's Mother?" Kstawl asked. "You know better than to keep her so long at the Council meetings." Her eyes had fixed expectantly on the door behind him, as though awaiting her appearance.

Cold, like a curling breaker, washed through him. "She's not here?"

"I thought she was with you!"

Cimmis blinked, stepping across the lodge to stare dully at her bed. Her favorite robes were missing. He turned, expecting to see her small bag of ornaments resting in its place, only to find the dirt bare.

"Merciful gods," he whispered. "We have to find your mother! She may have wandered off, gotten lost."

She pointed to a basket, its contents covered by a wicker lid. "A man brought that not more than several fingers ago. He said it was for you."

Cimmis, an incipient panic rising, lifted the lid. In the dim interior, he could just make out Red Dog's blood-streaked face, the matted hair gluey with gore, the eyes half opened.

"I do not tolerate betrayal," he murmured. "Gods, we've got to find your mother. Quick. Go wake White Stone. I want this village turned upside down!"

As Rain Bear walked through the darkness, his bones had a rickety feel, and he kept stumbling over little irregularities in the rocky surface. The tension in his muscles reminded him he wasn't a young man anymore.

Overhead, the stars were gleaming in a frosty wash across the sky. They cast just enough light that Rain Bear could see the outlines of their camp. His warriors were bundled in their blankets, most snoring fitfully. For some, exhaustion vied with anxiety about the coming battle. For the rest, fatigue momentarily had the upper hand.

In my next life, I'm going to be a simple hunter. Hunters, he figured, got more sleep than chiefs did.

He rubbed his gritty eyes and pinched the bridge of his nose, as if doing so would squeeze the weariness from his head. It didn't.

He turned faltering steps toward his flickering fire where it glowed near the middle of their camp, and was surprised to see Evening Star sitting on his robes. She had a long stick that she used to play with the flames, lighting the end, then lifting it until the yellow tongues died before poking it back into the coals.

"I'm surprised that you're still awake."

She glanced up, shot him a radiant smile, and shrugged. "I knew you had to make one last inspection. I thought I'd see if you wanted company tonight?"

He glanced out at the slumbering warriors.

Her lips turned up wryly. "It's not as if they didn't already guess. Besides, we'll stay dressed. If I'm half as tired as you look, neither one us will have the energy for anything but sleep."

He nodded, loosened his cape, pulled off his moccasins, and climbed under the thick buffalo robe beside her.

For long moments, they held each other, the combined warmth of their bodies leaching the misery out of his bones and muscles.

"We made better time than I thought we would," she said.

"We got a break in the weather. If it had been snowing, we'd have covered half the ground."

She tightened her hold on him. "Will we make Whispering Waters Spring in time?"

"I think." He filled his lungs and tried to exhale the tension inside him. "So many things could go wrong."

"For Cimmis as well," she reminded. "It's up to the gods."

He reached up, running his fingers along the curve of her soft cheek. "If we live, will you be my wife?"

She hesitated. "You're a Dreamer."

"As long as I can Dream you."

She smiled, and he felt the foggy warm sensation of sleep creeping through his soul.

Yes, enjoy this. If you know nothing else, it's that you have this one moment of bliss. After tomorrow, you may have nothing but eternity.

Fifty-seven

Pitch jerked awake and stared around the lodge, his heart hammering. In the faint glow of the fire, he could see Dzoo where she sat upright, a sea-grass blanket over her shoulders. From the blank expression on her face and wide glassy eyes she might have been seeing something far distant across time and space.

He was starting back to sleep when he heard the voice: a hollow whisper. He could barely make it out, the words unintelligible. Sitting up, he frowned.

"Dzoo?"

At his call, the voice stopped short.

Dzoo raised a warning hand; her face remained slack, emotionless.

The faintest rustling came from behind the wall, as if hide clothing had scuffed the bark.

"Who was that?" Pitch demanded.

"Coyote."

Pitch blinked and felt his heart skip. "He's here? Just outside the lodge?"

"Oh, yes," she said simply. "He comes and goes. Mostly, he just listens at the wall. Tonight he came to warn me."

"Warn you of what?"

Her eyes moved; then her face began to melt into a ghastly smile. "That our joining approaches."

"Dzoo, we have to get out of here. Given the choice of Cimmis or Coyote, I'd rather take my chances dying while trying to escape."

"There is no escape," she said simply. "Ever since Antler Spoon's village, I've been working to lure him ever closer."

Before Pitch could ask, shouts came from outside. "Now what?" he muttered.

He reached for his shirt. As he slipped it over his head, the voices grew louder. He was already on his feet when a warrior threw back the door flap.

"Grab your things!" He was young, skinny, with a melon-shaped skull.

"Why? What's happening?"

"We're leaving Fire Village."

"Now? In the middle of the night?" Pitch stood and tied his pouch to his belt. "I thought we were leaving at dawn."

"Hurry. The chief wants us out of Fire Village within one finger of time."

Dzoo was still smiling her eerie smile. Gods, was she actually looking forward to this? Pitch swung his cape around his shoulders and ducked beneath the door flap. Another warrior, older, with hard eyes, stood outside.

"Follow me," the man said, and turned to walk up the trail.

Some of the warriors carried torches, which illuminated a knot of people who stood near the palisade gate.

Pitch leaned toward Dzoo, whispering, "I still think we should make a break for it."

The young guard prodded Pitch's back with a spear. "Quiet. Walk."

Pitch walked.

Star People glittered across the midnight sky with an icy crystalline brightness. In the plaza, people hugged each other, and he heard weeping as they said good-bye to this place that had been their home.

A coil of gray smoke rose from the dying plaza fire and trailed across Fire Village like a sleepy serpent. The air smelled pungently of burning sagebrush.

"Stop at the gate. The great chief is coming."

Pitch stopped and glanced at Dzoo. In the faint light, he could still see that enigmatic smile. It brought a shiver up his back. Through the gate Salmon Village was visible farther down the mountain slope. Distant warriors bore torches—but pinpricks of light—while people trotted around the palisade, carrying litters and bundles.

It took Pitch a moment to recognize Cimmis when he hobbled out of the darkness. Could this be the same Cimmis who had scared the soul half out of him earlier? His face was a mask of worry, the eyes glittering as if lost. The man walked with a slight limp, his withered left arm hanging from his shoulder. He wore a blue shirt beneath a hide cape. He looked like an ordinary warrior. Nothing more. He'd even coiled his gray hair into a bun at the base of his skull—like every other warrior standing close by.

At that moment, War Chief White Stone came trotting at the head of a small party of warriors.

"Great Chief," he called. "We have discovered what happened to the matron."

Cimmis spun on his feet, crying, "What? Where is she? Take me to her!"

White Stone stopped short, his head cocked, puzzlement on his face. "Well, it seems that she has already left."

"What? Left how?"

"Deer Killer was on guard at this same gate earlier today. He said that the great matron—carried on her litter by four warriors—passed through the gate."

"I don't understand!" Cimmis bellowed. "Was she a prisoner? Was she . . . Was her soul loose?"

A frightened young man stepped forward, visibly shaken. "Great Chief"—his voice quavered—"I swear, she was fine. She sat atop her litter and gave orders to the warriors carrying her. She seemed completely in control of her senses. She—"

Cimmis stepped forward and slapped the man across the face. "Why? Why did she leave me?"

The blow wasn't that powerful, but the warrior collapsed to the ground. His voice was almost a wail when he shrieked, "I heard her say she'd see you at Wasp Village!"

Cimmis bent down over the huddled figure. *"Why didn't you stop her?"*

"She's *the Matron!*"

Cimmis blinked, stepping back. "Yes. She's the matron." He shook his head in confusion. "Did she say anything else?"

"Yes! I heard her bid Fire Village farewell. But that's all. I swear it on my life, Great Chief!"

Cimmis straightened, turning to White Stone. "Then let's get this column moving. Someone inform my daughter."

Where she stood beside Pitch, Dzoo leaned her head back. The sound of her laughter rising on the cold night air was unnerving.

"Separate them," Cimmis ordered, flicking his finger between Pitch and Dzoo. Then he turned and stalked down the slope toward the muscular warriors who stood with the Four Old Women's litters on their shoulders, awaiting orders to move. The old women resembled dark mounds of flapping hides. More litters lined the trail, loaded heavily with packs and roped with grass cords.

"I'll see you later," Pitch cried hopefully as Dzoo followed the shaken Deer Killer off into the night.

People stood alongside the Four Old Women's litters, calling last words. Several wept openly and tore at their clothes.

The warrior called Thunder Boy hissed, "I swear it's the end of our world."

His companion, Ground Hog, a young man with wide blue eyes and copper-colored hair, shook his head. "Not yet. The reckoning is yet to come . . . when we meet Rain Bear."

Wind Woman's cold breath fanned Pitch's hair around his shoulders. He took a deep breath and gave Fire Village one last look.

Fifty-eight

Hunter tried to look confident as he strode toward the gate. He could feel Dzoo's presence, like a malignant wind, blowing a chill onto his back. His hair was prickling, as if someone rubbed a phantom foxhide over his skin. Of all the luck, why did Wind Scorpion constantly order him and Deer Killer to guard the witch?

The Raven People slaves milling around the fires hushed as they passed. They resembled lean hungry wolves. The few Raven People who'd decided to remain had already piled their belongings in front of the lodges they would be claiming and had posted family members to protect them, but he suspected there would still be fights. He could feel the tension in the air. When the elite were finally gone, there would be a great tumult of greed.

Dzoo's soft steps padded behind Hunter as he walked through the gate. He glanced back to see Deer Killer, shaken and wobbly after his experience with the great chief. He was the last man who should have been assigned to this duty.

Soon, the three of them would be marching out in front of the procession like the triangular head of a snake. All night long, he'd been praying to every Ancestor Spirit he could think of that Deer Killer wouldn't bolt, or fall first in the battle.

Blessed gods, what will I do if I suddenly find myself alone with her?

The thought must have stopped him in his tracks, because Dzoo walked up beside him. She stared him in the eyes for a long time, as though reading the path of his soul, before she walked ahead.

Hunter fought to steady his nerves.

Deer Killer gave him a weak grin. "Try not to throw up. Everyone is watching."

Hunter grabbed him by the cape ties. "From now on, *you're* leading the way." Then he shoved Deer Killer ahead.

Deer Killer glanced over his shoulder and said, "I was just joking!"

Tsauz lay in the cold windswept darkness, listening. All around him, fragrant branches whispered in the moving air, the sound mixing oddly with the snores of tens of warriors.

They had traveled for two days through the forest and up into the alder thickets west of Eelgrass Village. Rides-the-Wind slept beneath the hides to his left, his back to Tsauz. The rest of the camp was behind them, scattered across the slope.

Tsauz reached out and put a hand on the old Soul Keeper's shoulder. He just needed to touch someone.

Each step he took, he was getting closer to home, but he had to keep reminding himself that he wasn't going home. Fire Village would never be his home again.

Rides-the-Wind patted his hand and whispered, "Are you all right, Tsauz?"

"I'm not sleepy."

"What's wrong?"

Tsauz blinked at the darkness. "Chief Cimmis could still win the battle, couldn't he?"

"Yes."

"What will happen if he does?"

Rides-the-Wind yawned. "The North Wind People will probably continue their march to Wasp Village, where they will live until the Raven People finally overwhelm them."

"Are you sure?"

"Some things are inevitable." Rides-the-Wind put a warm hand on Tsauz's arm. "You've done everything you can, Tsauz."

He sucked in a deep breath and held it. He'd flown on Thunderbird's rain-scented back, diving and soaring through the glistening Cloud People. He had glimpsed the future, but Thunderbird had told him they were just things that *might* be.

He looked up and searched the blackness.

Father once told him that Mother had become a tiny point of light in the belly of Old Woman's enormous sky. He tried to imagine where she would be shining. Every day since she'd died, he'd longed for her. Tsauz closed his eyes and lifted his hand, holding it out to her.

If I die, Mother, will you please come for me?

"Tsauz, you mustn't dwell on these thoughts. They siphon your strength. Bad thoughts are like tiny holes in a water bucket. Pretty soon they'll make you dry and empty."

Tsauz closed his eyes. He tried to calm himself by imagining the countryside. "I know."

He smelled water.

They hadn't traveled long enough to be near Whispering Waters Spring. They must be on Water Storage Plateau. He and Father had camped here on the way north. The flat expanse of lava was covered by wind-carved potholes. When it rained or snowed, the holes filled and served as cisterns.

Rides-the-Wind flipped onto his side. His hair smelled of wood smoke and sweat. It had been a long hard march, and Rides-the-Wind had held his hand the entire way, guiding him around brush and away from holes where he might fall and break his leg.

"Where are we? Would you tell me what you see?"

Rides-the-Wind sighed and lifted his head. "Tens of black humps."

"Sleeping warriors?"

"Yes. And more stand on the high points, keeping guard over Water Storage Plateau. Every so often the obsidian points of their spears glint in the night."

"Elder, do you think . . ." He paused, hating to ask, unable to help himself. "Do you think Thunderbirds can lie?"

"Why do you ask?"

Tsauz smoothed his cheek over the soft buffalohide. "I've just been wondering, that's all."

"Well, I've never heard of a Spirit Helper lying, though they often play tricks on people."

"No, I mean, would a Spirit Helper try to turn a battle in favor of one side?"

"Of course he would."

Wind Woman breathed across the plateau, and the foot of their buffalohides flapped. Cold air ate at Tsauz's bare feet. He didn't say anything for a while, just breathed in and out as he remembered what Thunderbird had said about his father.

Apprehensively, the old Soul Keeper asked, "Which side do you think Thunderbird might be favoring?"

Tsauz swallowed hard. "The North Wind People."

"Why would you say that?"

"I—I don't know. It's just a feeling." He rubbed a hand over his aching heart. "Right here. It hurts. Like I can already feel a spear point lodged in my lungs."

Rides-the-Wind put his hand over Tsauz's heart. "I wouldn't worry. That's probably the dried fish you had for supper. I swear Rain Bear has had that fish for cycles. It looked a little green to me."

"Did it?" Tsauz asked hopefully. Anything would be better than thinking his Spirit Helper was Trickster in disguise.

"You wouldn't sound so happy if you'd seen it. I would have rather chewed on a moldering dog leg. I was just too tired to go out and hunt one down."

"Elder, do you fear death?"

"Not as much as I fear Rain Bear's cooking."

Fifty-nine

Gispaxloats glanced uneasily at Kitselas. Their small fire had burned down to ashes, and as the first faint light of dawn sent rose colors through the thin high clouds, it was apparent that the great matron's soul had fled. What was even worse, they were lost. He had no idea where the trail was that they were supposed to take, and without Astcat to tell them, all he could do was stumble on ahead and hope he was doing it right.

Blue Hand and Spotted Arm both sat across the fire, blankets around their waists as they yawned and rubbed their eyes. That didn't hide the worry as they shot quick glances at the matron.

She lay in her litter just west of the fire, where the evening breezes would drift the fire's warmth over her. This morning, however, her face was slack, her mouth hanging agape. Drool slipped silver down the side of her chin.

Gispaxloats shook his head, muttering, "What now?"

They had stopped for the night and set up camp in a shallow cove just up from a stream crossing. The location was bounded on three sides by basalt outcrops and partially screened by brush. Thick grass had made for good bedding, and enough snags had been snapped from the nearby conifers to keep the fire going all night.

"We follow our orders," Kitselas said with resignation as he watched the old woman's shallow breathing. "She is the great matron. That's all there is to it."

"But it doesn't make any sense!" Spotted Arm muttered as he stood, watched his frosty breath in the cold air, and then walked into the brush to relieve himself.

"Who cares if it makes sense?" Blue Hand, his younger brother, kicked his blankets off, rose, and followed. From behind the screening of brush, he added, "Kitselas is right. She's the great matron of the North Wind People. We keep going."

"Cimmis is going to pull our hearts out of our chests and boil them while they're still beating."

Gispaxloats pulled his war bag over, lifted the flap, and stared inside. "There's enough food here for one breakfast. I say we cook it, eat it, and do as the matron told us."

"Yes. Let's," Kitselas agreed. "We might as well eat it all. I've always wanted to die with a full stomach."

Blue Hand stepped out of the brush and ran his fingers through his hair as he stared at the listless Astcat. "Why did she choose us for this?"

"Because we're the best." Gispaxloats tossed more firewood onto the coals. "Kitselas, take that bladder over there and walk down to the stream. Bring me some water. I heard that the great chief always trickles water into her mouth when her soul comes loose."

Kitselas took the water bladder and stood. "What if the great chief catches us before we can complete the task we've been given?"

"Then he'd better find the matron receiving the best of care." Gispaxloats stared hopefully at Astcat. "I just hope she brings her soul back in time to explain for us."

Reluctantly Blue Hand said, "Well, let's get about it. We have the matron's orders. I'll build up the fire. You go cut green branches. If she wants a big smoke, we'll make it so that the whole country can see."

"Yeah," Spotted Arm muttered as he stepped out of the bushes. "It's a toss-up as to who is going to find us and kill us first."

Do you see the smoke, my Chief?" Young Thunder Boy called.

"What smoke?" Cimmis asked.

Over ten tens of people twisted at once to look back at Cimmis. He felt like he was gazing into a writhing sea of disembodied faces. The North Wind procession resembled a snake with a chipmunk in its belly as it wound down the ridgetop trail. The triangular head of the snake was composed of three people. Immediately behind them, a group of around five tens of warriors marched. A bulbous circle of spear throwers encircled the Four Old Women's litters. Another group of warriors brought up the rear, and the tail of the snake slithered out behind.

Just ahead of him, the Four Old Women shifted on their litters to see what the commotion was.

Thunder Boy said, "Someone is sending a signal down along the base of the mountain." He swung around and pointed to the southwest. "You can still see the column of white smoke where the wind has blown it back into the trees."

Cimmis stepped away from his guards to get a good look at the location. He knew this terrain; every groove and bump was familiar. If Rain Bear was sending the message, he couldn't be too far from the spire. Probably . . . there. Less than two hand's run from Water Storage Plateau.

"Are you sure that was a message and not just some hunter drowning a campfire?"

Thunder Boy swallowed hard. "It was a white plume of smoke, Great Chief. We thought you should know."

Cimmis turned, beckoning to Wind Scorpion, who walked several paces back. The grizzled old warrior trotted forward.

"Yes, Great Chief?" When Cimmis pointed, the cunning old eyes turned to where the faint white plume of smoke rose over the distant trees.

"Do you know what that might be?"

Wind Scorpion's eyes narrowed. "A signal of some sort, I suppose. The first thing that comes to mind is that Rain Bear has split his forces. One group is signaling to another. He surely wouldn't attack here. This ground is too open."

He gestured down the slope. A fire five summers ago had denuded the slope where the trail followed the ridge down toward patches of trees.

As they walked, Cimmis couldn't help but glance periodically at the plume of white. It seemed to strengthen, and then diminish, only to be replenished again. It looked to him more like a beacon than a signal smoke. Beacon? For what? For whom?

As if he had overheard Cimmis's thoughts, Wind Scorpion said, "The threads of Power are being drawn tight."

As the sun rose ever higher in the sky, Hunter kept shooting wary glances at the witch, as did Deer Killer; but Dzoo had her unblinking eyes focused on Ecan. She seemed possessed of an absolute stillness. With her dark hood flapping around her beautiful face, she looked almost godlike.

"Witch!" Hunter called. "Are you sleepwalking?"

She didn't appear to hear him.

"I asked you a—"

"Red Dog's soul is stalking yours." She said it so calmly.

Deer Killer cried, "Red Dog? No one's even seen him for days. Word is he ran off to Rain Bear."

Hunter glanced warily around; the very notion of something stalking his soul chilled his blood. "What makes you think he's dead?"

"A witch whispered it to me last night."

"We were guarding you all night. No one came close." Deer Killer thumped his chest in emphasis.

"I shall miss the two of you," she said simply. "Give my regards to Red Dog's spirit when you see it. Tell him I will always honor his memory."

"That makes no sense," Hunter muttered, but he kept glancing over his shoulder to see if a ghost was there.

As Dzoo walked, a heaviness lay in her heart. She had liked Red Dog. When Coyote had whispered that he'd killed him outside of Salmon Village, her heart had deadened. She had known that Red Dog cared for her, had seen it grow in his eyes while he healed under her care.

Scoundrel that he was, she would miss his wit, the dogged persistence of his character. He would never have filled the hole left by her Pearl Oyster: She had had one husband, one love of her life.

She could feel Ecan's presence long before she was aware of him marching up to her.

"Hunter, Deer Killer, leave us." The Starwatcher made a gesture with his hand.

The guards faded off to each side, leaving a bubble of space around them. Dzoo sniffed, catching the subtle odor of damp moss. "You are tainted, Starwatcher." She glanced at his pinched expression. "What was his reaction when he laid hands on his fetishes again?"

Ecan missed a step. And recovered, one hand to his breast. "What . . . what are you talking about?"

She let the faintest of smiles bend her lips. "I'm talking about the bargain you struck with Coyote. Was Red Dog part of it, or was killing him Cimmis's idea?"

"Cimmis deals with Coyote?" Ecan seemed genuinely surprised.

"Of course. But for a thread of Power, Coyote would have already killed Tsauz and removed him from the complex web we find ourselves in. Curious, isn't it, that he didn't kill Matron Evening Star that night in her lodge?"

Ecan was watching her as if she could spin miracles. "Coyote was sent to kill both Evening Star *and* Tsauz?"

"You owe your son's life to the Soul Keeper, Rides-the-Wind. Why do you think the old man went to Rain Bear in the first place? It was to save the boy."

"For which I shall reward him when the time comes." Ecan seemed suddenly reserved, as if putting new pieces into an old puzzle. "As to Evening Star, I would prefer to deal with her on my own."

"If *he* will let you."

"I control—"

"Is that what you think?" She laughed at the man's temerity. "What makes you think he would *serve* you?" She lowered her voice to a hiss. "You're no doubt congratulating yourself on having drawn him away from Cimmis. Do you really think Coyote would choose to ally himself with a dead man?"

He barked a sharp if unsettled laugh. "You keep calling me that, and my heart keeps beating."

She shrugged. "Even without your prompting, he would have killed Cimmis and Astcat sooner or later."

Ecan's face went ashen. "I would *never*—"

"You still don't understand, do you?" She searched his eyes, seeing all the vainglorious arrogance welling behind them.

"Understand what?"

"The reason he took your payment, the reason he'll kill Astcat and Cimmis in the end. You see the reason he left Evening Star alive is because he needs her to be his matron. When this is all over, *he will be great chief!*"

Sixty

From his place in the line of march, White Stone watched as Ecan staggered away from Dzoo. The Starwatcher stopped in the middle of the trail, his eyes focused on something in the distance. White Stone gazed curiously that way, but could only see Raven Bay, Gull Inlet, and the distant islands.

Dzoo, meanwhile, was looking down the slope ahead of them, where patches of firs grew. He followed her gaze first to the low rise to his left—at which she smiled for a time—then down to the grove of firs. Dzoo's face turned stoic enough to have been carved from some pale hardwood.

White Stone lifted his war ax and called, "Hunter! Close up on the prisoner." She wouldn't think of trying to escape into those trees, would she?

As the procession continued plodding down the winding trail toward the trees, the ocean breeze mixed with scents of mud and damp firs to form a heady fragrance. The Four Old Women on their litters hissed questions to each other. Everything was going as planned, and they were ahead of schedule.

He watched his two lead scouts trot into the trees. He had almost forgotten Dzoo's interest in the trees when two warriors in mangy hide capes charged out from the timber. A half heartbeat later, a screaming horde broke from cover. Keen obsidian points glinted on the tips of their spears.

White Stone shouted, "Get into position!"

Just as Cimmis had planned, three tens of spear throwers separated from the circle around the Four Old Women, and the men behind moved forward to take their places. The first group ran downhill to form a solid wall against the attackers.

The litter bearers quickly set their burdens down and huddled around the Council and the matrons accompanying the party.

All except Kaska, who stepped off her litter, shoved through the ring of guards, and looked down the slope at the Raven People. White Stone smiled at the thought of her confusion. By now, according to her plan, Sand Wasp should have been looking to her for orders.

Instead, the Salmon Village war chief stood tall, his jaw set, not two paces from White Stone. White Stone said, "Sand Wasp, have your warriors form a second line behind the first!"

"Yes, War Chief!"

For a moment, when he turned around, Sand Wasp's gaze touched Kaska's. The man seemed to freeze; then he motioned to his warriors. "You heard White Stone, form a second line!"

Three tens of Kaska's warriors ran down the slope and knelt behind the first row of defenders.

"Ready!" White Stone called as the Raven People dashed up the slope, their spears over their heads. Casting uphill was risky at best, but on the run?

As they neared casting range, the Raven People split in half in a clumsy pincer movement.

Blessed gods, they're fools! White Stone watched the ineffective tactic develop. The attacking warriors were panting from their long run up the hill. Worse, their formation was disintegrating as they scrambled over the rough hillside.

White Stone filled his lungs. "First line, cast!"

Sunlight flashed down the polished shafts as the spears arced into the sky, seemed to hover like birds for a few eternal instants, then plunged down.

The lethal missiles met flesh; the screams began—ragged, breathless. At least half of the Raven People fell. Most writhed on the ground, trying to jerk the shafts of wood and stone from their bodies. Some stood dumbfounded, staring at the carnage. Others threw down their weapons and ran, but a few kept coming.

The few enemy spears gleamed as though afire as they lanced through the sky. Three of the throwers in the first line went down. Then two more.

"Second line, cast!" White Stone ordered.

Kaska's warriors took aim and threw.

White Stone turned to look at Dzoo. She stood tall, utterly un-afraid, watching the battle. Cimmis had hoped that by leaving Dzoo out front, it might stem the ardor of the enemy spear throwers. The great chief had apparently miscalculated.

"Ready!" White Stone's remaining warriors nocked spears in their atlatl hooks.

"Let them get closer, closer . . ." When the Raven People were less than two tens of paces away, he shouted, "Cast!"

Several went down instantly, but the others charged forward, screaming like gutted birds.

"Use your clubs!" he shouted, and as his men rushed to obey, tens of spears clattered onto the ground.

The war chief who led the enemy warriors headed straight for White Stone. He was stocky, with a scarred face and granite-headed war club.

White Stone lifted his ax, braced his feet, and waited for the man to come to him.

"Meet your death!" The Raven warrior swung his club at White Stone's head.

White Stone sidestepped, pivoted, and drove his ax into the pant-ing man's back as momentum carried him around. The Raven war-rior let out a surprised yip as the blow severed his spine. He tumbled to the ground, screaming, his upper body flopping helplessly. Several others went down around White Stone as Sand Wasp waded into the onslaught.

Then, abruptly, the few remaining Raven warriors broke and ran.

"Hold!" White Stone bellowed to keep his warriors from dashing in pursuit. Nevertheless, a handful did, carried away by the moment. He ground his teeth. Better if they were killed by the fleeing Raven warriors than if they had to face his wrath for disobeying orders. At the calls of their fellows a couple turned back, glancing sheepishly in his direction.

Cimmis came striding down the line. His gray bun had come un-pinned and hung around his wrinkled face. White Stone watched as Matron Kaska lifted the hem of her cape and fell into step behind Cimmis.

As Cimmis passed the Four Old Women, he ordered, "Lift these litters! Be ready to move at my command!"

In less than five heartbeats they'd hoisted the litters and stood stiffly waiting.

"Where is Rain Bear?" Cimmis demanded when he arrived. His

sharp old gaze darted over the dead and wounded that scattered the slope.

"I didn't see him, my Chief."

"Where could he be? Still in the trees?"

White Stone shook his head. "It isn't like Rain Bear to hide in the trees while his men go out to meet the enemy. He usually leads the charge."

"Hunter?" Cimmis sharply called. "Go and search the bodies for Rain Bear."

"Yes, my Chief!"

White Stone turned to watch Hunter kick over the first body and barely heard the soft grunt behind him.

He turned back in time to see Sand Wasp stagger as Kaska repeatedly drove a stiletto into his back. The war chief didn't even try to fight back, but wavered as his knees buckled and he collapsed at her feet.

Sand Wasp gasped, "Forgive me, Matron. I did not wish to . . . to do it, but . . ." His gaze flickered to Cimmis, as if caressing his face.

White Stone clutched his ax a little more tightly and noticed the two new shiny copper nuggets that gleamed on the dying war chief's throat.

Kaska shouted at her warriors, "You obey my orders now, and mine alone! Return to your positions. We must make it to Wasp Village as soon as possible!"

White Stone glanced at Cimmis and raised a questioning eyebrow. *Kill her now?*

The great chief shook his head.

White Stone wasn't sure he agreed, but perhaps this really wasn't the time.

Cimmis whispered, "I'll have my special agent attend to it tonight. When everyone else is asleep."

White Stone nodded.

Kaska's warriors muttered, stared forlornly at Sand Wasp, then started back to regroup in front of the litters.

Kaska had turned her hard glare on Cimmis, knowing full well he was going to kill her, and calmly went back to climb onto her litter.

"That's a brave woman," White Stone said softly.

Cimmis ground his teeth. "Yes, much too brave. I want her separated from her warriors."

"But my chief, we need every—"

"It would demoralize our men to have to kill their own people, War Chief. Do as I say."

He bowed stiffly. "Of course."

Occasional screams still rose from the firs down the slope, but White Stone had no way of knowing if they were torn from his men, or from Raven warriors.

Hunter trotted back up the slope and said, "My chief, I have looked into the eyes of everyone lying on this slope, alive or dead. Rain Bear is not here."

Cimmis wiped his mouth with the back of his hand. "Then who are these people? They are Raven warriors, aren't they?"

"They are Raven warriors," White Stone said. "It took me a few moments, but I recognized the man who attacked me. He was the war chief of Shell Maiden village."

Cimmis seemed to be considering that. "I may have underestimated Rain Bear."

"I hope not. He is the one man in the world I would not wish to underestimate. Especially not now when we are tired from marching all night. Our quivers are half empty, my chief. If this was some kind of diversion, it did work to weaken us."

Cimmis rubbed his chin. "Tell our warriors to pick up every spear that can be thrown, even if the point's broken. Then we'll go. We won't be safe until we're in Wasp Village."

White Stone lifted his ax and shouted, "Move through the meadow. Collect every spear!"

People ran through the grass, picking up spears, pulling stilettos from the bodies of dead warriors.

He turned, looking down the mountain's flank to where a green thumb of land protruded into Raven Bay. A faint blue haze of smoke could be seen.

Their haven still lay a hard march away.

And somewhere out there, Rain Bear and his warriors were waiting.

Sixty-one

Rain Bear sat quietly in the shadowed patch of timber that over-looked Whispering Waters Spring. Below him, he could see the grassy meadow where he fully expected Cimmis to stop for a midday rest.

To his right, Evening Star crouched over the body of Cimmis's scout. He had already been stripped, Falcon Boy donning his clothes so that he could wave the all-clear when the North Wind procession arrived at the spring. If all went according to plan, they would begin to relax, and then, as they let down their guard, Rain Bear's warriors would charge down the hill.

The advantage of surprise would be his. Cimmis's people would be tired, off their guard. The terrain here favored an attack, allowing momentum to carry his people through their lines. Better, the defend-ers would be casting uphill at rapidly moving and bobbing targets.

As soon as his people had broken the lines, Kaska's warriors would rally to their aid. If it worked as planned, within moments, Dogrib would have taken the Four Old Women. That was the key. Hold them, and all North Wind opposition would crumble.

He glanced back at the low knob above Raspberry Creek where the curious white plume of smoke had appeared. They had seen it a hand of time ago as they moved into position. It looked like someone was burning green branches to make so much smoke. Like a beacon.

But for whom? He had dispatched Sleeper and a handful of scouts to find out, fearing a flanking move by Cimmis.

"He's dead," Evening Star said as she stood. The scout's body looked pathetic and forlorn in the meadow grass. "Look at him there. Just one more young man who has lost his future. All of his Dreams are gone, Rain Bear. Within days, his flesh, too, will be stripped away. By this time next year, the grass will have grown through a few white bones. Porcupines will gnaw at his remaining ribs, and mice will build a house inside his skull."

"It's how Song Maker made the world." Rain Bear gave a shrug. "It's such a waste, but what can we do? Name a single people who don't make war, who don't raid."

She nodded. "I know, but I don't have to like it."

He glanced at the warriors who had lain down in the shade behind him. He wanted them as completely rested as they could be.

A day this warm was unusual for the middle of the winter. Just days ago snow had coated these same trees. Now the needles looked green in the bright midday sun. It felt like spring.

Evening Star cocked her head. "Did you hear that?"

"What?"

"It sounded like someone shouted in the distance."

He listened, hearing the soft sigh of the breeze through the fir branches, the melodic trill of a chickadee.

"Definitely shouting," she said, her blue eyes narrowing.

Rain Bear shrugged, wondering if age had robbed him of hearing as well as flexibility in his joints and muscles. "If there's anything to report, Talon will let us know. He and his scouts are keeping—"

"Great Chief!" Sleeper called from below. The war chief was waving for all he was worth.

Rain Bear frowned. "Curious. Stay here. I'll go down to get his report."

He started down the ridge, nodding to his warriors as they dozed, checked their weapons, and waited.

As he stepped into the sunshine, it was to see Sleeper's small party of scouts weaving through the trees, followed by what seemed to be a litter. The dress of the bearers couldn't be mistaken for anything but North Wind.

Sleeper's expression immediately set Rain Bear on edge.

"Did you find that fire?" Rain Bear asked.

"Did we ever." Sleeper's eyes were wide. "You were right. It was a signal for us. We crept up the Raspberry Creek bottom, and look what we found." He extended his arm toward the litter bearers.

Rain Bear read the awed expressions of Sleeper's warriors. These were the men who had shadowed Ecan, definitely not callow novices.

He stepped forward to meet the litter. The four young men carrying it were muscular, fit-looking. Beautifully dyed blue war shirts hung to midthigh, and each was decorated by a wealth of stone, shell, bone, and copper beads. They carried themselves well, each as alert as a hawk sailing into an eagle's territory.

Rain Bear raised a hand. "What is your purpose?"

As one, they slowed to a stop, the right-hand man asking, "Can you take us to the great chief, Rain Bear? We come in response to his promise of safe passage."

That caught him by surprise. "I am Rain Bear. If your purpose is peace, your safe passage will be honored."

The speaker smiled uneasily, and at a gesture, lowered the litter. "I am Gispaxloat. I am here on the orders of our great matron. We place ourselves under your protection, Great Chief, and invoke the honor of your oath."

"What is this?" Rain Bear stepped forward, hands raised. "I grant you my protection, but why are you here? Who's in the litter?"

Gispaxloat carefully reached over, pulling back the corner of a stunningly decorated and painted robe to reveal an old woman, eyes sunken, her mouth agape. He'd have thought her dead but for the faint rising and falling of her chest.

Gispaxloat stood stiffly at attention. "Great Chief, I present the matron of the North Wind People, Astcat. She has asked us to tell you that when her soul returns, she wishes to speak with Matron Evening Star, Soul Keeper Rides-the-Wind, and the boy Tsauz."

Wind Woman blew Evening Star's long red hair over her face. She brushed it away and stared out at the vista. From the top of the timbered ridge, she could see down the coastline and along the rugged terrain. On the distant point below them, Wasp Village could be seen. It seemed so peaceful on such an unseasonably warm day.

Movement caught her eye, and she turned to watch a man trotting down the hillside. His white hair shone like polished seashells. Glancing down the backside of the ridge, she wondered what was keeping Rain Bear. He'd been gone nearly three fingers of time.

"Is that Dogrib?" Rides-the-Wind asked and pointed with his walking stick. He sat on a rock not far from the dead scout's body.

"With blazing white hair like that? It's got to be. He's back sooner than I'd have thought."

"Perhaps they're closer than we think and he didn't need to run farther."

Dogrib trotted up and stopped. He bent, his chest rising and falling as he caught his breath. His gaze searched the people nearby before he whispered, "Where is Rain Bear?"

Evening Star said, "Sleeper returned from a scouting trip. Rain Bear went to take his report. What did you find?"

"I met our scout, Salt Boy." He gave Evening Star a suspicious look, as though not certain he should trust her with the information. "He was running down the trail as fast as he could. There was a battle up on the old burned ridge."

"I don't understand? Who was fighting?"

"The renegade chiefs who refused to support Rain Bear mounted their own attack at the spring."

Evening Star took a deep breath, expecting the worst. "And?"

Dogrib shook his head. "Salt Boy said Cimmis's warriors cut through them like an obsidian knife through hot fat. Apparently Bluegrass's faction managed to gather about six tens of warriors. They were badly outnumbered to start with and bungled the attack."

"The fools!" Rides-the-Wind spat the words and clutched Tsauz's hand more tightly.

Evening Star absently stared at the old alder leaves blowing up the trail. "Cimmis isn't anyone's fool. He'll think it was a trick, a way to make him lower his guard for the real attack."

Dogrib nodded, a new respect in his eyes. "I agree, Matron."

"What of Kaska's forces? Did Salt Boy see them?"

"He watched the battle from that point, Matron." Dogrib pointed to a hilltop north of the spring, where a thick stand of firs grew. "Salt Boy said he couldn't tell one group of warriors from another, but they all worked as one, obeying Cimmis's orders. However, when the battle was over, he's sure he saw Matron Kaska plunge her stiletto into Sand Wasp's back. Many times."

Rain Bear's familiar steps sounded behind her, but she didn't turn. "What happened then? Did Cimmis kill Kaska?"

Dogrib shook his head. "Salt Boy says no."

She tucked windblown hair behind her ears. "If he's smart he'll wait. He won't want to alienate her warriors when he might need to use them against us."

She waited while Dogrib made his report to Rain Bear.

Rain Bear stared at the ground, kicking pensively at the old leaves and duff. "Do you think there's any chance our decoy scout can just wave them in?"

"Not any more. We must choose another place," Dogrib said. "A place far enough ahead that we will have time to get into position. If we attack at dusk, close to Wasp Village, when they're utterly exhausted from running and fighting, we'll have an advantage."

"They've been hit once today; they'll be waiting for us around every bend."

Evening Star touched his arm. "Think about attacking at Gull Inlet. It's close to Wasp Village. They will be rushing to get there, thinking they are almost safe."

Rain Bear nodded; then his black brows drew together. "Red Dog said they expected our attack there."

She saw his mind wasn't on war and asked, "What is it?"

"Something unexpected has happened. I'm not sure what to do about it."

"What?"

"Matron Astcat has taken me up on my offer."

Evening Star blinked. "What offer?"

Rain Bear turned and used his chin to gesture. Evening Star frowned down the hill at the litter being carefully placed in the shade. Four blue-shirted warriors were watching carefully as Sleeper and his men kept curious warriors at bay.

"I don't . . . ," she started, then stopped. Yes, she did understand. "She didn't. She wouldn't!"

"She would and did." Rain Bear lifted his brows, silently asking her what he was supposed to do now.

Evening Star looked at the litter again. "Is she all right?"

"She's alive. But her soul is gone."

Dogrib said, "What are you speaking about?"

"See that new litter?" Rain Bear asked.

"Yes."

"That's Matron Astcat."

Dogrib looked like he'd been bludgeoned. *"What?"*

Rides-the-Wind stepped forward, and his gray beard flapped in the wind. "Great Chief, Astcat has placed a strand of Power in your hand. How will you pull it?"

Rain Bear made a calming gesture with his hands. "I just need some time to think."

Evening Star's gaze drifted down the coastline, noting every unusual rock formation and the way the surf curled against the cliffs. "Well, you had better think fast. With each step, the North Wind People are closing the distance to Wasp Village. Once they are behind that palisade, you won't be able to strike at them."

"And you are now responsible for the great matron's welfare," Rides-the-Wind reminded. "If anything should happen to her all of your hopes will be dashed like a clamshell on the rocks."

Rain Bear stepped out of the trees to stare down at the distant Wasp Village. "I am very aware of that, Elder."

Evening Star watched him stroke his chin, a reservation behind his dark eyes. He stood so deeply lost in thought that he might have been stone.

He stiffened as if struck, a light behind his eyes. He glanced at Evening Star, then at the Soul Keeper. "Having the matron complicates things, but I think I know how to do this. If we are to succeed, I need your help. And you, Dogrib, can you carry out a particularly dangerous task?"

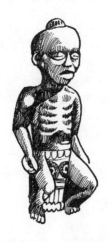

Sixty-two

Rides-the-Wind held Tsauz's hand and looked over the side of the trail to the surf below. Mother Ocean raged beside them, throwing water at the passing people as though to wash humans from the face of the world. In the distance, Thunderbirds hunted a dark wall of Cloud People, flashing and soaring. If he concentrated he could hear the deep boom of thunder on Wind Woman's breath.

Immediately to the south, Gull Inlet cut a wide notch in the cliffs. The trail split just before the inlet. One branch ran up over the cliffs, then followed the ridge where it jutted out into Raven Bay. The other branch, which Rain Bear's warriors currently followed, ran parallel to the ridge.

If Rain Bear's audacious plan worked, Rides-the-Wind could see a way out of their current dilemma. So much depended on timing and Rain Bear's control of his warriors in battle. Even more depended on Evening Star's courage, and Matron Astcat's condition. May the gods help them if her soul returned too soon. If the North Wind lines held and Rain Bear's warriors fled the wrong way, they'd end up cut off from retreat and would be driven into Gull Inlet. He could imagine tens of people fleeing into the surf, trying to swim through the rough swells. Many would drown.

Astcat's four litter-bearers seemed tireless as they bore the great matron onward. In fact, their pace only seemed slowed by Rides-the-

Wind and Tsauz. His old bones were hobbling along as fast as they could go, but already he was tired, fearful of his heart where it hammered so hard against his ancient ribs.

They had one hand of time, maybe.

"Soul Keeper?" Evening Star called just above a whisper.

He turned. "Yes?"

"I have a little dried fish left in my pack, and Tsauz has some dried seaweed. It's not much, but anything will help keep your strength up."

"Your kindness is appreciated." Rides-the-Wind was freezing and hungry. "Pull the yellow bag from my pack and we can chew the last of the pemmican as we go."

"Yes, Elder."

As Evening Star reached to fish around in Rides-the-Wind's pack, she almost pulled him off balance. She handed sections to him, Tsauz, and the litter bearers. They all ate as they walked.

"Is she all right, Elder?" Evening Star indicated the litter.

"I think she's alive, though I can't prove it."

Tsauz bent around to peer blindly at Rides-the-Wind. Worry tightened his young face. "But she's breathing, isn't she?"

"Not that I can tell, but that may mean nothing. Several times in the past six tens of summers I have sat beside people who did not seem to be alive. They did not breathe. They had no heartbeat. Yet, two or three days later, they awakened and smiled at me." He stared at Astcat, catching glimpses of her face. Damp locks of hair spread across her blankets like a dark gray halo.

"She'll get well, Elder. I know it." Tsauz seemed so sure of himself.

"I pray you're right."

Tsauz was genuinely concerned. He could see it in the boy's eyes and the worried set of his mouth. "Was the matron kind to you?"

"Oh, yes. After Mother's death she used to speak to me when no one else would. I think people were frightened by my blindness, but Matron Astcat treated me just the same as she had before Mother's death."

"She has guided her people well."

"She tried to, but when her soul started to fly away, things changed."

Evening Star's delicate brows lowered. "How so?"

"Father said the Council of Elders had become like a boat without a paddler. There was no one to tell it which way it should go. It just seemed to flounder without her. Then Old Woman North decided to make the decisions."

"And we all know what that led us to," Evening Star said darkly.

Tsauz nodded. "We only started attacking the Raven People after Matron Astcat's soul left her body."

It surprised Rides-the-Wind that the boy knew what a bad decision that had been. He hadn't gotten that from his father, since Ecan seemed to thrive on murdering Raven People.

In a barely audible voice, Tsauz said, "I want to marry her, Elder. I *have* to."

Evening Star turned. "What will you do if you become chief, Tsauz?"

He wiped his nose on his sleeve. "Stop the war. Then I—I'll free all the Raven People slaves. I have to. I've seen it."

"Seen it?" Rides the Wind frowned. "You mean in a Dream? Thunderbird showed it to you?"

Tsauz's blind eyes seemed to be drifting over the white-crested waves that tormented Mother Ocean just below their trail. "No, this is a Dream I had the night I went blind. Mother was . . . was dead, and Red Dog left me sitting alone on a hillside with the people who'd been hurt in the fire. They all died, of course; and I was scared. I tried to climb off the rock and fell and hit my arm." He wet his lips. "Father later said that once I got used to being safe again, I'd stop having the Dream, but it's never gone away."

"What happens in the Dream, Tsauz?"

Tsauz looked nervous, his feet feeling for the trail as he held Rides-the-Wind's arm. "After I have made peace with the Raven People I'm swimming in a lake of blood trying to save a baby boy who's drowning, and there are strange feathered Spirits—"

"Ah," Rides-the-Wind said in a soft voice. "I know that Dream."

Tsauz jerked his head around, almost falling. "You do?"

"Oh, yes. As a matter of fact, I've never known a Dreamer who hasn't had that Dream at least once in his life. The greatest Dreamers have it many times."

"But why, Elder? What does it mean?"

Rides-the-Wind gestured uncertainly. "I think it's a warning. Something far in the future, I fear."

As though trying to memorize it, Tsauz whispered, "A bloody boy far in the future."

As they wound down the mountain trail through the leafless alder groves, Ecan gradually dropped to the rear of the procession to walk beside Pitch. No one seemed to notice. Almost everyone had shifted positions after the battle. Cimmis now walked in front, beside Dzoo. Kaska's warriors followed them; then came the three concentric circles of warriors around the Four Old Women. Kaska's litter was the last in line as they descended the steep trail, and she had new litter bearers—Cimmis's warriors. Cimmis had effectively separated her from her people.

She had to know that upon arrival at Wasp Village, they would separate her permanently.

With Sand Wasp dead, her warriors were like a headless serpent, writhing about aimlessly. Ecan had heard two disheartened men whisper that they should just go back to Salmon Village and live out their lives without a matron.

Pitch walked two paces to Ecan's left, the Singer's narrow face a stoic mask, his gaze trying to keep track of Dzoo way up at the front.

Ecan shifted to watch her through the weave of people. Ahead, the gray cliffs of Gull Inlet scooped out the coastline. Her eyes seemed to be on the wind-twisted firs that crowded the rim.

Is that where Rain Bear has set up his ambush?

The trail made a wide curve around a thicket of head-high alder saplings. Ecan saw Cimmis gesture, and two warriors sprinted to the thicket and began thrashing it with their spears, trying to flush any enemy warriors who might be hiding there.

Cimmis was saying something to Dzoo.

When her soft laughter echoed in return, the entire procession backed away.

Ecan narrowed his eyes. *Coyote will kill him after we arrive at Wasp Village. And if Dzoo is right, I have to kill Coyote as soon after as possible.*

He shot a glance back at Kaska where she rode the litter. He was going to need a great matron. His first attempt to whip Evening Star into submission hadn't gone so well. Would he have better luck with Kaska? Would she be willing to divorce her husband and marry him, say, if he were to save her life and the life of her daughter?

Coyote. How do I kill Coyote?

Gods, he didn't even know who the man was!

Sixty-three

At the call from the guards at the main gate, War Chief Tsak left his son in charge of the final inspection of the lodges. In all of his years in Wasp Village, this was the most upsetting of times. He kept glancing up at the sun as he walked across the plaza toward the main gate. They couldn't already be arriving, could they?

No, he needn't look at the sun; all he had to do was see his lengthening shadow to know that by the time the sun set, he would no longer be the war chief of Wasp Village. He might indeed serve his matron, but his authority would be subject to White Stone's approval.

Dwelling on the notion wasn't something that made Tsak overly fond of the coming commotion. He would be courteous and respectful, of course, and greet the Council and Cimmis with the homage due them, but inside, part of him would be dying.

As he walked, he took in the new lodges with a sidelong glance. Where Wasp Village had once been airy and spacious, it now resembled an overstuffed hive. In every open spot, the slaves had built new lodges, most of them larger and more imposing than those of the original inhabitants.

"Maybe it won't be so bad," he muttered under his breath. He was lying to himself, of course. He had known White Stone for years. They had a mutual respect for each other's abilities, and a formal relationship that had never been strained by long and intimate association.

"No," he corrected, "this is going to be a disaster."

Down in the depths of his soul, he wondered if Rain Bear needed any volunteers. The thought tickled the rude and obnoxious part of him that he had spent most of his life trying to keep under firm control. He just couldn't help it—that little voice inside was always making fun, or mouthing off in the most disrespectful way. People often saw a wry smile on his lips and wondered why.

He approached the eastern gate, where the two guards stood looking up-country, their spears resting butt down on the ground.

"What is it?" Tsak asked as he stepped between them and stared up the main trail past the slave village. The ridge was open for two spear casts before a stand of fir and spruce masked the trail. There, in full view, he could see a litter being borne by four blue-shirted warriors. Behind them came a small knot of people: a woman, an old man and child, and a ratty looking—but heavily armed—party of perhaps five tens of warriors walking five abreast.

As word of their arrival spread through the slave village, Raven People trooped out in the muted afternoon sunlight to watch.

With a sinking sensation, Tsak looked down to see his shadow gone. A quick glance over his shoulder showed that a dark cloud had obscured the sun. Gods, the weather had been too good to be true. By nightfall, it would be raining again.

Turning his attention back to the approaching party, he steeled himself and walked out the gate, motioning his guards to accompany him. His heart beat like a sodden drum. Who were these people? The four leading warriors were certainly Cimmis's: They wore blue, the fabric dyed from a combination of octopus blood and larkspur petals.

He threw his head back, calling, "Who comes?"

"The great matron, Astcat, and her party," came the reply from one of the blue-clad warriors.

Tsak waited with the finality of a man doomed. As they came close, he could recognize Astcat's bearers: Gispaxloat, Kitselas, and the Raven warriors. And behind them, yes, that was Matron Evening Star, whom he had thought a fugitive; and there was the Soul Keeper, Rides-the-Wind, also supposedly with the Raven People at Sandy Point Village. The first tingling of unease grew within him. Especially as he got a good look at the hard-jawed ranks of warriors coming behind.

"Please lower the litter," he called, reaching for his war club. "I want to see Matron Astcat for myself."

Gispaxloat nodded to his companions, and they carefully eased the litter to the ground. Kitselas pulled a corner of the ornate blanket back to expose the matron's lax face.

"Her soul has fled," Rides-the-Wind said as he stepped forward.

"We would like to take Astcat to her new lodge as quickly as possible."

Tsak hesitated. "Matron Evening Star? I thought you were Outcast?"

"Enslaved," she said bitterly. "It's not quite the same thing." She tilted her head toward the litter. "The great matron has seen fit to reinstate me."

Tsak glanced at Gispaxloat, but the stern warrior betrayed nothing. "And you, Soul Keeper? Is it true that you were staying among the Raven People?"

Rides-the-Wind thrust his face uncomfortably close. "Is it true, Tsak, that you're going to keep us waiting out here answering stupid questions while the Great Astcat is in need of shelter, food, and water?"

"But these warriors?" He indicated the hard-eyed warriors who had formed a knot on the trail behind them. They looked nervous as they fingered their weapons and appraised him with wolfish eyes.

"Are the protective escort for the great matron," Evening Star said hotly. "If you're not going to allow us entry, let us know so we can tell Chief Cimmis to turn the entire procession around and send it back to Fire Village."

"He's close?"

"A hand or two behind us. Cimmis deemed it *important* to bring the great matron ahead." She crossed her arms, those imperious blue eyes narrowing.

He hesitated for a moment, some voice of warning crying out inside him. But it made sense. If Astcat was incapacitated Cimmis would want her stowed away somewhere out of sight.

"Yes, yes," he muttered. "Go on. Inside, all of you." He turned his attention to the warriors. "Who is in charge here?"

A wiry young man in a torn cloak, mud-spattered moccasins, and grimy war shirt stepped forward. "I am war chief."

"Camp your men just inside the gate. I'll figure out what to do with you later."

Gispaxloat had already raised Astcat's litter. And so it was that she, her party, and Sleeper's five tens of warriors were ushered past Wasp Village's gate, War Chief Tsak trotting at their heels.

On the ridge above Gull Inlet, Dogrib experienced fear like he had never known it. His mouth was dry, his hands damp. His skin crawled as alternately fear-sweat beaded on it or shivers traced patterns across it. He hated the runny feeling in his bowels. His jaw was clamped so hard his cheeks were spasming.

He had hidden himself and four other men in a patch of raspberries just off the Wasp Village trail. They had burrowed down into the old musty leaves, thorns scratching and burning any exposed skin. He and his warriors now waited, each locked in his thoughts as the long moments passed.

He heard them coming, talking among themselves. Then came the moment of greatest terror. The North Wind scouts jabbed halfheartedly at the brush while, huddled in the center, Dogrib and his warriors shivered.

And then they passed.

Dogrib exhaled the terrible tension from his body and grinned at his companions through a hole in the thorns.

White Stone had commanded superb discipline at the burned ridge. When he broke Bluegrass's attack, most of his warriors had stood firm, refusing to break formation. Now, everything depended on Dogrib, on his ability to break that control.

Dogrib lifted his head, wary of exposing his white hair. Through the tangle, he could see Great Chief Cimmis walking beside Dzoo and White Stone. In that moment, he saw what fate had granted him. *Cimmis* . . .

His heart hammering like thunder, he wet his lips. *Let them come closer.*

Wait. Just wait. That's it.

Then, as they were almost even, he rose, shouting, *"Now!"*

He cast, putting all of his body behind the atlatl as it catapulted his finest spear. The missile flew true, as if drawn toward Cimmis's heart . . .

White Stone was caught completely by surprise. With one arm he shoved Cimmis, and slapped out with his other, touching the shaft, deflecting it at the last instant. It was enough. The spear meant for Cimmis's heart drove deeply into the bone of the old man's hip.

At the same time, Dogrib's other warriors had cast. He had no time to see the results. He shouted, *"Run!"*

They thrashed their way out of the raspberry patch, ripping their skin, tearing their war shirts. Feet beat the ground behind him as they raced toward escape. He heard screams, curses, and then the most glorious sound: White Stone bellowing, *"After them!"*

It was working! A quick glance over his shoulder showed warriors pounding in pursuit. A spear thudded into the ground ahead of him, the shaft vibrating with the force.

He leaped a fallen log and hurtled down the steep hillside almost out of control. He couldn't have stopped if he'd wanted to. His only hope was to guide his headlong flight around obstacles—like boulders—that might kill him. Another spear hissed past him to shatter on an angular basalt boulder.

"It's Dogrib! Get him! Run faster!" an enemy warrior called.

Over his shoulder, Dogrib shouted, "Eat maggots and die, you worms!"

Two more spears came close enough that he could feel the wind of their passing. He shot through a small hollow surrounded by trees and headed straight for an opening in the far side.

"Oh, my Ancestors, please help me!"

Just when Dogrib was certain he was dead, he heard Rain Bear shout:

"Hold . . . hold! *Cast!*"

Spears glittered as they shot from the trees ten paces ahead and to either side. Dogrib dove for the ground, hit, and rolled, the wind knocked out of him. In a retching agony, he covered his head. The sound of the spears cutting through the air above him was like tens of falcon wings hissing by. When they'd flown over, he jerked around to look.

The spears arced into the midst of the enemy warriors. Every man in the front row shrieked, tumbled as if broken, and fell writhing to the ground. Some jerked futilely at the spears embedded in their flesh. Others stared in disbelief, mouths open in horror. Others whimpered with pain and fear.

The remaining warriors rushed onward, coming ever closer. Dogrib figured that if he stood, he'd look like a mouse who'd roused a porcupine.

"Hallowed Ancestors," he whispered, "let me live through this and I promise I'll never—"

"*Cast!*" Rain Bear shouted.

Another volley hissed angrily through the air barely ten hands over Dogrib's head. He tried to curl into an invisible ball in the grass.

The screaming grew louder. A man fell on top of him. Dogrib stared into the fellow's wide, panicked eyes. The spear had taken him through the heart, but his body didn't know it yet. The man struggled to rise, a horrible sucking sound coming from his impaled chest.

Dogrib looked past him to see another two tens of warriors racing down the hill, straight into Rain Bear's trap.

When the few surviving North Wind warriors turned and ran, a great roar went up.

Dogrib held his breath, waiting.

Then he heard it. On the hill above him, White Stone ordered more warriors down the hill. Their distinctive North Wind war whoops ululated as they ran.

"Come on!" Rain Bear cried and burst from cover. "Keep them running!" He pointed to the fleeing North Wind warriors.

Dogrib watched his fellows rush from the trees, screaming their war yell—a sound like the hoarse throaty caws of a flock of ravens.

Within moments, the ululations and caws mixed with the whistling of spears to form a terrifying sound that resembled an avalanche tumbling downhill.

Dogrib froze until the last of the Raven warriors dashed by him; then he rose. His four warriors poked their heads up, wide-eyed as they gasped desperately for breath. He could see the amazement in their expressions. Like him, they were stunned to be alive.

Dogrib began to laugh. Starved for breath, surrounded by maimed and dying men, peal after mad peal of laughter shook him.

His men took it up. Together they laughed with the intensity of the insane.

Sixty-four

Pain was an old companion. Cimmis ground out a cry as Deer Killer tried to pull the slim spear from his hip.

"The stone tip is lodged in the bone, Great Chief." Deer Killer looked as if he was going to throw up.

Cimmis blinked, his vision sliding in and out. He couldn't seem to catch his breath. "Just pull it out! You, Hunter, grab on to that shaft and yank!"

They both grasped the polished wood, looked at each other, and pulled. The scream tore out of his throat, deafening even to him.

He felt his body jerked, and then both Deer Killer and Hunter tumbled backward, the slim shaft clutched in their hands.

"Quick, you fools! Take my cloak. Wad it up. Use my belt to bind it over the wound to stop the bleeding."

By Gutginsa's balls, where was a Healer? He considered calling Dzoo for a moment, and decided against it. She might take the opportunity to finish the job that three-times-accursed Dogrib had started.

"Great Chief?" Deer Killer asked, his voice tight with fear.

"What?"

The warrior held up the spear as Hunter attended to his wounded hip. "The point, Great Chief. I think it's still inside. The binding gave way."

Cimmis blinked, staring at the end of the spear. Although blood-soaked, he could see the broken sinew that had once held a keen stone point. "Men have lived with points in them before."

He almost bit his tongue as Hunter pulled the makeshift bandage tight. Gasping and sweating, he asked, "How is the fighting going?"

Deer Killer turned his attention from the spear to the fighting below. "Our warriors are after them. I think it was just a small party."

"Yes, well, there will be a larger one waiting. Call up Kaska's warriors and be ready for a counterattack. If I know Rain Bear, this won't be as easy as it was at the burned ridge."

Rain Bear led his forces to meet the howling North Wind warriors, leaping brush and deadfall, bursting through the tall grass. The spears of the enemy glinted like tens of membranous wings.

When they were within thirty paces, the voices of his men rose to a roar. Spears whistled by as his warriors cried out with the thrill of battle or shrieked in pain. He saw gaps in his line after the North Wind warriors cast their first volley—but he kept going, leading his men headlong into the North Wind warriors. They met with a clattering of spears, wild shouts, screams, and howls.

A tall North Wind warrior headed straight for Rain Bear, his mouth wide open in a scream of rage.

Rain Bear drove a spear through his chest. All around him men clashed in a snarling, grunting chaos.

He waded into a tangle of North Wind warriors and brought his club down hard on a man's head. The warrior fell like a limp strand of sea grass.

"Rain Bear!" Wet Fern shouted. "Behind you!"

He leaped sideways as a club smashed into his left shoulder. Pain staggered him, and the North Wind warrior whooped in victory as he lifted his club to finish the job. Rain Bear ducked the blow meant for his head and broke his attacker's ribs. The man's breath shot from his lungs in a loud *whoosh.*

Rain Bear's next blow took him squarely in the chest. Amid the screaming and shouting, he barely heard the man's breastbone crack.

The familiar odor of battle permeated the air: a powerful mixture of sweat and the coppery tangs of blood and torn intestines.

Rain Bear pushed himself up the hill. He could see White Stone.

The war chief stood like a sun-bronzed statue, his face stern as he shouted orders. Dzoo was poised slightly behind him, her long red hair blowing around the dark frame of her hood. Where was Pitch? Ecan?

And in that instant, the North Wind line broke, went tumbling back. Warriors dropped their weapons to flee up the hill. Rain Bear shouted in triumph, knowing that this single greatest victory would have to be surrendered.

"We can take them!" Talon bellowed as he smacked his war club into the back of a fleeing man's spine. The warrior staggered. Before he could fall, Talon split his skull.

"No!" Rain Bear cried. "Follow the plan! You *must* follow the plan!"

He might have been a whisper in a gale. His warriors went charging past him, heading up the hill.

"No! Do not do this! You are making the same mistake Bluegrass did!"

"Bluegrass led cowards!" Three Shells bellowed in reply as he charged headlong up the hill. Rain Bear watched as Three Shells ran down a straggler, beating the man's head in with a stroke of his club. "For War Gods Village!"

"For War Gods Village!" The cry was picked up by the charging warriors.

On the ridgetop War Chief White Stone separated from the group of warriors that surrounded the Four Old Women and strode forward, shouting orders.

"Back!" Rain Bear shouted after his warriors. "Come back! Follow the plan!"

A few of the Sandy Point warriors glanced at White Stone, longing in their eyes, but instinctively moved closer to Rain Bear.

The others rushed past, their excitement a living thing. He could feel it creeping through his own blood like tiny worms. Every fiber in his being cried to follow, to take the fight to Cimmis.

"Hold!" he ordered his remaining warriors. "We've got to prepare. They've got their blood up now, but they'll be headed back soon."

"But great chief!" one of the warriors cried. "If we don't support them, they'll be killed."

He stomped toward the men, anger building. "Yes! They will, unless we devise a plan to save them!" He thrust out his club. "You and you, into that patch of brush. Robin, I want you and others to take cover in that patch of fir trees." He searched their frantic eyes, knowing he was about to lose them to the fever of combat. Imploring, he asked, *"Do you remember the plan?"*

It was Bark Hare who said, "Yes, Great Chief. I do." He looked at the others. "Gods, yes. It's up to us. We've got to lay the ambush."

"That's it." Rain Bear slapped his shoulder. "Hurry. We don't have that much time. Gather as many spears as you can. We're going to need them."

He quickly placed his warriors, judging which route his absent warriors would take when they fled the fight. Looking down the hill, he could see where Dogrib should be, the war chief still assuming that the plan was working.

"When we go, you run there!" Rain Bear pointed to the gap in the rocks. "After we pass, we set up another ambush. Remember how it works?"

The craziness of battle had been replaced with a rabid excitement. He'd held them.

Even as he laid his trap, the first of the Raven warriors, a man streaming blood from a head wound, came pelting past. He was but the first of a flood.

Up on the ridge, Rain Bear knew that White Stone had called in his reinforcements. Kaska's warriors would have joined the fight.

Now warriors fled in absolute panic past Rain Bear's position. As the first of the North Wind warriors came whooping down in pursuit, Rain Bear stood, signaling his warriors. Each picked a target and cast.

Rain Bear turned and ran for all he was worth.

A flood of warriors rolled down the hill with him. "The gap!" he called, pointing. "Make for the gap!"

He shot a quick glance over his shoulder. The North Wind warriors were close, but some slowed as they stopped to kill a straggler.

"My warriors!" he screamed against his tearing lungs. "Stay with me! Stay close and don't lose your weapons!"

He led the way through the gap, followed by wheezing and gasping men. As he passed the rocks, he could see Dogrib, a spear balanced in his hand. Yes, blessed gods, Dogrib was where he should be.

Past the rocks, Rain Bear pointed to the stony outcrop below. "There! We'll set the next ambush there!"

Lungs laboring, he scrambled up into the rocks in time to look back. Screams erupted from the gap as Dogrib and his men stood, bodies twisting as they speared the first pursuing North Wind warriors.

Then Dogrib and his three remaining companions turned and ran for all they were worth, headed straight past Rain Bear's outcrop.

The race would be long, fraught with danger, and if he failed to cross the finish line ahead of Cimmis, a great many people were going to die.

Sixty-five

Tsauz sat beside Matron Astcat and listened to her labored breathing. She hadn't moved at all since they'd arrived in the spacious new lodge in Wasp Village. The place smelled of sappy wood, green bark, and freshly cut vines. Packs had been placed along the walls, and a row of magnificent shields stood across from him. He had run his fingers over them, learning their size and shape. On one, the figure of Killer Whale had been created out of round beads.

Longing tingled in his chest. He needed to speak with her, to ask her advice.

"Just fill Matron Astcat's bowl with broth," Evening Star had said. "No meat." Then she had gone back outside to ensure that the prisoners were safely locked away and guarded. War Chief Tsak's shouts of rage and disbelief as he was marched off at spear point still echoed in Tsauz's ears.

Tsauz lifted his pointed chin, and the cold ocean breeze tousled his shoulder-length black hair. The rich scent of fish soup made his empty stomach growl, but he was saving it for Astcat.

A flash.

Tsauz tilted his head and stared toward what he assumed to be Mother Ocean. The roar of her voice grew louder, and tiny fleeting spots of brightness lit up the dark curtain behind his eyes.

"What's the matter, Tsauz?" Rides-the-Wind asked as he entered the lodge.

"Are—are the Thunderbirds coming?" Fear stung his veins.

"Yes. Why?"

He swallowed hard. "I see them."

"See who?"

"Their flashes are bouncing around behind my eyes."

Rides-the-Wind tucked a bowl into Tsauz's hands and grunted as he sat down. "Eat, Tsauz. If Thunderbird is coming for you, you'll need to have a full stomach."

Tsauz felt for his horn spoon and tasted the soup. The flavors of the fish and venison pemmican created a mouth-watering combination.

Rides-the-Wind slid across the sand, and the matron's blankets rustled.

Around a mouthful of pemmican, Tsauz asked, "What are you doing, Elder? May I help?"

"No, you just eat. I'm arranging the matron's head on my lap so that I can try to feed her."

After a few instants Rides-the-Wind said, "Matron Astcat, I'm going to put a few drops of broth in your mouth."

Tsauz heard Rides-the-Wind stir the broth—the spoon raked the sides of the wooden bowl—then Rides-the-Wind said, "That's good. See if you can swallow a little more."

"Is she eating?" Tsauz asked hopefully and touched her soft cheek.

"She's taken two swallows so far. I'm slowly trickling another spoonful into her open mouth."

Tsauz heard her swallow this time; it sounded difficult, as though she might be on the verge of choking.

"I'll just pat her hair, Elder," he said, and drew his hand away from her wrinkled cheek. When he started stroking her hair, she gasped suddenly and coughed with such violence he jumped back.

"What's happening?" he cried. "Is she choking?"

She drew in a sharp breath.

Rides-the-Wind's voice went so gentle Tsauz almost didn't recognize it. "Matron? Can you hear me?"

"I . . . I hear you . . . Holy Hermit."

Tsauz's eyes jerked wide at the hoarse sound of her voice.

"Please, lie still. Don't move too quickly. Your soul just came home. We want it to stay."

"How . . . long?"

"Have you been gone? I don't know, Matron. Your warriors brought you to us for safekeeping. But I think you've been away for at least a day."

She took several deep breaths, as though enjoying the feel of air moving in her lungs. "R-Rides-the-Wind," she asked in a pitifully small voice, "do you have any . . . willow bark tea? It seems to help fasten my soul down."

"I do, Matron. Let me get it from my pack."

Rides-the-Wind rose, and his pack rustled.

"Matron, are you all right?" Tsauz asked, and edged as close to her as he could.

She took several breaths before she said, "I always feel confused, empty, for a time after I return. But I think I'm all right."

He could feel her staring at him as she asked, "Did you fly very high on Thunderbird's back?"

"All the way to the Star People, Matron."

"I do not understand this."

Tears welled in his eyes. "I don't understand it either, Matron. I just know that you need me."

She let out a breath, and her hand crept out and found his. "I saw you in a Dream, boy. You were standing, tall and bloody. You had stones for eyes."

"Will you marry me?"

"Your mother was one of the Raven People."

Tsauz blinked. Bolts of lightning shot around behind his eyes again, flashing so brightly they hurt. "Thunderbird . . . Thunderbird said that Father murdered her because she was Raven." He winced. "I asked Rides-the-Wind if Spirit Helpers ever lied."

"In that case, no." She seemed sad. "Red Dog told me about it."

"Why would Father do that? He loved her."

She said nothing, but he could feel a sad anger brewing within her. When he looked her way, he could see a glow behind his eyes.

Frightened, he said, "Does that mean you don't want to marry me? Because of my Raven blood?"

She squeezed his hand with no more strength than a sparrow. "Quite the contrary. Power is all around us. And in the end, you can't fight Power."

"No," Rides-the-Wind whispered from the side.

"Poor Cimmis. Oh, gods, this is going to hurt him."

"There is no way out of this that isn't painful, Matron," Rides-the-Wind said. "Not for you, or for Cimmis. Each of you must make choices. Power will be the judge."

"Very well." The matron's fingers felt icy in Tsauz's grip. She swallowed and said, "Do you give me your oath . . . that you will be a good and faithful chief? That you will always put the good of both peoples before your own happiness?"

Tsauz's throat constricted. "Yes, Matron. I will try very hard to be a good chief."

"Then I think perhaps I will take you as my husband."

Tsauz wet his lips nervously. He'd heard her say those words before, when he'd been riding Thunderbird's back, but they sounded different, kinder, coming from her own lips. "Thank you, Matron."

Dzoo crouched over a dying warrior, placing a finger on his neck to feel the pulse weakening. As she did so, she slipped an obsidian knife from his belt and tucked it into her legging. When she straightened, it was to see the Four Old Women staring bug-eyed at Cimmis where he was being placed on a litter by Deer Killer and Hunter. Blood smeared the bindings on his hip, scarlet in the slanting light.

Dzoo looked just in time to see the last of Rain Bear's warriors break. Even as they turned and fled, they were being run down. As with the dying warrior, she could do nothing for them. Idly she turned her attention to the brown stand of cattails that filled a hollow to the south of the trail. The dry stalks were head-high, winter-brittle, and rattly.

Cimmis had ordered Kaska's warriors forward, but for the moment White Stone was keeping them out of the battle. They didn't look happy about it. Many grumbled and stamped their feet, eager to be in the fight.

She could see Ecan leading Pitch down the slope to stand at the head of the party. Presumably so the Raven warriors would see him. Hunter and Deer Killer had taken positions on either side of Cimmis's litter. Her own guard, Wind Scorpion, had disappeared. She looked again at the cattails. Threads of dark Power filtered through the stalks like a malignant mist.

"Of course we're winning!" Old Woman North shouted gleefully from her litter. "It will only be a matter of moments before we push the Raven People into the sea!"

Old Woman South lifted her wrinkled chin and said, "Good riddance. The Raven People have always been thieves and maggots."

Chuckles burst from the others, and Dzoo's heart went cold.

Old Woman North called, "Warriors! Prepare to move. We are going closer to get a better view."

"But, Elder!" one of the guards objected. "The battle could shift! You should remain here where it's safe."

"I said we're moving lower on the mountain! Accompany us!"

Dzoo's attention fixed on Cimmis. She had seen the warriors pull the spear from his hip, but how badly was he wounded? He was propped in his litter, calling orders, using his shriveled arm to point this way and that.

She glanced at the cattails. *Yes, it is time, my stalker. The final Dance has begun.*

She glanced out at the storm brewing over Raven Bay. Sunlight outlined the tall bank of clouds in a halo of gold. She waited for another crack of lightning. In the rolling growl that followed, she stepped into the cattails.

A cheer went up when Cimmis's forces charged after Rain Bear's fleeing warriors. With that as cover, she made another step. And then another.

She sniffed: The dank odor of cattails barely masked the mossy scent she had come to associate with him.

Step by step she made her way through the stalks and leaves. With a careful hand she parted the dry plants, looked around, and was in the process of taking another step when a shape rose from one side. She started to turn as the whistling club slashed through the cattails and blasted lightning behind her eyes.

As she fell, she heard the Thunderbirds booming in defiance. *Yes, Coyote. How clever you are. Ever the patient one . . .*

Sixty-six

Despite the pain Cimmis smiled to himself as his litter swayed. A runner had arrived with word that the great matron was waiting in Wasp Village. A weight, like a huge stone, had lifted from Cimmis's chest. He still didn't know why she had gone on ahead, but by Old Woman Above, she was safe.

From his perch atop his swaying litter, he watched as the remains of his party wound through the last stand of firs and into the clearing. In the growing dusk, he could see the welcoming palisade of Wasp Village just ahead. The gates were open, warriors standing at them, spears in hand.

It was over. They had made it. Though White Stone had only made a quick count, it seemed that some seven tens of warriors were missing after their final fight with Rain Bear. But given the extent of the rout, most of them would come trickling in through the night, jesting and waving trophies taken from the dead.

As he studied the meadow before Wasp Village an idea came to him. "White Stone?"

His war chief dropped back to walk beside the litter. "Yes, Great Chief?"

"I'm thinking about setting a row of poles on either side of the trail here. Tomorrow, I want you to send a party of warriors out to cut the heads off the dead Raven warriors. We'll stick a head atop each of the poles. It should create quite the stir among the Raven villages, don't you think?"

White Stone gave him a sober look, and asked, "Are you all right, my Chief?"

"A little dizzy."

White Stone shot a speculative look at the slave village just to the north of the village gates. "It might not be such a bad idea after all."

Cimmis smiled as White Stone trotted back to his advance guard.

Behind him, the Four Old Women chattered like ruffed grouse in spring. The young Singer, Pitch, marched with his head down, a dazed look in his eyes. Yes, well, his head could join the others.

Dzoo, perhaps to no one's surprise, was missing. Slipped away like smoke.

Let her enjoy it. In the end, I'll send Coyote to bring her back.

Ecan walked like a man in a trance, his eyes slightly out of focus. The expression on his face was that of a man who had unexpectedly rounded a forest turn and found himself eye to eye with a spring-starved grizzly.

Cimmis blinked, dizzy again. He took a deep breath, feeling oddly light-headed. Touching a hand to his wadded cloak, he found it saturated with blood.

"Set me down. Starwatcher! Bring me your cloak." As great chief, he wasn't going to make his grand entry dripping blood like a beheaded rabbit. Besides, the time had come to put Ecan in his place.

The warriors lowered him gently to the ground. Ecan stepped over, eyes dull. He hardly seemed aware as he slipped off his snowy cloak and handed it to Deer Killer.

Cimmis winced as Hunter and Deer Killer untied his belt. Swiftly, efficiently, they wadded Ecan's white cloak and bound it tightly to keep pressure on the wound.

When they were finished, Cimmis beckoned. "Ecan, a word please." He placed a hand on the Starwatcher's shoulder when the man bent over him. "Well, we are here. The Raven People have taken not one but two defeats, and we have flushed all of our adversaries."

"We have indeed," Ecan agreed despite the distance in his eyes. "I assume that I can bargain for the return of my son now."

"Bargain?" Cimmis smiled in a fatherly way. "I don't think you have the talent for it. You're not good at making deals with people. You don't seem capable of reading their true souls." He shrugged. "The way I heard it, you'd bargain away your future for a sack of stone trinkets."

The color drained from Ecan's face.

If he placed Ecan's head on the first pole outside the gate, he wouldn't have to walk so far to see it. Better, he could place a wager with White Stone as to how long it would take for the flesh to melt away from the bones.

But who should I appoint as the new Starwatcher?

When Ecan stumbled back, the strength seemed gone from his legs. Cimmis chuckled and shot a glance behind him. The silly old women were preening in their litters, arranging their jewelry.

Four paces in front, White Stone was staring pensively at the distant Wasp Village gate, as if worried. Cimmis squinted at the clouds blowing in from the west. What did White Stone have to worry about? It wasn't like the storm was going to catch them out in the open.

"Yes, War Chief?" Cimmis gestured toward the gate.

"Nothing, Great Chief, just a feeling. As if something terrible is about to happen." He smiled. "Are you comfortable?"

"Oh, quite. Everything is finally in place."

Y*ou are a dead man!"* Dzoo's words echoed inside Ecan's hollow soul. So, too, was his son. He'd seen that in Cimmis's eyes. No matter what happened, the boy was going to die.

Without his cloak, Ecan felt the chill as he stepped away from Cimmis's litter. The great chief was talking light-headedly with White Stone while the Four Old Women attended to their appearances. The rest of the remaining warriors lounged and chatted about the battles, their talk filled with animation. The threat was vanquished, and the time for bragging had arrived.

"You'd bargain away your future for a sack of stone trinkets." Coyote had betrayed him.

Ecan threw his head back and looked up at the dark clouds rolling down upon them from the sea. Lightning flashed. Distant thunder rolled.

It would come in the night, silently, without warning. The next morning someone would go to wake the tardy Starwatcher—only to find Ecan's mutilated body lying in his blood-soaked bedding.

How did it come to this?

He felt at his belt, but had no weapon. He turned, seeing Kaska, surrounded by her guards.

Is that how I want to go? But perhaps there was still a way to save his son and perhaps save himself.

No weapon.

He crouched, cupped his hands around an angular piece of basalt, and lifted. The stone loosened in the damp soil, then peeled free.

Ecan lifted, savoring the head-sized stone's weight. He turned, took two steps, and raised the heavy rock high.

"For my boy," he said softly.

Cimmis had just looked up, his eyes going wide. Ecan slammed the stone squarely onto the great chief's chest.

He heard the thump, the cracking of ribs, the gush of air blown from the old man's throat. The expression of shock and surprise gave way to a rasping gasp as Cimmis struggled for a breath.

It took a moment of stunned disbelief before Ecan realized what he'd done. He was still staring into Cimmis's eyes when a voice whispered, *"Run"*

Ecan leaped Cimmis's litter, pelting full tilt through the following warriors, shoving slaves out of his way as he raced for the screen of fir trees. It was a blind flight, spurred by panic. He had no idea where he was going, how he was going to escape.

He had just reached the trees when White Stone's spear impaled him from behind. The force of it staggered him, and an odd tingling chill like spearmint mixed with the sharp pain.

Sixty-seven

Coyote carried Dzoo into the winter-bare alders and gently laid her on a pile of old leaves. Her long red hair, matted with sticky blood, spread across the leaves in glistening waves. She looked serenely beautiful. He touched his fingers to the side of her head, feeling to make sure the skull wasn't broken. Then he raised his fingers to his nostrils and savored the coppery scent of her blood.

He'd deliberately pulled his blow, hitting her only hard enough to temporarily cause her soul to fly. She would wake soon. She had to, because he wanted to look into her eyes when he took her.

He ran his finger down her jaw and could barely contain himself. The need within him was alive, a palpable presence that churned in his guts and bones.

He bent down and nuzzled his cheek against hers, then whispered in her ear, "Are you ready? We are together at last."

He'd waited so long for this that he feared he might rush and ruin it. But it was getting dark, and a storm was breaking. He didn't wish to do this in the dark while rain pelted their naked bodies, so he had to hurry.

He held out his shaking hands and flexed his fingers several times; then he reached down and untied the laces of her cape. When he threw it back, he saw the beautiful crimson dress she wore. The shell beads that covered the bodice winked and glimmered in the flashes of distant lightning.

She was limp as he lifted her and slid the dress from her smooth pale skin. Carefully, deliberately, and with great tenderness, he arranged her on his cloak. Rolling her dress, he made a pillow for her head, and then like an artist painting a shield, he stretched her matted hair out so that the red tresses lay like rays of sunlight on the dry leaves.

Fighting to still his trembling, he massaged her full breasts. At the touch of her smooth warm skin, an electric sensation flushed his veins. He ran his palms over the curve of her ribs, down the dip of her waist, across the bone in her hips to the flat above her pubis. His fingers traced the downy softness of her curly pubic hair. He bent down and filled his lungs with the scent of her womanhood.

He ripped off his war shirt and stared down at his stiff penis where it jutted out from below his muscular belly. Need, like a fire, burned inside him. His erection had become a tingling ache as he positioned himself between her muscular legs.

He whimpered as he lowered himself onto her. His fevered penis slipped along the inside of her thigh, and he gasped at the point of ejaculation.

You're going too fast! You've Dreamed this ten tens of times! You are supposed to savor her! Use your tongue to taste her before you—

Dzoo opened her eyes.

His face was less than a hand from hers. He was panting as he thrust his fingers into her and opened her to his manhood.

She didn't struggle, but rolled her hips back ready to receive him. Her dark luminous eyes began to drink his soul. She must have wanted him as badly as he'd wanted her.

"Are you ready?" he whispered huskily.

She was dry when he forced himself inside; her eyes widened slightly.

Gripping a handful of her red hair, he took it into his mouth. He could taste her blood; it stoked his desire even more. He sucked at her hair and thrust as hard as he could. Her legs were rising, tightening around him. He should have removed her leggings! Then it would only be her skin against his sides, across his back.

By the gods! Yes! Yes! He felt the tingling sensation building at the root of his penis. She was watching him, a gleam in her eyes, a faint parting of her lips as she anticipated the explosion of his loins.

His whole body convulsed with each jetting of his seed inside her.

From the corner of his eye, he saw her reach for her legging. Then her pale hand lifted . . .

Sixty-eight

From the platform within Wasp Village's walls, Evening Star stared in amazement as Ecan plucked a head-sized stone from the ground and crushed Cimmis's chest. She watched White Stone start at the sight, barely hesitate, and then race in pursuit of the fleeing Starwatcher. She saw the war chief's arm whip back as he sent a spear flying after Ecan. Gods! Had she just witnessed what she thought she had?

In confirmation, the North Wind party broke into shouts and began running back and forth in confusion. White Stone turned back, bellowing orders, and the litter bearers bent over Cimmis. From her vantage inside Wasp Village, Evening Star could see Cimmis's legs as he writhed and kicked in pain.

She glanced at Sleeper, himself gaping in disbelief. He asked, "Should we attack them? Even with our five tens, there could be no better time. They're disorganized, stunned."

"No." She shot a quick glance at the lodge closest to the gate. "Stick to the plan. Be patient."

He nodded, looking unsure.

She glanced back across Wasp Village. At the far end she could see ten of her warriors surrounding the two lodges where they had confined Tsak and his warriors. Here and there she could see her people prowling, swinging their axes or cradling spears as they ensured the rest of the villagers stayed put in their lodges.

She remembered the stunned look on Tsak's face as she stepped up and pressed a bone stiletto against his throat. Even as the Wasp Village warriors had begun to understand, Sleeper's warriors had surrounded them, sealing their fate. Rather than die, all but a handful had surrendered. The bodies of those who had not lay hidden under a cover of sea-grass matting.

Turning her attention back to Cimmis, she could have predicted what happened next. His warriors packed him up on the litter and charged for the gate. As they neared, they cried, "Make way! Make way for the great chief! He's wounded. We need help!"

Sleeper climbed nimbly down the palisade, dropping to the ground. "Let him in! And then let the Four Old Women in. After that, try to close the gate with the warriors outside."

Evening Star leaped to the ground as Cimmis's litter was borne through the gate and carried to the Council Lodge. As the four bearers lowered it to the ground, she gestured, sending several of her warriors to surround them.

The four bearers looked up in astonishment as Evening Star stopped before them. "We have no wish to kill you. If you wish to save his life, you will surrender your weapons and walk peacefully to that lodge." She pointed to the large storage lodge where Tsak and his warriors waited under the vigilant noses of Dogrib's warriors.

"I say we do it," the first muttered as he took measure of the hard-eyed warriors surrounding him. The others nodded, tossing stilettos and war clubs to the ground.

As they were being led off, the Four Old Women were being ceremoniously borne through the palisade. Evening Star shot a glance over her shoulder in time to see Sleeper's men roll the gate closed in White Stone's face.

Angry shouts broke out as the North Wind war chief howled in protest.

Then Rain Bear emerged from the lodge where he'd been hiding. He shot her a smile, but looked haggard, still breathing hard from his long run. His body remained sweat-streaked and filthy. An ugly bruise had swollen and discolored his left shoulder. She watched him climb painfully up the rickety palisade. He cupped his hands and shouted, "We have Cimmis and the Council! You will disband, surrender your weapons, and leave this place!"

"Rain Bear?" White Stone cried in dismay.

"It's over. We have won."

The shout caught everyone by surprise. Not only that he could do it, but that a man with a crushed chest could muster the volume.

Cimmis shouted, *"Attack! Kill them all!"*

White Stone waved his men back, Cimmis's order ringing in his ears. Attack! His chief commanded.

"Assemble here!" He pointed to the grassy flat just out of casting range from the palisade. "I want someone to run to the forest for a log! Not a rotten one that will splinter on impact, but one that will take that gate down!"

Ten of his warriors turned on their heels and left at a run for the distant stand of firs.

White Stone paced back and forth. Everything was out of control. He shot a glance at the masking trees behind them. Ecan was hit; he was sure of it. Some part of his soul insisted that he send warriors to hunt the Starwatcher down. Sense told him he needed all of his strength here.

He studied the Wasp Village palisade again. No way around it—this was going to be a bloody affair. His people would die on the way to the gate. With Kaska's forces, he had enough warriors to storm it, but once inside? Who knew how many capable fighters Rain Bear had behind him.

Rain Bear? He was supposed to be fleeing southward around Raven Bay. How in Gutginsa's name had he gotten into Wasp Village in the first place?

Kaska stood as her guards set her litter down and went trotting up to join White Stone's assembling warriors.

She blinked in amazement. No doubt about it—that was Rain Bear's silhouette above the palisade. No one could mistake his voice as he warned White Stone not to attack.

She pushed her way forward and stormed up to the war chief. "You're not seriously thinking of attacking, are you?"

White Stone gave her a cold glare. "My chief has given me an order."

"It will be a bloodbath!"

"Then it will be a bloodbath, but those are my orders! *I have sworn to obey my chief!*"

She could see he didn't like it, but a lifetime of obedience ruled him where sense should have.

"Is this what we've made ourselves into?"

She turned, taking stock. Her warriors stood to one side, shooting uneasy glances at her, White Stone, and the Wasp Village palisade. Unlike White Stone, they certainly didn't have any illusions.

She hurried forward, fully aware that she had little time before White Stone had her either killed or silenced. She lifted her hands to the storm-filled twilight and shouted, "My warriors, listen to me! It is time for you to choose!"

Her men knew something had gone terribly wrong. They must be confused, frightened. Would they obey her?

Kaska stabbed a finger at Banded Eagle. "You are now my war chief. Prepare to lead our warriors against the people who murdered Matron Gispaw!"

Banded Eagle's eyes glowed. He whirled around and shouted, "Follow me! For the matron! Let's teach these fools a lesson they'll never forget!"

"Prepare!" Kaska shouted as she took a position beside Banded Eagle. She would live or die with her warriors.

"Kaska!" someone shouted.

"Kaska! Kaska! *Kaska!*" her warriors began to shout. She raised her arms in time to rhythm. *"Kaska! Kaska! Kaska!"*

White Stone was staring, astonishment writ large on his face. One by one his warriors began to shift behind him, some almost dancing away as they realized the seriousness of their situation.

"Come on," Kaska growled under her breath. "Give up. Can't you see? It's over."

White Stone stood rigid, his back arched. Then he sagged and made a weak gesture to his warriors, calling, "It's over. They have won."

Kaska stood tall and straight, trembling, praying, wondering if she had just saved her people, or condemned them.

Sixty-nine

From his position in the Council Lodge, Rain Bear studied Great Chief Cimmis. The North Wind chief lay under a blanket, breath wheezing in and out of his crushed chest. A double strand of rope had been tied around his hips to keep the compress over the spear wound. Firelight flickered like burnished copper on his sagging cheeks. The old man's eyes were fevered, pain-bright, but he was alert, knowing full well what was happening.

Behind him, the Four Old Women sat silent, owl-eyed, still stunned as the realization of their captivity sank in.

"What's to talk about?" Talon thrust out his arm and looked one by one at the occupants of the Council Lodge. The place was huge, but when the old women had ordered it built, they'd had no idea what its first use would be.

"Kill them," Sleeper agreed. "For the pain they have caused our people, I say that we boil them alive and leave their corpses on the beach for the gulls and crabs to pick at."

"Yes!" Goldenrod agreed.

"Death." Black Mountain slapped a hand to his thigh in agreement.

Rain Bear glanced at Evening Star and Kaska, who watched with uneasy eyes.

Rides-the-Wind eased back from where he'd been inspecting Cimmis's wound. "You may kill them most gruesomely if you wish, but I would ask you, is that the message you want to send to the rest of the North Wind People?"

"The time of the North Wind People is over," Black Mountain growled. He looked at the two matrons. "Besides, Evening Star and Kaska have served us well."

Kaska flared, "I do not serve the Raven People, Chief. My goals are not yours."

"We'll remember that," Black Mountain said darkly, "later."

Rain Bear interjected wearily, "This isn't about peoples."

"Then what is it about?" Goldenrod asked bitterly. "For years we have served the—"

"And they have served *us*!" Rain Bear thundered. "Like I said, this isn't about peoples; it's about them!" He pointed at Cimmis and the Council. "It's about the decisions they made that led to the murder of tens of tens of people, Raven and North Wind alike!" He rose painfully to his feet, glaring. "What we do here will affect everyone. Don't you understand? It's our families that we're talking about. If we choose the wrong path here today our sons and daughters will continue to kill each other until we are all so weak the Cougar People or the Buffalo People will move into our lands, and we will be *their* slaves."

"He is right," Evening Star said. "We must confine our punishment to the Council and the great chief alone." Images of her dying family flickered in the back of her mind. "Death."

"Death," the others assented.

"Life!" a sharp voice barked.

All eyes turned to see Matron Astcat standing in the doorway. She held Tsauz's hand. Carefully, she walked into the Council Lodge and braced herself. She shot a fond look at Cimmis. "Hello, my husband."

He couldn't seem to find words, but nodded a faint greeting as he labored for air.

Astcat turned, taking in the chiefs. Rain Bear felt the Power in her as their eyes met. She gave him the briefest of nods.

"Oh, yes," Astcat said wearily, "something must be done to atone for the Wolf Tails, and the raids, and the fear." She narrowed her eyes, staring at the Four Old Women. "You have ruined the Council. You have brought us to the teetering edge of destruction. Because of you, our time is done."

"You don't—" Old Woman North began.

"Quiet!" Astcat cried.

"Why shouldn't we kill them, Great Matron?" Rain Bear asked reasonably.

Astcat gave him a wary smile. "I will bargain with you, Great Chief. If you will allow me to declare them Outcast, I am prepared to divide up the North Wind clan grounds among the Raven People. We will surrender our villages to you, live among you, and teach you everything that we know. We will work beside you, gathering clams, digging roots, and fishing."

"Great Matron!" Kaska cried in dismay.

Astcat fixed her with keen eyes. "My soul has been away for a long time, Kaska. I was lost in a vision of the future, and this is how it shall be. We are losing ourselves as it is. Let us make the process as painless as possible, shall we?"

"But our traditions," Evening Star cried. "Who will keep them alive?"

"We all will." Astcat pointed to Rain Bear. "Look at the great chief! His daughter is my granddaughter. She is married to a Raven Singer." She pointed to Pitch, who watched soberly from the side. "Tsauz here is half Raven, and he will be my husband."

Talon made a hacking sound as he cleared his throat. "We can have all of your territory anyway, Matron. What if we just take it and turn the tables, enslave the North Wind People as they have enslaved us? Why should we do it your way when we can do it ours?"

Astcat's keen gaze bored into him. "That's a fair question, but the Wolf Tails are still out there, and I am the great matron. At my order, they can either disband, or you may awaken some morning to find your children headless—assuming they survive the wars. I assure you the North Wind People will fight for their lives. I offer you an opportunity to let your children grow up, War Chief. How do you want it? Easy, or hard?"

Talon had visibly paled. "You would do that? Disband the Wolf Tails?"

She nodded. "I never liked the idea anyway."

"And who would follow you?" Sleeper asked. "What if we ended up with someone like Old Woman North as great matron? Or an Ecan as great chief?"

"Evening Star will succeed me as great matron. If she hasn't earned your trust, no one can."

Rain Bear took a deep breath. "Chiefs, I think there is a great deal of wisdom in the great matron's words."

Astcat turned, her face like carved wood as she met her husband's eyes. "Cimmis, you and the Four Old Women are hereby declared Outcast! I order Matron Kaska to assign a party of her warriors to bear you across the mountains to the lands of the

Striped Dart People. There, she will leave you with any who wish to accompany you. You, and your followers, and any such descendants as they may have, may never return to our lands under pain of death."

"Why," Cimmis whispered, "my wife?"

Her voice, tight with love and pain, almost broke as she said, "It is the price of my people's survival, husband."

She turned, eyes like wounds, and hobbled slowly from the Council Lodge. Tsauz clutched tightly to her withered hand.

Ecan curled on his side. He lay screened from view by a skirt of low-hanging fir branches. Brittle fir needles prickled against his sweat-hot cheek and stuck to his skin. His breath came in fast gasps. With each inhalation, with each heartbeat, the spear sticking through his body moved.

Ecan opened his mouth, blinking against the pain and fear. His belly was on fire, burning as gut juices leaked from his torn intestines and gurgled inside him. The stink of it clogged his nostrils where intestinal fluids and blood continued to leak out of the wound.

He heard them, the rapid pounding of feet as two warriors hurried past. Twisting his head, he could see them through the screening branches. Cimmis's men, they ran with a purpose.

Hunting me?

But they didn't even look his way, trotting past, casting anxious looks over their shoulders. Fleeing. But from what?

Ecan lowered his head back to the duff, his hands gripping the spear point that stuck out from just to the right of his navel.

Gods, he was dying. The spear had caught him from behind, lancing through his right kidney, angling down through his stomach and intestines. He'd cut enough people open, listened to their screams as he'd pawed through their living guts, to know how he was hit.

I'm dying! The thought sent a shiver of fear through him.

"I am to be great chief," he whispered to the shadows where he lay. "Do you hear me? Great chief!"

It was all so unfair! He'd been betrayed at every turn. Betrayed by Evening Star, White Stone, Coyote, Cimmis—all of them!

He blinked, aware of the hot blood that dribbled from the spear shaft onto his hands. He tightened his fingers around the spear, feeling the keen edge of the point. Did he dare pull it out?

Could he? The very thought of feeling that long shaft sliding through his guts sickened him.

Fear coupled with shock and sent a feverish heat through him. Sweat prickled on his skin just before his body jerked, and he threw up great gouts of clotted blood.

Whimpering, he lay back, the stench of his wound rising to tease his nostrils. Tears leaked from his eyes and turned the world silver.

Movement! Something creeping through the branches. He blinked to clear the glassy sheen from his eyes. Then blinked again.

Yes, it was a puppy! A little black dog with a white face.

"Runner?" he gasped. The puppy was watching him intently, studying him.

But if Runner was here, was Tsauz close by? His heart leapt. Tsauz! Yes, his son had come for him!

"Tsauz?" he tried to cry, having a hard time finding the breath.

The world seemed to shimmer and float in a way that was watery and liquid. A warm haze began to gray Ecan's vision. Only Runner remained in focus as he stepped ever closer, his black shiny nose sniffing warily.

"Take me to Tsauz," Ecan gasped, fighting to keep the world in focus. All he could see was the puppy. It was smiling now, wagging its tail in anticipation.

Then he remembered War Gods Village, recalled driving the spear into the little puppy's side, hearing the shriek of pain and fear. Gods, was that why Runner was here? To claim him?

As if in answer, the little dog threw its head back and yipped in delight.

As his soul loosened from his body, Ecan knew the true taste of fear.

Seventy

 hat are you feeling?" Rides-the-Wind asked as he crouched next
to Cimmis. The great chief lay on his litter, a blanket covering all but
his head and arms. Around them, people passed. They shot uneasy
looks in Cimmis's direction, whispering behind their hands. Two
guards ensured the old man's safety.

Cimmis managed a bare whisper. "Rage." Blood caked his lips.
When blood from his punctured lungs built up, racking coughs ex-
pelled clotted phlegm. The pain had to be excruciating.

Rides-the-Wind looked down into the old man's pain-glazed eyes
and felt, what? Sympathy? No, more curiosity than anything else. "I
have often wondered if for every good there is an evil. A balance in
the way the world was first Sung."

"There is only suffering," Cimmis whispered dryly. "If I could
stand, only for a moment . . ."

"You would do what?"

"I would choke the life from her body!" He winced with the vehemence of his words.

"Do you have so little love for her?"

"No," the old man whispered. "It's because I still love her that I
want so badly to make her pay." He turned his head away, tears leaking from the corners of his eyes.

"Do you wish to tell me anything, Cimmis?" Rides-the-Wind considered the old man. "You will be standing before Gutginsa's spear soon. I am curious as to how you will be judged."

"I'll live," he swore. "Just wait and see! From exile, I'll come back, and when I do . . ."

"Yes?"

"I will see them scream in agony."

"Have you no room in your heart for anything but anger?"

He reached up, gasping from the pain in his crushed chest, and wiped his eyes. "I loved . . . her. . . ."

"Then," the old Soul Keeper mused, "perhaps there is hope."

"Hope . . . is a myth."

Rain Bear stepped around the edges of the Joining ceremony, heading to where Rides-the-Wind knelt beside Cimmis. He'd been there all day, right at the edge of the palisade, talking with the captive chief. A hard-eyed guard of Kaska's warriors ensured his safety.

Pitch's voice carried in the clear morning air. "And will you, Astcat, matron of the North Wind People, accept this man Tsauz as your husband, to become great chief of the North Wind People?"

Astcat took Tsauz's hand and called in a loud voice, "I accept Tsauz."

Over ten tens of people had come, including many from the once slave village. They watched with wary but curious eyes. Tsauz stood to Astcat's right, a tall boy with his chin up, wearing Pitch's red ritual cape.

"So, it is done," Evening Star said as she walked up and took Rain Bear's hand. "And now, I have a question for you."

"Yes?"

"Will you, Rain Bear, great chief of the Raven People, join with me, Evening Star, of the North Wind People, to be my husband, and to eventually become the great chief of the North Wind People?"

He studied her for a moment. "Are you sure you want to do this?"

Her steady blue eyes seemed to bore into his soul. "If I have to build a new world for my people, I want to do it with the man I love. My people will trust you."

He hesitated for a moment, just staring into her eyes. "Yes, Matron, I will Join with you."

Great chief?" Dogrib said. "You had better come see this."

Rain Bear left the Council Lodge where he, Evening Star, Talon, and Kaska had been talking.

"What is it?"

"Dzoo." Dogrib shot him a grim glance. "She just appeared headed this way down the trail."

"Is she all right?"

"She looks fine. She's leading a party bearing someone on a stretcher."

"Thank Gutginsa she's safe." They'd been worried. Dzoo's blessing would be critical if they were going to maintain the fragile peace. "Do you think she found Ecan?"

"I can't say, my chief. No one has found him yet."

As Rain Bear followed Dogrib through the gate he could see her. In the clear morning light, Dzoo walked at the head of a small party of former slaves. They carried a litter, upon which a person lay.

The way Dzoo moved was magical, almost as if she floated above the ground. Her body dipped and swayed as she sang a melody that was at once haunting and joyous.

Above her, a column of crows wheeled and cawed, as if drawn by the bizarre sight.

Rain Bear and Dogrib stepped out to meet her, and both men shivered as Dzoo's voice rose to a high pitch and ended in laughter.

"Dzoo?" Rain Bear asked. "Are you all right? We've had warriors searching for you."

When her large eyes fixed on his, he felt the world sway, and reached out to brace himself on Dogrib's shoulder.

"I thank you for your concern, Great Chief. I have been Dancing with Coyote. It has taken a while to teach him to fly."

"Coyote? Fly?" He glanced at the litter, noticing for the first time that the bearers looked scared half out of their wits.

At a gesture from Dzoo, the litter clattered to the ground—and no sooner were the bearers free of the poles than they broke and ran like quail from a weasel.

Rain Bear stepped forward, frowning, trying to make sense of what he saw. The gruesome thing indeed looked like a huge bloody bird.

"Wings," Dzoo whispered as Rain Bear puzzled over the flaps of skin that hung down from the spread arms. "Skinned wings."

The organs had been removed from inside the torso, leaving a blood-caked hollow, the spine visible where the ribs curled up. The eyes were gone; the face had been carefully sliced away from the underlying bone. But the thing that drew the eye was the erect penis that stuck up from the crimson-caked pubis. A stick had been inserted to extend it far beyond human dimensions.

A dizzying sense of Power whirled through the air, and Rain Bear stepped back, wincing. Dzoo caught him and kept him from falling. Dogrib was making a sucking sound, as if he couldn't quite fill his lungs with air.

"It's all right, Chief Rain Bear. He can't hurt you." She smiled as she held up a blood-streaked obsidian fetish. It had been carefully chipped into the shape of a coyote's head. "I've placed Coyote's soul in here. It's obsidian, so sharp and brittle. All I have to do is snap it in two, or crush it under a rock, and his soul is gone forever." Her smile was predatory. "And he knows it."

Dogrib had turned away, a green color rising in his face.

She pulled the familiar coyote-tracked bag from the belt at her waist and dropped the fetish inside.

Rain Bear would have sworn he heard a faint, high-pitched scream.

Night

After everything we'd done together, everything we'd been through, she cast me aside like a cracked cup. I can't believe it. I loved her with all my soul." I force a difficult breath into my lungs.

They have been waiting for me to die. But I continue to fool them. For three moons I've been devouring myself from the inside out, until now I feel like a drum; all beating heart, but no insides.

"She had to make a choice: you or the survival of two peoples. You know that. Just as you know that she made the right choice."

"Perhaps, but I have been betrayed. I feel completely empty."

The old Soul Keeper's voice is gruff: "It is emptiness that makes a vessel useful. What would a bowl or cup be without its hollow interior?"

"Well, then, my wife has turned me into something very useful—I have become a yawning black abyss." Anger tinges the words. My love has turned into a huge burning ache. More than anything, I wish I could have betrayed her in kind. A great many women would have flocked to me, worshipped me.

"Very soon now you must decide whether that abyss will be eternally filled with anger and resentment or love and peace. Which will it be?"

As he rises, the Soul Keeper's cape flutters then flaps in a gust of wind. He smells spicy, like the leaves of the Spirit plants he's been using to Heal me.

He doesn't know it, but I already understand his words—only too well.

It is the empty chamber that makes a drum beautiful, or a flute melodious. Without emptiness there would be no music.

Emptiness is also what makes love possible. If a human being felt full and contented, he would have no need for love.

But at this late date, what does such knowledge bring me? I understand that I am now the perfect vessel. Waiting to be filled . . . but with what? Perhaps I just need a purpose. Any purpose, beyond simply dying and ridding the world of my presence, would be welcome.

"Do I have a purpose?"

Through hazy eyes, I see him watching me. "If I could Heal you, what is the first thing you would do?"

I wheeze the words, "I would seek her out, and strangle that boy before her eyes."

He nods cryptically. "Despite what you would have me believe. You are not empty, Chief. Unfortunately you are still full."

Full? Of what? I wonder as the darkness closes in around me. At first it is soft and gray. The world is fading as I fall toward . . . what?

Epilogue

The small camp was located in the floodplain beside the north bank of the great river. A cool stand of cottonwood trees gave respite from the oppressive heat that came rolling out of the arid uplands. Summer here, in the dry plateau, was brutally hot compared to the cool damp coast where the people had lived. Deer Killer had chosen this spot out of necessity. Not only had Cimmis needed the shade, but Rides-the-Wind suffered under the direct sunlight.

Cimmis's dead body lay beneath the hides, his eyes staring wide into the distance of death. His shriveled face bore the faint sheen of sweat. Beads of it dotted his lashes.

Since the day Kaska's small band of warriors had left them and turned back to the mountains, Cimmis and his group had wandered the sagebrush barrens. Making a living had depended on the few strong young warriors who had accompanied them.

But for the gift of the camas roots, they'd have starved in the first few weeks. Deer Killer, despite his Raven People blood, had become their chief. No one had said anything when Kstawl moved her robes to his lodge and began sharing his bed.

Rides-the-Wind thoughtfully studied the dead man before he reached over and pulled Cimmis's eyelids closed.

"Soul Keeper?" Kstawl called. "How is he?"

Rides-the-Wind replied, "His soul is hovering inside his nostrils."

She took a breath, head bowing. "Then, my father is finally dead?" She pinched the bridge of her nose. "I'm sorry, but it's a relief."

Rides-the-Wind picked up a stick that he'd placed to one side and held the end in the smoke. He kept it over the heat until it began to smolder, then held it under Cimmis's nose.

Kstawl knelt beside him and saw that it was a lock of gray hair tied to the stick. The smoke came from a smoldering bundle of sweet grass and cedar bark that lay in the ashes.

"You're smoking Father's hair?" Kstawl asked in disbelief. Then she realized what he was doing. "You're *sealing* his soul in his body? For the sake of the gods, let it go!"

A perfectly cut square of buffalohide rested beside Rides-the-Wind's knee. He tucked the smoked lock into the hide, then folded it up and tied it with a sea-grass cord. When he tossed it into the ashes, it landed with a thump and began to blacken. The first tongues of flame caressed its edges.

Kstawl gasped in horror, backing away. Her disbelieving eyes went from the fire, to Cimmis, to Rides-the-Wind.

"It isn't time for his soul to be set free," the Soul Keeper said. "It must stay here, with his bones."

"Why, Elder?"

Rides-the-Wind stood, and his gray hair and beard whipped around his face. One by one he looked into the sober eyes of Deer Killer's small band. "Everyone deserves the chance to stand before Gutginsa and explain his actions. Even Cimmis. Though it may be a long time before Cimmis understands what he did and Gutginsa allows him to go free."

"How long?" Kstawl demanded.

"Who knows? That is up to Cimmis's soul. It may be for a people long removed from us to finally send him to judgment."

As he walked across the grassy silt, he looked out at the wide river, at the bluffs wavering in the midsummer sun beyond. Terrible sadness had settled upon his aged shoulders. "I will leave tonight. I have no more business here."

In the haze, far to the west, Thunderbirds played over the distant mountain peaks; lightning leaped through the clouds.

"Do you think that's true?" Kstawl asked Deer Killer as she studied her dead father. "That everyone deserves the chance to explain?"

Deer Killer shrugged. "Who are we to judge, my wife? For the moment, I am more concerned with making a grave for your father. As to his soul, well, that's up to Gutginsa's spear."

Afterword

So, who were the first people to arrive in North America?

The question has tantalized archaeologists for over a century, but we are only now just beginning to piece together the answer.

When we wrote *People of the Wolf* in 1988, it was generally accepted that the earliest peoples to arrive in North America were Mongoloids, American Indians, and that they came down an ice-free corridor between the massive Cordilleran Ice Sheet and the Laurentide Glacier around 12,000 years ago. In the past fifteen years, new information derived from archaeological excavations and technological advances has altered that view.

We now know that the Indian peoples were not alone in the Americas—not in North America and not in South America. Kennewick Man and Stick Man in the Pacific Northwest, as well as the Spirit Cave Mummy in Nevada and Horn Shelter Number Two Man in Texas, prove there were Caucasoids—traditionally described as light-skinned people—in North America between 9,000 and 11,000 years ago. "Luzia" and many other specimens in Brazil prove there were Australoids—a dark-skinned people common to the southern hemisphere—in South America over 12,000 years ago.

Surprised? We all were.

The simple fact is that less than 5 percent of the land in the Americas has been surveyed for archaeology. We do the best we can with the information we have, but there *must* be many more dramatic surprises waiting for us.

The earliest reliable dates for human entry into the New World now come from a variety of geographic regions: Dry Creek I in Alaska, the Manis Mastodon Kill site in Washington, Meadowcroft Rockshelter in Pennsylvania, and Monte Verde in Chile all reliably date to between 14,000 and 14,500 years ago. The Cactus Hill site in southern Virginia dates to around 15,000 years before present, and many other dates from sites across the Americas suggest human beings may have arrived here as early as 20,000 years ago. These are pre-Clovis cultures. Clovis sites, left by the famed big-game hunters who used a very distinctive "fluted" spear point, date no earlier than 13,500 years ago. But by 13,000 years ago, Clovis hunters had colonized much of the North American continent. They moved rapidly, and they took their remarkable culture with them wherever they went. Human occupation of the Queen Charlotte Islands in Canada, and Prince of Wales Island in Alaska, dates to around 12,000 years ago.

We are also fairly certain now that the first peoples did not strictly come by land down the ice-free corridor along the face of the Canadian Rocky Mountains. We suspect they also had boats and paddled down the coastlines, fishing, hunting, and gathering as they traveled.

It is likely that the earliest inhabitants of North America lived along the Pacific coast of Canada and the northwestern United States. We say that for two reasons. First, the greatest diversity of Native American languages is found along the Pacific coast. It takes time for languages to diverge. They are most different in areas where people have lived longest. Second, though much of the northern Pacific coast was covered by the Cordilleran Ice Sheet 16,000 years ago, parts of the Queen Charlotte Islands in British Columbia and Prince of Wales Island in southeast Alaska appear to have been ice-free. As well, recent geological evidence indicates that the continental shelf, which was exposed by lowered sea levels 13,000 to 14,000 years ago, was also free of ice. The ice had, in fact, retreated from British Columbia's coastal mountains by about 13,000 years ago. By 10,600 years ago, lowered sea levels had exposed large areas of the Hecate Plain east of the Queen Charlotte Islands, the bottom of Queen Charlotte Sound, and the areas adjacent to the north and west coasts of Vancouver Island.

But what were the food resources?

Paleobotany, the study of pollens, seeds, and phytoliths—the silicate skeletons of plant cells—tells us that those ice-free areas were vegetated. By 14,000 years ago, southern British Columbia supported heath, a variety of grasses, sedges, and herbs. There were also conifers present. By about 12,000 years ago, lodgepole pine and poplar grew on the Queen Charlotte Islands and had spread to southeast Alaska. Close behind were sitka spruce and hemlock.

In addition, from 8,000 to 12,000 years ago, Prince of Wales Island supported brown bear, black bear, red fox, otter and ermine, and other small mammals, as well as fish resources.

People of the Raven is set at about 9,300 years ago in what is now Washington and southern British Columbia. This was a period of extreme stress for the two distinct cultural traditions that inhabited the region: the Pebble Tool Tradition and the Stemmed Point Tradition. At the same time that sea levels were rising rapidly, the land itself was "springing back." This is called "isostatic rebound." Imagine putting a block of ice on a piece of foam. As the ice melts, the foam "springs back." Continents do the same thing. As the massive weight of the glaciers vanished, the land rose. But it seems to have happened at different rates in different places. For example, the sea level on Prince of Wales Island between 9,000 and 9,500 years ago was about twenty feet higher than today. Farther south, 9,300 years ago, the sea level on the Queen Charlotte Islands was approximately 475 feet higher than modern sea level (Josenhans et al., 1995, 1997)!

Sediment cores taken off the Oregon coast show that wind patterns also reversed at this time, weakening the coastal upwelling and reducing marine productivity (Sanchetta et al., 1992).

Adding to this problem, as the Cordilleran Ice Sheet continued to melt it flooded the rivers, streams, and finally the ocean with silt-laden fresh water. This decimated shellfish beds and lowered salmon runs, affecting the food chain and reducing the numbers of sea mammals, birds, and human beings who could survive.

Of the thirty-nine individuals found in North America who date to more than 9,000 years ago, only two are fairly complete: Spirit Cave Mummy from Nevada and Kennewick Man from Washington. Even with these limited data we can glean critical details about who they were and what happened to them.

Keep in mind this is a period of rapid transition from the Pleistocene Ice Age to the warmer Holocene period that we now enjoy. Most of North America's earliest inhabitants endured periods of starvation. Malnutrition temporarily interrupts bone growth and leaves mineral deposits that we call "Harris lines" in the limb bones; it also appears as ripples in the teeth called dental hypoplasias. We see changes in the skull as well. The girl from the Spirit Cave site in

Nevada showed multiple growth interruptions in her teeth, indicating a life of repeated nutritional privation. The Spirit Cave Mummy (10,700 years old) had a number of Harris lines in his limb bones, as did the Buhl Woman from Idaho (12,800 years old). The lines on the Buhl Woman's femur, or thigh bone, were so regularly spaced that hunger seems to have been a yearly occurrence. The bones of the man from Horn Shelter Number Two in Texas (11,200 years ago) also show he suffered extreme hunger in his life.

But what did they look like? How long did they live? What did they die from?

The Spirit Cave Man who lived in Nevada almost 11,000 years ago died in his middle forties, and he had wavy black hair. We know because he still had patches clinging to his mummified head. His physical features most closely resemble those of the medieval Norse and the Ainu, the aboriginal people of Japan. Both populations have long been characterized as Caucasoids—light-skinned people. Kennewick Man (9,300 years old) may have lived into his fifties, and his features, too, most closely resemble those of the Ainu. The man from Horn Shelter Number Two in Texas (11,200 years old) falls into this same category and is the least "Indianlike" of all. He has a long narrow skull, massive overhanging brow and close-set eyes. He died at around age forty.

Though afterlife traditions can only be guessed at, the treatment of the dead gives us clues to what they might have believed, and given the diversity of burial styles, their religious traditions appear to have been many. Ten of the thirty-nine were cremated. Thirteen were buried. Two were "bundle" burials, that is bundles of cleaned bones wrapped in beautiful blankets and deposited in caves or rock shelters. We call these "secondary" burials. We occasionally find grave goods. The Buhl Woman in Idaho and the woman from Colorado's Gordon Creek site were buried with stone knives. The Horn Shelter Girl, Marmes I, and Buhl Woman all had needles as grave offerings. Buhl Woman also had a badger's baculum—penis bone—with her. A beautiful group of spear points accompanied the man from Browns Valley. The man at Horn Shelter Number Two in Texas had more than one hundred grave offerings, including a large chert knife, two antler wrenches for straightening spear shafts, sandstone slabs for working bone or shell, and a necklace of four canid teeth surrounded by more than eighty snail-shell beads from the Gulf of Mexico. Red ocher is the most common offering; it was used to coat the bodies of the people found at the Gordon Creek site; the Anzick site in Montana; Browns Valley; the woman from Arch Lake, New Mexico; and probably Stick Man from Washington. We also find raw lumps of the pigment included with the dead—as though they would need it in the afterworld, just as they would need knives, needles, and spear points.

Eight of the earliest skeletons are children. The Anzick child (12,000 years old) was about eighteen months old. The Horn Shelter girl lived to be around twelve.

Interestingly, only the men show dramatic injuries, which tells us a great deal about how they lived and died.

Spirit Cave Mummy had fractures to his skull, spine, and hand. Stick Man and the Marmes III Man also had skull fractures, as did Kennewick Man. The Grimes Burial Shelter teenager tells a similar story. One cut on his rib contains obsidian fragments—residue left from the weapon used to inflict the wound—and there are two cuts present, indicating that the youth's assailant stabbed him at least twice. Since no healing is apparent, it's probable that the teenager died from this assault.

Kennewick Man shows, by far, the most traumatic injuries—all of which he survived. Several months, or even a few years, before his death, his chest was crushed, breaking several ribs. He also had an infected wound in his skull, on his left temple. He was relatively tall for the time period, five feet nine inches, and was around fifty years old when he died. In addition, Kennewick Man had a "Cascade" spear point embedded in his hip.

In our current collection, 67 percent of the males from this time period demonstrate serious injuries. This is a very high rate, especially when compared to European burials. Mary Brennan, who was working on her doctorate at New York University, studied 209 skeletons from southern France dating to between 10,000 and 100,000 years ago, and found only *five* fractures, or a little over 2 percent. As another example, Thomas Berger and Eric Trinkaus studied over 1,200 skeletons from modern humans and Neandertals and found less than one hundred injuries, or around 8 percent.

The high rate we see among Paleo-American males could be sampling error—we don't have many examples to learn from—but it probably represents interpersonal violence. We only find skull fractures on males, and most of those occur on the left side of the head, toward the front, as if caused by a blow delivered by a right-handed opponent.

Women, on the other hand, show few such injuries. Only the Minnesota girl had a fractured rib. But women also had a much shorter life span than men. While men often lived into their forties or fifties, or even older, Paleo-American women generally died between the ages of eighteen and twenty-three. We don't know why this disparity exists, though the physical and nutritional stresses associated with childbearing almost certainly played a role.

Lastly, in a recent study Dr. Richard Jantz and Dr. Doug Owsley showed that the most ancient skeletons in North America fall into two distinct groups: one group that has features similar to the Ainu or Polynesians and a second group that appears very Indianlike. These groups are so different from each other that Owsley and Jantz propose they are from two distinct populations of people who migrated separately into North America.

What's surprising about this is that it surprises anyone. After all, we know that Europe and Asia were "melting pots" long before humans arrived in North America. At least some of the ancestors of ancient Americans surely traveled across Europe, into Asia, and finally into North America—and they undoubtedly mixed with other peoples as they traveled.

The remarkable thing is that it has taken us this long to find the evidence, but that's archaeology. The research is never finished. We do not know enough to reconstruct the past completely. We never will. All we can do is take the best information we have . . . and try.

Selected Bibliography

Bancroft-Hunt, Norman, and Werner Forman. *People of the Totem.* Norman, Okla.: University of Oklahoma, 1988.

Beck, Mary. *Heroes and Heroines in Tlingit-Haida Legend.* Anchorage: Alaska Northwest Books, 1989.

Benedict, Jeff. *No Bone Unturned.* New York: Harper Collins, 2003.

Bonnichsen, Robson, and Karen L. Turnmire. *Clovis: Origins and Adaptations.* Corvallis, Oregon: Center for the Study of the First North Americans: 1991.

Bringhurst, Robert. *A Story as Sharp as a Knife. The Classical Haida Mythtellers and Their World.* Lincoln: University of Nebraska Press, 1999.

Bryant, Vaughn M., and Richard G. Holloway. *Pollen Records of Late-Quaternary North American Sediments.* Dallas: The American Association of Stratigraphic Palynologists Foundation, 1985.

Capes, Katherine H. *Contributions to the Prehistory of Vancouver Island.* Pocatello, Idaho: Occasional Papers of the Idaho State University Museum, Number 15, 1964.

Chatters, James C. *Ancient Encounters: Kennewick Man and the First Americans.* New York: Simon and Schuster, 2001.

Cove, John J. et al., editors. *Tricksters, Shamans and Heroes: Tsimshian Narratives I and II.* Ottawa: Directorate, Paper No. 3, Canadian Museum of Civilization, 1987.

Crawford, Michael H. *The Origins of Native Americans. Evidence from Anthropological Genetics.* Cambridge: Cambridge University Press, 1998.

Dauenhauer, Nora, and Richard Dauenhauer. *Haa Tuwunaagu Yis, for Healing Our Spirit: Tlingit Oratory.* Seattle: University of Washington Press, 1990.

Dixon, James E. *Bones, Boats and Bison.* Albuquerque: University of New Mexico Press, 1999.

Emmons, George Thornton. *The Tlingit Indians.* Seattle: University of Washington Press, 1991.

Enrico, John, and Wendy Bross Stuart. *Northern Haida Songs.* Lincoln: University of Nebraska Press, 1996.

Fagan, Brian M. *Ancient North America: The Archaeology of a Continent.* Third edition. London: Thames and Hudson, 2000.

Fienup-Riordan, Ann, ed. *Our Way of Making Prayer. Yup'ik Masks and the Stories They Tell Us.* Seattle: University of Washington Press, 1996.

Gunther, Erna. *Ethnobotany of Western Washington. The Knowledge and Use of Indigenous Plants by Native Americans.* Seattle: University of Washington, 1999.

Harkin, Michael E. *The Heiltsuks. Dialogues of Culture and History on the Northwest Coast.* Lincoln: University of Nebraska Press, 1997.

Harris, Arthur. *Late Pleistocene Vertebrate Paleoecology of the West.* Austin: University of Texas Press, 1985.

Jaffe, A. J. *The First Immigrants from Asia.* New York: Plenum Press, 1992.

Josenhans, H. W. et al., 1995. "Post Glacial Sea-Levels on the Western Canadian Continental Shelf: Evidence for Rapid Change, Extensive Subaerial Exposure, and Early Habitation." *Marine Geology* 125: 73–94.

———. 1997, "Early Humans and Rapidly Changing Holocene Sea Levels in the Queen Charlotte Islands–Hecate Strait, British Columbia, Canada." *Science* 277: 71–74.

Judson, Katharine Berry, ed. *Myths and Legends of the Pacific Northwest.* Lincoln: University of Nebraska Press, 1997.

Kan, Sergei. *Symbolic Immortality; the Thlingit Potlatch of the Nineteenth Century.* Washington: Smithsonian Institution Press, 1989.

Krober, Paul D. *The Salish Language Family; Reconstructing Syntax.* Lincoln: University of Nebraska Press, 1999.

LaBlanc, Steven. *Constant Battles.* New York: St. Martin's Press, 2003.

Linderman, Frank B. *Kootenai Why Stories*. Lincoln: University of Nebraska Press, 1926.

Martin, Paul. *Quaternary Extinctions: A Prehistoric Revolution*. Tucson: University of Arizona Press, 1989.

Matson, R. G., and Gary Coupland. *The Prehistory of the Northwest Coast*. San Diego: Academic Press, 1995.

McFeat, Tom, ed. *Indians of the Pacific Northwest*. Seattle: University of Washington Press, 1989.

McIlwraith, T. F. *The Bella Coola Indians*. Toronto: University of Toronto Press, 1948.

Miller, Jay. *Tsimshian Culture, a Light Through the Ages*. Lincoln: University of Nebraska Press, 1997.

Millspaugh, Charles F. *American Medicinal Plants*. New York: Dover Publications, 1974.

Owsley, Douglas W., and Richard J. Jantz. "Archeological Politics and Public Interest in PaleoAmerican Studies: Lessons from Gordon Creek Woman and Kennewick Man." *American Antiquity*, September 2001.

Pielou, E. C. *After the Ice Age: The Return of Life to Glaciated North America*. Chicago: University of Chicago Press, 1991.

Reid, Bill, and Robert Bringhurst. *The Raven Steals the Light*. Seattle: University of Washington, 1988.

Ruby, Robert H., and John A. Brown. *Indians of the Pacific Northwest*. Norman: University of Oklahoma, 1981.

———. *Dreamer-Prophets of the Columbia Plateau: Smohalla and Skolaskin*. Norman: University of Oklahoma Press, 1989.

Samuel, Cheryl. *The Raven's Tail*. Vancouver: University of British Columbia, 1987.

Sanchetta, C. et al., 1992, "Late-Glacial to Holocene Changes in Winds, Upwelling, and Seasonal Production of the Northern California Current System, *Quaternary Research* 38:359–370.

Savinelli, Alfred. *Plants of Power: Native American Ceremony and the Use of Sacred Plants*. Tennessee: Native Voices Publishing, 2002.

Smith, Harlan I. *Ethnobotany of the Gitksan Indians of British Columbia*. Hull, Quebec: Canadian Museum of Civilization, Paper 132, 1997.

Steward, Hilary. *Totem Poles*. Seattle: University of Washington Press, 1990.

Straus, Lawrence Guy et al., eds. *Humans at the End of the Ice Age: The Archaeology of the Pleistocene-Holocene Transition*. New York, Plenum Press, 1996.

Suttles, Wayne, ed. *Handbook of North American Indians: Northwest Coast.* Washington: Vol. 7. Washington, Smithsonian Institution Press, 1990.

Thomas, David Hurst. *Skull Wars. Kennewick Man, Archaeology and the Battle for Native American Identity.* New York: Basic Books, 2000.

Turner, Nancy J. *Plant Technology of First Peoples in British Columbia.* Vancouver: University of British Columbia, Royal British Columbia Museum Handbook, 1998.

———. *Food Plants of Coastal First Peoples.* Vancouver: University of British Columbia, Royal British Columbia Museum Handbook, 1995.